The Best of

Bad-Ass Faeries

Edited by

Danielle Ackley-McPhail

eBooks

Stratford, NJ

PUBLISHED BY
eSpec Books LLC
Danielle McPhail, Publisher
PO Box 493,
Stratford, New Jersey 08084
www.especbooks.com

ISBN (paperback): 978-1-942990-50-5
ISBN (hardcover): 978-1-942990-69-7
ISBN (ebook): 978-1-942990-51-2

Bad-Ass Faeries originally published in 2007 by Marietta Publishing and in 2009 by Mundania Press.
Bad-Ass Faeries: Just Plain Bad originally published in 2008 by Marietta Publishing and in 2009 by Mundania Press.
Bad-Ass Faeries: In All Their Glory originally published in 2010 by Mundania Press.
Bad-Ass Faeries: It's Elemental originally published in 2014 by Dark Quest Books.

Cover Design: Mike McPhail
Interior Design: Danielle McPhail
Cover Art: © katalinks
Interior Art: © Ed Coutts
Copyeditor: Greg Schauer

Bad-Ass Autographs

Brian Koscienski

L. Jagi Lamplighter

Chris Pisano

John L. French

Keith R.A. DeCandido

James Daniel Ross

Adam P. Knave

Robert E. Waters

Jesse Harris

Kelly A. Harmon

James Chambers

D.L. Thurston

Danielle Ackley-McPhail

Patrick Thomas

John Passarella

Jody Lynn Nye

Jeffrey Lyman

Lee C. Hillman

Bernie Mojzes

N.R. Brown

C.J. Henderson

DEDICATED TO

JEFFREY LYMAN
L. JAGI LAMPLIGHTER
LEE C. HILLMAN

THANK YOU FOR MAKING THIS A BAD-ASS SERIES!

AND TO THE MEMORY OF
C.J. HENDERSON
TRULY THE BEST OF BAD-ASS FAERIES.

YOU ARE MISSED.

Contents

Bad-Ass Faeries

Ballad of the Seven-Up Sprite

Brian Koscienski & Chris Pisano

DEADWILLOW WAS A PIXIE-DUST MINING TOWN INDISTINGUISH-able from any other. Faeries with sunken cheeks and hardened brows ended their day by spending their hard-earned pixie dust on honeysuckle cider, wild forest nymphs and a tulip petal bed to lie on only to repeat the process the following day. The main street, worn dirt bare, passed through the town like an afterthought, leading from the thick forest to the pixie-dust mines. Taverns and inns, carved deep into the trunks of the trees that lined the street, flourished no more or less than any other tavern or inn in any other town. Then, for one brief, glimmering moment in time, the town became much, much different—he arrived.

La-la-li sat on an acorn chair, her doll in her hands: the body in her left hand, the doll's head in her right. She sat on the porch outside her father's tavern, and, even though cheerful song and laughter spilled out from the windows, she sobbed. Her favorite toy—her best friend—broken. Her heart had made plans to sob all day, but her eyes saw something that made her heart concede. A shadow of enormous proportions glided across the dirt street, and then circled in front of the tavern, in front of La-la-li. But as it circled, it became smaller; with each swirl the shadow halved. Just as La-la-li saw what caused the unprecedented shadow, it settled within the soft cloud of dust it created and looked her in the eye—a large, crimson cardinal.

The other birds tied to the tavern's hitching post chirped, flapped and hopped, agitated by the arrival of a newcomer. Sparrows and starlings, with the occasional chickadee, kicked dirt and pebble as they danced defensively. La-la-li watched in

stunned silence, her tears refusing to stop. She knew this bird, knew of the stories and tales abound, knew who it belonged to—the Seven-Up Sprite, the most wanted faerie in the land.

La-la-li noticed right away the faerie's spurs as he dismounted; so rare for a faerie to walk instead of fly. She assumed why when she saw his wings—gnarled and torn, pock-marked with holes, short and aggressive like a horsefly's rather than full and regal like a dragonfly's, the typical accoutrements of most faeries. Other than the shocking condition of his wings, it was said that this faerie was rather unassuming, neither tall nor short, ate only when hungry, but didn't work unless he had to. La-la-li wondered why people feared him so. His spurs clanked and his long, tattered jacket flowed as he made his way across the porch to the tavern door. The spurs' noises stopped only when he did, to cast a stare at the little faerie girl sitting on an acorn chair, holding a broken doll.

"Can...can you fix her?" La-la-li asked, not knowing what else to say.

Tipping his wide brimmed hat, he replied, "M'afraid I can't sew," and pushed open the swinging doors. His spurs once again clanked as he entered the tavern.

The music stopped. The singing and merriment ceased. Bewilderment became the new companion to every soul in the tavern as the Seven-Up Sprite sidled up to the bar. Shocked by the sight, many of the faeries forgot how to use their wings to hover and fell to the floor.

Awkward situations would be nothing new to the Sprite, had he the propensity to feel anything other than terminal indifference. Deadwillow was no different from any other town, and this tavern was no different from any other he had stepped in before. He ordered a honeysuckle cider, his request breaking the utter silence. His first few sips echoed through the room, until other patrons gathered their wits and whispered among themselves. Halfway through his drink, conversations grew in volume, now nothing more than idle chatter. By the time he ordered his second cider, the music returned, as did the cavalier atmosphere. Just like every other tavern he had been to before—except for one thing. A woman.

From the corner of his eye, the Seven-Up Sprite caught a glimpse of her at the other end of the bar. He did his best to keep from looking at her, because he knew what kind of magic a forest nymph like her possessed; a magic not learned in any book or apprenticeship, but the nature-given magic of effortless beauty. With skin as dark as tree bark and hair as green and thick as summer meadow, he knew she was trouble. To his surprise, though, she was receiving it, not giving it.

During his second cider, the Sprite saw a half-drunk faerie approach the nymph. Being twice her age and cross-eyed, the rancid faerie made proposition after proposition. His ears worked as well as his mouth, slurred and sloppy, because no matter how many times she shunned his advances, he came back for more. By the time the Sprite finished his fourth cider, the dullard across the bar grabbed the nymph by her wrists, ignoring her protests.

"Let go of me!"

The Seven-Up Sprite knew what was right and what was wrong. The law never seemed to agree with his opinions on the topic, but he had them nonetheless. And what he witnessed was wrong. He needed to make it right. "Best be lettin' go of her, partner."

"What!?" the miscreant faerie snapped, fire in his crossed eyes as well as his words. "What'd you say?!"

"You stupid before or after cider? Let. Her. Go. Partner. Hear better now?" The Sprite emphasized his point by brushing his jacket open, exposing his holstered magic wand.

The tavern fell silent again, this time in reverence for the sight of the old, tarnished wand. It looked like any other six-shooter around, but was made far more lethal by the faerie that owned it. Half the silence came from the faerie folk wondering how such a relic could do what the legends said it did.

"That ol' thing don't scare me! And I ain't scared of you, neither!" the drunk faerie slurred.

"You should be," the Sprite whispered as he took another sip.

"What? Why don't you come here an' say that again?"

"Wouldn't waste my time nor breath on you. My spit, neither."

The drunkard released the nymph so he could slam both hands on the bar top. "That's it! Outside! Draw at high shroom!"

Wondering why fate always forced him to do this, the Seven-Up Sprite finished his cider in one swig and sighed. He walked out the tavern door and into the street paying no attention to the faerie he had offended.

Old women gasped and old men pulled shutters closed. Young women swooned at their overly romanticized notions of a wand-fight while young men maintained an air of bravado, as if they participated in wand fights every day. The tavern owner shielded his daughter, La-la-li, with his body, but she managed to peek around to see what was happening. The Seven-Up Sprite just wanted to get this over with.

The outlaw faerie twisted his body so his jacket did not hinder the path from his hand to his wand. He watched as the drunkard stumbled his way onto the street while fastening his wand holster around his waist. The morricone mushroom in the clock tower was getting ready to whistle a long eerie whistle, as it did every hour on the hour. The Sprite prepared himself to draw upon the mushroom's whistle until he noticed something peculiar about his adversary...his eyes, no longer crossed, darted to a nearby roof top.

Drawing his wand early, just as the honorless faerie did, the Seven-Up Sprite fired. The jagged bolt of magic from his wand met his opponent's, nullifying whatever spell he might have cast. To keep his opponent off-guard, as well as any who observed, he did what none thought he could — he flew.

Blasts of magic from many different wands fried and charred the dirt road beneath his feet as the Sprite launched himself into the air. His wings beat fast, a violent tympanum that sent chills down the spines of all who heard it. Now that he had a better vantage point, he saw the source of the magic blasts. Four snipers, obvious partners of the lecherous faerie who prompted the showdown, stared from rooftops, mouths agape at the faerie with gnarled wings flying high above them. It made them easy targets for his ire.

Four targets, four shots, four hits. One sniper turned into a pile of sand, the second a collection of caterpillars, the third a bouquet of tulips, and the final gun-faerie was frozen forever as a wooden statue of himself. That left only the rogue who tried to ensnare the Seven-Up Sprite in an ambush.

Returning to the ground, the Sprite walked toward his adversary. Bolts of magic flashed past him; the rogue faerie's hand shook too hard for an accurate shot. Once the faerie saw the futility of his actions, he spread his wings and flew straight up, hoping beyond hope to escape the legend he tried to connive. He could not. A red beam of magic from the legend's wand turned him into a brief, yet brilliant, fireworks display for the town-faeries to behold.

The Sprite turned to the onlookers, expecting either applause or wonder, and depending how hardened the pixie-dust mines had made these faerie folk, maybe even mild apathy. He did not expect what he saw in their faces: surprise. However, they were not looking at him, rather directly behind him. He turned to see the forest nymph he originally tried to defend pointing a magic wand at his head.

"Surprised?" she asked.

"A bit," the outlaw faerie replied. "Nice set up."

"Why, thank you," the nymph said, doing a sarcastic curtsy. "It was a win-win situation really. If they got you, then I'd take them out and collect the bounty for you. But since they didn't get you, you had to waste all six shots of that antiquated wand of yours. And since you're now unarmed, I get to take you in alive."

With squint-eyed grin and stubbled chin, the Seven-Up Sprite asked, "Do you know how I got my name?"

"Sure do. Everyone knows the story. The first group of law-faeries sent to bring you in were all found turned to sticks and stones. Seven of them. All on the ground, face up."

"Meaning?"

She huffed a snort of contempt. "Meaning that even though you're a criminal faerie with no name, you obviously didn't shoot any of them in the back. Very noble. But...oh wait," her voice faltered. "There were seven of them...seven...NO!!!"

Realization hit the nymph like the blast of magic from the Seven-Up Sprite's wand. As he watched the smoke clear, he said, "Yep. This here wand's been modified to hold seven shots, not six."

Stunned silence, the way the town-faeries looked at the renegade faerie as he bent over and picked up the remains of the forest nymph—a doll. Gasps ran up and down the street as he took the doll to La-la-li, the one faerie not scared of him.

"Still can't sew," he winked as he handed the doll to her.

Excitement consumed La-la-li to the brink of oblivion, unaware that the Seven-Up Sprite mounted his cardinal and flew out of Deadwillow, never to return. She was just happy to have a favorite toy again, a new best friend. And this one was even better than the last—it blinked and made funny noises when she tickled it...

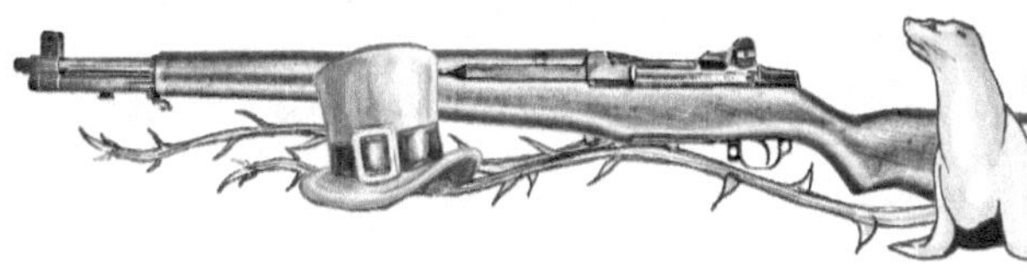

House Arrest

Keith R.A. DeCandido

The house faerie had been sitting in the small, drab room in the eastern wing of the castle for over half an hour before somebody finally walked in. The home of the Lord and Lady who ruled the city-state of Cliff's End, the castle was also the workplace of many of the nobility and others who served the demesne. This wing housed the headquarters of the Cliff's End Castle Guard, who were tasked with maintaining law and order in the port city. This was the first time the faerie had entered the Lord and Lady's Seat.

But then, as a house faerie, he had reason to stay inside his own home.

Being confined to this room, however, was frustrating for the faerie, as there wasn't enough room to fly about, and there wasn't anything in the room to hold his interest. The décor was rather pedestrian: a table surrounded by three chairs, two on one side, one on the other; a lantern that cast odd shadows; and nothing else. The house faerie had been brought here by two large members of the Guard "for questioning," along with the humans who lived in the house for which he was responsible.

Well, all but one of the humans. The one they didn't bring was also the reason why they had been brought to the castle: Alvin, the middle son, had died.

The house faerie regarded his new visitor, a tall man with long red hair and a thick red beard that obscured virtually all of his face, save an aquiline nose and probing green eyes. He wore an earth-colored cloak, indicating his rank of lieutenant, which also meant that he was tasked with the solving of the more

elaborate crimes—such as murder. The cloak covered leather armor decorated with the gryphon crest of the Lord and Lady.

"Good afternoon," he said, closing the door to the small, drab room behind him as he entered. "My name is Lieutenant Torin ban Wyvald."

The faerie had been pacing. "It's about time somebody showed up. I was going barking mad in here."

"My apologies. I'm afraid that this case is rather complex."

"I can't even sit, thanks to those blessed backed chairs, and the place is too small for flying. These wings ain't for show, I'll have you know, Lieutenant."

"Again, my apologies. I'm afraid we don't have any stools. Feel free to sit on the table."

With a loud groan of annoyance, the faerie did so, crossing his green legs and folding his green arms. Indeed, the faerie was entirely green, save for his wings, which were more of a teal color.

Torin would normally have sat in one of the two chairs with their backs to the door, facing the person being questioned, who was in the chair on the other side of the table. But the faerie's position on the table's edge made that awkward, so Torin remained standing. "Now then, you are the house faerie of the Grabodlik residence, yes?"

"Right."

"I'm afraid I was never able to get a name for you—what are you called?"

Smiling sardonically, the faerie said, "The house faerie of the Grabodlik residence'll do the trick, thanks. 'Fraid you couldn't pronounce my name."

"You'd be surprised what I could pronounce, good, ah—good sir."

"Not properly." The faerie sighed. He went through this every time a non-fae tried to call him by his name. "See, us fae, our language don't just use the throat—the vibration of our wings're a part of it, too. Like I said, they ain't just for show. So you're not physically capable of pronouncing my name, and if you try it, it'll sound wrong."

"Very well, good sir faerie." Torin nodded and leaned up against the wall. "I assume you know why we've brought you here?"

"I'm guessing it's got to do with poor Alvin's death?"

"Correct."

"Well, at least it got me out of the house. Honestly, I almost never leave. Don't have much call to, really—I mean, as a house faerie, I got a job to do, and it ties me to the place most of the time, y'know?"

"Understandable."

"The castle's nice—not so sure about this room, though. Rather drab. I thought you lot had a whole troupe of fae working here."

Torin half-smiled. "The Lord and Lady do employ a swarm of house faeries, yes."

"Obviously, they forgot this room the last time they swept through." The faerie didn't even try to keep the disdain out of his voice.

Seeing no need to explain that the room was kept drab on purpose, Torin pressed on. "We're here to talk about young Alvin Grabodlik."

"Right. How'd he die, anyhow?"

"That, in fact, is what we are trying to determine. My partner and I have been interviewing the members of the Grabodlik family."

The faerie shook his head. "You have my sympathies, Lieutenant."

"Oh?" Torin said with a bushy red eyebrow raised.

"Look, I don't mean to speak ill of the folks or anything, really," the faerie said, unfolding his arms to hold up his hands in a gesture of reassurance. "I mean, they're decent enough, for humans. But—well, I've been the house faerie of that place since the Lord and Lady founded Cliff's End, and the place has seen better owners. Seen worse, too, really, but these guys ain't hardly the best I've seen."

Now Torin did sit in one of the chairs, taking care to pull it away from the table. The faerie winced when the wooden legs dragged on the stone floor. "I'm afraid we haven't been able to determine the provenance of the house. Who were the prior inhabitants?"

Looking up, as if the ceiling would aid in remembering, the faerie let out a breath before speaking. "Well, it started out belonging to a couple who'd been fishers all their lives, the Tosbrats. They were nice—always gave me a saucer of fresh milk in exchange for cleaning the house. Then they died, and it went to some rich sod at the estate sale—one of the Cynnis boys. He rented it to a young fellow who was getting married. Everything was fine at first, until they had a kid. Then it all went to hell. They kept forgetting to put out milk, let the kid knock over the charms—well, I can't work under those conditions." Again folding his arms, the faerie shook his head. "I refused to keep the place clean unless they performed the rituals right—they didn't, so I stopped."

"How did that get resolved?"

"The place was such a pigsty that the kid got sick and died. The wife committed suicide after that, and the man—don't know what happened to him. Then the Cynnis boy rented to a healer, who lived alone with her cat. She was great, real nice, but the cat was a little monster — kept drinking my milk." Smirking, the faerie added, "Not that little, really. That was one fat old moggy. When the cat up and died, she moved to Iaron, and next up was another couple, the Forgrins." The faerie shuddered. "Never forget those two — didn't even acknowledge my existence." At Torin's questioning gaze, the faerie explained: "Temisans."

"Ah, yes," Torin said with a nod. "If I have my theology correct, Temisa frowns on the fae, does She not?"

"Temisa can go hang, for all I care." The faerie pointed a green finger at Torin. "I'm just trying to make an honest living here, I don't need some goddess sticking Her nose into my business. Okay? So after they left — "

Holding up a hand, Torin interrupted. "Wait a moment, please — why did the Forgrins depart?"

"It's all well and good to disbelieve house faeries, but then you need to pick up the slack, don't you? Mrs. Forgrin was the world's worst housekeeper, and Mr. Forgrin was allergic to dust. So they left, and Cynnis couldn't find anyone, so *he* moved in. Used to entertain his lady friends every once in a while."

"Which Cynnis was this?"

"Jared."

Torin blinked. "Isn't he married?"

Grinning widely, the faerie said, "That's why it was only every once in a while." The grin dropped quickly. "Was kind of frustrating, too, 'cause the only time he'd leave out milk for me was when he was entertaining. Mind you, he'd leave a huge bowl of the stuff, so I'd make the place cleaner than the Lord and Lady's china — but then the place'd go to pot between trysts. I remember one time his wife caught him at it — I didn't see him for months. I swear, I was this close to sucking on a cow."

His face scrunched up in mild disgust, Torin said, "It never came to *that*, I hope."

The faerie shook his head. "No, Jared couldn't keep it in his tights that long. Anyhow, it wasn't long after that that his investments all went bad on him and he had to sell the place. This was about ten years ago."

"Ah, yes, right after the crash." At that, Torin got up and started pacing the room. "That was shortly after I began working for the Castle Guard."

"Yes, well, it was great for me. I got the best family since the Tosbrats: the Melkins. They were the best of all possible worlds—neat freaks who didn't drink milk, so everything they bought went to me."

"I can see how that would be appealing to you."

"Oh, it was great. One speck of dust, and they were putting up charms and putting out the big bowls of milk. Now to be honest, I don't care *that* much about the charms. It's just cheap symbolism, really. But the milk—I *live* for the milk!"

The faerie got a bit of a faraway look, until Torin cleared his throat and said: "According to what Mr. Grabodlik told us, he bought the house from Mr. Melkin after the latter's wife died, yes?"

"Yeah, it was some dinner party or other. The cook made something with a 'secret ingredient,' which turned out to be milk. She up and died right there."

Torin scratched his thick beard. "So what happened after that?"

"The Grabodliks came in. Nice enough folks, I suppose, but a little odd. I mean, Mr. Grabodlik spends all his time in the library. Won't let me in there at all—put up wards, even."

"Were you closed off from any other part of the house?"

"No, just there. The old sod *loves* to read, I guess." The faerie folded his arms again. "Didn't matter to me none. Mrs. Grabodlik was the laziest woman who ever lived, and she was more than happy to let me do all the work. Lazy women are the best thing for a house faerie, that's a fact."

"And I daresay active women are the best thing for lazy house fae?"

The faerie glanced over at Torin, as if never having considered that before. "I suppose so, but I wouldn't know. Don't matter to me none, I'm just in it for the milk."

"Of course. What of the rest of the family?"

Shrugging, the faerie said, "The children're all nice enough. Especially Alvin. Very good boy, he is. A shame he had to go and die like that. How'd you say he died again?"

"I didn't." Torin stopped pacing and walked over to the table. The faerie's small size meant that he towered over the creature. "If I may ask, how often did the Grabodliks require your services?"

Again, the faerie shrugged. "About like usual. Not as often as the Melkins, but enough. I'd say twice a week, maybe three times if the children got rowdy."

"Or if there is a rash of accidents."

"I'm sorry?" The faerie squinted.

Torin walked toward the door and leaned against it. "According to what Mrs. Grabodlik told my partner, there have been a rash of strange accidents lately. The looking-glass on her vanity broken, the kitchen utensils all on the floor, the kerosene draining out of the lanterns."

"I remember cleaning up that kerosene. Foul stuff, let me tell you. I almost held out for more milk for that one."

"That would have been a bit of a hardship."

"Whaddaya mean?"

Now Torin started walking slowly back toward the faerie—who, for his part, was shifting on the table. "Well, you are, of course, aware of the bovine malady that has struck Cliff's End?"

"What's a bovine malady?" the faerie asked, sounding genuinely confused.

"A sickness among the cow population. Approximately a quarter of all of the cows used by Cliff's End for food and dairy had to be slaughtered and destroyed due to an illness." By now, Torin was again face to face—or, rather, face to neck—with the faerie. "I'm surprised you were unaware of that."

"Look, I told you, I'm in the house all day. That's *my* job. The comings and goings of cows are hardly my lookout, is it?"

"Perhaps, but since your payment comes in the form of milk, it would perhaps behoove you to be cognizant of it."

Now, the faerie stood up on the table so he was nose to nose with the detective. "Look, I feel bad for those poor cows and all, but what's this got to do with Alvin? You've yet to tell me how he died. Don't you lot have a wizard on staff to do a peel-back spell on crime scenes?"

"Yes, we do." Torin folded his arms. "The problem is our magical examiner was unable to determine the specifics. We know only that he died in the living room of the house, apparently of a broken neck."

Again, the faerie's voice was tinged with surprised. "You couldn't tell what he slipped on?"

"No, that was obscured in the peel-back—which indicates that there is some minor magic at work."

"Minor?" The faerie sounded almost offended by that.

"There are types of magic that can be unseen by a peel-back, but this type of obscurity—according to our M.E., at least—indicates actions by a magical creature."

"Really? You mean to tell me there's some *other* magical creature I don't know about wandering about the house?"

Torin smirked. "That is *one* possibility, yes. Tell me, were you upset when the Grabodliks cut back to only requiring your services once a fortnight instead of once or twice a week?"

"What're you talking about?"

"Just what I asked. You see, my partner and I, we asked the Grabodliks what had changed recently to account for the accidents. They told us that the price of milk had gotten so high, thanks to the cows being sick, that they were forced to cut back on their use of your fine services. Mr. Grabodlik's job at the book dealer does not pay especially well, you see."

In a subdued voice, the faerie said, "'Fine services'? That was what they said?"

Torin nodded.

"Huh. Nice of them to say." The faerie flapped his wings, which filled the room with a mild buzz, and started levitating and moving toward the door. "Well, look, Lieutenant, I'm getting very tired, and I'd like to fly on home, so if there isn't anything else?"

Torin moved to stand between the faerie and the exit. "There's quite a bit else, good sir faerie. You see, what I think happened was that you had become dependent on a regular source of milk. After being so horribly rationed by the irregular schedule of Jared Cynnis, you positively gorged under the care of the Melkin family. So when the Grabodliks cut you back to only once or twice a week, and then to twice a *month*, you were livid. You started arranging accidents in the house to make your displeasure known."

"That's a fine story, Lieutenant, but—"

"How did you know that Alvin slipped on something?"

That brought the faerie up short. The buzz dimmed as his wings flapped more slowly and he descended a bit. "What?"

"You asked me a minute ago if we couldn't tell what it was that Alvin slipped on. I never said he slipped on anything—merely that he broke his neck in the living room."

Turning his back on Torin, the faerie flew back to the table, alighting on the chair, but not sitting. "Well, it stands to reason, doesn't it? I mean, how else does a boy break his neck in the middle of a living room?"

"Quite a number of ways, actually. That you were so sure it was slipping on something indicates to me that you were the cause."

"And what if I was?" the faerie angrily snapped. "I need dairy, don't I? I'm a *house faerie*—milk is what we *live* on! And I got—well, let's just say I was accustomed to more than I was getting from the Grabodliks. They should have—"

"They had no *choice*. They could not afford—"

"How was *I* to know that?"

"So you killed young Alvin to show your displeasure?"

"No!" In but a moment, the faerie's anger and outrage burned to ashes. "I mean—hell, Lieutenant, I didn't *mean* to kill him! I just used some elbow grease."

Torin squinted in confusion. "I beg your pardon?"

"Elbow grease—the stuff we secrete from our elbows?" The faerie talked slowly, as if to a not-very-bright child. "How you think we get things so clean?"

After hesitating a moment, Torin smiled. "I must admit I hadn't thought about it that closely."

"Well, that's where it comes from. I squirted out an extra bit on the floor when I knew the kid was walking through. I just wanted him to fall down and look stupid, that's all. I didn't think he'd break his neck."

"So you confess to the crime?"

The faerie let out a long breath. Now that he'd told the truth, it was as if a weight had been lifted from his wings. Fae are creatures of truth, after all—while misdirection and being overly literal was part and parcel of their lives, out-and-out deception was not an easy thing for them. It had just been a matter of time before Torin outlasted him. "I suppose I am. Dammit." Staring up at the lieutenant's green eyes, the faerie started pleading. "Look, I just wanted my milk. Is that really so wrong?"

Torin walked over to the door and opened it. "It is when a person is killed. Guards?"

"Yeah."

Two Guards—the same two who had brought the faerie and the Grabodliks to the castle—came in. "You'll be taken to the hole," Torin said, "until the magistrate is ready to see you."

"The hole" was the colloquial name for the holding dungeon in the basement of the castle. One remained there until the magistrate decided on your sentence. If you were lucky, it was to return to the hole. The faerie was unlikely to be so lucky.

The faerie let out a long sigh. "I'm really sorry about all this, Lieutenant, you must believe that. He was a good kid."

"Yes, I'm sure he was. Take him away."

The Guards nodded and each of them grabbed one of the faerie's small arms.

As they carried him out, the faerie's legs dangling in the air beneath him, the creature called out, "Lieutenant?"

"Yes?"

"They have any dairy in the hole?"

Torin considered, realized he wasn't sure. "Perhaps."

"I hope so. I've been without for almost a week now—I'm getting the milk shakes."

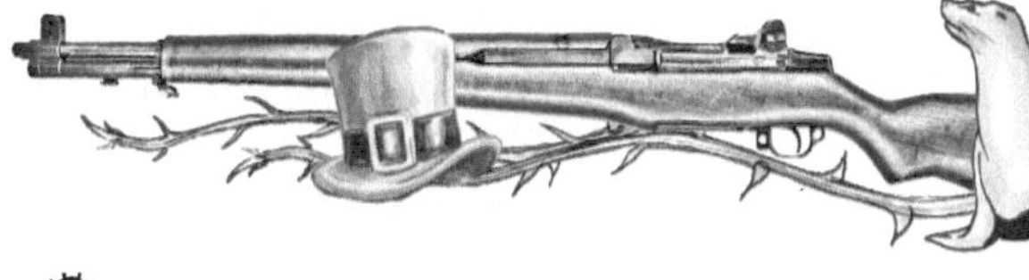

Futuristic Cybernetic Faerie Assassin Hasballah

Adam P. Knave

I ONLY TOOK THE JOB BECAUSE I NEEDED THE MONEY. I ONLY needed the money because Bunny needed the money. Bunny needed the money because she owed it to Kleigschtomper. Kleigschtomper wanted his money.

Regardless, it was a warm, sunny day when I sat on a rock in the open field we always met in and talked to Jenhoff, my agent, about the job itself.

"Hasballah, I couldn't give less of a damn about why you're taking the job…"

"I'm telling you about Kleigschtomper here. He…"

"I know Kleigschtomper. I've worked with Kleigschtomper. Bunny should have known better than to get in debt to Kleigschtomper." Jenhoff shook her head slowly, her sharply sloping ears poking out under her long dark hair. Her wings buzzed annoyance and she fidgeted with a folder that sat in her lap like a bomb.

"Fun name though, isn't it? Kleigschtomper. I just like saying it."

"You like saying it when it isn't being gasped out of you with his hand around your neck as you beg for life."

"I don't deny this. Fine." I ran a hand through my shoulder length blond hair and took a deep breath, settling my own wings so their movements wouldn't betray my anxiousness to get the job and get it done. "You don't care about the deeper causes and meanings of my existence, or Bunny's.

"What's the job?"

"It's shit."

"Thanks, Jenn. Build morale some more, why don't you?"

"Not my job. My job is to hand you, Mister Killer man, a file." She tossed a folder into my lap. "And tell you to kill someone. Him, in the file. Kill him."

With that, she got up and left me alone in the field, folder unopened in my lap. Sighing — I did a lot of sighing, it felt like — I stood and wandered out of the field, flipping through the folder as I went.

The target's name was Ugh, no last name given. He was an Ogre. I mean a real Ogre: large, smelly, lived in a cave, tusks...the works. I felt another sigh coming on. Ogres weren't exactly easy to kill. Not even for the best of the best. Which would be me.

There weren't many assassins who were faeries to begin with, these days. We were considered too small to be a serious threat to the larger races. All too often, it was one of the larger races someone needed assassinated.

Since the fall of Man and the return of Magery and our older ways, most disputes were settled in a civilized manner: sword to the face, mace to the neck, acceptable societal situational handlers.

It just so happened, though, that sometimes it didn't work too well that way. You might have the moral high ground, but a weak sword arm. Times like those, you wanted an assassin. If you were really smart, you wanted an assassin who was small enough and fast enough to not be caught. Too many people didn't think of that part.

Furthermore, the really critical point, you wanted an assassin who had cybernetic implants and fought dirty on your behalf. Sure, I traded in my left arm for a hunk of metal and wires, and an eye, and my liver and right foot and a few other bits and pieces here and there, all in the name of old Man tech. It made me a whole lot more fun to be around, but we all had to make a living.

I filled a niche.

I took to the air and buzzed my way back to the tree. Flashing my metal eye at a sensor hidden under a leaf deactivated the security. I walked in to see Bunny sitting around, counting what was left of her money.

"Hasbutt," she said merrily, kicking her feet against the legs of her chair, "did you get a job?"

"I got," I said, waving the folder, "a job. Ogre, though."

"Ooo, man, I hate Ogres."

"You don't have to kill this one."

"Well that's good, considering that I hate them and wouldn't want to even get close to it. Besides, you're the guy."

I walked over to her and ruffled her hair, laughing. What most people never realized was that Bunny was the dangerous one. Oh sure, I can take down a bunch of Man-sized beasts and do it so no one ever really notices me, but Bunny is the dangerous one. You just never find out about it until you're dead.

It lowers the number of people who talk.

She hopped off her chair and hugged me tight, giggling like a madfaerie. Yup. Deadly beast is she. Trust me on this. I've seen her take out Ogres without too much trouble. Hells, she could take out this one for me, but she wouldn't. Bunny had a thing about chores. She didn't want to do any if she didn't have to. She saw my work as a chore, of course, so she would only help out in the preparation and the cheer-leading.

Bunny owned pompoms.

I stumbled as I landed on the tree and fell against the eye sensor hard enough to hurt. At least it still read my ID and opened the door. Bunny perked up as I staggered through the door and met the carpet face first.

"Hasballah," she asked, concern in her voice, "what the..."

"*Mmmrf*, Bunny. We should... Well, I left here, right?"

"Right, you left here," she agreed as she helped me up and over to the couch.

"To kill Ugh."

"The Ogre?"

"Yeah, him. He was home," I said slowly.

"Good place to kill him," Bunny agreed.

"Sure, but he knew I was coming I think, I just...Ow, stop that."

Bunny shook her head and continued to poke and prod at my wounds.

"But, Has, you're bleeding all over the couch. I keep my art near the couch," she sighed.

"Right, sure. So he surprised me," I admitted ruefully.

"Not the other way around?"

"No. Get me that battery over there?"

Bunny nodded and flounced over to the work table I kept on one side of the room. She studied the assortment of gear: batteries, replacement lenses and wires, and so on.

"The black...?"

"Yeah. Anyway, as soon as I got through the door, he clubbed me."

She came back, handing me the battery, and resumed her makeshift nursing attempts, eyes going wide.

"*Ooohh*, one of those big..." she started.

"An Ogre club, of course, what else would he...?"

"I don't know. Here, let me see your arm."

Bunny reached for my cybernetic arm, dabbing at it with an oil cloth.

"Arm's fine. Rebooting," I told her, moving it away from her. Bunny wasn't great with electronics. "So he clubbed me, and then he did it again and..."

"And you blasted him to bits?"

"No, I fell down. A lot. Those clubs hurt."

"Well, why'd you get hit?"

"He surprised me, I told you."

"Oh. Right."

"So I...Help me plug this in, quickly?"

"What's the rush?"

"Well I got away from him."

"Ugh. The Ogre."

"Right. Except..."

"There's an except?"

"He followed me..."

"Here?"

"Well, not here, yet. Tree's still standing."

"Oh, Has, oh, oh, Has, that's not...that's not good, it's just...that's... oh, Has, not good."

I agreed with her, in principle at least. I stood, shakily, and grabbed some new weaponry: a couple of grenades, an extra knife, a bag of the good dust, a bit of glue...just some basics. Bunny followed me around fussing as we traced circular paths in the place. I circled back around and grabbed the little chip out of the desk. Something felt off about all of this, and I hated to be caught cold.

"Time to bail," I said. "We'll use the back."

Bunny nodded and leapt out of the window with a little squeak, her bag of goods clutched tightly in her hand. Her wings slowed her as soon as she cleared the windowsill and I followed in short order.

Except my wings weren't up to snuff. They're hybrids, my wings. Semi-mechanical. They have to be; my originals got mostly blown off years ago. I felt like crap, though, and the mechanical systems were still a bit shaky from damage, so I fell like a stone. While I twisted and turned in the air, I caught a glimpse of Bunny getting clear and avoiding something.

Something I landed on with a *whuff* and thump. I held onto the lumpy mass tightly, not wanting to slide down and hit the ground, until I noticed that the lump was breathing. Sighing, I peeled an arm away and took a good look at what I was holding.

"Hey, Ugh, no hard feelings?" I asked the Ogre as I clutched his head tightly.

"Ugh no like you. Ugh use club."

"All right, Ugh, if you need to." I sighed and unhooked a grenade from my belt. Ugh hit himself in the head with his club, narrowly missing my toes. He growled and drew back for another swing.

Crawling around Ugh's head some, I squirted a large gob of glue into his left eye and crammed the grenade into the sticky mess, taking the pin back as a souvenir.

I hit the ground hard, but luckily my side was there to take the fall. As I fell off Ugh, his club swung by my ear and right into his own. I took off at a sprint, counting to myself. I reached six and got bowled over by the concussive force of a grenade exploding behind me.

I picked myself up off the ground for what seemed like one time too many in a single day and glanced behind me. Half of Ugh's head was missing, and he seemed to be looking for it on the ground.

Damned Ogres and their ability to keep moving. They were like chickens that way: you can remove their heads but sometimes they just keep going. I watched him for a minute or two, Bunny coming up to my side and watching with me, until he fell down. Hard.

"Bunny, go back inside," I told her as we stepped over Ugh's body.

"What about you, Hasbutt?" She grinned and went back to jumped up and down on Ugh's body a few times.

"I have to go finish the job."

"Ogre's dead. Job's done. Right?"

"Normally. But not this time."

"If you're sure, I mean shouldn't you take some time and..."

"Nope. Now go on."

Huffing lightly, Bunny nodded and got off the Ogre carcass to fly back into the tree. I resettled my weapons and tried to fly, finding my wings sore, but workable.

⚜

The door to Jennhoff's office was open. She was sitting at her desk, the window behind her open to allow a cool breeze in. She looked up as I came in, the tips of her ears twitching.

"Ugh taken care of?" she asked me as she looked back down at her desk and whatever she was doing.

"*Mmm*, you could say that, Jenn."

"I just did say that."

"Sure. There's just one thing..." I sat down on the edge of her desk and gave her a cold grin.

"Yeah?" she asked, trying to hide her annoyance and failing.

"He knew I was coming," I said as I pulled a knife from my belt, "and I gotta ask myself how he knew."

Jenn started to stand up, stopping when the edge of my knife found itself a few inches from her eye.

"Has, what are you trying to...?" She managed to hold her voice level but her eyes kept flicking between my knife and my face.

"At first I just headed here to...I thought you might be able to work out who...but then it clicked. How much?"

"How much what?" she asked archly, growing annoyed as her initial fear faded. That's the problem with pulling a knife on someone. When you don't use it quick enough, they assume you won't use it at all.

"Don't...just don't. We've worked together for too long. I'll ask once more, seeing as how we've taken all this time to build a lasting and meaningful relationship. How much?" I inched the knife closer to her face and tried not to smile as she flinched.

"Has, you're wrong about..."

Her words cut off with a scream as my knife slid along her cheek, parting the skin easily.

"Next it's an eye. C'mon, Jenn. Don't do this...or make me do this."

"The money was too good. I got four times a normal job for it, all right?"

I sighed and lowered the knife some, "So that's all I'm worth to you, four jobs all rolled up in one easy moment?"

"Don't put it like that, Has..."

"No? How should I put it, then?"

"Well..."

"Right." I hopped off her desk and walked towards the door.

"This doesn't mean we can't still work together, Has. It was just business," she insisted, standing up and starting to move around her desk.

"Jenn. Don't even try that shit with me."

I closed her office door behind me and took off from her ledge, doing everything I could to look uninjured and strong.

I was even able to keep it up for a good three minutes, before I bobbled in the air a bit, almost swerving into a tree. I was doing fine. Really.

⚜

Kleigschtomper sat on a rock, idly playing with a knife. He was big for a faerie, about twice again my height and weight. Not that any of the extra weight was body fat; no, Kleigschtomper was all muscle and bad attitude.

"Hey, dude, got a sec?" I asked as I landed behind him.

Kleigschtomper spun around and threw his knife hard before he even saw me. I dodged and shook my head with a laugh.

"Is that the best you got for me, Kleig?"

"Hasballah," he said, and spat on the ground. "You really are stupid, aren't you?"

"That's me. The stupidest with the...Oh, the hell with it."

I threw a handful of faerie dust at him, my own special blend. It hit the air and shimmered bright hues of silver before falling towards him. I counted to three and dove for cover.

The dust sparkled brighter, I assume, since I couldn't see — face down like I was — and then exploded. The exploded part I'm sure of. That much I felt and heard.

Potent batch.

Kleigschtomper yelped and thudded to the ground. I stood up after an extra second of waiting to see him lying prone on his back in the grass.

"Kleig," I asked as I walked over to him, "I know you're still alive. Why are you trying to kill me?"

"B-bunny," he muttered, his eyes opening slowly and painfully, "owes me money."

"So you try to kill me? How does that work? Try and kill her, like an honest kinda guy."

"She works for you…"

"Mmm right, that makes it all make sense. Sure. Admit it, Kleig, this is because…"

"Don't start that!" he bellowed. He sat up slowly and rested his hand on his knees, spreading his wings wide to feel for damage. There was none; exploding faerie dust can be lethal, but I knew how much to throw at a faerie.

"It's true, isn't it?"

"Mom always liked you best!"

"Klieg," I said as I sat down next to him, "we're not related."

"Yes we are, our mom is the…"

"Unfortunate result of a time-traveling cloning experiment. I explained this all *last* month."

He glared at me and patted at his belt before finding and pulling a fresh knife out of a sheath.

"I still don't…"

"It's a long story. Just deal with it and move on. Now how much does Bunny owe you?"

He waved the knife around some and pointed it at me in a fairly menacing manner. I slapped it away with my metal arm and primed the laser, the small red light blinking to show a full charge.

"I wanted you dead!"

"I know, dude," I told him softly, the primer light still blinking at him. "It's just that things get complicated in my life. It isn't you. So why don't I settle the debt, and we'll start fresh."

"I'll kill you eventually, Hasballah, you know that."

"Sure. Just not today. I tell you what…" I dug my free hand into a pocket slowly and rummaged until I found the chip, "I'll give you this, and you can go kill me."

"What," he asked, snatching the chip out of my hand, "the hell is this?"

"Time machine. Tiny. Effective. Programmed to take you to my future where I'll be nice and old, and you can kill me. Deal?"

He studied the chip, frowning at it as he turned it end over end in his hand.

"Well, I mean, I guess, sure…if you…"

"And we'll call the Bunny-thing even. You get to kill me, after all."

"Yeah, all right, Hasballah."

Kleigschtomper gave the chip a good squeeze and vanished before my eyes. Dumb semi-half-brother faerie. He never thought to ask how he would get home again.

This is why not even Bunny knew about our relationship. I was ashamed of him.

I told him the truth, though—that chip would take him to my future. I should know; that's where I got it from. Years ago, an older version of myself came back and handed me the chip, telling me to send Kleigschtomper back to him eventually, for the laugh.

I laughed as I stood up and beat my wings against the air, rising into the sky.

I laughed long and good.

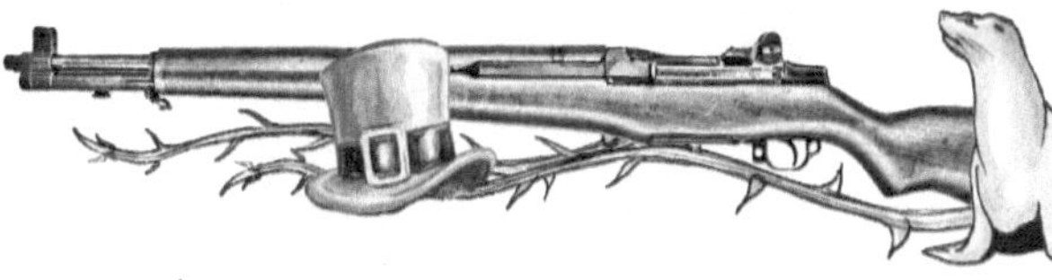

Hidden in the Folds

Jesse Harris

Swallowed by the unforgiving mountains of Etchu Province
Battle-worn ronin flees the looming end of an Emperor's reign
Fangs of thick, grey clouds menace low in the sky
His only comfort an onimori clutched close to his heart

Battle-worn ronin flees the looming end of an Emperor's reign
Shifting mud sucking at his feet, cold rains drench like despair
His only comfort an onimori clutched close to his heart
Fear of pursuit, fear of worse, drives the ronin on

Shifting mud sucking at his feet, cold rains drench like despair
Treachery among slick rocks, fissures spew hot, heavy breath of demons
Fear of pursuit, fear of worse, drives the ronin on
Light from a distant lantern beckons and brings hope

Well after sunset, through blustery wind and driving rain, a weary *ronin* sought shelter at a small, well-kept temple tucked away in the folds of a bamboo grove. As he passed under the *torii* gate, the pugnacious wind ceased its mordant bluster, though he could still hear its vehemence and see the branches of the nearby cedar trees flailing beyond the grove. Peace settle over him, though, as he felt cupped in the protective embrace of this hallowed dell. The warrior drew a bamboo *onimori* from around his neck and gave it a thankful kiss as he turned to what he hoped would be a reprieve from an another harrowing night's sleep.

Shinemawa were wrapped around the gate's supports and also on a nearby boulder. A faint smile caressed his lips at a familiar thought, for he always wondered how long it took to twist the straw into strands, or to fold the paper prayers into such intricate, zigzag designs.

Painted paper lanterns adorned the rafters, and as he passed through the curtain that adorned the doorway, tallow candles illuminated the inside and pungent incense stung his eyes and nose. His gaze then fell to the center of the room where a stone carving of *Saruta-hiko* sat. Without wasting another moment, he crossed the wooden floor and knelt before the stone god of travelers, clasped his hands together and offered a fervent prayer of thanks.

"A visitor, on a night like this, you must be lost or mad."

The *ronin* turned at the shrill voice, but when he regarded the speaker, he rose in surprise and put his hand to the hilt of his sword. Before him was a small creature right out of a faerie story. It stood no taller than his sword, with skin as red as the paint on the torii gate, and a nose at least three hand widths in length. It was dressed in priestly garb, held prayer beads in its hand, and its head was shaved bald. But the thing that startled him the most, though, was that it had wings and claws where its arms and hands should have been.

"Please close your mouth, it is very impolite."

As if he were ordered by a daimyo, or the Emperor himself, the warrior closed his mouth. So unnerved was he that the *ronin* tripped over a step as he backed away in disbelief. "But...you are..." the warrior could not say its name. Stories from his childhood flooded his mind; mischievous pranksters, capricious imps, vengeful, easily insulted...

"I am now a monk, atoning for my sins; nothing more." The creature's piercing voice pricked at the hair on the back of the warrior's neck. He could not take his eyes off it as it hopped across the floor. It picked up a straw broom in its claws and began to sweep. "So, which is it?"

The *ronin* struggled to keep up. "Which is what?" He could not hide the mistrust in his voice.

The creature continued to sweep the floor and took no perceptible notice of the warrior's wariness. "Are you mad, or are you just lost?"

The warrior, determined to regain his composure, drew his sword. "You are *tengu*." Confidence and strength replaced the temporary shock.

The *tengu* paused from its errand and sighed, "I am a monk; you are a warrior; I am *tengu*; you are man. One should not judge by labels."

The *ronin* was taken aback, flushed with confusion, like a hand that had just clapped him on the side of his head. "What are you doing?" He wanted to ask more, but how does one question a creature that up until now was thought a mere child's story told to instill obedience?

"I am sweeping the floors." Only a hint of irritation could be heard in the imp's response. "Other than that I am trying to start a civil conversation. If you are opposed to that, let me finish my chores and I will take my leave of you." The tengu redoubled his sweeping, obviously annoyed at the turn that this conversation had taken.

"No," the *ronin* said as he put up his hand. "Please, forgive me. I meant no disrespect." The little goblin paused once again, took a deep breath and let its shoulders sag as if to let some of its tension and irritation release. The young warrior continued, "I have only known of *tengu* by the stories I heard as a child."

A cackle escaped the puck's crimson, bulbous lips as it continued its sweeping. "Let me guess...your mother told you that if you were not good, a *tengu* would carry you away and feed you to its younglings."

The *ronin* smiled as he nodded in agreement. After a moment of uncomfortable silence, the *tengu* snuffed its nose and resumed sweeping, "So, you never answered my question."

"I am lost. My name is Toushi, Yamakazi Toushi," he said as he slid his sword back into its sheath with a click.

A stillness hung in the air, neither sure how to continue the conversation. Only the sound of straw scraping against the floor disturbed the awkward silence. The *tengu* then smiled and said, "Well, friend Toushi, you are free to spend the night...Sleep well."

The *ronin*'s curiosity, however, could not be so easily dismissed. "Please...tell me," he asked. "Why you are here?"

The *tengu* turned back to Toushi and its look of surprise and marvel could not be hidden. "You really wish to hear my story?"

"Yes I do." A broad smile crossed Toushi's face. "I was rude earlier, and it would be my honor to listen while you regale me with your journey." The warrior bowed, and then sat down on the floor, legs folded beneath him, his back, straight and strong. "Tell me good *tengu*, what adventure brought you into the priesthood?"

The *tengu* jittered with delight. It dropped its broom, and folded its legs underneath itself. The sight, however, perplexed Toushi, for instead of sitting on the floor, it hovered in the air. The gremlin saw Toushi's expression and set its taloned feet on the floor once again.

"Please forgive my inconsideration. If you prefer me to sit on the floor I will, but..."

"No, that will not be necessary," Toushi said. "It is just something I never thought I would have to get used to. Please...go on."

A wide smile adorned the *tengu*'s face as it once again hovered in the air. "There is not much to tell...but your mother's stories and faerie tales were true. I and my brothers and sisters carried off many children, but it was more than that. I regret to say that there were many times that I was party to tipping over ornate palanquins filled with painted geisha, or snatching travelers from their path and taking them to far away cities where we would drop them with little clothing and no idea how they got there."

⚕

"One day, not too long ago, I was waiting in the lofty perch of a Cryptomeria tree when an old woman walked by and I could not help myself. I swooped down and snatched her off the ground. She fought harder than I anticipated and she slipped from my grasp. All I had left was the pack that she had carried. With her screams dwindling in the distance, I returned to my cave with my plunder. When I looked at what I had acquired, I was astonished."

The *tengu*'s eyes and voice softened and became distant, "As I unwrapped the bundle, I saw what could only have been a *bohivitsu*, a future Buddha. The baby was beautiful and without blemish, his skin pale like milk, and his hair was like gold. It seemed to glow with a light like that from the rising sun.

He looked at me with eyes as blue as a mountain lake and spoke to me without words. He told me that my deeds went against the teachings of the Buddha. To pass into paradise, I had to turn from my mischievous nature and serve at a temple. So from that point, I have worked here, and have served faithfully, and I pray that one day, the Buddha will find me worthy to pass into the Land of Paradise."

"How long have you been faithful to your vow?"

"It has now been over 200 years."

The warrior could not contain his disbelief. He sat up straighter, unable to grasp so staggering a number. The *tengu*'s smile broadened, pleased by the reaction. "Please close your mouth; we have already talked about this, it's impolite."

Still stunned by the revelation, he asked, "Two hundred years? What have you been doing for two hundred years, sweeping floors?"

The cackle burst forth from the *tengu*'s and echoed from the walls. "No. Each day I write down a copy of the 'Diamond Wisdom Sutra' and make these." And the *tengu* pointed up.

Toushi looked up at the ceiling. From the rafters hung thousands upon thousands of origami, all of different shapes and sizes and colors. *"Gacho-n!"* The sheer magnitude of awe could not be expressed in so simple a phrase, but the incredulity that showed on the warrior's face made some semblance of rectification for so gross an understatement.

Upon a closer look, Toushi's shock turned to wonder and admiration for not one matched another. Each one was brilliant in color and shape and design. Each piece was intricate in construct and form, meticulously folded to find the perfect marriage of harmony and peace, while still maintaining the intent of the desired image. Animals and flowers, boats and bridges, birds and fish, and every other imaginable shape one could dream of. Toushi marveled at how beautiful and delicate each piece was.

"You made *all* of these?" Toushi said, still enthralled by the origami's beauty.

"Yes; one for each day I have served my oath." The *tengu* then paused for a moment, "Do you like what you see?"

"I have never seen their equal. Even the sacred jewels of the *Minamoto* would pale in comparison."

"I am so glad you like my work." The *tengu* floated closer and a grin alighted on its face. "And because you have been so nice to me, I have decided to teach you how to do this."

Toushi beamed and cocked his head as if to talk to the *tengu* without taking his eyes off the captivating origami. "You...would teach this to me?" Toushi thought of how a skill like this could get him back into the graces of a *daimyo*, and regain his honor and rank.

With a gracious wave of its hand, the *tengu* patted the young *ronin* on his back. "It would be my honor." At its tug and with reluctant step, Toushi tore his eyes from the origami and allowed the *tengu* to lead him towards the back of the temple, though each moment he could, he stole another enamored glance at the origami.

He was led into a small room filled with a foul smell, like that of a dog that died in its own excrement. The stench made Toushi's eyes water and his hand instinctively came in front of his face.

"Please forgive the conditions in which I live, but we *tengu* are not the same as you. Give me a moment to light some incense to make things more pleasant. Please, make yourself comfortable." The *tengu* floated across the room to a brazier and lit it with a long, wooden match. It then lit some candles and a small hearth, and the room suffused with a golden glow that was bright, warm and dry.

The *tengu* was true to his word, the room was soon imbued with a strong scent of spice and tang, like cinnamon and orange, that washed away the powerful stench that only moments ago could have set the *Ksitigarbha* statue on Mt. Osore to crumble. Toushi settled down on a *zabuton* and seemingly melted into its folds. Never before had he felt anything so soft. Before he was even aware of it, the *tengu* stood before him with a small black-lacquer tray on which sat a polished, jade teapot with a twisted straw handle, and two matching cups filled with a steamy brew. Lax and languid in both mind and body, Toushi reached forward and lifted one of the cups off the tray. The smell of jasmine and ginkgo surfeited his senses as he sniffed the concoction, and a contented sigh escaped his lips. He drew a savory and pleasurable sip from the cup and let the exotic taste of the blend dance on his tongue. The heat of the liquid gave a warm and pleasant shiver that helped settle him into an even more relaxed repose.

For the moment, there was no time; there was no rain or wind. The days of mountain travel were naught but a transient dream. It was comfort, and warmth. Toushi lounged on his pillow and savored each sip taken, and each moment indulged.

"Forgive me, my Lord."

With a moan of assent and a listless smile on his face that spread from ear to ear, the man opened his eyes and could not help but start as his mind focused on the red-skinned, bald-headed, bulbous-nosed imp that obtruded his sight.

"The paper is ready; do you wish to begin the lesson?"

Toushi sat forward and rubbed his eyes, yawned and stretched in one veritable motion, and then with prodigious effort, stood. With limbs of lead and tree stumps for feet, Toushi lumbered forward at the *tengu*'s lead. It took a moment for his eyes to adjust and refocus, but when they did, he found himself at a table filled and dazzling with all colors and patterns of paper imaginable; each piece as vibrant as priceless jewels or precious metals.

A few more steps and Toushi felt the gentle claws bid him sit on a plush, covered stool.

"Before we start, we need to know what you want to make."

Toushi turned as the *tengu*'s hot breath brushed against his cheek. "What do you mean?" he responded, distracted by the size of the imps nose.

"Don't be doltish. We need to figure out what shape you would like to fold the paper into. But not just anything," it said as it raised its finger. The smile the *tengu* gave grew even wider and seemed to distort and stretch its whole face. "We need to find out what your shape is.

The trick is, especially for the first time, to think of a shape that you love." His eyes shined like burnished coins. "Think of a fond memory...the fondest one you can think of. Let your mind wonder, and let your heart speak to you.

"What is the one shape that could sum up all your happy moments?"

A grin spread across Toushi's face, a mixture of achievement and nostalgia. The *tengu* nodded and sniggered in approval, and without a word being said, the *tengu* reached into the heap of paper and drew out a parchment the color of cedar. Toushi looked at it, and then to the *tengu*, and approved of the choice. He then took the sheet and turned it around several times, and studied all facets of the paper. A tone of gold enhanced the color of the cedar; and before his eyes, it looked as though the surface and texture emerged from what once seemed flat.

"Remember to take it slow." The tengu's words were paltry distractions as Toushi's mind raced and remembered. "Think long and hard of the object you want to make. See it in your mind. See every possible detail, every conceivable feature of your shape. Let it become real in your mind."

Toushi was so engrossed that the rest of the *tengu*'s words were lost to him; a mere babbling, chanting rhythm, absent of meaning compared to his task. His hands moved back and forth as the paper took its form, but Toushi's eyes stared off into nothingness. He saw the shape in his mind's eye: His father's boat, tied up to the pier.

Never had it looked more beautiful as it rocked back and forth on the waves. Deep cedar beams made the hull, tall strong oak made the mast and a pure white sheet made the sail. It looked so magnificent when set against the bright azure sky and white, wispy clouds.

He could hear the crash of the waves against surf and pier. He could smell the salty breeze as it blew across his face, a good strong wind that made one long for the open sea. The tide was going out and the sun was high and bright, and burned the eyes to look upon it.

With a rush of anticipation, he leapt onto the boat, untied the ropes, and caught the northern winds in his sail to blow him out to sea. He was free at last, back on the waves. The sea mist dampened his face and the land at his back shrank into the distance.

The boat sliced through the waves like a sword. He felt at home with the screech of the birds in the air, and the crash of the waves against the hull as the deck rocked and pounded beneath his feet.

A thrill of satisfaction filled his spirit to overflowing and a deep sigh accompanied his beaming smile, when suddenly he felt a tug at his heart. He turned to the west and his smile disappeared like the sun.

Thunderclouds blotted out the brilliant blue sky. The crisp, refreshing breeze grew into a blustering squall, and down from the ominous, black sky to the turbulent ocean reached a funnel of swirling black clouds as large as *Fuji-no-Takane*.

Each rise and fall of the ship caused the beams and planks to shudder and groan, and threatened to tear the ship apart. Toushi used a rope to fasten himself to the mast and said a fervent prayer, but before the knot could be fastened, he and his boat were sucked up into the powerful vortex.

His boat shattered into countless pieces and he was set adrift in the tsunami, tumbling and plummeting in uncontrollable terror. With despair and desperation, he cried out to every god he knew, and begged for salvation; each lamentation a plea for mercy.

Toushi gave up all hope. The gale sucked him dry of tears. His throat raw from his screams. His body broken and his very soul, shattered. The thought of death was a welcome release. He closed his eyes and let himself go to the storm.

The howl and bawl of the tempest seemed to rejoice. A malevolent laughter echoed within the thunder. The wind sped up and Toushi felt as if his very life was being drawn out of him.

Warmth then touched his cheek. At first, Toushi disregarded it, but it persisted despite the cyclone. Weary with battle and desperate for oblivion, he looked in the direction of the touch and was surprised to see a golden light break through the miasma. It reached out for him. As he looked to the light, it urged him to come towards it.

A spark ignited in his soul and his spirit rekindled when a form emerged from within the center of the beam, a shape at first he did not recognize. Somewhere from within he found a renewed strength, and despite the pain and exhaustion, the warrior reached out for the light.

The storm seemed enraged by Toushi's efforts and redoubled its fury. It ripped at his body and stole the very air from his lungs. It beat down on him with a ferocity that felt as if it would tear the skin from his bones. He tumbled and tossed and spun so much that tendrils of unconsciousness reached around the edges of his vision and threatened to draw him in. But still he kept his eyes on the form within the golden light.

Closer and closer the light came, and each moment the form took clearer shape. Through tear-blurred eyes, Toushi at first thought he saw a child, which in an instant was replaced by a lotus. His arms stretched out, his hand splayed, desperate to reach the light. A scream of rage thundered through the clouds.

With a start, Toushi opened his eyes and found himself back in the small, filthy, stench-filled room. He was soaked through with sweat. On the table before him lay a drab scrap of mangled paper that somewhat resembled a ship. In his hand he held the splintered remains of a bamboo tube, his *onimori*; and a copy of the Lotus Sutra that was given to him by a young acolyte he had saved during the battle.

Before another thought could pass through his mind, a pair of claws wrapped around his throat and wrestled him to the ground. The *ronin* reacted on instinct and went with the roll. He broke the hold and launched himself out the door. As he scrambled away and picked himself up, he looked back. From the doorway poured an ominous black smoke that shimmered with burning embers; and from the top of the smoke grew an *oni*, a demon of such size and horror that its head and torso burst through the temple ceiling. Its arms and hands scattering cedar beams like windblown rice.

"You think you are clever hiding that Sutra on me, do you?" Its voice rattled the air like thunder, and each step it took shook the ground. "You will soon find out how powerful my magic can be."

In its red hand, a great *bisento* sword as large as a tree appeared and it swung a mighty blow. As Toushi dodged to the side, the blade sunk deep into the soft, wet ground and sent mud, and Toushi, flying. Rage distorted the demon's ugly face and a fierce howl bellowed from its lips as it pulled the sword free and swung again.

Toushi slipped and lurched through the mud, but everywhere he stumbled, the colossal sword cleaved into the ground only a hair's breadth from him. Finally, a flash of lightning distracted the *tengu* enough for Toushi to dive behind the boulder near the *torii* gate.

"Come out, Toushi. You cannot hide forever." The behemoth stalked among the bamboo grove, its massive sword ready in hand, metal glinting from the lightning flashes. Raindrops hissed as they drenched its crimson hide, enshrouding the devil in a cloud of sulfurous steam.

Toushi trembled behind the boulder; his mind searched for any clue that could help him survive, and a thought struck him like the kick of a horse. *"Mochiron-yo!"* Toushi took a strong grip of his sword. After a deep breath and a quick prayer, he stepped out from behind his refuge, wishing he still had his lucky charm around his neck. "You red-faced dog," he yelled. "Take your foul smelling hide and leave before I cut your oversized nose down to size."

The *tengu* let loose a thunderous roar and came at Toushi with indiscriminate cuts. Toushi, however, took to a sprightly defense. He jumped from side to side, front to rear, and rear to front again, mocking the giant *oni* with jests and stinging insults, always followed by a peal of ringing laughter. Round and round went the *tengu*'s sword, always striking either the air or the ground, and ever missing its adversary.

Toushi then stood his ground, and the tengu swung with all its pent-up rage. This time, Toushi was prepared. The warrior side stepped the blow, and jumped as high as he could. The move allowed him to avoid the splash of mud and he landed on the giant fiend's arm. As fast as he could, he raced up the arm, and before it could react, Toushi imbedded his sword deep into the demon's neck.

The devil bellowed in pain and rage, and hurled the warrior to the ground. Its blood mixed with the mud. As the brute struggled, it shrank in size, smaller and smaller, until it was hard to see through the driving rain.

When the struggle ended, Toushi walked over to where the *oni* last lay. All that he found was his sword, and next to it lay next a dead kite with a broken neck.

With nowhere else to go, Toushi picked up his sword and went back into the temple. It seemed that the demon was only an illusion, for the temple was once again whole. The warrior clambered inside and leaned against the wall with labored breath and exhausted body.

His eyes first drifted to the straw broom that lay in the middle of the floor, then up to the ceiling where all the origami still hung. To his surprise, a glittering, azure mist formed around the origami and now drifted down to the floor. Thousands of little spirits materialized as the delicate paper ornaments that held them evaporated into nothing.

His amazement could not be hidden when from the mist; a figure took form, dressed in priest's robes and carrying prayer beads. He drifted to the floor and came forward to stand before Toushi. Nothing was said, but with a bow of his head and a humble smile on its aged face, the *kami* turned and followed the rest out the window.

Toushi bowed his head in response, "You're welcome."

Just Plain Bad

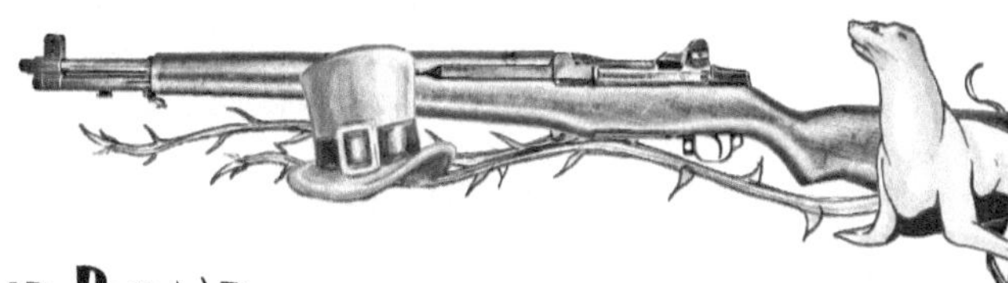

Way of the Bone

James Chambers

A DOZEN UNDRESSED PEOPLE LAY SCATTERED AROUND THE ROOM like wilted flowers.

Gorge spotted his drummer, Dev, sprawled across one of the sofas, still garbed in his immutable costume of denim and motorcycle boots, snoring, his limbs entangled with three women sleeping nude. Empty beer and liquor bottles littered the floor amidst booze puddles drying in the hazy sunlight. Pills peppered the coffee table, and a torchiere lamp protruded from the cracked screen of the wall-mounted television.

Picking a clear path through the carnage, Gorge opened the first adjoining room and peeked inside. Roald, his guitarist, sat meditating by the open balcony, bed empty, room clean. Gorge retreated quietly and closed the door. In the next room his bass player, who looked like he hadn't yet slept, entertained four women in a bed disheveled with hurricane frenzy. Three of the women stared at Gorge's naked body with open lust. The fourth pressed her face against a pillow as she moaned with ecstasy.

"Sound check at four o'clock. I'll have your balls if you're late," Gorge said. "I fucking mean it, Tank. Don't screw up this gig."

The bass player lifted his head from the soft arc of a perfect buttock and nodded.

Gorge cherished the abandon these people brought to their celebrations, chaos sweetened so much by their mortality and the real prospect of dying for a good time. He had known excess before his exile but bland in comparison, inconsequential and therefore cheapened. His mortal musicians and their groupies lived on the hard edge of a genuine abyss, and he found it addictive. The drugs and alcohol didn't affect him the same way they did the others, but he got off well enough on the atmosphere of risk and blind defiance. This was the way to live: one's ego and libido unchecked, forever flipping the bird at convention.

He returned to his own room and opened the curtains. His skin soaked in the midday heat. An old melody from the Faerie Kingdoms came to mind. He sat on the edge of the bed, picked up his guitar, and strummed while he sang. The song conjured his past when every day had been a thousand times more glorious than this one, and he had been worshipped and lived among kings. But the melody—heard perfectly in his head—could never be played as intended here. He set down the guitar in frustration and told himself, as he had daily for more than half a century: *Now I am free.*

Behind him Delilah uncoiled from the sheets and cupped herself against Gorge's back, wrapping her legs around his waist. Her skin, still damp with sweat from a morning spent in passion, plastered itself to Gorge. The gnarled knobs of flesh above his scapulae tingled as she cleansed their weeping scars with a moist washcloth from the nightstand. She caressed them with her fingertips, her lips, and then dried them with a soft towel.

Delilah hugged him tight and whispered in his ear. Her words reached him on the palanquin of her honeyed breath.

"Tell me again about how it was in the Faerie Kingdoms," she said.

Gorge caressed the silky tops of her thighs.

"Which version do you want today?" he asked. "The paradise I sacrificed for my life here with you, or the gilded cage from which I broke free to save my soul?"

"How do *you* see it today?"

"Today, I see through new eyes. Today the Kingdoms are a delicate fruit rotten at its core, which I will destroy before it spreads its taint."

"How will you do it?"

"I will open the Way of the Bone."

Delilah glided her tongue over Gorge's neck and slid her hands along his chest and abdomen, toward his cock. He stopped her with a gentle touch.

"You'll keep me here all day if I let you," he said, flashing a wicked grin. "I've got interviews, a sound check, and preparations to make."

Pouting, Delilah rose, and moved to the bathroom. Gorge watched captivated by her swaying, blue-black hair and the sublime way her curves and muscles shifted when she walked. She hadn't aged since he met her more than five decades ago; he'd brought enough magic with him for that at least when he'd been banished here.

While Delilah sang in the shower Gorge dressed in black leather pants, a faded orange Killing Joke T-shirt, and a black jacket. On his way out of the suite, he dialed up the Motörhead playlist on Dev's iPod, cranked the stereo volume to full, and then let the door swing shut as the feverish opening riff of "Ace of Spades" kicked in. Guitars roared. Bass and drums thundered. Then came the shouts of a dozen sleeping people blasted awake.

Checking himself in the elevator wall mirror, Gorge spent a touch of glamour to fix his appearance. He never let the public see him absent black lipstick, eyes circled with kohl, and wild, short spikes of black hair rising from his hawkish face. His transformation to a human body had dampened his native faerie features, but the remnants provided for an exotic appearance he liked to emphasize. His plans demanded he play the monstrous rock god to perfection today. When Red Gorge played Madison Square Garden tonight, they wanted the devout attention of millions watching their live-televised performance. It was the first step in the last leg of the journey Gorge had begun before he'd been cast out of the Kingdoms.

On the twelfth floor a black man built like a pro wrestler met Gorge and guided him toward the concierge suite. "They're gathering," he said.

"I saw them, Snow" said Gorge. "They've been all around us the last few days."

"I counted a couple of dozen different types, but mostly blackjack sprites."

"Vicious, little attack dogs." Gorge grimaced. Bloodthirsty blackjack sprites had chewed his fiery, gossamer wings from his body before they'd left him in iron chains in the desert.

"There are some I still don't recognize," Snow said.

Gorge nodded. "You take to my training exceptionally well, but some things will always stay beyond your ability to perceive them. I sensed a trio of elementals, probably the Winds of Change. A handful of fey from the Choruses are here too. As if they could turn song against me."

"So, how do we play it?"

Gorge squelched the wise-ass comment that rose to his lips and put a reassuring hand on Snow's back. "We stay alert. Take down any of them that comes within ten feet, and we do what we've always done—play the fucking show. Let them come. They think I'm weak. They expect if they punish me long enough, I'll repent, give up, or die. They have no idea how close I am to destroying them."

"Glad to hear it." Snow opened the concierge suite door. "Keep your guard up, boss, 'cause me, I got bills to pay."

Gorge laughed then shifted his attention to the young man waiting inside the suite. Silver piercings glinted on his face. Gorge sensed his nervousness and played on it, sizing him up with a stony glare, before he flopped onto an easy chair across from him.

"So, what the fuck do you want to know?" he said.

The man stammered, introducing himself as Kenny Choi, editor for *Guitar Gun* magazine. For half an hour he questioned Gorge about his early underground recordings, his influences, what he thought about streaming music services and the resurgence of popularity for vinyl, life on tour, and other topics. Gorge replied with whatever rude and indifferent answer occurred to him, grinding hard on his punk-inflected image.

"So, uh, *Way of the Bone*, your new album, out last month. The singles, especially the title song, have been burning up the charts, but it's kind of a concept album, right?" Kenny said. "What's the inspiration behind that?"

Gorge counted silently to ten and then said, "It's my fucking life story."

"Wow. So, like, it's a metaphor?"

"Yeah, exactly." Gorge slid into his stage voice, its effect on Kenny immediate. "It's about a musician who was the greatest musician who ever lived. Imagine having headphones plugged directly into the music of the spheres, and that's the kind of music this guy could make. He composed symphonies that brought tears to the eyes of the dead. His songs made virgins' loins tremble. They made royalty melt. And though he lived in a place where musical talent was a natural gift nearly everyone possessed, no one played better than him. So, this guy, he becomes friend to kings and queens, the confidante of emperors and empresses. They even initiate him into the Flock of Eternity, the 1,000 entrusted with all the secrets of the great Kingdoms."

Gorge kicked his feet up on the coffee table in front of him and sneered. "Except it all turns out to be a steaming load of dog shit."

He dragged out his pause to let his story breathe in Kenny's mind.

When he sensed the reporter about to ask a question, he continued.

"It was all nothing more than a way for these uptight pussies to break him, to keep him in an invisible prison, and make sure he did what they wanted. When he'd finally had enough, he spurned their laws and castrating traditions, and pursued music they'd forbidden. So they mutilated him and cast him down to what they considered Hell. But he only got stronger there and rose again. He reclaimed his music, and with it came serious fucking magic. Now he's going to bring darkness down on all Creation."

"The Way of the Bone?"

"The dark way. The music that makes devils of men."

Kenny scribbled in his notebook. "Giving me fucking chills here, man. Tonight's so gonna rock."

"I know," Gorge said, satisfied with the light he'd fired in Kenny's eyes.

He wanted everyone who heard his story to believe in its meaning if not its facts, even if only subconsciously, so that when they retold it or wrote it down, they imparted some of their belief to others. Gorge's tale resonated powerfully with the band's fans, especially the young, so many of whom sensed that better worlds existed beyond this one, although they could never reach or properly perceive them. They grappled with anger they didn't understand, with rage born of soul-deep frustration and the primal knowledge that they were unjustly cut off from great glory. They were left only to dream, and Gorge was happy to inspire them. It had taken years to gather so many fans, and tonight as Red Gorge performed *Way of the Bone* in its entirety, millions would listen enrapt in Gorge's story, focused on *his* life and desires. He would gather the power needed to wedge open the Way of the Bone. His gain would seem small for the effort spent to obtain it, but the power would enable him to collect more from around the world, until he could finally, fully open the Way, and bring all the wild, dark, slavering things in the universe right to the doorstep of the Faerie fucking Kingdoms.

Kenny stood. "Thanks for the interview, man. It was awesome to meet you. I've been a fan for practically my whole life. Your music is the real fucking deal."

"No shit. Keep dreaming, Kenny."

"Count on it."

As Kenny pocketed his digital recorder and his notepad and turned toward the door, Gorge spied it: a faint, bronze shimmer along Kenny's spine, like a shirt-seam dusted with glitter. He recognized it at once and flew from his chair, shoved Kenny to the floor, and wrenched free the glimmering, semi-invisible thing that had grafted itself to the editor's back. Kenny howled. The door banged open. Snow barreled in as Gorge stood, wrestling a flickering winged lightning bolt. The creature whipped around, trying to fly free, dragging Gorge against the coffee table, but Gorge held tight, squeezing so hard, his knuckles turned white, until the thing gave up, shimmered, and became fully visible. The slender creature had a snake's body topped by the miniaturized torso, arms, and face of a man. Its wings were like white crow's wings, and at the end of its tail dangled a knobby, spiral stinger.

"Holy... shit...," Kenny said from the floor.

Snow wrapped a hand around the gun holstered under his jacket. "You okay, boss?"

Gorge nodded. "Look what I've caught."

"A dragon pixie."

"Correct."

"We're compromised."

"No, don't you see? They don't know what's coming. They sent this pathetic little thing to find out. They're as fucking clueless as ever. Isn't that right?"

The dragon pixie trembled and hissed at Gorge.

"Don't you know who I am? What I am?" Gorge said.

"They call you the Death-Singer, black-hearted from the day you were spawned."

"Yes." Gorge smiled, pleased. "And well they should."

"Holy... *shit*," said Kenny. "It's all fucking real? The magic shit? That's so mind-blowing!"

"Snow?" Gorge said.

Snow yanked Kenny to his feet, maneuvered him into the corridor, and said, "See you at the show tonight, kid," before he slammed the door shut. Turning back to Gorge, he asked, "So, what do we do with it?"

"Do you understand, little pixie, what I'm about to accomplish?" Gorge asked.

"You think you can open the Way of the Bone, but they'll stop you," said the pixie. "She'll stop you."

"She? Who?" said Gorge.

Realizing it had said too much, the pixie clamped its lips tight.

"Is it Soniella? I don't fear Soniella," said Gorge. "The Flock has no idea what's coming, else they wouldn't have sent you here to find out. They'd just have killed me outright. But the law is the law. They sentenced me to exile, not execution so they can't do that. I know them much better than you, little wyrm. There's nothing more revealing of someone's nature than being the object of their hatred and subjected to their torture. You're about to learn that firsthand. I'm only going to release you after I've blinded you, sliced out your tongue, and cut off your hands, so you can't share anything you know with my enemies. You'll be my message to them. I'll leave you your ears so that when the great destruction arrives on a crashing wave of sound, you may witness it."

The pixie squealed and thrashed, but Gorge pressed it against the table. It lashed out with its tail, landing its stinger deep in Gorge's arms several times. Gorge ignored the wounds, and when Snow handed him a knife, the first thing he sliced away was the pixie's tail, chopping off its sting with a single blow. The rest went fast. Soon Gorge released the decimated creature out the window, cleaned up the room, and called for his next interviewer.

They ended the sound check with "Soniella," the ballad Gorge had written for the woman who'd been his lover in the Faerie Kingdoms. She had also been his betrayer and tricked him into surrendering himself for exile. Only Delilah knew the story, so when she stormed backstage during the song, her fury seemed inexplicable to all but Gorge.

Her reaction upset him. They were each other's sanctuary, each the only one the other trusted with their life and soul. In his old existence Gorge had never known such devotion, but he found it essential in this world of cruelty and filth. She had found him in Death Valley, ruined and chained to rocky ground. Mistaking her camera for a weapon, he attacked her at first, too weak to do any damage, but then she freed him and gave him water, brought him to her city apartment and nursed him. From Delilah he learned how to live in his new flesh of dust and ashes. If not for her, he'd have shriveled up and dried in the desert sun until he rotted away to dander to be blown across the sand.

He found her in his dressing room, drinking beer and scratching a charcoal stick across one of her countless sketchpads.

"I'm sorry," he said.

"It's fine. It's just... you promised me you'd never play that fucking song again."

"I need to prepare myself. I think she's here."

"How can she be?"

"I caught a spy this afternoon, and he said, 'She'll stop you.' He couldn't mean anyone else. Agents of the Kingdoms will attack tonight, probably during the concert."

"Shit," said Delilah. "Why send her?"

"They think I won't be able to fight her. Maybe they think I still love her."

"Do you?"

Gorge met Delilah's dark stare and said, "I love only you," feeling the nearly palpable truth of the words as he spoke them.

"Will she try to kill you?"

"No, she's of the Flock, and so, supposedly, above such things. But she knows my music better than anyone else. She might be able to disrupt it. There are faeries from the Choruses, elementals that control the wind, blackjack sprites, others. Everything must be played perfectly for the Way to open. If they distort the sound or stop us from playing our full set, it could exhaust the magic I've gathered in this world and leave the Way closed."

"Will you die?"

"No," said Gorge "You might if they wipe me out, and I can't replenish my magic soon enough. Last time, I had an edge, having brought some with me from the Kingdoms. This time I'll have to spend everything I have to crack open the Way. After that, I'll be starting at empty. It could take a century for me to recover fully."

"Find her and kill her now."

"There's no time. I'll be the strongest I've ever been as a mortal during the concert. Better to face her then. Soniella will only show herself when the balance of my spell is most exposed. I'll be ready. I won't let her harm you. I won't let her destroy what we have." Gorge lifted Delilah's chin toward his face. "I promise you. You're my night-haired beauty. You saved me, and I'll save you. We're meant to be together for all time."

He kissed her, stirring to the heat of her lips. He folded himself against her on the couch, feeling her tremble and clutch at him. They slid out of their clothes and moved together, and afterward lay there until it was time for the show to go on.

Four songs into their set, Red Gorge had already driven the crowd to frenzy.

The audience danced and slammed against each other, screamed lyrics from raw throats, and surrendered to the deep rhythms rising from the band. Their faces resembled ghost buoys bobbing on a dark sea. Dev, Roald, and Tank played like never before, the best Gorge had ever heard them: tight, fast, and with a will that would've left entire cities dead in their wake had they been an army on the march. They thrived on the excitement of the crowd and the fulfillment of their deepest wishes of greatness; it flowed into their music. Gorge worked his voice to its limits, ascending scales in rapid succession as he wove ethereal song over the hard terrain of the instruments. Together they created Red Gorge's signature sound: the grinding, irresistible progress of guitar, bass, and drums elevated by transcendent melodies and Gorge's unearthly voice. In the Kingdoms, where many more notes and musical scales existed, their music would've sounded crude, but in this world, it surpassed anything people had ever before heard.

As Roald bit into a guitar solo, Gorge raised his microphone stand and speared it against the stage. He drifted from the spotlight while guitar notes blistered the air. At the side of the stage, Delilah and Snow looked distracted by worry, and to Gorge they seemed immeasurably fragile, like paper and wax toys vibrating in the barrage of sound blasting from the arena's speakers. Part of him wanted to grasp Delilah's hand and comfort her. Another part wondered why he bothered with such a trivial creature such as a human woman who should've died ten years ago—and the moment that thought formed he knew his enemies stood nearby. He hadn't even noticed their attack begin, so subtle had it been, influencing his thoughts. Now he'd sensed the arrogant taint of the Kingdoms creeping into him.

It knocked him momentarily off balance and he almost lost his cue, but then he launched back into the song with a roar that shook the walls. The audience responded with thousands of voices that together barely measured up to the power of Gorge's amplified singing. The band tore into the song's climax with terrifying force, and didn't skip a beat launching into the next one. The others sensed Gorge's urgency and played with fantastic speed, as the lyrics emerged from Gorge like a cyclone slamming cars together along a rain-slashed highway. The arena rumbled. The force of the audience's energy connected with Gorge. A feedback loop opened as he absorbed it, skimmed away what he wanted, and kicked it back to them through the music. It was the moment he'd been working toward; the opening had begun.

The people nearest the stage thrashed to the beat, writhing like panicked animals. Security guards struggled to contain the melee from the rest of the crowd. Gorge watched the sea of people shoving, dancing, fighting, some even fucking in the dark. He swelled with pride for what he'd wrought. Like a living thing, the song grew around them in the shadows, stretched itself in the flashing stage-lights, reached its thunderous crescendo, and then segued straight into the next number, the title song from *Way of the Bone*.

Dev assaulted his drums and Tank's fingers ripped along the bass. Rhythm ruled for two measures then Roald's hands moved over his guitar strings, creating a riff that filled the arena like a jet of molten noise. The world wavered, as if the walls and roof, the advertising posters, and the overhead jumbo television screens were peeling back from reality so that the audience existed only within the music. Gorge rose at the edge of the stage like a crane about to dive into the air and sang:

Born in a moment
Born in pain
Nothing's ever the
same again

Chained in the desert
Chains in my mind
Wings bit off by
my own kind

Once, lord of lyrics
Once, prince of peace

Now a demon let
off his leash

And I will find the way
the Dark way, the way home
the way to Hell
the Way of the Bone

His voice soared, hounding the melody along a gouging assemblage of sound that lifted and enhanced it. A hundred voices joined in, a thousand, then ten thousand, and more as the crowd sang. The seal on the Way of the Bone loosened. The arena faded away. Power flowed into Gorge, and he sensed the universe trembling at his hubris, for the Way of the Bone would bring only death and stir only the carrion eaters and the blind things that stood hungry in the night. It was the forbidden Way, submerged in the deepest pockets of reality, and Gorge was slipping his filthy fingernails in around the edges to pry it loose for his pleasure.

Empress loved me
King smiled down
Until I stepped upon
hallowed ground

Music surrendered
Love became dread
Cast away, scarred, and
left for dead

But I will find the way
the Dark way, the way home
the way to Hell
the Way of the Bone

First came the blackjack sprites, swarming across the darkness like oversized wasps. Gorge swept his gaze in their direction as he repeated the chorus and vaporized them on a burst of sound, hurling them back to the Kingdoms. Next came the Winds of Change, howling, driving down on the band, forcing Roald and Tank to the stage floor, rattling

Dev's drums like dice. Red Gorge played on, kept the rhythm, and hit every note with practiced precision and the smoldering passion of fifteen years of hunting a dream. The Winds clutched at the sounds. Gorge watched the whirling elementals as they lashed out with airy tendrils, trying to grasp individual notes, to warp and change them, but the music carried on unaltered. His enemies hadn't had half a century to become acclimated to this world like he had, to understand how music worked here. As he started into the song's final verse, Gorge funneled some of his power upward to create a countervailing gale that sent the Winds of Change home.

Sing to me of shadows
Of stars gone dark
Of death and lies,
the hideous art

A light glowed across the arena. As Roald and Tank drove into a synchronized barrage of notes, a new sound rose over the music, although only Gorge heard it at first. It came in harmony, three voices singing a gentle tune ill-conceived for how sound worked in this world, yet effective nonetheless, especially when joined by a fourth singer with a much more powerful voice.

One Gorge knew intimately.

Soniella.

She flashed across the black expanse.

She'd brought three of her best from the Choruses. They sang, but not to disrupt Gorge's song as he'd anticipated. Like him, they were singing to open a way. The light glowing around them grew brilliant, almost blinding, at least to Gorge, who perceived it fully, and perhaps to Snow and Delilah, whom he'd trained to see as he did. The audience could only glimpse enough to think it was part of the light show.

Notes flowed outward from Soniella and her singers, rising from their lips like delicate snowflakes etched from candle flames. They amassed to form a ragged, swirling oval, and through its heart Gorge saw the place he'd once called home: his conservatory in the Kingdoms, untouched from the day he'd last left it. The half-finished composition he'd been writing still sat propped up beside his instruments. The faeries' magic slowed time, so that each single note Red Gorge pumped out lasted what seemed like minutes, while Gorge stared at the indescribable beauty beyond the opening, astonished by how it exceeded his memories, how much sweeter the air flowing out of it was than the air of this dingy gutter world, how much more sublime were the sounds.

Soniella descended to the stage. Gorgeous beyond Gorge's capacity to describe with a mortal mind, she stood bathed in light and clothed in transparent, iridescent cloth that revealed every measure of her perfection. Her hair moved like liquid gold, and from her back sprouted glorious double wings of blue and yellow. Once their beauty had been equaled only by Gorge's wings, and when they'd flown together entire villages had stopped to watch them pass. Gorge met her eyes, dizzying in their depths, and watched her lips move as she sang, struggling to form the sounds right in mortal air. Then her singers held a long, trilling note. Reality seemed to freeze.

"Come back to us, Gorge," Soniella said. "We wronged you. We see that. Return and be restored. My guilt has never faded, and I miss you, my love."

Gorge's eyes wandered over Soniella, over the view of the Kingdoms, and then he looked at Delilah, who, in comparison, appeared crudely formed, like a statue fashioned of cinder and silt. The sight of Soniella's glorious wings caused his wounded shoulders to ache with phantom wings.

"We can heal you and restore your wings. You'll fly again. You and I can be as we once were," said Soniella.

Gorge had never considered that the Flock might offer him reconciliation; that all he had forsaken might be restored, his lost glory renewed. The entire arena swirled awash in magical energy, barely contained by his and Soniella's efforts. Yet he felt cold to his core. Here lay a choice he'd never anticipated. His anger, nursed for decades, seemed like surf breaking over an eternally rocky shore. It would be madness to refuse. He stared into his conservatory, remembering his days there, and his eyes took in all the wonders he'd once possessed. Its allure ached within him — until he spotted a crystal square engraved with musical notations and carved to act like a prism, always surrounded by color. A gift from Soniella. Once he'd cherished it. The memories it held were the most potent Gorge possessed from the Kingdoms — and the most painful.

Gorge peered into Soniella's flickering eyes. Working magic in the mortal world strained her, but she'd accumulated a great deal of power since he'd last seen her.

Gorge let her approach and embrace him.

He whispered, "I have a gift for you, love," then kissed her and stroked her dusty, silken wings, holding her close enough to feel the tension leave her as she decided she'd won him over. He pressed his lips against hers. She let down her guard. Gorge inhaled, sucking a blast of magic from her body and into his. His power surged as her's withered. He made a claw of his hand and ripped away the top quarter of her left wing. Shoving her aside, he released a burst of energy, nearly all he'd accumulated that night, and Soniella's spell shattered. The brilliant opening vanished, taking with it the three singers. Gorge's view of the Kingdoms closed. The music thundered back to full life and speed.

Gorge sang:

My gift to you
My gift to them
Nothing's ever the
same again

And I will find the way
the Dark way, the way home
the way to Hell
the Way of the Bone

The song rumbled toward its ending. Soniella — shocked and wounded — ghosted to nothingness and faded back to the Faerie Kingdoms. Roald led the band to a crashing finale, and when the music ended, Gorge alone sang out:

And I will find the way
The Way of the Bone

The crowd exploded with applause, and Gorge collapsed to the stage.

He struggled with what magic remained inside him to keep the Way open, but he lacked the power. Everything around him snapped back to substance as the Way slammed shut. He would gather no more magic tonight.

The band rushed to his side. He couldn't move, couldn't stand.

Delilah shoved past Tank, knelt down, and took Gorge's hand. Before she could speak, he grabbed the back of her neck and pulled him to her, kissing her, and as he did, he released all the magic left inside him, delivering it to her body, recharging the magic already there. He watched Delilah quiver with shock, and then Gorge's eyes shut, and saw only darkness.

⚕

Gorge ached when he awoke. Delilah's face at his side eased the pain. There was sunlight and quiet. Gorge lay in a hospital bed.

"Shhh, don't move," Delilah said. "You collapsed. The doctors don't think there's any permanent damage, though."

"She came to take me home and I said no," Gorge said.

"What do you mean?"

"Soniella offered to give me back my old life, my wings. I refused."

Tears welled in Delilah's eyes. She held Gorge's hand, pressed it to her cheek.

"You feel so cold. You sent all your magic into me. It filled me up when the Way closed. Why, when you were so close?"

Gorge shut his eyes and pictured Soniella as she'd appeared last night: glorious and vibrant and powerful, and yet deep in her eyes there had dwelled black terror curling like venom in a place where he only ever saw warmth and love from Delilah.

"If I'd exhausted my magic, you would've died. What would opening the Way mean without you beside me? What would anything mean without you? The magic is my gift to you. In the Kingdoms, they fear me. That's enough for now."

Gorge pulled Delilah into bed beside him. It was only in the halo of Delilah's warmth that this life felt right and his way felt good. She nestled her head against Gorge's chest and they lay there, each listening to the other's breath, to the indifferent rhythms of the city outside, to the breeze humming past the half-opened window.

Gorge chose then to remind himself, as he did everyday: *Now I am free.*

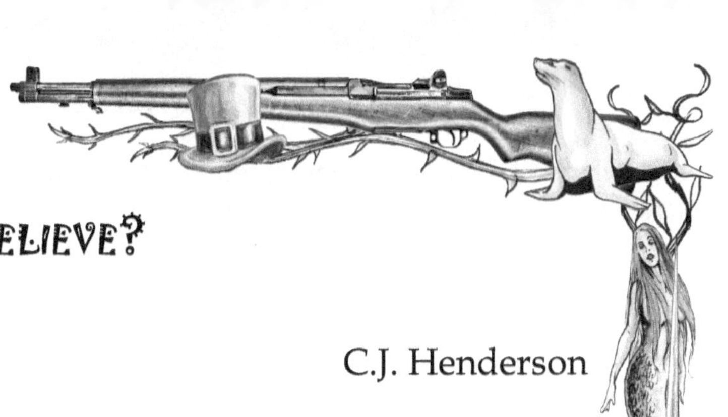

Do You Believe?

C.J. Henderson

"Do you believe in faeries? Say quick that you believe. If you believe, clap your hands."

J.M. Barrie

C'MON, FELLAS," THE NEWSMAN SHOUTED PITIFULLY, "GIMME A break!"

It was the horrible sincerity the figure before him could muster, with his pitifully outstretched arms and quickly moistening eyes, that made the balding man grin so. Turning to his friends, he shuddered in mock horror, then asked;

"Well, what'daya think? Can we tolerate his presence?"

"I don't know," added another at the table, a tall, thin gentleman with intense blue eyes. "I do hate it so when his lower lip starts quivering."

"Did I mention," offered the newsman with practiced timing, "that the next round is, of course, on the network?"

"Now I could be seein' my way to forgivin' the lad his indiscretions," offered an aromatic type of extremely disreputable note. "Considerin' his warm proposal of a proper makin' of penance, as it were."

"Oh, good," chuckled the balding man, "now I'm in the dubious position of not only supportin' the local pariah, but also havin' it known that I agreed with Darby on somethin'."

Most who were gathered there that night got the joke. The newsman was Marv Richards, head anchor and main producer of *Challenge of the Unknown*, the only network news show dedicated to covering the strange and the supernatural. He was also one of the only media personalities ever to be allowed within the walls of the Narkane. On every world, there was one spot where all dimensions met. In some it appeared to be a marketplace; in some a temple; some a school. Often it was a library. Whatever the shade of a particular reality, however, that same set of square footage was always a place where people gathered, reverently, to engage in social discourse.

In the reality where they called the third planet from the yellow sun in their Sol system "the Earth," that spot was the Narkane, Manhattan's most exclusive night spot, and a focusing point for all manner of things. It was known across the widest band of the dimensional spanway as quite possibly the most interesting club experience in the "Hip" universe. Within its walls, any two creatures, entities, or semi-mobilized philosophies could bump up against each other.

The Narkane was, of course, a natural haven for scoundrels determined to transport illicit goods across inter-dimensional boundaries. Which meant on any night there you might be rubbing elbows with smugglers bent on moving anything from Romulan ale to the square eggs of the Andes. In a nutshell, it was the ultimate Spe'keasy—a place where anyone and anything could take to the dance floor. Which was more than proved by the crew at table 15, who were finally waving Richards over.

The oldest was Professor Zackery Goward. Doctor of philosophy and theology, he had spent the better part of his life in search of the strange and the bizarre. Paul Morcey, the balding man next to him, was not nearly as cultured as "the Doc," but, as a detective working out of the London Agency, he had come across enough of the strange and the bizarre to last most men several lifetimes. And completing the trio was one of the least reputable beings for miles around wherever he went. A storyteller known simply as Darby, he was the last word in "odious," the kind of person who made those rare strains of sentient toilet scum feel good about themselves.

As Richards turned the threesome into a quartet, he indicated to one of the bartenders that the table should be hit once all around by pointing to the claw hammer hanging above it. Sliding into one of the table's two vacant seats, his ears leaped into the conversation as Darby growled;

"Oh, auk now—it t'weren't so bad."

"Not so bad," sputtered Goward. "You had sex with a blind nun by telling her you were Jesus."

"Well and sure, now hasn't every young scamp played a merry prank or two in his time?"

"Yeah," drawled Morcey, grimacing as anyone would who had to admit to knowing Darby, "but you made a tape of the evenin' and sent it in to 'America's Most Embarrassing Videos.'"

"That was you?" All heads turned toward Richards. His eyes filling with admiration, he said, "They won Sweeps hands-down with that. Forced ad revenues up for their network three points. Nice work, dude."

"Sweet bride of the night," groaned Morcey. "Now we got two of 'em." The detective's mouth hung open a moment, as he listened to a chuckling Richards say;

"I'm telling you, oh, when you told her 'This is my body, take therefore of it and eat,' oh, oh my God..."

The anchorman broke down into hysterics at that point, first at the memory of Darby's carnal comedy, then at the pun of his own calling on the Almighty during that story. Pounding the table with his fist, waving his other hand, he choked out a few words—

"And then, then...oh, and then, when...when you blessed her with your 'holy water'...*ahhahhahhahaha...*"

And then fell into a tittering fit that left the professor and Morcey looking at each other askance, and Darby simply sitting back, enjoying his pipe. Richards was saved from death-by-fluster, however, in a timely fashion by the arrival of a medium-sized carnivore of some sort or another management had somehow stuffed into a tuxedo, which had brought the new round of drinks, including a Scotch for Richards, his usual, and a complementary bowl of house mix—a random mangerful of goodies in which one could find anything from Raisinettes and Crunchy Frog to golden apple chips or bits of the True Cross.

"So," said Goward, tossing a noncommittal fragment of conversation into the air, "it seems the theme tonight is something of an Art Deco by way of Kate Hepburn/Flash Gordon."

The others agreed. It was one of the more fascinating, yet subtle things about the club, the fact that the decor and design changed on an almost nightly basis. For instance, if Monday the band was blowing big band cool, Tuesday was just as likely to be a combination of jitterbugging and hip hop as it was to be superheroic polkas. The management had long before decided that the easiest way to keep any one faction from dominating the clientele policies was to maintain an ever-changing atmosphere. Thus, if Wednesday the universe's best Klezmer band was on stage, then Thursday might be Jazz James Bond Night, Geeks-Rule Eve, Barbie Night, or who knew what.

"All right, fine — the decor is swell," responded Richards, never one to let an interesting conversational opener interfere with his primary objective of self-promotion, "but who's got something good for me?"

"Hey, Marv," answered Morcey, setting down his bourbon, "give it a rest, will you?"

"C'mon, you guys," the anchor pleaded. "It's a cold, cruel world out there. I've got my third season justification pitch coming up. I need something new. Something with a little pizzazz. Some kind of shambling creepie, or slinky hell babe —"

"Well," responded Morcey, grinning, "Truth told, I could go for a slinky hell babe myself."

"Yes, quite," said Goward. His fourth Rob Roy firmly in hand, he added, "what a provocative idea. Make that two, would you?"

"Go on, yuk it up," groaned Richards. "I'm still desperate here. Doesn't a finder's fee interest anyone anymore?"

"By the by," said Darby dryly, "I might have a tale you could spin them." Goward and Morcey turned with interest. Foul and repugnant and just downright cootie-a-fied as Darby was, there was no doubting that when it came to storytelling, he was the king of kings. Richards also flashed his interest at the lumpy Irishman, but his was powered by a need far more intense than the desire to be entertained. Turning the full intensity of his personality upon the storyteller, Richards signaled for a waiter while saying;

"Do tell? What kind of story?"

"Well now," answered Darby. "Have you ever heard tell of...the cockroach faeries?"

"Hey, that sounds grea —" the anchorman cut his cheer short as his hearing caught up with his enthusiasm. "What?"

"You heard me...the cockroach faeries. Do you know of them?"

"I've heard of faeries," said Morcey. "And bein' a New Yorker, it's obvious I know about roaches. But what do the two of them have to do with each other?"

"Let me pose a question," said Darby. Draining his glass as the waiter approached, he indicated he would like three more of the same, then said, "You're all men of substance. All of you over a hundred and fifty pounds, at least. Now, you tell me — is there a man among you who, in his time, that hasn't stepped on a roach, tryin' your best to eradicate the wee beastie's mortal existence?" All three of the others affirmed that they had.

"Of course you have. Now, tell me, how many times have you done so, to then lift your foot and watch the blessed thing run off with nary a harm done to it?" Again, all three affirmed that such was the case.

"I thought so," answered Darby. "That's because there are roaches in this world, and there are faeries—true is true. But the thing most have nary a clue over is the secret of the cockroach faeries."

As Darby downed a full-throated swig of his Baggins Brew Dark Ale, Harry Hausen, a skeleton in a tuxedo complete with top hat and spats, ambled out onto the Narkane stage to introduce the members of the band. Realizing this meant it was time to order a last rounds of drinks for the moment, the club's clientele went into an uproar, calling for everything from Pan-Galactic Gargle Fizzes to Cherry Rolling Rocks. Once the commotion died down, and the Narkane's All Cephalopod Dancers had taken to the stage to mambo to the haunting strains of Kip Bisseldorf and his Elegant Lads, Darby returned to his story.

"Now, as I was sayin'...the cockroach faeries.... Well, first you have to understand, I'm not tryin' to tell you that all cockroaches are faeries, or that all faeries are cockroaches. No. You see, a long time back, there was a group of faeries, the Kel'derna, that, well, I hate to cast aspersions, but they were, shall we say, not appreciated amongst their own kind."

"Why's that?"

"They had what some judged to be, bad habits. They weren't as interested in helpin' kindly cobblers or paintin' rainbows as they were stealin' the milk from cows and runnin' away with human babies and the such."

"Faeries from the wrong side of town, like?"

"Oh, aye, Mr. Richards, that they were. And they caused the rest of the faerie community no end of trubble—that they did. Well now, it wasn't long before they weren't welcomed in any neighborhood, district, or region by any type of pixie, sprite, or other winged imp. Their brand was as unwelcome as an undertaker at a wedding. Why, they made the traveling Jews of the fourteenth century look like the Prodigal Son, they did."

Darby drained one of the various mugs before him, then hoisted another with a wonderfully smooth motion, as he continued.

"Now, it was around about the time of the Greeks — I mean, when they were the big kahunas, philosophically speaking — that things came to a boil for the Kel'derna. Gettin' a bit full of themselves, don't cha'know, they managed to upset just about every branch of the magical world. I mean, if you think the faeries were mad at them, oh and now, I'm tellin' you true as dew in the mornin', there wasn't a harpy, hydra, or demi-god that wouldn't swat one as soon as give 'em a glance at their sun dial. They were in it, sure'nd true."

"So that's when they turned into cockroaches?"

"Don't interrupt him," cautioned Morcey. "That'll just cost you more drinks."

And, indeed, the balding man was correct. Darby had the anchor signal another waiter who was given the order to simply start bringing random drinks of any type in any quantity to the table. Morcey smiled, saying;

"This ought to be good. I want to see you drink a mint julep right after a Coconut Pepper Zombie."

The storyteller's only response was to instruct the waiter to combine the drinks just mentioned in one pitcher, add a can of Foster's Lager, a raw egg, and two chicken bouillon cubes and to then bring it to the table with a stalk of celery he could use as a stirrer. As Goward turned a touch green, Darby continued telling the history of the cockroach faeries. And fascinating it turned out to be.

Over roughly the next forty-five minutes, while consuming an Eclipse, a Dubonnet Fizz, a Thunder, two Ninitchkas, a Bulldog, a Bronx Terrace, three Fallen Angels, two Pink Whiskers, and a small tub of Pousse Café, along, of course, with his initial special order, Darby told those assembled the remaining history of the Kel'derna.

Gathering all their remaining clansprites in the forests of Gaul, the outcast pixies debated as to how best protect themselves from a hostile world. The decision was made that the simplest way for them to survive was to disappear. The Kel'derna would be no more. It was decided they would retreat back into the most inaccessible reaches of Gaul, and create a society for themselves alone. Impossible thoughts such as "hard work" and "moral responsibility" were bandied about, but the clan had brought such down upon themselves, and there was no getting around it.

Now at the time, the common cockroach was not the fearsome and hated creature it is today. A simple, sturdy survivor from prehistoric times, the Kel'derna began to breed them along specific lines. One thing, Darby emphasized, was the importance that they become both delicious and indestructible. If the creatures were to be the cows as well as the horses of the race, they would have to become tasty as well as sturdy.

The Kel'derna bred the race of cockroaches in secrecy for centuries, for both size and speed for when they would be used as steeds, as well as for their further applications after life. The clan increasingly enjoyed the taste of the cockroach, of that there was no denying, but they also found myriad other uses for them, as well. Their wings, especially, became not only shields, but the basic building blocks of Kel'dernian industry.

Homes were made from them, as well as boats, umbrellas, cutting edged tools, serving bowls, et cetera. The roach became marvelously useful to the Kel'dernian community, but their greatest use was yet to be discovered.

"Indeed," said Darby, his voice low and eyes glistening, "that moment dinna come until the Kel'derna had been breeding roaches for nearly a thousand years. By then, Gaul had been overrun with people, and as the Kel'dernian population was finally startin' to show a bit of an explosion, itself, it was decided that some of the younger, more adventurous of the clan might set out on their own. And, dinna they have the marvelous luck then that the Pope, in his infinite greed and deviltry, called at that time for the first of the Crusades."

Richards' hands flew through page after page of notes as the storyteller related how the movement of people out of the cold and damp north into the southlands and back again, over and over for the next few hundred years became the catalyst for the spread of roaches across the face of the world. Morcey and Goward looked at each other a trifle askance, but did not interrupt, wanting to see just where Darby was going with his tale.

And where he wanted to go proved interesting to both of them. As he told it, wanting to see the rest of the world, or at least some of its drier segments, the Kel'dernians decided to venture out from the protection of the dark wood. It was then, as they began to move about in the world at large once more, that they noticed the greater aversion humans had to their friends, the cockroaches, than they did other insects.

The reason, it was assumed, was the roaches' habit of invading the homes of man on a far more permanent basis than the occasional fly or bee that might wander in. Even ants always went home after they found what they wanted. But, the human reaction to roaches was so much greater than these that it was soon decided the Kel'derna would become as closely associated with their livestock as possible. Soon cloaks were added to the utilitarian function to which their cattle were put. The clan also soon began experimenting with a form of rudimentary genetics, breeding themselves to darker and darker shades.

Over the hundreds of years of the Crusades, the clan became more and more adept at mimicking their mounts. They learned to run across floors like them, run in wild circles to avoid destruction, and to vibrate at just the right frequency while standing still in a sudden burst of light so as to appear to be insects. Truth to tell, the secret the Kel'derna learned was the more they pushed their way into the homes of the aristocracy, the less people bothered to look at them.

"It's a sad commentary on folk, but it's true," Darby sighed, stirring a half keg of General Harrison's Egg Nog with his celery stalk, "We live in an age now where Kel'dernian magic has the world completely under its spell. You know as well as I do, some folks, as soon as they see a roach, why, they grow completely irrational, slammin' and bangin' away at the poor dears with anything at hand, while others go completely in the other direction and will turn the lights back out and just tip toe away."

"But, I don't get it," said Richards. His face showing his puzzlement clearly, he said, "When there aren't any faeries around, why do people get so upset over just simple roaches?"

"It's the magic — the magic that the Kel'dernians used to breed their roaches, it's in all of them now. The clan is in every city in the world; they still find it easier to live off what they can steal from human society. Even after spending near an entire millennia on their own, as soon as they came out into the world again...well, sigh — I guess it's just in their blood, the little devils. But as I was sayin', the magic they used to breed their roaches has infected the entire species. Now, people can't be around them without reactin' far different than they do with any other bug."

Darby sat back, taking a long swig of no one knew what. Morcey hooded his eyes and gave Goward a what-do-you-think look. The professor smiled, not quite knowing how to answer. Not noticing the non-verbal conversation on the other side of the table, Richards jerked his head back involuntarily once he realized the storyteller had finished his tale, and barked;

"That's it? That's the big story? I shelled out..." he did a quick bit of mental calculating, then shrieked, "nine hundred and eighty-five dollars just for *that?*"

"Did you be wanting' more?" As the anchorman's glare blasted its way across the table, Darby moved a bit in his seat, reaching inside his coat, saying;

"Auck, you TV people and your visuals. Well, mayhap this might be of some assistance."

Darby withdrew his hand from the moldering tatters of his overcoat, bits of thread and other debris clinging to it. Then, putting his loosely-closed fist down in the center of the table, he opened his fingers to reveal a large number of roaches. Everyone else's immediate reaction was to grab his drink and move back a bit. Then, the previous conversation sinking in, they all leaned forward again to find they were not looking at roaches at all — or, at least, not merely roaches.

Several of the figures Darby had set to rest next to the table's candle and the wicker basket of half-eaten house mix were indeed roaches, but two were not. Richards leaned in even closer, at first not believing his eyes, then not believing his good fortune. Morcey and Goward leaned in as well, joining him in his former disbelief if not his latter joyfulness, for there on the table were two miniature human beings, faeries if either had ever seen one, but of a type they had never previously beheld.

Tall and thin, one male and one female, the pair were as brown as mahogany and as spiteful as an Old Testament deity. They wore helmets adorned with long antennae, vests, and cloaks made of cockroach wings, and leggings and boots fashioned from some other part of roachian anatomy no one wished to question. Two of the roaches that had been set down along with them stood calmly aside their masters, obviously outfitted with saddles and reins. Rubbing his eyes, Richards stammered;

"But, but...I can see everything so clearly. When they're in my kitchen, I only see...I mean—"

"Ah, an' that's easy to explain," answered Darby casually. "When you snap on a light and you see one of these fellows, your mind thinks 'roach,' and so that's what you see. But, now that you know what you're looking at, well, you see what you know. You know?"

The anchorman nodded absently, his eyes studying the two figures on the table with a growing fascination. He asked a score more questions, but everything Darby told him about the Kel'derna only made him more and more desperate to take the two pixies away with him that night. Finally, they made a deal for a figure that choked the working stiffs at the table. After the storyteller and Richards shook hands, however, Darby added;

"Of course, this is all moot if the Kel'derna won't go with you."

"Go with me?" questioned the anchor. "I thought they were, I don't know, pets, or something."

As tiny hands went for their swords, Darby leaned forward quickly, shaking his hands and speaking in a bastardized elven dialect that hurt the ears. After making Richards' apologizes for him, then calling for another round of too-many-drinks, this time including a set of thimbles so the Kel'dernians could help themselves, the storyteller asked;

"So, what say you two? You've been with me a while, and there's all the fun in that, but this fellow, now...he wants to put you on the tellie. What do you say...would you like to be exploited for ratings?"

"Did I mention," offered the newsman with practiced timing, "that practically anything you might want is, of course, on the net-work?"

The offer brought a chorus of high-pitched giggles that seemed to delight Richards and Darby equally. Indeed, negotiations went so swimmingly after that point that it was but a matter of seven minutes before the anchor was on his way to the front door with his new stars, and Darby was signaling furiously for a waiter.

"That was a remarkable bit of history, Mr. Darby," offered Goward as a waiter approached. The storyteller asked for a heavy-duty first aid kit then responded to the professor.

"What, oh, *heh heh,* sorry, but you might not want to be repeatin' any of that for one of your classes."

Morcey groaned, pulling a hand down over his face as he said, "*Owwwww,* suckered again."

"Now, now," said Darby as he removed a great wad of blood-soaked linen from beneath his coat, "it was just a harmless bit of fun either of you might have pulled. I mean, well and sure, now hasn't every young scamp played a merry prank or two in his time?"

"You mean to say, sir, that there are no cockroach faeries?"

"There are," said Darby with assurance. "Two, to be exact. Fred and Maxine, and you just met them, may the devil take their hindquarters, the ungrateful little bas—"

Morcey started to laugh as the waiter returned with the first aid kit. In moments, Darby was washing out his left arm pit with hydrogen peroxide while the waiter prepared to sew shut the ragged holes in his arm still dripping blood and loose bits of flesh. While the storyteller groaned at the first threading puncture, he explained;

"I might have promised the two of them a place to stay after a Halloween party a couple of years back. They went as cockroaches. I lost some sort of bet. I can't be too certain of the details, all I know is after drinkin' perhaps a wee bit too much, I woke up with those two livin' in me armpit, and no way in hell of gettin' them out except comin' up with a better deal for them."

"So," said Goward, his knuckles turning white as he unconsciously gripped the stem of his Rob Roy far too tightly, "you're telling us that for several...years, *years*...you've had a small horde of cockroaches and faeries...livin' in your armpit?"

Darby nodded sadly, pleading that anyone can get himself into a spot of trouble now and again. The waiter bit off the last piece of thread knotting closed the last of the wounds in the storyteller's arm. Gathering up his kit, he removed it, along with twenty-some of the empty glasses, mugs, and thimbles, the emptied house mix basket, and the remaining roaches. As he left, Goward sighed;

"I'm sorry to hear the tale was a fiction. It did explain a great deal about cockroaches. I've always sworn the damnable things were magic on some level or another."

"Oh," responded Darby absently as he tested his arm, "but they are. Dinna you know? It was one of the outer gods or the other, created them just to cause trouble, it did."

"Do tell..."

Darby looked up, discovering Morcey and Goward looking at him with interest. Finding his arm reasonably repaired, the storyteller told them;

"Oh, indeed. What a tale I could tell you, if it t'weren't for my terrible thirst..."

The two men looked at each other for a moment, shrugged, and then signaled for a waiter while Darby said;

"It was the Daemon Sultan, itself, the primal chaos men say sits in its court at the center of the universe..."

And, while his story went on, drinks were served, vampires mingled with insurance salesmen, faeries stole mints from the bowls at the bar, and cephalopods danced, as they did every night at the Narkane.

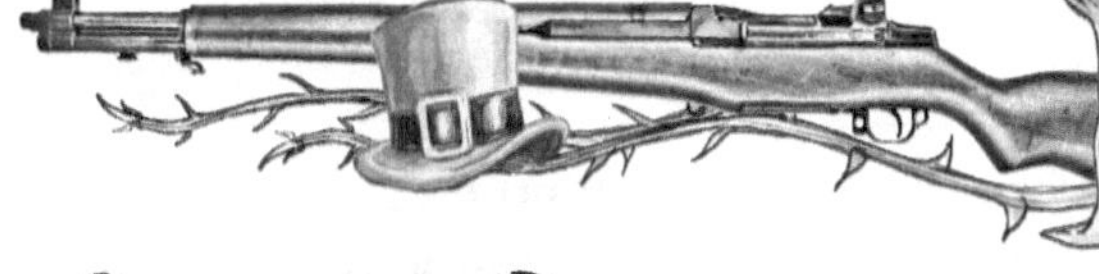

Within the Guardian Bell

Danielle Ackley-McPhail

SUZANNE WAS WORRIED. VERY WORRIED. LANCE HAD NEVER FELT so much anxiety from a fae as what flowed through her now. The pillion pad behind him remained empty, but the unmistakable sensation clinging around his right arm concerned him. Sparing a fleeting glance from the road, he looked down to where the black muscle shirt left his arm bare. The tattooed image of his lady had shifted as only magic could allow. Right now the skin art hid itself between his arm and the curve of his chest, all four limbs wrapped tight around his biceps as if it were a lifeline. It was the closest he'd ever seen Suzanne get to being clingy.

Magic had seamlessly healed her body from the encounter with the *Dubh Fae*, but her spirit still bore those absent scars. Lance knew she was worrying about him. He even understood. Hell, he shared her worry. Not because someone had decided to target him, but because they'd hurt Suzanne, and she still wasn't over it.

Neither was he.

It had left him raw and sent him raging if he thought on it too long. This was the first time he'd left her side since he and the club rode to her rescue. He didn't like it any more than she had but it couldn't be helped...he rode on AMA business that couldn't be put off. He'd been on the road a week.

Suzanne wasn't handling the separation well.

Again: neither was he.

The second they cut him free he'd jumped on his bike and headed home. Didn't gear up, didn't check the weather. Didn't even take the extra time to call and let them know he was on his

way. That's how his fool ass ended up riding unprotected in conditions even a SQUID would have had more sense than to ride in. Of course, the weather had been nice when he'd headed out. Not so much now. His teeth ground against one another and he resisted the urge to rev his engine.

Suzanne waited safe at *Delilah's,* surrounded by the other members of the club. He had to keep telling himself that. Though mindspeaking was not one of his gifts, Lance thought real hard at her. *I'm coming, babe. I'm coming.*

The power of his engine thrummed through him, making him one with leather and chrome and steel. If he listened real close, he almost dared believe he heard the mad tinkling of the tiny pewter guardian bell Suzanne had attached to his swing arm before he'd left. No way was the bell actually audible over the sounds of the engine, but he certainly sensed its magic, subtly flavored by Suzanne's special touch.

Behind him, the hiss of four wheels on wet pavement blended with the muted rumble of some cager's engine, a reminder Lance needed to keep his mind on the slab. As if to reinforce his thoughts, a Q-Tip in an equally ancient Buick passed too close on Lance's left, sending the bike swerving toward a rainbow-covered puddle.

"Ah, crap!" Lance swore as his tires hit the slick and lost their grip on the road. The Knucklehead dipped sideways, surely setting the bell to ring wildly. His stomach lurched hard until he brought the bike vertical once more.

"Get some glasses or give up the license, Grandma!" Lance yelled after the oblivious old woman.

He fought the skid and won, but it was close. If he'd wiped out in this weather he'd have surely earned himself another set of broken wings.

That settles it, he thought, *time to get off the road a while.*

A quick glance down at his gas gauge confirmed it was time for a fluid exchange, anyway. Lance moved into the Bike Lane and opened the throttle, triggering a string of horn blasts from the cagers to either side as he passed them by.

⚶

As the biker rode away down the center of the road, the puddle bubbled and seethed. Up from its shallow depth popped an odd, tiny creature, clutching at its ears. "Smear doesn't like the faerie-man. Not at all. Or his bloody little shrill bell. Smear wants to grind his face, crush the bell." Crouched upon the road, he slammed his thick, meaty fists against the asphalt.

Microfissures formed: the conception of a pothole.

Another of his kind crawled up through the fissures, and then another, expanding the damage to the roadbed until the puddle drained away. A troupe of inch-high gremlins stood where it had been. They appeared identical in every way: Skin as grey as asphalt, with an oily, rainbow shimmer. Hair long and thick and spiny, like a porcupine mated with a box of nails. A thick white line marked the center of their faces like war paint, and along their arms ran thick, black squiggles. Like tats or tribal markings, only with the dull gleam of tar snakes. Each finger looked like a spike, reminiscent of those found at toll booths, only jointed. The miniscule troupe rumbled and grumbled as they watched the bike speed away.

"Smear doesn't like him, wants to snap his bones, crumble a fender," one of them muttered. "Smear doesn't like him, wants to bash his head, crack the tranny," added another. Each of them offered up the world of pain they planned to inflict upon the biker and his cycle; each of them punctuated their threat by pounding upon the blacktop, splitting it further.

Why do you wait? He escapes you! a lethal voice hissed into each of their heads. As it did, their eyes flared bright green instead of red. The voice sounded beautiful and horrible all at once, leaving them as cold as icebound pavement.

"Why? Why? Smear doesn't wait! We go! King-fae says we can; says we must. Smear listens," they vowed in one voice. "But King should know, biker's been belled."

Go, now! I will take care of the bell, the king's voice answered.

Cackling a sound like shattering windshield, one gremlin grabbed the next, each of them melding until there stood only one the size of a particularly ugly cabbage patch doll. It crouched upon the roadway as a Mustang went zooming by. With supernatural precision Smear reached out, his spiky digits piercing the vulcanized rubber as if it were water. Swinging up, he perched on the rim of the wheel, his fingers still in place. It wouldn't do to have the ride spin out...until after Smear reached his target, anyway.

As they sped away, the only sign the gremlins had been there was a scattering of nail-like spines and the crumbling edges of a pothole just waiting for the next car to come along.

The rain had settled down to a pissy mist by the time Lance pulled into the truck stop and right up to the pumps. Kicking down the stand, he unscrewed the gas cap, setting it on the saddle as he got off the bike. In minutes, he'd topped off both his gas tank and the reserve and headed inside. With the rain letting up, he didn't want to stop long, just enough to fill up and drain.

"What'll you have?" asked the hot, young mattress cover in a waitress uniform. Lance kept his expression neutral as she gave him the once-over, making it clear she offered a bit of distraction along with whatever he wanted from the menu. She was good. He practically felt her gaze run from his segmented ponytail clear down to his ass. Too bad he also felt the ribbon of malice spiraling through her, focused on him. One of the dubious benefits of being an empath....

He'd never even seen her before, so what was her hang-up? He might have suspected she was a part of the *Dubh Fae's* crowd, gunning for the halfling, only he couldn't sense anything fae about her and that crowd loathed humans nearly as much as they did halflings.

"I'm good," he answered. "Just looking for the way to the john..." She acted disappointed on the surface, but Lance sensed her satisfaction, as she pointed down the hall.

By the time he came back the waitress was nowhere in sight. Lance frowned and glanced around the diner before hurrying outside. Nearing his ride, he discovered where she went. He stalked up behind her and cleared his throat.

"Oh!" She spun around. Her hand slid into her apron pocket while her eyes shifted to the side as if looking for where to run. Instead she laughed, slipped on that fake invitation smile, and let her eyes roam over him suggestively once more. "I just had to come out for a closer look. Nice ride..."

"My old lady likes to think so," Lance let a bit of steel creep into his voice. "Now, how about stepping away from the bike..."

Again, that flash of malice deep in her eyes.

Before she could say a word, a couple of drivers came strolling out of the truck stop. "Hey, Jolene, Mac's lookin' for ya," one of them called out. With a huff, Jolene hurried away, her eyes slicing across Lance in a much different manner than moments before.

"Whack job," he murmured as he inspected his scoot. Everything seemed in order. He couldn't find anything that she might have disturbed in the short time she was alone with the bike. Even the bell still hung in place. Dismissing the episode from his thoughts as just one more example of everyday craziness, Lance pulled out his cell phone and hit the speed dial.

"Hey, bro," he said as Gavin answered. "Just checking in. Nah, I'm about half an hour out.... No, everything's fine. Tell Suzanne I'll be there soon."

He flipped the phone closed and slipped it into his pocket, then he swung onto the bike and gunned it out of there.

Not far past the truck stop, Smear released his grip on the wheel where he'd hitched, letting the spikes shred the treads as they pulled away from the rubber. As he flipped himself to the ground, there was a *pop,* and the tire blew, followed by the crunch of crumpled metal. Not as glorious as Smear would have liked; just a bit of bent steel and a bumped head, no blood or flame or final breath. Several Smears broke away from the whole and, despite all reason and their one-inch size, they shoved the 'Stang and its unconscious driver out of sight of the road where the biker would not see it before scampering back to meld once more.

"Faerie-man, crunch your head, hose your ride," the gremlin chanted. "Dance in your blood and wear your stupid bell as a hat."

Continuing to mutter, Smear stalked to the center of the road and called every bit of Smear from every crack and crevice, every slick spot and crumpled zone. As they rallied forth like blowflies to roadkill, the gremlin beefed up, absorbing all that came until he was the size of a Pitbull, and then a Rottweiler. He stood there in fine fae challenge, idly whirling a bit of chain swept up from the side of the road.

The roar of the cycle drew near. Smear crouched at the ready, blending with the asphalt like a chameleon on a log. Only a chameleon never had such teeth.

Lance throttled down. His head came up, and his muscles went taut. If he used Jolene's malice as a baseline, what he sensed now shot off the charts. Pure malevolence pounded him from every direction except above. He strained his senses trying to pinpoint the threat, but his perception seemed off now that his fae nature dominated the human, rather than the other way around.

(He still didn't know if he should thank Gavin for that, or redesign his anatomy. Of course, the encounter at the crossroads would have gone quite differently, possibly even fatally, otherwise.)

Anyway, if Lance believed what he sensed right now, surrounding him were a crowd of people who hated him...only they were all invisible.

Not totally impossible...he should know...but frankly the only ones that hated him that bad were all fae, and he didn't sense them.

Lance kept going, but took it slow, just in case this wasn't his empathy acting screwy. Drawing a deep breath, he gathered in magic slow and easy. His body shook in reaction as the energy filled him up. He grinned at the still-new sensation of his shoulder fins unfurling. Every nerve ending seemed to dance in reaction to the magic trailing from those fins as they rose through the slits in his muscle shirt to form his wings.

Man, I almost sympathize with those 1%ers addicted to meth. If it feels *anything like this, no wonder the craving's damn hard to shake.*

Ready to blast whatever came at him, Lance rounded the bend. He could see no source of threat. The road remained smooth and bare. Writing it off as his body adjusting to the recent changes, he opened up the throttle. This close to home he had no interest in taking it slow.

Out of nowhere, the wind rose, sounding like ground glass and a cackle mixed in a blender. The Knucklehead hit a bump camouflaged by the roadway. Again the front wheel threatened to skid. Lance growled and fought it, only to hit one on the other side.

All around him the wind both whispered and howled.

Goin' down, faerie-man, crunch your head, shred your wings.

Goin' down, faerie-man, spill your guts, blow your gasket.

Goin' down, faerie-man, skin nothin' but rash, bike nothin' but trash.

Goin' down...goin' down...goin' down....

"What the hell?!" Lance swore. There was nothing around but him, the wind, and the road.... So what was the deal with the voices in his head? Mindhearing wasn't one of his gifts any more than mindspeaking was. His lip twisted in a snarl and his brow dipped low, as he opened up the throttle all the way, ready to power through this creeped-out stretch of road.

What was that Irish blessing?

Oh...yeah.... *May the road rise up to meet your feet....* Someone needed to tell them that wasn't necessarily a good thing.

Before his eyes, the road rucked up in front of him. Malice met his gaze from bright red eyes glowing like lit brake lights. A chain whirled idly in the creature's hand. Any moment Lance expected the links to fling out, tangling in his rims. Maybe that was why he wasn't quite ready when the chain dropped to the asphalt, and what could only be a road gremlin incarnate launched itself straight for him.

Yeah, there was that hatred loud and clear now. It still streamed from all around, but that made sense; Lance was surrounded by nothing but road...and gremlin.

"Bring it on, skidmark." Lance sneered. He had faith in the bell Suzanne had gifted him, knew its magic firsthand; it served the sole purpose of either warding off gremlins or trapping those already in residence on any bike. And as it was a gift from a loved one, its power was doubly potent.

Between the bell's protection and his own magic Lance felt little threat from the gremlin.

Goin' down, faerie-man....

"...Yeah, right!"

Even as Lance watched, the Knucklehead collided with the creature. The gremlin shattered into countless pieces. Only they didn't fall away. Each one grimaced with hatred, trying to stare him down with light-bright eyes.

They cackled and again he heard the grind of shattered glass on the wind. That was when Lance realized something was wrong with the bell. The swiftest of glances confirmed it still hung from his sidearm, but the clapper remained silent and he could no longer sense its magic. Then he remembered Jolene, crouched by his bike, and he cursed with enough venom to put a goblin to shame.

Goin' down, faerie-man...crack your balls like a walnut, crumple your pipes real good...chew you up into itty bitty bits.

One of the buggers chomped on his earlobe, making him regret he hadn't yet replaced his shattered helmet; another slammed a fist full of spikes through his engine block. The others followed suit, in one manner or another attacking him or the Knucklehead. Lance snarled and fought to keep the bike stable while smacking the creatures away. But there were too many of them. He could hear the bike start to fail; smell fluids he ought not to have been able to smell...both his own and the bike's.

Tearing one of the creatures from his neck, Lance roared and slammed the bike into a skid, laying her down on the road, scraping dozens of the gremlins off as he surfed the asphalt. Both his wings and the cycle sent up sparks. Little puffs of acrid smoke peppered the air where the gremlin bits ignited. He felt some satisfaction in that, but there were too many of them left for it to count. He leapt to his feet, leaving behind a good bit of both leather and skin, but snatching up his bell on impulse and pocketing it.

His left arm felt rawer than ground chuck, and his pants were almost as torn up. The road rash would hurt like a bitch later, but right now it just stung.

Goin' down, faerie-man, goin' down right now, put you out like a candle.

"Come on and try it, slick," Lance growled. "See how fast I jack you up."

The gremlins hissed at him as they gang-banged back into one creature. Its bulbous nose twitched and its finger spikes flexed. It stalked forward, now roughly the size of a bull mastiff, only much uglier.

Lance's wings crackled behind him as he lashed out with a side kick at his adversary. The kick sent the creature flying, slamming it right into the downed bike. Lance winced at the added damage; the gremlin, on the other hand, merely exploded back into a thousand smaller selves. They scrambled to meld back together as Lance stalked forward and brought the heavy tread of his biker boot down on a choice few of them, leaving nothing but smears on the pavement. But too many remained. He quickly faced a once-more unified foe.

Bloody bells! Bloody biker! Smear smash 'em and crash 'em and leave 'em in pieces!

The gremlin fairly frothed as it spat and cursed. It also gave itself away. Lance knew what to do. He again dropped the creature with a kick. This time, the gremlin anticipated the strike and mostly kept itself together. However, while it was distracted reabsorbing the few bits that popped loose, Lance drew out the bell.

With a vicious grin, he held it up high, dangling a silent threat. But was it an empty one? Lance could see the clapper was gone, hastily ripped out by the bitch at the truck stop.

Still...nothing that couldn't be overcome... He might not have been able to manipulate magic until recently, but that didn't mean he had no understanding of how it worked. Drawing a bit of magic to his fingertip, he drew it down the slope of the bell. There sounded a subtle hum that turned Lance's grin wolfish. In his thoughts, he pictured a clapper of pure, hard light. The more he focused, the more solid it became. For a fraction of a second, the creature missed a step.

No! Turn you to pizza, tear you to shreds, crush the fucking bell like a bug!

The gremlin's raging took on a frantic edge as it launched itself at Lance's hand, spikes extended as if to slice the bell. With a laugh that any member of the club would have known to back away from, Lance sent the bell ringing right in the gremlin's face.

Once in flight, the gremlin had no hope of avoiding the hollow. Caught fast by the mage-energy clapper, every bit of the creature disappeared within the depths of the tiny bell. It rang even more, frantically swinging as the gremlin fought his new prison.

Nothing escaped the bell but sound.

Lance smiled and gave the bell a little shake of his own...noting that it rang with a new tone, like screeching metal against metal. The sound delighted his ears. With a satisfied grin he slipped the bell into his pocket and righted his battered bike. That's when he noticed a Mustang buried in the brush on the side of the road. Propping the Knucklehead beside it, he pulled out his cell phone, hitting speed dial as he flipped it open.

"Yeah, Delilah.... I need you to send out the Wrench...."

Twilight Crossing

John Passarella

George Thorogood was playing on the jukebox when I tossed Ollie Janks out on his ass. Wasn't the first time. Wouldn't be the last. Or so I thought, when I said, "Nothing personal, Ollie."

Little did I know everything was about to change.

The grizzled drunk staggered to his feet and made a half-hearted attempt to brush off the seat of his bib overalls. Lacking the coordination to complete that simple task, he decided to flip me off instead. "The fuck, Ray?" he shouted. "My money ain't good enough for the Willowbrook Tavern?"

"Not when you confuse Shirley's ass with the produce aisle."

"Practically keep this dump in business," Ollie said, "much as I spend here."

"We appreciate your support," I said. "But Shirley's not on the menu."

"And what do I get for my hard-earned dollars, eh? Watered down liquor and the bum's rush, that's what!"

"Time to walk it off, Ollie. Or should I call you a cab?"

"Need no fuckin' cab," Ollie said with a dismissive wave of his hand. He plodded toward the shoulder of the road. "Live three damn blocks away."

Shaking my head, I returned to the dark confines of the Willowbrook Tavern. By morning, Ollie wouldn't have the slightest recollection of the events preceding or following his unceremonious ejection from his favorite watering hole.

Something happens often enough, you begin to expect it. That's when you need to worry.

Moments later, the door hinges creaked behind me.

I turned, bracing for round two with Ollie, but the drunk had stayed true to form. Instead, a slender young man with dark hair and a harried expression on his gaunt face brushed by me, tossing a mumbled apology in his wake. My first thought was: *Underage.* My second: *Trouble.*

The clock above the bar displayed midnight.

Then the red second hand began to descend.

Ignoring the social invitation of the bar stools or the shadowed privacy of the side booths, where most of the evening's crowd were huddled, the young man chose the nearest of three unoccupied, wobbly tables, and dropped into one of the four rickety chairs that surrounded it. A hanging brass light fixture seemed to deconstruct his face into pale slivers of flesh and harsh shadows. Otherwise, he looked unremarkably ordinary in a green and tan Rugby shirt, dark jeans and black running shoes. One heel beat an insistent tattoo against the warped floorboards, as if he were keeping time with a frenetic drummer.

About ready to vibrate out of his skin.

Wearing her customary red-and-white-checked blouse, jeans, a beer-stained apron, and calf-high leather boots, Shirley strolled over to the table to take his order. She gave him a one-second appraisal. "There's a law against serving minors."

The young man looked at her, gauging, challenging. "Is that so?"

"That's what they tell me," Shirley said, punctuating the comment with a little chuckle. "So what can I get you?"

"Whatever you've got on tap."

"Gotcha. Back in a jiff, hon."

I shook my head in disbelief. *She's flirting with him! Ben finds out, he'll break that kid in half.*

"Thanks." He tapped both index fingers against the side of the small bowl of pretzels in the center of the table, ran one hand through his hair, then heaved a sigh.

I drifted back to my regular booth, first one on the left, and picked up the well-worn baseball I'd snagged at a Phillies' game over a year ago. Foul ball, unsigned, no sentimental value, but it helped me think. And I needed to understand what was happening.

From my booth, I could observe the entire front half of the tavern, and peek down the short hall to the back room, with its side-by-side pool tables. Only the modest kitchen, with its small grill and deep fryer, was hidden from me. Although, occasionally, through the porthole window in the scuffed kitchen door, I caught a glimpse of the bald head of Oscar, our night cook. With Ollie gone, the place was relatively calm, but I sensed trouble brewing, an inexplicable prickling of the short hairs on the back of my neck. Wasn't sure from which direction the trouble would come. But I knew its target. Had since the moment he bumped into me.

I scanned the crowd, seeking anything or anyone unusual. The tavern was less than a quarter filled, all regulars, fewer than twenty people, huddled in the booths that lined the walls. A few pairs quietly conversed. Some loners scanned the sports pages or worked crosswords, while others watched the muted TV over the bar, tuned to ESPN's continual stream of scores and highlights. Steady night, not too busy. Sometimes the back room could get rowdy. Tonight, there was a companionable game of eight ball in progress. Nothing more. As the Thorogood tune faded, the only sound rising above the whispered conversations was the muffled thwack of billiard balls colliding. An expression came to mind....

The calm before the storm.

Shirley delivered the young man's draft in a stein. He paid attention long enough to hand her a five and tell her to keep the change. Instead of drinking the beer, he traced his fingertips along the surface of the glass, creating parallel trails in the condensation.

I was the Willowbrook Tavern's resident bouncer. At six-one and less than one-hundred-seventy pounds, I hardly looked the part, but I maintained order with the fairly rough trade that frequented the place. I'd needed a job and convinced Quentin Avery, the owner, that I had mastered some inscrutable far eastern martial art whose name I'd made up on the spot and had since forgotten. Self-defense came naturally to me, on some instinctual level I was reluctant to question. In my first two weeks on the job, I proved I could handle the bullies and belligerent drunks, as well as the occasional knife wielders and those making death threats with the borrowed courage of a tire iron or baseball bat. Compared to them, Ollie Janks was a cream puff. Since then....

How long had I been rubbing my arm? Where the young man had bumped into me, my skin felt as if it had been charged with a current. The sensation was spreading, as if he had infected me with his nervous energy. I debated leaving my booth to have a little chat with him, to determine what the hell was happening, when the front door burst open.

Cloaked in shadows, I settled back into the booth and watched as three burly men in black leather garb strode down the length of the tavern, their boot heels striking the floorboards like a succession of hammer blows. Could have been bikers, but I would have heard motorcycles arriving. Two took positions around the nervous young man, one to each side, while the third, presumably the leader, stood in front.

Here comes the storm.

Behind the bar, Shirley tucked a bottled-blonde strand of hair behind her ear. Nervous gesture. She cast an expectant look in my direction. Hank, the greying bartender, stood by the cash register, drying glasses with a frayed cloth. Despite his casual pose, I noticed a slight tremor in his hands. Oscar cast a wide-eyed look through the porthole window, decided it was none of his business and ducked out of view. Most of the bar patrons darted curious but discreet glances at the three men, careful not to draw unwanted attention to themselves. Dan and Elaine, a young couple in thrift shop clothes but with no shortage of common sense, slipped from their far corner booth and practically tiptoed out the back room exit. Resigned to witnessing whatever mayhem ensued, the rest of the crowd seemed to lean a bit further away from the leather-clad trio. The instinct for self-preservation had begun to assert itself.

I leaned forward, my right hand pressing the baseball hard against the tabletop as I studied the new arrivals. All three stood several inches over six feet, had reddish hair and fine facial features, almost delicate in an odd way. *Brothers,* I thought. Though the leader's hair was cropped short, the other two sported locks halfway down their back. Belatedly, I realized they were twins. All three had knives in scabbards looped through their belts. I wondered about concealed weapons.

"Well now," said the leader to the seated young man. "Look what we have here."

"Do I know you?"

Genuinely puzzled, I thought, surprised. *He really doesn't know them.*

"Name's Darius," the leader said. "My brothers, Maleck and Mortenn. And you would be Kevin. Kevin Robb, to be precise. Correct?" The young man nodded nervously, as if confessing a felony to a police officer. "Don't expect you know us, but...." He reached into the chest pocket of his jacket and took out a snapshot. After a quick glance, he nodded and tossed it on the table in front of the young man. "Bet he looks familiar."

As the three brothers leaned forward, into the pale cone of light, to witness Kevin's reaction to the photo — my breath caught in my throat. "What the hell —?"

At first I thought something dark and slimy crawled along their skin and clothes, but then I realized it was some sort of dark *light* or energy rippling around them, a visible aura, something malevolent, if my gut reaction were any judge. I scanned the bar, wondering if anyone else could see the strange phenomenon enveloping these men. Everyone seemed oblivious to it —

— except Kevin Robb. Something had rattled him. Sweat glistened on his brow. His lips trembled as he said, "That — that's a picture of me. Dead. But that's impossible."

"You're half right, Kevin," Darius said. "He is most certainly dead. Did the honors myself. Three days back."

Kevin gulped. "Three — three days?"

"Yep," Darius said. "Problem is, you ain't him."

"Of course not!"

"You've just been pretending to be him," Darius said. "Ain't that right, boys?"

The twins nodded. Mortenn, who stood closest to me, said, "Nine years running."

Jasper Long, a toothless old geezer with a perpetually grizzled jaw and a hollow leg he liked to fill on a nightly basis, demonstrated an alarming knack for bad timing by heaving himself up out of his booth, which was nearest the brewing confrontation, and attempting to sidle past Kevin's table. Maleck's right arm reached out in a blur, palm flat against Jasper's barrel chest. "Stand down, old man," Maleck said. The unspoken threat was clear in his deep voice and steady glare.

With an impatient shrug, Jasper said, "Gotta take a piss, is all."

"Later." With a quick motion, Maleck shoved Jasper back into the booth.

Jasper was no fighter. I heard him grumble, "Young punks got no respect," but that was the end of his protest.

Normally that scuffle would have been my cue to intervene. But something held me back. Something about Kevin and the three leather-clad thugs.

Perhaps hoping to take advantage of Jasper's distraction, Kevin tried to stand, but Mortenn clamped down on both his shoulders and forced him back into the chair. Kevin shook his head. "Listen, there's some kind of mix-up. I have no idea who you are or what this is about."

Darius chuckled unsympathetically. "Your being kept in the dark, figuratively, don't matter much. Our job is to put you in the dark, literally."

With practiced ease, Darius reached back under his loose jacket and pulled a dark automatic from where it had been tucked into his waistband.

"Wait!" Kevin leaned back in the rickety chair, hands raised, palms out. "Why?"

Darius extended his arm, the gun's muzzle aimed at the center of Kevin's forehead. "Because the price was irresistible."

The moment Darius reached for his gun, I was out of my booth and rushing toward the brothers. No conscious thought involved. Later, I would realize I hadn't waited to act out of doubt or fear. I had been gathering as much information as possible before unstoppable events began their inevitable motion. Later, I would marvel that my rush down the aisle over warped floorboards made not the slightest sound to betray me. Later, I would recall how time seemed to slow, how the reactions of Shirley, Hank and the other bar patrons seemed to be frozen in amber. Later, many things would resolve themselves. At that moment, my response was pure instinct, that other-self taking over my actions, my own sense of self-preservation choosing, as it always had, fight over flight.

Sensing movement, Mortenn glanced my way. As his long hair whipped around his head, I noticed a slight point to the tip of his exposed ear. He shouted a warning to Darius: "*Fae!*"

Too late.

My arm had already whipped around and was coming forward, the baseball leaving my fingertips at a speed any major league radar gun would have clocked over one hundred miles per hour. Trust me. And my control was uncannily precise. The regulation stitched cowhide ball slammed into the grip of the automatic, knocking Darius's arm off the mark. A 9mm round ripped a furrow into the floorboards. Darius yelped in pain as the gun flew from his hand.

Kevin heaved his chair backward. The rear legs struck an uneven floorboard and split under the force directed against them. The chair collapsed, taking Kevin with it, but he recovered quickly, crab-walking out of the danger zone, momentarily forgotten.

Decorative wagon wheels had been nailed to support beams on either side of the open table area. I grabbed the rim of the nearest one in both hands and swung my legs up and around. My right heel caught Mortenn in the throat. Cartilage crunched. Choking and sputtering, he dropped to his knees, a panicked look in his pale grey eyes as he struggled to breathe, hands pressed to his neck.

Maleck hadn't been idle. During my aerial assault, he went for his knife, slipping it expertly from its scabbard. The blade and hilt were flat, I saw, balanced for throwing. As his brother dropped in agony, he shouted: "Mortenn!"

Rusted nails creaked and the wagon wheel pulled free of the post.

I landed awkwardly, the wooden wheel falling into my lap.

Maleck cocked his arm. A blur of motion and a flash of silver.

Again, reacting instead of thinking, I hoisted the wagon wheel in front of my face, a fatally flawed shield, and with a split-second twist, caught the point of the blade in one of the wheel's spokes. Protruding through the back of the spoke, the tip quivered two inches in front of my right eye.

I sprang to my feet, wrenched the knife free and tossed the wagon wheel aside. The knife seemed to vibrate in my hand. I had the odd notion that it was imbued with some sort of mystical energy.

Maleck's eyes widened in sudden alarm. He darted a warning glance at Darius before returning his attention to me. The dark light of odious energy skittered around his frame. Some hint of recognition prodded the back of my mind, but the words remained too elusive to grasp. "It's him," Maleck said. "Silverthorn."

"Whisper Guard?" Darius said, then shook his head. "Can't be. Silverthorn was executed."

Shirley had crept around from behind the bar and had recovered Darius's gun. Too brave for her own good. Likely to get herself killed.

Raising my arms dramatically, I said, "My name is Ray Thorn!"

Maleck scoffed. "He doesn't know."

"So tell me!"

Abruptly, Shirley stood and stepped forward, arms outstretched, gun clutched in both hands, directing the barrel at Darius. Trembling, she nevertheless stood her ground. "Get out! Now! I'm calling the police."

"Take it easy, madam," Darius said in a soothing tone. His hand fiddled with his belt buckle. Nerves, maybe. I suspected another concealed weapon. But he raised his empty hand and waved it casually toward her. "You're too tired to hold onto that gun."

Something glittered in the light near her face, like a shower of dust.

"Too tired," Shirley repeated softly and yawned. Her eyes rolled back and her knees buckled. As she crumpled to the floor, Darius snatched the dark automatic from her hand, a look of triumph on his face.

Kevin lunged from a crouching position and swung a broken chair leg overhead like an axe handle at Darius, but he was too far away. Maleck stepped between them and took the brunt of the blow across the side of his head and left shoulder. He wrestled the young man to his knees and held him pinned there for the kill shot. Darius leveled the weapon.

I had already flipped the balanced knife, my thumb and fingers now pressed against the tip. Expediency chose my target. With a lightning flick of my wrist, I hurled it at Darius. He shrieked as the blade sank several inches into the meat of his forearm.

At that moment, Kevin pulled free of Maleck and flung himself against the wheezing Mortenn. Concealed from view, Kevin's hand darted toward the fallen twin's belted scabbard. Maleck's pale eyes blazed with fury. He bent over and grabbed Kevin's Rugby jersey in a white-knuckled grip. "Had just about enough of your shit, ch—"

Gasping, he staggered backward, and Kevin rose with him, both hands clutched around Maleck's knife, now buried to the hilt in Mortenn's abdomen. The dark energy sparked and spiked and sputtered around the twin's body. His face became gaunt before my eyes, his body sagging—no, *withering*, moment by moment. In contrast, Kevin seemed to swell with an influx of energy and strength.

Words came unbidden to my tongue: *"Soul blade."* Each one of the brothers carried a soul blade. That explained the energy I had felt vibrating along the hilt of Maleck's weapon.

The gleaming knife in Kevin's hands slipped free as the lifeless husk—all that remained of Maleck—crumpled to the floor. In a moment, the body faded away. Then Mortenn, witnessing his twin's death, made an enraged gurgling sound as he attempted to climb to his feet. Alarmed, Kevin reacted instantly. His right arm lashed out in a brutal backhand, plunging the bloodied knife between two ribs high on Mortenn's chest.

With a last, weary exhalation, Mortenn's wheezing ceased and he slumped back to the floor. A moment later, his lifeless body vanished into oblivion as well.

Not oblivion, I thought. *Otherworld.*

That word had bubbled to the surface of my mind, and I had no idea what it meant.

"What the hell is this?" Kevin said to Darius. "Who are you people?"

"Unbelievable." Darius grunted. He glanced at me and then nervously at Kevin, who still wielded a soul blade. He was out-numbered. And he'd dropped his gun again. "You two really have no clue."

"No," I said and strode toward him, "but you will tell us. Everything!"

"Like hell," Darius said. He raised a booted foot against the edge of Kevin's table and shoved hard. The untouched stein of beer went flying; pretzels scattered from the upended bowl; and the table slammed into Kevin, knocking him off balance. With a howl, Darius pulled Maleck's knife from his forearm. Not in the hands of an attacker at the moment, the soul blade posed no extra threat and had no additional ability to harm him, beyond the wound itself. Darius spun on his heel and hurled the knife toward me, then scooped his gun off the floor and thundered down the hall to the rear exit. "This is not over!" he called. "My brothers will be avenged!"

Despite Darius's haste, his knife throw was uncannily accurate. Reflexively, I twisted my head and torso aside and still felt the breeze of the blade's passing. It thudded into a supporting post behind me. I debated giving chase immediately, but Darius had the gun and his own soul blade, while I was unarmed. Instead, I yanked the knife from the post and caught up to Kevin.

Old Jasper lumbered past me, his gaze fixed on the front door.

I grabbed Kevin's arm. "We need to talk."

Gulping air, he nodded.

With the apparent end to the violence, the rest of the crowd cleared out as if the tavern were ablaze, including Gus and Cal, retirees who had been playing eight-ball in back when the commotion began. A rush of overlapping voices trailed out into the night, "The hell was that?" "—those two just vanished." "Did you see—?" "—a fuckin' hallucination!" "Didn't see a blessed thing." "—the hell outta here!"

Most of the regulars had had more than a few drinks. I wondered what they would remember—or believe—in the harsh light of morning. A brief fight resulting in two deaths, but the bodies had disappeared. Literally vanished into thin air. I imagined a few of the tavern's patrons would begin the new day by entering a twelve-step program.

"Ray? What happened?" a woozy Shirley asked as she pulled herself upright, using a bar stool for support. "Believe this is yours."

My baseball. I took it and thanked her.

"What should I do here, Ray?" Hank said, "Call the cops?"

"Place is empty," I said. "Close early. Quentin will understand."

"What are you gonna do?"

"Hell if I know."

⚜

I paid cash for a room at the Riverview Motel. The place was a dump and the nearest river was five miles away. Not that it mattered. We needed a place to regroup and the motel was within walking distance of the tavern. Besides, we also needed to stay near the tavern. Add that to the list of things I knew without knowing *how* I knew.

I stared at the corpse in the photograph.

Throat slit. Eyes vacant. Definitely not a fake. Beyond that, I had my doubts. "There is a resemblance, but...."

"Resemblance, hell!" Kevin said. "That's me!"

"Setting aside the obvious rebuttal," I said. "Have you looked at yourself in the mirror?"

"What?"

"Your hair, it's not dark brown or wavy, it's almost golden and you have these little...ringlets." Weird thing was, I remembered his features from the tavern differently. But I was looking right at him now.

Kevin's hand brushed his hair, his fingers combing through the curls. He frowned, walked over to the full-length mirror on the back of the closet door and said, "Jesus! What's happening to me?" His hands pressed against the side of his face. "My ears, they're almost...pointed."

"They said you weren't Kevin Robb."

"They were mistaken."

"What if they were right?" I said. "What happened to you three days ago? When Darius said he'd killed the Kevin Robb in the photograph three days ago, you reacted."

"A panic attack."

Curious, I walked over to him and tried to recall the moment when he first burst through the door of the Willowbrook Tavern. No denying it: That Kevin Robb *was* different from this Kevin Robb. He was changing, his physical attributes metamorphosing slower than the conscious level of human perception. Something time-lapse photography would certainly reveal. "Explain."

"Three days ago I had my first panic attack, an overwhelming sensation that my life was in danger. I needed to get out of my apartment. I couldn't go to work. Certainly couldn't stay there for hours. I chalked it up to restlessness, lack of sleep. But every time I tried to fight it, to return to my normal routines, the sensation returned. Been living out of my car for the last two days, moving whenever I *sensed* danger. Until my car broke down, about a mile and a half from the tavern. I started walking. When I saw the tavern, something clicked."

"Clicked?"

Kevin shrugged. "Don't know. Like it was a safe haven."

I chuckled. "First time anyone's called the Willowbrook Tavern a safe haven."

"None of this makes sense."

"What happened nine years ago?"

"Nine years?"

"Something Mortenn said after Darius said you weren't Kevin Robb."

"Right," Kevin said, remembering. "I would have been ten. Not much.... Wait! The traveling carnival. Henderson Acres. My parents took me. I got lost."

"Tell me about it."

"All week long, I watched the carnies putting together these fantastic rides, like this fairytale city rising from the field. It seemed magical. I begged my parents to take me. I was so excited. So much to do, so many rides, and games, and the food. Stuffed myself on cotton candy, fries, and hot dogs. I felt sick and got separated in the crowd. Too much noise and confusion. I walked into the woods and got lost. Seemed like hours. Eventually, my parents found me asleep, curled under a bush near the edge of the woods."

"The edge?"

"Yeah," he said. "They wondered why I gave up so close to the carnival grounds, figured I must have been exhausted."

"Is it possible somebody left you there, where you were sure to be found?"

"No," Kevin said, "I was alone. Don't remember anybody else."

"Maybe you weren't supposed to remember."

"What are you saying?"

"There's a gap in your memories," I said. "And, since the moment you bumped into me, I've been *recalling* things I couldn't possibly know. Somehow, we're connected."

"Those men — or whatever they are — they recognized you. And how did you learn to fight like that. It was almost..."

"Fae."

"I was going to say 'inhuman.' What about 'Fae'?"

"The word Mortenn used when he first saw me."

"Maleck called you Silverthorn. And Darius, he called you something else..."

"Whisper Guard."

"He also said you were dead."

"Makes two of us," I said wryly.

"According to Maleck, you don't know who you are," Kevin said. "And I'm not who I think I am."

"What if they're right?"

"About us?"

"What do you know about the Fae?"

"Fae? You mean Faeries, right? Folklore stuff. Read about it in English lit. *A Midsummer Night's Dream.* Can't recall too much."

"Anything about changelings?"

"What? Alien shape-shifters?"

I shook my head. "Faerie children swapped for human children. The human parents unknowingly raise the Faerie child, while the Faeries raise the human child."

"Are you trying to say I'm a Faerie child? That I'm not Kevin Robb, that the real Kevin was raised by Faeries, and murdered three days ago? That's ridiculous!"

"More ridiculous than bodies disappearing in front of your eyes?"

"But I look just like the other Kevin Robb—"

"Past tense. You're changing. Reverting."

" — and I have his memories — *my* — memories."

"We've seen how memories can be tricked. How much do you really remember before that day at the carnival?"

"A lot, ten years of my...." Kevin pounded the heel of his palm against his forehead in frustration.

"What about your parents? We could call them, ask them about that day."

Kevin shook his head. "They died, fifteen months ago, electrical fire. Smoke inhalation. I was at a party when...." He sat on the edge of the bed, shaking his head. "Why? What's the point? This changeling nonsense."

"Maybe the Faeries thought you would be safe here," I said absently. I was staring at my own reflection in the mirror. The hair I had assumed was prematurely grey was, quite possibly, naturally silver. My ears, so like Mortenn's — and now Kevin's — rising in back, unmistakably pointed. As I examined events in my life, those remembrances began to tatter under my mental scrutiny, a life's scenery constructed from tissue paper, flimsy and unconvincing. Only the past year held the solidity of truth. And my name, Ray Thorn, perhaps only a half-truth. Could my life, my home, my job, all of it, be nothing more than a way station? Silverthorn was real. Ray Thorn was the illusion.

I had been in a holding pattern, marking time. Another word bubbled up to the surface of my consciousness and it held the sad ring of truth. Darius had thought me dead, but the hidden reality was a crueler fate. *Exile....*

Inevitably, the answer came to me. "Henderson Acres."

"What about it?"

"Those woods aren't far from here," I said. "Few blocks behind Willowbrook Tavern."

He nodded. "We should go. Agreed?"

"Not yet."

"When?"

"Twilight."

Though Kevin seemed too restless to sleep, I took the first watch. Made bad coffee with the in-room percolator and supplies. One sip and I swore off the stuff. I angled the ratty armchair toward the front window and widened the gap between the putrid orange curtains enough to reveal most of the parking lot — an island of fractured concrete under the pale wash of streetlights—while maintaining our own privacy. We'd been up most of the night, so the plan was to sleep through the morning and into the afternoon, to bide our time during the day and await twilight. I doubted it would be that simple. Darius had found Kevin once. I had no delusions about his ability to do so again.

I settled into the uncomfortable chair with my legs extended, feet crossed at the ankles. In fifteen hours, we could walk into Henderson Acres. A long time, maybe, but we had no choice. We would wait. And if the situation called for action, instinct would take over. It always had. I glanced at the bed and was not surprised to see Kevin asleep. He'd been on the run for three days. I, on the other hand, had only been drafted into service several hours ago.

Kevin's referring to my disreputable place of employment as a "safe haven" had brought a smile to my face. But I began to wonder if it had been the tavern that had lured him inside or its proximity to me, a trained guardian. *Whisper Guard.* We were connected in all the craziness. Would we find the answers we sought in the woods where a young boy had gotten lost nine years ago?

A weird sensation overcame me. Sitting in the lumpy chair, staring into the illuminated night, my awareness seemed to slip out of the moment. Disconnected from my flesh, in some sort of trancelike state, I heard an old woman's voice, a frail whisper on the edge of a dream.

"So soon you begin to remember, Sunray Silverthorn."

I spoke into the heedless dark of the hotel room. "Bits and pieces, Elder. Not nearly enough."

"Four years too soon," she said. *"But it was necessary to interrupt your* pretender *life. To protect the heir."*

"Kevin? Then he is one of the Fae?"

"Miles, last heir to Clan Evergreen."

"And who am I? Who is Sunray Silverthorn?"

"Also of our clan, disgraced of our clan, a captain of the Whisper Guard, slayer of a Royal in a duel sprung from a lover's jealous rage—"

With her words, a rush of images tumbled up through my mind, lost memories and forgotten faces revealed for a split second before falling away again. And with the images, glimpses into my past, the familiar sound of names lost to the shell of a man I had become. "Allemara chose me!"

"—betrayer of protocol—"

"Prince Raganel was the challenger. Honor dictated —"

" — *and, ultimately* — "

"He refused to yield!"

" — *an exile.*"

Remembering, I sighed. "A five-year sentence."

"By my proclamation," the elder said. The walls of the motel room faded into translucency, as insubstantial as my *pretender* life. Beyond these hollow walls, I saw a rich forest glade and, standing in its center, a majestically old woman in a shimmering golden gown with impossibly long silver hair, tinted emerald green. Despite her advanced age, her features were delicate and beautiful. Motes of light sparkled from her green eyes and took flight with an aerial dance akin to the passage of butterflies. *"Knowing the truth of which you speak, it was I, Ellisandra Evergreen, who waived the execution order and spared your life."*

"This is not a life," I said. "Not the life I was meant to live."

"You seek pardon? A commutation? Then do what you must. Bring the heir safely home to us and it may yet come to pass."

"I will not fail."

She nodded, pleased. *"Now tell me of his would-be assassins."* After I recounted the fight with Darius and his twin brothers, she frowned. *"As I expected, clanless rogues, no lasting allegiance other than to coin.*

"A rival clan, out of the Unseelie Court, seeks to steal our land and holdings without the consequence of retaliation. For years, we have been unable to expose them."

"Darius will talk."

"Remember, the heir's safety takes precedence. May fortune favor you, Silverthorn."

Pins and needles in my feet. The walls of the cheap motel room were solid again. Seemingly in the blink of an eye, my *other* awareness had fled. The gap between the curtains revealed it was nearly dawn. Almost two hours had passed. Other than the minor discomfort of my feet, I felt invigorated. Rising, I walked toward the bathroom.

Kevin sat up, yawned, and looked around the drab room. "My turn already?"

"That won't be —"

A sound like an explosion behind me.

I whirled as the door slammed against the wall. Darius rushed in, gun leveled in the hand of his bandaged arm. Kevin rolled off the far side of the mattress. Two rounds blasted into the headboard behind where he'd been sitting. I grabbed the coffee pot and flung the scalding liquid at Darius's face. A third shot, intended for me, slammed into the ceiling as he recoiled from the heat.

A spin-kick dislodged the gun from his hand. It clattered against the wall to my left. Without pause, Darius reached for his soul blade. I charged him, pinning his arm against his body as I drove him backward and slammed him into the television set bolted to the dresser. He grunted, regained his balance, then pushed off, using his superior height and weight to force me back on my heels. "I promise you a slow death, Silverthorn."

A glance over my shoulder caused me to adjust the angle of my retreat.

"If you hadn't interfered—!"

"It's in my nature," I said. *Just a little bit more....*

"Maleck and Mortenn will be avenged!"

I spied Kevin, circling around the foot of the bed, wielding the soul blade he'd snatched from Mortenn. *The heir's safety takes precedence.* I shook my head vigorously to stop Kevin. Darius frowned in apparent confusion. So I chose that moment to stop resisting and fell backward, using his forward momentum against him. I hit the floor and rolled on my back, tucking my legs between us, then pushing out with both feet, hurling him overhead with all my strength.

Upended, his body smashed through the bay window in a tangle of curtains and a shower of glass, and he fell hard against the pavement outside the motel room.

I rolled onto my hands and knees and scrambled for the gun lying against the wall, under the shattered window. Darius roared in anger a split-second before Kevin yelled, "Look out!"

Unable to secure the gun, I rose from a crouch as Darius hurled himself through the broken window. His shadow swept over me, the only light glinting off the soul blade clutched in his right hand, sweeping toward my chest. Peripherally, I saw Maleck's knife on the end table—out of reach.

Kevin yelled. "Catch!"

It all happened in a moment. My left arm shot out, seizing Darius's right wrist, below his injured forearm, to thwart his attack, even as my right hand opened to catch the soul blade Kevin had tossed to me. And again Darius's momentum worked against him. I slipped the point of the blade between us and his own charge drove it into his chest, up to the hilt, as we both fell against the side of the bed.

He grunted, fear ablaze in his eyes as he tried to pull away from me, but I held tight. Groaning, he staggered upright, lurched sideways a few steps, and fell to his knees. He pounded my right arm with his left fist, but I stayed with him, one hand pressing the knife into his flesh, the other keeping his own knife turned away from me. "Who hired you?"

"Go to hell!"

As he struggled, I felt myself becoming stronger, infused with a heady rush of power. I twisted the knife against his ribs for emphasis. "Which clan paid you?"

"Too late," he mumbled weakly.

Too late – ? The soul blade! "No!"

I tried to remove the knife, but he clamped his hand over mine, perversely holding it in place for the last few seconds of his life. The hilt was slick with his blood and slipped within my grasp.

He collapsed, spittle on his chin, grinning insanely as he held the knife inside his flesh, literally willing his life away in defeat simply to deny me a vital piece of information.

Before Darius's body faded back to *Otherworld,* I found in his jacket pocket, tied to a leather cord, an irregular chunk of dark crystal, the tip of which glowed when I waved it in Kevin's direction. One mystery solved, if not all of them. But the crystal was a potential clue to the identity of the Unseelie Court clan, so I took it with us as we fled the damaged motel room. We killed time in a diner a couple miles away, drinking coffee, exploring fragments of recovered memories as the day expended itself. Eventually, we made our way back on foot to Henderson Acres, and walked deep into the woods.

Instinctively, we ignored the will-o'-the-wisps, as they would only lead us astray, and we waited for the true path to reveal itself to us. Miles Evergreen had been kept safe, hidden among the humans as Kevin Robb for nine years, in anticipation of this twilight crossing. Fortunately for me, our paths crossed. Redemption was within my grasp.

At last, the path appeared, weaving through the underbrush, gilded in Faerie lights like a bridge into dreams. For me, it was a passage out of uninspired dreams and back into my true life.

With a flourish befitting a prince of a Seelie Court clan, I bowed from the waist and extended my arm toward the path. "After you, Miles Evergreen."

He chuckled. "I'll never get used to this."

"You'd be surprised."

He stepped onto the path to reclaim his birthright.

My road back was simpler, but no less important.

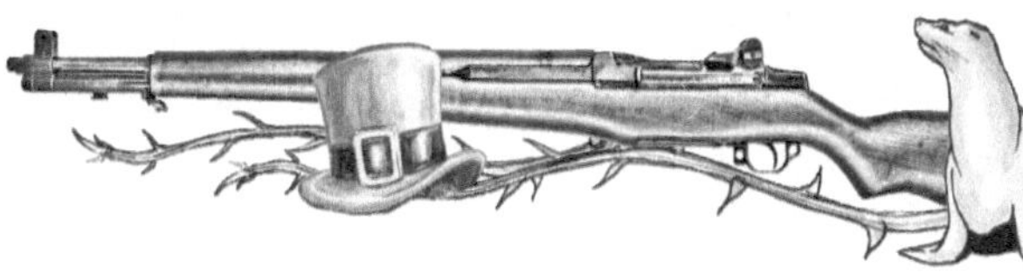

Grim Necessity

Jeffrey Lyman

FEATHERLIGHT AND HER PARTNER, REMY, STRODE DOWN THE corridor of the pixie wing of the maximum security prison, boots clacking on the floor. Remy tapped his billy club against his hip as he walked, a nervous habit. Full-sized bricks, painted white and stacked four high, had been used in the construction of the walls, and there was iron plating behind those bricks. Iron didn't bother Featherlight, but Remy said it felt like an uncomfortable itch.

"I can't believe Clank's getting a visitor," he said.

"Happens to the worst of us," she replied, keeping her eyes open for trouble. "I can't believe the warden's allowing her to see a visitor."

The corridor ended and P-wing opened up around them. They were on the top floor of four stories of cells, wrapped around a central, open core. The core had been strung back and forth with steel wire to keep the pixies from flying.

There were a lot of pixies inside today. The prison was on semi-lockdown because of an outbreak of fighting the day before. The warden was limiting the number of races out in the yards. Right now the brownies and faeries were out, and the pixies, ogres, and most of the dwarfs were inside.

Featherlight and Remy stopped in front of a cell. "Clankerbell. You have a visitor." Remy grunted.

She didn't agree with the warden allowing Clank to have a visitor.

All evidence indicated that she hadn't been in the fight, but Featherlight knew Clank had been involved somehow. She always was. Clankerbell stood from her cot, looking bored. Plastic dog tags hung proudly on the wall behind her. They

were a trophy, taken from the body of the Rottweiler that had bitten off her right wing.

"My reputation must be growing," she said, staring at Featherlight. "They sent the Big Pig to fetch me this time." She fanned her remaining left wing like a butterfly and glanced at Remy. "Who is it?"

She had gotten a new tattoo on her arm, Featherlight noticed. An inverted rainbow, meaning something like an upside-down cross. No matter how hard the warden tried, he couldn't keep the pixies from getting colors for their prison tats. They practically shat colors, so what was the use?

"I have no idea who it is and I didn't ask," Remy said. "He's either a dwarf or a short, hairy man. You ready?" Clank nodded and Remy bellowed back down to the guardhouse, "Open up number seventeen."

The bars of Clankerbell's cell clicked and whirred on their servos and slid to the side.

Featherlight tensed up. "You know the drill. Keep your hands to yourself and I won't crush you."

"Chill, Big Pig. We're cool." Clankerbell smirked and stepped out of her cell.

Featherlight was a protean shapeshifter who could change not only her looks, but her size. She could swell up in the corridor and mash Clankerbell into the wall in a second if there were trouble. She could also close up her wounds if someone knifed her. The warden always sent her into the fights, and the prisoners respected her abilities.

Clank carelessly sauntered down the corridor, whistling the same cheery song all Pixies whistled. Featherlight heard it in her head sometimes after long days. Remy walked behind them both to stay out of the 'crush zone' should Featherlight's abilities be needed.

They passed a smaller cell with a single bell hanging from the ceiling, and it rang off-key in time with Clank. An ugly gremlin peeked out below the rim and Featherlight pointed at him. "Go back to sleep, Smear." The greasy head vanished.

They passed through security, where Clankerbell was searched from top to bottom. Featherlight then led her through a mouse hole and into the secure visiting area. Birdcages hung where pixies could talk to their visitors. More docile inmates were allowed out into the larger Visitor's Room to meet with family members directly. Clankerbell had never been docile.

Featherlight and Remy locked Clankerbell into a birdcage securely.

"Yo, Feather."

Featherlight looked up as an elf guard leaned into the secure room. He was holding a telephone receiver.

"What?" she shouted.

"The Man wants to talk to you."

Featherlight quickly passed through pixie security, and, swelling to near-human size, climbed down to the floor of the guard booth. The elf, who was now shorter than she, handed her the phone.

"What's up, Boss?" She looked out the booth window and was surprised at how many visitors were in the room. With the tension in the prison, the inmates were only being allowed out a few at a time and the backlog of visitors was growing. All manner of husbands and wives slouched at tables, waiting. A gaggle of dwarf children chased a troll kit around. One of the prisoners, dressed like a harlequin, was juggling and failing to entertain them.

"Featherlight," the warden said. "Come on up. I want you to see something."

"I'm looking after Clankerbell."

"Remy's fine. Come on up."

"Sure." She hung up with misgivings and leaned down to her pixie partner. "Hey Remy, you got this?"

Remy nodded and flapped his wings. "If you gotta go, you gotta go. Odbottom will back me up. Besides, me and Clankerbell here are old friends, ain't we, Clank? She'll behave."

Featherlight hustled upstairs to the catwalks. As she headed in the direction of the warden's office, she took note of the dwarf entering Clank's small room. He wasn't someone she was familiar with, but then Clank rarely got visitors since her mother and grandmother were also incarcerated. Nothing looked out of the ordinary as he clambered up onto a stool and pulled down a phone receiver from the wall. Clankerbell lifted a tiny receiver in her birdcage. Guards in the booth monitored the conversation.

Featherlight pushed through an exterior door into late October sunshine and hurried down the catwalk, passing over the brownie basketball courts. Several elf-guards monitored from above, arrows half-drawn in their bows. She could feel the tension in the air. Yesterday's fight had been a bad one.

She nodded to the guards, glancing down at the heavily muscled, shirtless brownies scuffling below over bright orange, squeaky-balls.

The brownies used toy basketballs, and the noise was always riotous. Today it was worse than ever, and she could barely hear herself think. They were dribbling as hard as they could. Featherlight had always thought using a dog's chew-toy was degrading, but the brownies, as tough as they were, loved the noise.

Next came the dwarf-yard on her right, if you could call it a yard. It was all concrete, elevated a few feet above the ground. There was no way the dwarfs were going to tunnel out through that, though they were constantly kicking and scuffing at it, and frowning. Looking for cracks, the guards used to say. Because of the lockdown, there were only four dwarves out today. One was bench pressing a massive weight. Two were braiding each other's beards. The fourth glared and shouted insults over at the adjacent faerie yard. He was new, came in with a number of faeries dressed like pirates a week before. He looked like all the other dwarves now in prison-orange.

The modestly-sized faerie yard on Featherlight's left was completely enclosed in a Kevlar, mesh cage. The faeries couldn't tolerate the usual steel chain link fences, and the prison had to box them in somehow.

A few blues were hanging from the west end of the cage, their wings drawn up tight. A few reds were clustered on the east end. They could hang there for hours, trading insults and hatred. Today they were joined together in common cause, shouting insults back at the dwarf. Below them on the ground of the yard stalked the pathetic non-fliers with broken or damaged wings. Faeries could be vicious when they fought, going after each other's wings first.

She passed through another security gate and into the Admin Wing. It was warmer here. She shook off the early season chill. She always got cold so fast.

"What's up?" she said as she opened the warden's door. He was on the phone, but he waved her in with a sausage-fingered hand. He was a brownie, as fat as brownies came when they dined on too many cakes and bowls of milk a day.

"So? What do you think," he said when he hung up.

"About what?"

"Clankerbell."

"Did something happen?" Featherlight immediately thought of Remy. He was a fighting pixie, but Clankerbell was Clankerbell.

"Not yet. Take a look." He gestured to the bank of video screens along his wall. Several were trained on the Visitors' Rooms, on

Clankerbell's in particular.

Featherlight dropped onto a seat. She hadn't created wings for this body, so she didn't need to use the wing-cutout at the seatback. "If you think Clank's up to something, I should be there."

"No, you should be out here because something *is* up. That fight yesterday was bigger than any I've seen in my thirty years here. And Clankerbell, who always fights, didn't fight. Then she gets a visitor today, her first in years. It's all tied together somehow."

"Did you send over more guards?"

"I've got four extra on the catwalks above the Visitors' Room, that's it. I don't want to drain my resources if trouble breaks out elsewhere."

A siren wailed. Featherlight scanned the screens. The brownies and redcaps were quiet. The ogres sat in their cells, staring at the stone walls, which always seemed to fascinate them. She pointed to the screen showing the dwarf and faerie yards.

"They're trying to rip through!" she said.

One of the insults must have hit home, because two of the four dwarfs were pressed up against the Kevlar mesh, trying to pull it apart. There was no sound, but it looked like they were screaming as they strained. Kevlar was strong, but an angry dwarf might be stronger. Blue and red faeries fluttered everywhere inside of the cage. Several were right up in the dwarves' faces, yanking at their beards through the mesh and shouting back.

"I'm going out there," Featherlight said.

"Sit tight! The elves can handle it, and I'll call in a troll or two if need be. This might be a distraction, so keep an eye on Clankerbell."

Elves fired pixie-dust tipped arrows down into the dwarf-yard, but the dwarves were too worked up to go down easily. Nearby faeries began falling from the top of the cage like bugs from a hot lightbulb as the dust grew thick.

Suddenly the squawk-box on the warden's desk erupted in shouting and a cacophonous barking. It quickly clarified into Wheezer's voice. Wheezer was the head troll over the mess hall.

"Warden! We've got a situation!"

"What's going on?"

Both the warden and Featherlight stared at the security screens and the scrum of brown, furry bodies in the mess hall.

"The faeries all dumped their trays into the Selkie watering hole. I've got pissed off seals everywhere!"

"There she goes," Featherlight said, pointing up at Clankerbell's screen.

Clankerbell's dwarf visitor stood and smashed through the Plexiglas wall separating him from her birdcage with one powerful punch that must have broken his hand. Undeterred, he tore her cage from its anchors and charged out into the Visitors' Room. An elf guard jabbed him with an electric-stick but he shrugged it off and continued his bowlegged run for the front security door.

The two guards at the security station and the four additional guards that the warden had sent lined up at the door, while behind them the ogres pulled down the steel shields. Arrows were drawn and Featherlight looked to the warden, wanting permission to go.

In a blink, a table crashed into the guards. Then another. Featherlight stood. There were other dwarves amidst the visitors, helping Clankerbell. Guards sprawled and arrows sprang disjointedly from bows to land into the crowds of panicking civilians. People fainted from errant clouds of pixie dust. Three dwarves rushed forward. The two ogres at the door hunkered down at the ready. The dwarf carrying Clankerbell's cage hadn't slowed his run.

The Warden started slapping buttons.

"What are you doing?" Featherlight's head was spinning. Clankerbell was getting away. Conversely, Clank might get injured in her own riotous escape. Ogres were excitable, and pixies were squishable.

"I'm neutralizing the situation with pixie-dust bombs before someone gets hurt," he shouted. "We don't want a hostage situation, and I can't let Clankerbell escape. And I can't spare more guards for her or for the Mess Hall until that damned dwarf stops tearing up my Kevlar cage. If he gets it open, we'll have faeries flying for the hills."

The screens showing both the Visitors' Room and the Mess Hall blossomed into white like swirling snow, as pixie-bombs exploded *en masse*.

"You shouldn't have let her have visitors," Featherlight said.

"Just go out make sure everything's settled. I want everyone in full lockdown, in their cells with the doors closed."

"The brownies, too?"

"Yes, the brownies, too. But they're the least of my concern. What are they going to do, break out and clean my office?"

Featherlight stood. "Something's not right."

"Is it that obvious?"

"No, Clank had to know we'd gas her in the Visitors' Room. She's not stupid."

"So go check on her after you check on my Kevlar." He poured himself a quick shot of milk and tossed it back.

"I'm on it." Featherlight hustled back out to the catwalk.

There were eight elves above the dwarf yard now, dropping arrows like pennies into a wishing well. There was a thick cloud of pixie dust below them, and one dwarf was staggering. The other was still bellowing and madly trying to tear his way in at the faeries. The red and blue faeries who hadn't succumbed to the dust were pressed against the far side of the pen, as far away as possible. Still, there were probably thirty sleeping bodies stretched across their cage.

"He's going down!" someone crowed.

Featherlight leaned over the railing, studying the Kevlar. The dwarf had managed to stretch the weave big enough to get his arm through. They'd have to replace that section before the faeries could come out again. Faeries were like those octopi in the nature specials, they could wriggle out through anything. Cartilage for bones.

She wasn't needed here.

She hurried on, over the brownie pen where the small men watched the commotion with agitation, squeaky balls held at rest. They hated pixie-dustings. All that mess just upset them.

With barely a thought, she dropped down into the form of a huge black dog, loping along the catwalk. It hurt for a moment as her bones reconfigured themselves, and then it was done. Her shaggy fur ruffled in the breeze of her own swift passing. She wanted to be ready for anything.

She raced through the door at speed, stirring up clouds of recently settled pixie dust. She snorted and sniffed at the air, but couldn't smell anything over that dust. Her sharp eyes immediately discerned Clankerbell's open cage on the floor near the room's main door. Clank's dwarf accomplice was simultaneously trying to wedge the doors open a crack with a table leg and trying to breathe fresh air through that same crack. The rest of the dwarves who had been involved were unconscious amidst guards and children. Had Clank escaped?

No, Featherlight was certain of that. Clank was up to something. The open door had not yet been used. She raised herself back up into bipedal form and scooped a handful of pixie dust from a table-top. She walked to the frantically working dwarf and tapped him on the shoulder. When he turned, she blew the dust directly into his face. He shouted and leapt off-balance like a drunk. In a second, he was snoring.

She jogged up the stairs in the now terribly silent room and walked carefully through the vacant security gate. The guards were sprawled, asleep. No sign of Clank. Also no sign of Remy.

Featherlight crushed herself down tight into pixie shape and walked into the pixie corridor. The door to the corridor was open and dust had drifted in. She reached the fourth floor of P-Wing and walked past cell after cell of sleeping or groggy inhabitants. She slowed as she approached the open door of Clankerbell's cell. The steel bars had been torn and bent open. Two doll-sized oven mitts lay on the floor, obviously Clank's protection when she ripped apart the steel.

"Is that you, Big Pig?" a muffled version of Clank's voice called. "Come on in."

Featherlight stepped into the door opening and took in the scene: Clankerbell sat on the edge of her bed wearing a gasmask; Remy and Odbottom out cold and in a pile on the bed next to her. She held a plastic dog tag like a guillotine blade over Remy's neck, ready to decapitate him. It wasn't sharp, but she was plenty strong enough to do it.

"Where did you get that?" Featherlight said, pointing to the gas mask. She took a step forward. If she could swell up, maybe she could knock Clank and her dog tags back up against the wall.

"You could search a dwarf's beard for three days and still not find everything he's hidden there," Clankerbell said. "How do you think we get our drugs?"

"We should shave the dwarves when we bring 'em in," Featherlight said softly.

Clankerbell actually laughed. "The bleeding hearts would scream about cruel and unusual punishment. So tell me, how is it you're breathing when all of the other pigs are down on the deck?"

"You were expecting me," Featherlight said, ignoring the question. She reached out and grabbed the bent bars of the door with her bare hands, showing Clankerbell that steel didn't bother her.

"My grandmother told me you were the Big Pig in her day, too. She said that if I ever tried to escape, I had to handle you or it would never work."

Clankerbell launched herself straight into Featherlight's stomach, tearing her hands from the bars and hurtling her over the railing and into the empty space over the common area four stories below. Featherlight felt the pain of her feet leaving the deck, the panic of not touching ground. She felt powerless for the first time in years. She flailed and struggled.

Clank laughed as they clipped one of the steel wires the prison had strung above the open area. Featherlight's hand was cut cleanly from her arm. She screamed in pain as they went spinning from the impact. A second wire chopped through both of her legs. Clank leapt clear, twisting out of the way as several more staggered wires cut greater and greater parts from Featherlight's body: her pelvis, then torso, then her head from what was left.

Blackness descended and she lost vision for a moment, until her head cracked and bounced across the floor. That woke her up. She could hear other parts of her body slapping wetly to earth. Clankerbell whistled and sang from behind her gas mask and swung back and forth from wire to wire on her way to the floor. Other pixies had ventured out into the common area, pixies far enough from the entry corridor to have missed the full dose of dust.

Featherlight shut her eyes. No use in broadcasting she was still here and in pain.

Clank landed in an awkward clatter as her one wing failed to keep her balanced at the last minute. The pixies cheered anyway.

"That, ladies and gentlemen, is how it's done," Clank crowed, pulling her gasmask off with steel-burned hands. "Big Pig is down. Separate the head from the body, and I dare you to find me anyone that can survive. Now who's with me? The front door's open and I've done all the hard work. You just have to hold your breath long enough to fly across the Visitor's Room."

Again the cheers. Featherlight had heard enough. Clankerbell's carefully laid plan was nothing more than brute force—arrange for the faeries to riot outside, arrange for dwarves to riot in the Visitor's Room, and wait for the warden to start dropping bombs. Featherlight had been hoping for something more. Clankerbell's grandmother had been a master of subtlety.

She formed a body out of the concrete floor below her head and climbed to her two, new feet. Her broken head wobbled a little on the neck until she could settle it and heal the broken skull. Silence fell and pixies rapidly backed away.

"Hey Clank," Featherlight rasped, then cleared her throat.

"What the hell?" Clankerbell was brought up short, her eyes wide. "I ripped your damned head off your body!"

"Whatever."

Clankerbell shrieked and charged again, but Featherlight was ready this time. She swelled up one of her hands until it was six inches tall and grabbed Clank roughly. The pixie struggled in vain, spewing curses and blasphemies.

"Anyone else want a piece of me?" Featherlight shouted. She almost laughed when she realized she was surrounded by pieces of her old body.

The pixies, shocked, shuffled back to their cells. Featherlight dragged her huge hand and Clankerbell up the winding stairs to the top, and out through the entrance corridor. She swelled her body size to match her hand, and waited for the cavalry to arrive. She *was* the Big Pig. She was the last defense; always had been.

"How did you survive?" Clank demanded as they took her away to a long stint in solitary confinement. "What kind of a faerie are you?"

Featherlight shrugged and returned to the catwalks. Elf guards passed her, slapping her on the back and congratulating her. Her new body ached with all of the wounds of the old one, so she escaped the crush of medical personnel helping visitors and guards gathering troublemakers, and climbed to the roof.

There, amidst the mushroom-shaped fans and air conditioners, she watched the sun set.

She was not a faerie. She had been once, but not for a long, long time. She was the prison Grim.

Formerly a prisoner in the old jail, over four hundred years ago now, she had been executed for her crimes. Lucky her, they had buried her under the foundations of the new prison as the guardian Grim. Forbidden to leave the prison, even to fly for a second, she would prowl the catwalks and corridors day and night, night and day, until they tore the prison down and released her.

But hey, at least she was free to climb up to the roof and smell the fresh air. After so long, she didn't want to leave the prison. She would protect it and keep the inmates as safe as she could, from each other and from the guards. Even Clankerbell, her great-great-great-great granddaughter.

Moonshine

Bernie Mojzes

Prohibition be damned. At Pogo & Bud's, the booze flowed like the music: hot and sultry, drums and bass laying down the groove as the piano tinkled like ice on glass, a splash of saxophone across the bar and into darkened corners. Bryn Mawr debs in feathers and fringe danced with nattily dressed negroes from the city. Lazy ceiling fans mixed dense clouds of tobacco and marijuana in the hot June air.

Tom Marich leaned back against the bar with closed eyes, letting the music wash over him, fingers tapping echoes of the melody against his whiskey glass. He wasn't the only regular attracted more by the music than the speakeasy's other offerings. Young musicians who pushed the boundaries wouldn't—couldn't—find work at more respectable venues like the Dunbar. However dubious his other concerns, Bud McGarritty made a point of booking some of the most innovative jazzmen in the country.

"It's the only thing makes having *that*," McGarritty had said to Tom once, glancing toward an unmarked door at the back of the room, "bearable."

Tom had crossed that threshold once: through that door, and up a staircase, carpeting worn and stained and smelling of piss and mold and less savory things, wallpaper dirty and bubbled and peeling. A single bare bulb casting it all in flickering contrast. He'd paid a man for passage, enticed by a pale slip of a girl whose name he'd never known. Beyond lay another world, one of shell-shocked men with haunted eyes—veterans of the Great War—and sometimes others: sharply-dressed men with girls on their arms, giggling couples or threesomes looking for an exotic kick. The opium smoke was sweet as nectar, and the sex sweeter, but once the excitement of the forbidden—and the drug—had worn off, the sight of wasted men and women scattered like casualties in hospice, lost in dream and decay, made him swear to stick to jazz and whiskey from then on.

Tom chain-smoked through the set, watching the flappers dance as he sipped his drink. When his last smoke threatened to burn his lips, he caught the attention of the Lucky Strikes girl, a tantalizing redhead with the cigarette tray. She was new, and Tom wondered who got paid what for the order to come down to Bud to show the Pall Mall girl the door.

He tossed three nickels on the tray, smiling as the girl opened the pack and tapped a cigarette out for him. She leaned forward with a lighter, and after the tip glowed red, she handed over the rest of the pack. Her fingers brushed his, and she grinned and winked at him. "My name's Mary," she said. "I'm new."

"Tom. And it's a pleasure."

"You a regular here, Tom?"

"Long as the music's good," he said.

"Then I hope the music stays good," she tossed over her shoulder as she walked away.

After the set, Tom waved his empty glass at McGarritty, but the bartender was down at the end of the bar in distracted conversation with a small man that Tom hadn't seen at Pogo & Bud's before. Man? Tom reassessed—there wasn't even a hint of stubble on the boy's face as he gazed innocently at McGarritty's scowl. His oversized jacket and pants made him seem even skinnier than he probably was. Tom drew his bar stool closer for a listen...and for a place at the front of the queue once McGarritty was pouring again.

"That ain't the way things are done," McGarritty was saying. "In this world there's rules, and even a punk kid like you knows it's bad for your health to go making side deals."

The kid took off his hat. Fine brown hair fell to his—her?—shoulder.

Tom blinked in surprise. All thoughts of the Lucky Strikes girl vanished.

"No side deals, Mr. McGarritty," the kid said in a woman's low alto, the words falling like music, "I'm simply asking you to sample my wares, and, if you find them satisfactory, provide an introduction to the appropriate people in the supply chain. I believe that with the endorsement of a fine businessman such as yourself, we can forge a long and lucrative partnership. For all concerned."

There was something slightly alien in her voice: the accent of a girl who had come to America in early childhood. Tom struggled to place it. A first-generation Serb growing up in a neighborhood of immigrants, he had a lot of experience with accents, but this one eluded him with a familiarity that lingered just out of reach.

McGarritty hesitated. "I dunno..."

Tom set his empty glass on the bar between McGarritty and the girl. She jumped, just slightly, surprised by the sudden intrusion.

"I'll try it," he said with a playful smile, "if you'll join me. Hell, right about now, seems like it's the only way to get a drink around here." The last he directed to McGarritty, though his eyes never left the girl's face.

"Excellent," she said, pulling a tall, thin bottle from inside her jacket. The liquor that poured from the dark green glass was a translucent, milky white that glowed in the dimly lit bar.

"Is that Absinthe?" Tom asked.

She smiled. "Not quite, though it's quite potent in its own way. We call it Moonshine. That's what gives it that glow. I'm told that it's also a pun. This recipe has been in my family for a long time, and we felt that it's time to share it with the world. So, here I am." She raised her glass and clinked it against Tom's. "To world domination," she said, and her eyes glittered.

There was a mild burn, the licorice-gummy anise almost masking the bitter bite of wormwood that gave Absinthe its distinctive properties. Tom smiled knowingly, then his eyes widened in surprise. A secondary flavor washed the anise from his mouth with a harsh burn reminiscent of *Slivovics*, the strong plum brandy his father used to distill in the basement. But there was something else, something he couldn't pinpoint. Like the girl's accent, it was almost familiar, hovering at the tip of recognition, but when he thought too hard it slipped away.

"That's amazing," he said, as the warmth burned slowly through his limbs.

"Amazing how?" McGarritty demanded. "What's it taste like?"

"It's..." Words failed him. "Just try it, you'll see."

"Fine," McGarritty grumbled. He set out a third glass.

"Another?" The girl smiled as she tipped a bit more into Tom's glass, then poured for McGarritty and herself.

"Sure." It was good. Better than good. He felt warm and strong and sexy. Every sight was more vivid, every sound more tactile, every touch more flavorful.

A look of wonder crossed McGarritty's face. "How much?"

"This bottle? It's free. The rest? Well, that's going to depend on how big a piece your, uh, acquaintance is going to require. I think that we can find a price that will keep all of us happy. Maybe we could talk again on Tuesday? You'll arrange that with the relevant parties." It wasn't a question.

"Tuesday? Yeah, I'll see what I can do."

"You do that," she said, pushing the bottle across the bar toward him. "Or Wednesday I'll be talking to some Italians."

McGarritty nodded sharply. "Yes, ma'am. I understand. We got one shot at this."

"Good boy." She tucked up her hair and fit it back under her fedora. Tom wondered how he could have ever mistaken her for a boy. Maybe it was the puckish grin, accentuated as it was by her angular features.

"For the record," Tom said, "wherever this stuff ends up, that's where I'll be." He smiled at the girl. "I'm Tom, by the way. Tom Marich."

She held out a hand. "You may call me Evelyn." She pronounced it with a long 'e,' and Tom thought of apples and gardens and snakes, of the original Eve, standing up naked and unafraid to pluck the Fruit of Knowledge away from God. Her accent wasn't Irish, or English. It was more like the distant echo of a much older tongue. He could almost visualize it. He bent to kiss her hand, then surprised himself by leaning forward boldly and whispering in her ear. A smile played across her lips. "An interesting proposal, Tom Marich, if I were in a playful mood. And I *may* be in a playful mood." She fingered the collar of his shirt thoughtfully, slid her hand down his chest, then pulled back abruptly. Something burned fiercely on Tom's chest. Her eyes narrowed warily. "Or *not*," she said. She pushed her hat down firmly, tucked in a stray strand, and turned to leave. "Tuesday," she said, over her shoulder, to McGarritty. "Three o' clock."

Tom blinked and shook his head, suddenly clearheaded. He caught the Lucky Strikes girl's eye as she worked her way across the floor. She smiled as he rose to meet her.

"Would you like to come upstairs with me?" he asked, setting a glass of Moonshine on her tray.

Mary bit her lip. "I don't know. I've never..." She gestured helplessly. "And I'm working till ten."

He smiled, nodding toward the stage, where the band had started tuning up. "I'll be here."

⚜

Brogan O'Connor checked himself in the mirror of the car before he got out. One of the boys handed him his hat, and he set it carefully on his head, then straightened his suit.

Evelyn watched this display from her seat outside the lunch counter two doors down from Pogo & Bud's. She sipped her coffee, determined it tepid, and warmed it discretely. O'Connor adjusted his cuffs and his bow tie. Only then did he walk through the door one of his boys patiently held open for him. He was on time. *How conscientious.*

She waved for another cup of coffee.

O'Connor was properly agitated by the time Evelyn slipped past the man at the door. He'd taken a corner table against the wall, where he sat with his legs crossed, sipping a Manhattan. He checked his pocket watch, polishing it before putting it away. Compared to the men who flanked him on either side, he looked harmless. Evelyn appreciated the illusion, even as she perpetrated her own. She walked up to the table without introduction, and without a word, set a bottle of Moonshine in front of the man.

"What the hell's this?" O'Conner stared at her as if she was a bug.

Evelyn kicked a chair back from the table and sat, not waiting for an invitation. "This is Moonshine, Mr. O'Connor," she said, putting one foot up on the table and hooking a thumb under a suspender. "I've got a shipment coming into Philadelphia on Thursday, and I'm bringing it here, to Pogo & Bud's. Because I like the music. But Mr. McGarritty was insistent that I speak with you, first."

O'Connor turned to the man on his left, a creature trollish of features and build, with fists clearly larger than his brain. "Remind me to have a little chat with Bud."

"Yes, sir." The troll chuckled.

Evelyn nodded. "Yes, I think it's only right that you thank him personally."

"Yeah. Y'know what I'm thinking, Miss...?" O'Connor paused expectantly.

"Evelyn."

"What I'm thinking, Miss Evelyn, is..."

"Just Evelyn. I don't give out my full name to anyone."

"Just Evelyn, then. Fine." O'Connor glanced at his fingernails. "Don't let this place fool you. We're a quality operation, and we take great pains — more pain than you can imagine, little girl — to procure the finest refreshments from the most reputable manufacturers. You are very far from Alabama, or wherever the fuck you crawled out of, so maybe you don't realize it, but there is no market for backwoods corn squeezins' in this city."

O'Connor smiled coldly and reached for his Manhattan.

As good a time as any: Evelyn shifted in her seat, tapping her heel against the edge of the table. A small gesture, but it shoved the heavy, oak table several inches toward O'Conner. His drink slid past his hand and over the edge, into his lap.

O'Connor uttered a pleasing gasp, as both of his men reached for their guns.

Evelyn placed her hands on the table and leaned forward. "Moonshine is not 'corn squeezins',' and it is infinitely better than what you're wearing."

⚜

Bud McGarritty was not a vulgar man, and unused to cussing, which meant that the words swirling through his head were mispronounced and misused, almost certainly, and probably all out of order, to boot. How the girl had gotten into the bar without his notice — or the notice of O'Connor's boys at the door — was beyond him, and putting her in front of O'Conner without a proper introduction was bad enough. But she seemed bound and determined to antagonize the man.

That would get her a bullet in the brain, if she was lucky, and a lot worse, for a lot longer, if she wasn't.

He scrambled for clean glasses, and pulled the half-empty bottle that Evelyn had left with him that first night from the safe under the bar. God, he *never* messed up the combination, and here he was starting over a third time!

Okay, bottle in hand, he stacked the glasses, and... cracked one in the process. He did *not* have time for this.

"I think you'll want to take your 'Moonshine,' *Miss* Evelyn," O'Conner was saying, "and shove it up your ass." He spoke coldly, then smiled easily and leaned back in his chair, which, in McGarritty's experience, was prelude to things going south very quickly.

He grabbed for more glasses, more than there were people at the table, so there was room for further breakage, and, scooping the mass of them up in his arms, hurried around the bar as fast as he dared.

O'Connor was making a production about how amused and self-controlled he was, which meant that everything was dangerously close to being completely out of control. "You'll pardon my French, of course," he said. He straightened his shirt and tie, checked his collar. "And please, if you have any problems making it fit, let me know. I'll have one of the boys help you out."

Evelyn laughed. *Laughed!* "These boys?"

"Gentlemen!" The glassware clattered onto the table from McGarritty's shaking hands. He caught the glasses before they rolled off the edge and set them straight. "And lady. This ain't the way to start out a business relationship." He fussed nervously, mopping the table with a towel, then hesitating as he contemplated the wet spot on O'Connor's pants. He uncapped the bottle. "Let's just calm down and share a drink. And, uh, calm down." He poured three trembling shots of soft, white light, knocked one back without waiting. Tension uncoiled visibly as he exhaled and he refilled his glass. He held it up and looked at Evelyn and O'Connor expectantly. "To future friends?"

"That seems unlikely."

"Please, sir, just try it."

O'Connor looked at the glass suspiciously. "Her first."

"To future friends," she said, draining her glass.

O'Connor scowled, sipped tentatively. He licked his lips. "It's..."

"A hundred dollars a case," Evelyn said. "That's what I want. Anything else is purely between the two of you."

"A hundred dollars for a drink nobody's ever heard of?" O'Connor made a small gesture and one of his associates refilled his glass. "Eighty would be generous."

"I'm not asking you to be generous. A hundred will do."

After a long moment, O'Connor took another sip, scowled, and nodded, and McGarritty could breathe again.

⚶

Mid-September, but it felt like August. There was no relief from the heat. The ceiling fans merely blew the thick, humid air around the oven that was Pogo & Bud's, mixing the smoke into a dense, uniform haze that stuck shirts to skin, beaded up and ran in thin, greasy rivulets down faces and throats. Even the most fastidious of the negro gentlemen had shed jackets and loosened ties. Tom had lost the tie entirely, and unbuttoned both his collar and his cuffs, something that would have been unthinkable only a month ago.

Tom sipped his Moonshine and listened to the band. They weren't very good: an insipid swing reminiscent of gumdrops. Mary leaned her head against his arm, her hair clinging damply to her face. It was hot, oppressive, and only guilt kept him from telling her not to touch him.

"Do you want to dance?" she asked, looking up at him with disinterested eyes. She was shivering, despite the heat.

Tom looked out at the dance floor, where bodies moved in time to the music with frantic exhaustion. There was something almost desperate there—souls seeking something elusive, something they had once held, but somehow lost. It had been said that Heaven's greatest pleasure was to see clearly into Hell and watch the torment of one's former oppressors. But perhaps the reverse held more truth: that Hell's greatest torment was to see clearly into Heaven and think, next time you'll make it. Next time you'll get there for sure.

"No," he said.

Mary laid her head back against his shoulder. There may have been relief in her eyes.

On the dance floor, two men bumped and scuffled. Punches were thrown and a knife was pulled. There was blood, but not much, before bouncers pulled the men apart. It was the heat. A week-long heat wave was bound to make tempers flare, and all the extra ice McGarritty put in the drinks wasn't going to change that. Tom reached for his cigarettes. The whole town was a tinderbox. There'd been daily murders for the past month. People were on edge, angry, rude. It *had* to be the heat.

But it felt like something more. It felt like the whole world was slowly going mad.

The pack was empty, and Tom cursed. He waved at the Lucky Strikes girl, who took damnably long to get to him.

"Hold your horses," she said, blue eyes and lipstick only accentuating the sneer behind her smile. "You think you're my only customer here? So, whaddaya want?"

Tom threw a penny on the tray. He wasn't giving this creature more than necessary, and what he needed was one cigarette. He couldn't remember when Mary had gotten fired. Last week? The week before? "I'll light it myself," he said, though the girl hadn't offered.

"Take me upstairs." Mary ran trembling fingers across his arm.

Tom closed his eyes and pulled hard on the cigarette, letting the smoke out through his nostrils.

"C'mon, baby," she said. "It's been days."

What might have been years or minutes later, Tom woke to the smell of vomit, and wondered whether any of it was his. All he could taste was ash. Mary lay next to him, her long, matted hair wrapped around his left arm. He untangled himself carefully. The breath caught in his throat as he brushed against her cold skin, and the memories flooded back: Mary pushing the needle into his vein—his first time, though apparently not hers—the pleasure flooding his body as she'd loosened the belt around his arm. He'd watched with detachment as she refilled the syringe for herself, watched her fall back against the cushions with a sigh before losing himself in dream.

She was breathing, shallow but steady, and fear eased its grip on his throat. But she didn't wake up when he shook her. He decided to wash up a bit and collect his wits. With the windows closed up and covered as they were, time was meaningless here, but apart from a few unconscious junkies, the room was empty. It had to be sometime in the morning.

Tom stumbled his way downstairs and stopped short at the entrance to the men's lavatory. The door had been ripped off its hinges. Inside, porcelain shards lay in a pool of bloody water. Sinks had been ripped off the walls, urinals shattered. A half-dozen bullets had splintered the wooden toilet stall, and blood seeped under the door.

He'd slept through this?

He rubbed his eyes and considered his bladder, and then pushed open the door to the ladies' lavatory, and he tried not to think of the sounds he'd heard coming from behind the splintered stall in the men's lavatory. The sounds of something feeding.

⚜

Pogo was the first one in. He burst through the door and ran around the room, checking behind the bar and sniffing under the tables, stopping briefly to scratch behind his ear. Then with a grunt, he set off in the direction of the men's lavatory. He stood in the doorway with the stub of his tail lowered, ears back, growling his confusion.

"Pogo, boy! Never mind that." Bud McGarritty followed slowly, slapping his thigh with his good hand to quiet the old Rottweiler. Pogo whined once, still bristling. His eyes darted from McGarritty's face to the lavatory. Something was upsetting him. Probably the blood.

McGarritty shook his head. "Good grief, Pogo. Look at the state of this place." Cigarette butts and broken glass littered the floor. Empty glasses and overflowing ashtrays covered the bar and tables. "They call this cleaning up?"

Pogo nuzzled his knee. There'd been bodies the night before. McGarritty didn't know what had happened to them, didn't want to know. That's what he'd said, when he'd woken up in the hospital with his arm in a sling and Pogo sitting on his legs, staring at him: "I don't want to know."

With a sigh, McGarritty started collecting glasses and stacking them on the bar, pushing trash onto the floor as he cleared the tables. Pogo nudged the door to the back room open. There was a push broom in the corner. He gripped the handle in his teeth and dragged it out to the bar.

"Good boy, Pogo," McGarritty said, and Pogo wagged his tail, confident, it seemed, that things would all work out.

⚜

"Gentlemen," said Brogan O'Connor with a smile. "I'm glad you could make time to visit the City of Brotherly Love." He looked around at the assembled East Coast mob bosses and their entourages. "Apologies for the mess. There was a small incident here last night. But our business here is important enough to put up with a little discomfort. Seems we're missing only one person, our perpetually tardy guest of honor."

"Oh, I'm here," Evelyn said, tipping her hat with a half-smile. She was leaning against the bar. "I've been here."

Pogo jumped, hackles raised, and started barking. "Hush," McGarritty said, to no avail.

For a city establishment, Pogo & Bud's had a lot going for it—music and madness, drink and dancing, and a lot of old, old wood. It spoke to Evelyn, stories of the people it had seen, the conversations it had overheard, and memories of the past, when this city had been forest. In fact, the only thing she didn't like about Pogo & Bud's was Pogo. She didn't trust him, and he certainly didn't trust her.

Well, she didn't trust Brogan O'Connor, either, but that was all part of the game. She smiled broadly at the assembly and took the empty seat across from O'Connor.

O'Connor tapped his fingers on the table. "Bud," he said, "you look like you're about to fall over. Why don't you go upstairs and take a load off your feet."

"Who's gonna mix your drinks?" McGarritty said. He gestured at one of O'Connor's troll-men. "One of these lunks? No offence, guys, just we all got our specialties, right?"

"We're talking distribution logistics, Bud, nothing that affects your house. Go on, make sure none of the junkies wanders down here and hears things they shouldn't. And take the goddamned pooch with you."

McGarritty sighed, defeated, and Evelyn shot him a grin.

"Don't worry, Mr. McGarritty, if they try anything that would hurt you, I'll set them straight." And she would. This was where her part of this started. It had been her choice, and no one would take that away from her.

And besides, there was very little to worry about. She cared little about how these people distributed Moonshine around the country, only that they do so. So far, they'd done an admirable job throughout the Northeast. The drink had become popular with stockbrokers in New York, and some shipments had found their way to both the White House and Congress.

The meeting today was to carve up the rest of the country between them, and to figure out how to best leverage the demand for Moonshine into national power. She had every confidence that they would work it out between them.

Her sister had said it would take decades, maybe half a century, for their plan to bear fruit, but the people of this place were even more susceptible to Moonshine's influence than they'd anticipated. Maybe in as little as ten years...

"Capone's the real problem," one of the mobsters was saying, his voice raised enough to break her reverie. "He's gonna do everything in his power to get at the source. He won't take to playing second fiddle without a fight, and we all know what a fight with Capone looks like."

"Who is Capone?" Evelyn asked.

"That, gentlemen," O'Connor said into the shocked silence, "is the crux of the problem." He leaned back, hands behind his head. "We're completely dependent on one single person. If something, God forbid, happened to her, where would we be? I think that it's time that that changes." He smiled. "Miss Evelyn, it's time to renegotiate the terms of our agreement. It's time for you to step aside and let the men handle things. We are, of course, extremely grateful for the opportunity you have presented us, and we've got an extremely generous offer for you."

Honestly, Evelyn had expected this moment months ago, before the myriad trading relationships that now existed had been established. Back when O'Connor might have thought of establishing his own monopoly. Seemed a bit late for it now. But here it was.

"Oh," she said. "Really?"

"We're about to go to war with Chicago over something that could up and walk out on us one day. That just ain't good business sense. All you've got to do is put us in contact with your supplier. We'll pay you enough to make sure you never have to work again."

Evelyn smiled. "No, I don't think so."

O'Connor shot a look at one of his men, a large Swede. "I'm going to ask you once more to reconsider, before we're forced to resort to alternative methods. Trust me. A suitcase full of hard cash is by far the more attractive option. Though Anderson here might disagree." The Swede grinned stupidly through broken teeth.

She shook her head sadly, though the smile never faded. O'Connor sighed, and then gestured with his chin.

Anderson grabbed her by the hair, pulling her roughly to her feet. He ripped her white button-down shirt open with the other hand, then threw her on the table.

"Not here, idiot!" O'Connor's eyes flashed. "Take her, I dunno, in there." He pointed at the ladies' lavatory. "Bring her back when she's ready to talk."

⚔

Tom Marich backed into one of the stalls in the Ladies' Lavatory as he heard the mobster dragging a woman into room. He eased the door closed as quietly as he could and locked it. Almost too late, he realized that his feet were visible, and perched on the toilet seat.

From his vantage, he could see the man O'Connor had called Anderson drag a slight slip of a woman, hardly more than a girl, into the room. He felt stupidly helpless. With the kind of muscle in the other room, anything he did to interfere would surely have only one outcome. Even after the fact, being able to only see a narrow vertical strip of either of them, it was unlikely he'd be able to identify either of them in a lineup.

The girl was fighter, though. She bit Anderson's wrist as he pushed her against the wall, but his slap took her to her knees.

"Is that all you've got?" she asked, as she got back up. With a sudden movement, she raked out with her hand, fingernails gouging deeply into cheek and lip and chin. A spray of blood spattered the floor in a line toward Tom's stall. The girl grinned.

"Bitch." The punch bounced her head off the wall and she collapsed, bleeding from her mouth and nose. Anderson laughed, an innocent, boyish noise that made Tom's blood run cold. He heard the sound of fabric tearing.

Anderson knelt between the girl's legs and readied himself. In a quick, fluid motion, she pulled herself up and kissed him. Tom could see Anderson pull back at first, and then respond in kind. His body relaxed, and the girl brought her lips to Anderson's ear.

"Blood to blood I bind thee," she said softly, and in that moment, Tom recognized her voice, "and seal it with a kiss." Evelyn pushed the Swede away. "I think we're done here."

Evelyn made her way unsteadily to her seat at the table, belt and suspenders holding her torn slacks in place, her shirt left tattered and open. Anderson took his position behind O'Connor.

"I guess that makes this a tittie bar," someone said. People laughed. Evelyn kept her feelings off her face.

O'Connor glared at them with displeasure. He took a deep breath. "Apologies, Evelyn, for these unpleasantries. Are you ready to give us what we asked for?"

"I've already told Anderson my answer. Perhaps he'd be so good as to deliver it?"

Anderson's gun roared and O'Connor's face dissolved, his blood splattering across the table and over Evelyn's face and chest. Brogan O'Connor slumped face-down on the table with a rustle of silk and a soft thump. There were more shots then, from a half-dozen guns—almost inconsequential, they seemed nearly silent after the first shot had torn the air. Anderson danced erratically before he dropped.

Evelyn ran a finger between her breasts, licked the blood off it and smiled, ignoring the guns aimed at her head, ignoring the grim faces. "Not bad," she said with approval, then: "I'm willing to honor the existing agreements at the existing terms. I will continue to leave the details of distribution to you and to you exclusively, for as long as your organizations continue to operate smoothly and efficiently. Unless there is someone else who would like to renegotiate? No? I thought not. Negotiations are such messy things." She wiped some more of O'Connor's blood from over her eye and suckled her finger once more.

"Actually," she said, "he's not bad at all."

✤

Pogo & Bud's grew quiet at last. Tom gave it a few minutes to be sure, and then took a tentative step off the toilet seat. His legs were cramped and he nearly fell. He resisted the urge for a cigarette. Get out while he could, that was the important thing. There would be plenty of time for cigarettes later. Once out of the stall, he tried to ease the cramping, alternately stretching and massaging his calves. He'd need to move quickly and quietly if he wanted to get out of this alive.

The door opened abruptly and Tom found himself staring straight at Evelyn. The girl who had introduced him to Moonshine. The same girl that the man named Anderson had almost... It seemed impossible that he hadn't recognized her, both her face and her voice, even from his limited view. And yet he hadn't.

But as much as he hadn't been able to see her as her, Evelyn's behavior was even more bizarre. She looked around the room, seeming not to notice him at all, then stripped off the remains of her shirt. Every time her eyes slid across him, something on his chest burned. It was the pendant he wore, an old iron amulet his grandmother had given him. That, he suddenly realized, was what she'd touched the first day he'd seen her, when she abruptly pushed him away. Maybe she hadn't simply been rudely pretending she hadn't seen him these past months. Maybe she really hadn't. After all, that first day, he'd been practically next to her without her noticing, until he addressed her directly.

She washed her face and body briskly over the sink, and Tom watched, heart pounding in his throat. Evelyn was a monster, he reminded himself, who had cold-heartedly gotten two people killed. But that didn't dull the longing that burned suddenly in him, longing that he'd barely remembered from the first time he'd met her. She dried herself with a towel and then looked closely at her face in the mirror.

Tom gasped, and she spun, looking around wildly. Again, her gaze seemed to slide right off him. Again, the pendant burned against his skin. He held his breath. He must have been wrong. Her face was bruised, her lip split, her nose crooked and probably broken, but she was still heart-stoppingly beautiful, in her harsh, boyish way.

Her reflection, on the other hand? The green, wrinkled thing in the mirror that mimicked her as she gingerly prodded her lip and nose bore only the faintest resemblance to Evelyn. It licked its lips as she did, wincing at the pain. "They died too quickly," she muttered.

Evelyn turned on the tap and threw a few handfuls of water on the mirror in front of her, spreading it over the glass with her hands. As the water ran in thin rivulets, the image behind it changed. The woman reflected shared some of Evelyn's features, the same thin, sardonic lips, the slightly angled eyes, but she had long, raven-black hair that matched the silk evening gown hugging her slight curves. Red-gloved fingers brought a long-stemmed cigarette holder to her lips.

"Little sister," said the woman in the mirror, each word a delicate puff of smoke, "you look a frightful mess."

"We all make our sacrifices, yes?" Evelyn touched her lip. "How are things in Germany?"

A slow smile. "The Germans love their *Bier*, but they seem to have found something they like even better. *Geistwasser* is now served in every bar in the country, and also in Austria. We have been exporting to Italy, but I think we need a new strategy. The Italians' capacity for self-absorption is defeating our best efforts."

Evelyn snorted. "Call it *Mente del Luna* and put it in a weird looking bottle."

"That might work. How go things in America? It looks like you've had some difficulties."

"No, no difficulties. Today we simply explained the hierarchy. It's all understood now. Tonight's the full moon harvest, and by next week we'll have national distribution. The way this is going, you know, things may happen much faster than we expected. These animals take very little prodding to start tearing each other apart."

"The Queen has no suspicions?"

"The Queen is an idiot who can't see past her own teats. Everything is fine."

"Still, the quicker this world falls apart, the better. Until we are established here, she remains a danger."

Evelyn nodded. "You shall make an excellent Queen, big sister."

"As shall you, little sister. I must run. I'm meeting with an Austrian artist with delusions of grandeur in a few minutes."

Evelyn left the tattered remains of her shirt on the floor and slipped back into the main room of Pogo & Bud's. Tom followed her quietly, then stopped dead in his tracks. The mob bosses had gone, but their minions remained. Two were frozen, bent over in the act of rolling a body into a carpet. Bud McGarritty had been scrubbing blood off the table with a wet rag while Pogo sniffed a second carpet that lay rolled against the wall. Another mobster had frozen while drinking a beer. The bottle had emptied, its contents running down his face and suit jacket. Tom looked at his watch, and then at the clock on the wall. The second hands on both ticked normally. The fans still turned. A fly settled on the sticky table. Another buzzed around it. Only the people, including Pogo, were frozen.

Evelyn poured herself a tall glass of Moonshine, tipped it back and downed it in three long swallows. "Lightweights," she said, and headed for the door.

Tom glanced toward the back of the room. Mary was still upstairs, but there was nothing he could do for her. He scurried after Evelyn. He didn't want to be anywhere close when those guys came unstuck.

⚜

Chico Borenko peered suspiciously through the narrow gap, then grinned widely as he slipped the chain and threw the door open.

"Tomislav!" He grabbed Tom and kissed him three times on the cheeks, left, right, left again, clapped him solidly on the shoulder, then grabbed him by the ear and dragged him inside. "Betty," he yelled, "your worthless, long-lost nephew is here! Put on some coffee!" He turned to Tom. "Come in, sit, please. You want coffee, yes?"

Tom couldn't help but smile. His uncle lived a grandiosely jolly life, evident in the dense belly that stretched his food-stained undershirt to its limits. His generosity never failed to leave his guests heavier in body but lighter in spirit. Tetka Betty was almost his opposite. She was soft and sensual, so small she seemed almost frail next to her husband, and in contrast to her dark skin, his ruddy features practically glowed with chubby pink cheerfulness.

"Hi, honey," she said, bringing a plate of cakes into the room. "Coffee's brewing." She kissed him on both cheeks in Balkan fashion.

"Thanks, Betty," he said. "Actually, I'm here to see Baba. I've run into some trouble, and I thought maybe she could help."

Betty looked at him with soft eyes. "I see. On the other hand, you could marry the girl. You're twenty-six now. Maybe this is God's way of telling you it's time to settle down and start a family."

Tom blinked. It took him a few seconds to understand what she meant. "Oh. No, not that kind of trouble. It's really a lot more complicated, and I don't know where else to turn."

Betty's eyebrows rose, but she didn't ask. "Ana's in the back. She likes the tree."

The back yard was a small plot the width of the house, surrounded on three sides with cinderblock walls. Raised beds dense with herbs lined the walls. Another raised bed in the center of the yard offered lettuce and cabbage and peppers and tomatoes. A dogwood tree raised its branches in one corner, and Tom's grandmother sat in her rocker, knitting in the tree's shade. She squinted at him with milky eyes.

"Baba Ana? It's me, Tomislav."

She smiled. "Ah, *mali Tomice. Sedi, sedi,*" she said, patting the chair next to her rocker. "Tell me what is wrong. Betty, *Tursku kafu, molim.*"

"You'll think I'm crazy."

"Whole world is crazy. I see when I go to market. So tell me."

"I came to you because of the locket. The one you gave me." His hand went to his chest. "I think it protected me. I felt it burn."

Ana nodded gravely. "Vodonoj kind of crazy. Yes. So, tell." She listened without judgment as he told her about Moonshine, about Evelyn and what he'd seen in the mirror. The tale was garbled and incoherent: the details were slippery in Tom's mind, but Baba Ana just sipped her Turkish coffee, speaking only to prod him now and again when he fell into confused and sheepish silence.

She rocked slowly, eyes closed, for some time after Tom finally rambled to a halt. He wondered if she was asleep.

"Your uncle, he is a good man," she said, at last. "He is a good son, and a good husband. There is never any trouble with him and Betty." She gazed at Tom. "Then one day he goes out, and when he comes home in the morning he stinks *ko javna kucha*, like a whorehouse, and he hits poor Betty so hard when she says something, I think he maybe breaks her neck. It is this Moonshine he was drinking. He does not drink anymore, only coffee. Take off your shirt."

"What?"

"I show you something. Please." Tom stripped off his shirt. Ana held the old iron pendant in withered fingers. "This protects. While you wear, they will turn away from you, not noticing. It guards against their charms, and fights their poisons. I make for you when you were born."

"That explains a lot."

Ana dropped the pendant and poked a crooked finger at an old scar on the left side of his chest. "This is other part. When you were baby, I cut," she paused, held her index finger and thumb apart just a hair, "very, very small part of your heart, and hide it." She laughed. "Your mother, she almost kill me, she is so angry."

"That's... Can you blame her?"

"When your heart is in two places, the *vodonoj* cannot find you. You slip from their heads just like they slip from yours. When you first met this Evelyn, she does not see you until you introduce yourself, yes? This is because of the pendant. And when she goes, she forgets you before she leaves the room. This is because of your heart."

"Oh." Tom rubbed his temples. "So, what do I do?"

Ana frowned. "The *vodonoj*, usually it is enough to protect yourself and they go find somewhere else to play. This Evelyn of yours, maybe protect just yourself, this is not enough."

"I know, I know. They want to start a war. I think they mean to break us and take over."

Ana pressed her lips together. "A man who fights the *vodonoj*, maybe he loses." She placed a wrinkled hand on his face. "Even if he wins."

"Yes. I understand."

"With your head you understand. Not yet with your heart." She shook her head. "With all things, there is balance. Where there is power, there is weakness. Everything they can do to us..." She hesitated, held both hands up equally with fingertips pressed together. "*Kako ze kazhe?* Where is here, can also happen here same way?"

"Reciprocal?"

Ana shrugged. "If the *vodonoj* can bind, then also they can be bound. With the right knowledge." She smiled. "Tonight is bingo. I talk to my friends. You come back tomorrow and we talk again."

✛

Tom stalked Pogo & Bud's from open to close for three days before he saw Evelyn again. His lungs felt like an ashtray and his kidneys ached.

Evelyn slipped past the doorman, making her way through the crowd without notice. She approached the bar and waved at McGarritty. He pulled out a pint glass and poured her a glowing drink. His smile was easy, but the muscles in his neck twitched.

Tom checked his pockets. The pouch his grandmother had given him felt cool under his fingers. He rehearsed everything in his mind.

Handing Mary some cash, he murmured, "Why don't you go upstairs? Wait for me, I'll be right up."

Mary looked at the cash. "Okay."

He pulled the iron pendant over his head and set it around her neck. "Hold on to this for me, okay?" He watched as Mary made her way to the back of the room. Once she was out of sight he pulled a stool up next to Evelyn. "Now that's how to drink," he said with a nod to Evelyn's glass. "Bud, can ya set me up with one like that?"

"I'm not sure that's a good idea, Tom." McGarritty gave him a warning look.

Evelyn laughed. "Oh, go on. Give the man a proper drink, on me." McGarritty shook his head as he poured the pint. Evelyn clinked her glass against Tom's. "So tell me, how is it Bud knows your name, but I've never met you?"

"Incredibly bad luck on my part, apparently." Bolstered by Moonshine, he reached out and touched her face, running a finger along her healing lip. "Tell me who did this, and I'll make sure he never touches you again." He was surprised to realize that he meant it.

"Don't worry, he won't." She held out her hand. "I'm Evelyn, and I believe I'm pleased to make your acquaintance."

"I'm..."

"Tom. Yes, I know."

Tom kissed her hand, then, heart racing, leaned forward and whispered in her ear. He tried to make it sound unrehearsed.

"That's a very interesting proposal," she said. "If you can finish that drink without falling over, I'll take you up on it."

⚕

They'd kissed in the taxi, long and sweet, and it was not difficult to forget the image of the hideous green creature in the mirror. It would have been harder to keep hold of it—it slipped around the edges of consciousness at the best of times. He felt dizzy as he led her up the stairs to his bedroom, and as he walked her into the circle cast by his Baba and her friends from bingo, he felt a twinge of guilt. But even that was hard to maintain. Her fingers were like fire as they tugged at his belt, as they sought the skin beneath his shirt.

He didn't want to do this. He ached to give himself to her, body and soul. With one hand, he dug in his pocket and pulled out the small pouch of salts and spices and whatever else Baba had put in there, tugged at the strings until it loosened. His other hand gripped her hair as he kissed her throat.

The first time he bit down on his tongue it wasn't hard enough. He bit harder and the sharp, metallic taste of his own blood filled his mouth. Then he pressed his mouth against hers and bit hard on her split lip. She gasped and tried to pull away as their blood mingled in each other's mouths.

"*Sa krvi ti si moj,*" he said. "With blood you are mine."

She looked at him with shock. "You can't." His heart ached with the betrayal.

His fingers shook as he poured the contents of the pouch into her mouth. She stiffened, fingers tensing with rigor. Her breathing slowed. "I'm sorry," he said, wondering if she could hear him. He kissed her rigid lips, and then turned away from her accusing eyes.

Baba Ana brought her friends, Ethel Berkowicz and Gwen Bythell, and Ethel's grandson Elijah. Evelyn's skin was rough and papery under Tom's hands, pale white like birch bark, as he lay her tenderly in the trunk of Elijah's Packard, taking care not to break any of the new growth. He kissed her one last time, then watched Elijah and the old women drive away.

The next day, a truck drove up to Tom's house and delivered three cords of green firewood and kindling. The men stacked it in the small back yard to dry. "You might want to put a tarp up over it," one of them said, "so it doesn't get wet in the rain."

Tom stared at the stacks of firewood for a long time after the men left, chain-smoking and chewing on his lip. It was impossible that he felt this way. He barely knew her, but she seemed more real to him than Mary did. After some time, he locked the back door and pushed the icebox in front of it.

⚜

The snow lay thin on the tombstones, but the sharp, grey air promised more. Tom laid his hand on the pine box and remembered holding her, but it was an empty memory, devoid of joy or grief or even love. Two days before Christmas he was putting his fiancée in the ground, and not even her parents had come to the funeral.

Bud McGarritty put a hand on Tom's shoulder. "Mary was a hell of a gal," he said. "I'm sorry."

"Yeah." Mary had died alone with a needle in her arm, the end of the path Tom had set for her. He still felt nothing, not even guilt. Just emptiness. Everything had gone to hell, even with the flow of Moonshine cut off. Maybe it was too late. Or maybe it would have been worse. It didn't matter. October of 1929 had brought the Crash and the world was spiraling toward disaster. This was just one more thing.

"I've been thinking about shutting down," McGarritty said. "Even before this. But where's a guy like me gonna get a job now that everyone's getting laid off? I got kids, you know."

"I know."

Tom walked home from the cemetery, stepping over the bums wrapped in newspaper for warmth. Some of these men had been successful, just a few months back. He ignored their pleas for money. There was nothing left to give.

Baba Ana had cooked for him and left the house warm, a modest fire burning in the hearth. Tom left the food untouched, reaching instead for his last bottle of Moonshine. It was a night for drinking, and he took a swig from the bottle.

Tom watched the dying flames for a while, until the chill began to creep in. Then, with a sigh, he threw another log of Evelyn on the fire, and listened to her hiss.

In All Their Glory

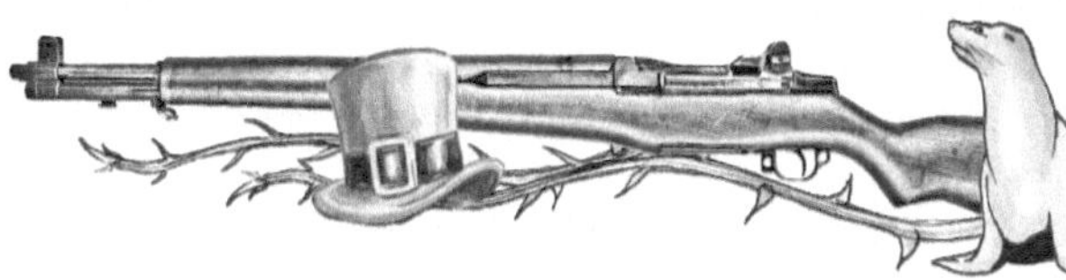

A Not-So-Silent Night

L. Jagi Lamplighter

Tis a true story I be telling ye, and if any should doubt a word of it, I'll pop him in the kisser!

Rat-tat-tat-tat. The guns rang out in the night.

"Stop that, ye wee wench. Ye be scaring the geese now!" I barked, popping me head out of the engine space and into the cockpit.

"Aye and let 'em be scared." Shauna pulled the plane up into a tight Immelman followed immediately by a second one. No easy feat on a cloudy night. Each time she executed the loop and roll with such perfect precision that I wondered if I had overestimated how much rum toddy she had poured down her gullet at the Officers' Christmas Eve party. Even half-bollixed, she was an ace behind the stick of a plane, me girl was.

"The sergeant will give ye quite the tongue-drubbing if he catches ye wasting ammunition." Leaning me pike against the side of the cockpit, I hopped up onto the dashboard and straightened me green hat with its shiny silver buckle. Then, I wagged me finger at her. "Ye know how hard it is to come by right now, what with the Germans bombing England day and night."

"Why don't they let women do this?" She fired off another volley. "Why are women only allowed to ferry planes?"

I thought about that, running a hand over me long red beard, which was neatly tucked into me belt. 'Twas a good thing, too, having a beard to warm the face, for the cockpit was icy cold. Shauna wore leather driving gloves and a ridiculous fluffy hat. Her breath formed cloudy puffs when she spoke.

"Has to do with the nature of men," I said. "What has a man to fight for, if his women and children are not safe at home?"

"*Hmmph*," she replied merrily.

I sat down cross-legged on the dashboard. It was narrow up here, but I was not entirely constrained by mundane space. "Besides, ye can't shoot worth a brass farthing."

"Aye, that's true enough." Shauna grinned. She was a big-boned girl with curly ginger hair, the spitting image of her great-great grand-mother. ('Twas due to her age, rather than her stature, that I addressed her as "wee".)

"Couldn't hit the broad side of the royal barn on a sunny day," I in-toned. "And that's one big barn!"

"Forget the broad side of a barn." Shauna snorted with amusement. "I'd be lucky if I could hit the Atlantic Ocean if I was positioned right dead above it."

"'Tis true." I nodded sagely. "Now, yer brother Paddy, rest his soul, he could shoot, that one could! Sixteen confirmed kills before he went down."

I did not add that five of those planes had been shot down by yers truly. Paddy did not always have time to both fly and shoot, and, well, me people took naturally to weapons. But I would nary speak a word of this to anyone. It would not do for the likes of me to be taking away from an O'Shaughnessy's legend.

She giggled. "But I could fly a Spitfire or a Piper Cub through a needle hole in the dark. Blindfolded if I had to!"

As if to prove it, she performed another Immelmann. I clung to the dash for dear life.

"Whoa, now! 'Tis hardly proper behavior on Christmas Eve," I chided, still grasping the edge of the dashboard with both me hands. "Ye should be home wrapping presents and hanging up stockings. Not flying this big lug of metal God knows where in the middle of the night. If ye had left at noon, we could have been home by now."

"If I had left at noon, I'd have missed the party," Shauna hiccupped. "Besides, my presents are wrapped, and I hung my stocking before I left, right between Mrs. Partridge's and Anna's."

"Still, it ain't right."

"If you don't like it, you don't have to come along."

'Twas more than any self-respecting guardian could be expected to endure. I jumped into a boxer's stance and put up me dooks.

"Hold it right there, ye wee lass! Ye're not getting rid of me. Ye'll have to fight me first."

"Whoa! Tom, whoa!" Shauna said laughing. "I'm not fighting you."

"Ye'll fight me before ye send me packing!"

"But you're a third of my height and can fade through walls."

"Up, I say!"

"It would hardly be a fair match!"

"Put 'em up!"

"Tom! I am flying the plane!"

"*Ock*, so ye are, but ye'll not be getting rid of me so easily!" I threw a punch or two at the air. "Have not I, Tom-O'-Thunder, been the guardian of the O'Shaughnessy family for longer than the traitorous Britains have been occupying Ireland? Was I not there to help during the potato famine? Did I utter even a peep of complaint when the family moved to America — across a giant ocean?"

"No, Tom. Not a peep, or so Grandpappy assures me," she said.

"Am I not here with ye now, in England, helping protect ye from gremlins — those no good Krauts! — while ye shuttle planes back and forth for the British Air Transport Auxiliary? Though why ye want to defend this tyrannical country that has oppressed the Irish for generations is a mystery to me."

Shauna snorted again. She said, "Think Ireland can defeat the Germans by herself once England falls, do you?"

When the wee girl was right, she was right.

⚜

Shauna flew on, singing Christmas carols at the top of her lungs, but her false cheer did not fool old Tom. Funny how 'tis the small things that trouble a soul. It was not the war that drove Shauna to drink too much this night, nor the constant blitzes, nor even the death of her beloved brother Patrick, God rest him. No, it was the future unhappiness of a little girl named Anna.

Anna was not even a member of the O'Shaughnessy family, just the daughter of the household where Shauna was bivouacking. She was a wee little thing, frail as a will-o-wisp. No one thought she would live to see Christmas next year. She was like the neighborhood's own Tiny Tim.

Many were surprised Anna had held on this long, but not Shauna. She knew what kept the girl going. 'Twas the wee child's dream — her longing to own a dollhouse made out of gingerbread, a gift she hoped to receive on Christmas day.

This Anna, she loved the story of the gingerbread man. One day, over six months earlier, someone had made the foolish mistake of promising to make her a house to go with her Christmas cookies. It was to be a gingerbread house built like one for dolls, with an open back and room to play. Perhaps, there was to be a bit of gingerbread furniture as well.

Since then, the child had spent hours, curled up in her bed, drawing plans for the little dwelling, or, when she was not well enough to draw, dreaming about where the walls would go and what the frosting roof might taste like.

It gave the wee thing something to look forward to.

'Twas not even Shauna who had made the promise, but me girl loved Anna. Tomorrow was Christmas morn, and it held nothing but disappointment for the sickly child. Shauna could not bear to be there when the time came.

See, gingerbread and frosting take sugar. And there was no sugar to be had during this terrible war, not for love or money.

Shauna knew this. She had tried her darndest at both. But neither wheedling nor bribery had produced a single grain of the sweet stuff.

❧

I took up me patrol again, me pike resting on me shoulder as I marched back and forth. All seemed quiet tonight, but one could never be too careful. Gremlins were tricky buggers. Not a single one would mess with me charge's plane, not while Old Tom was on duty. Since Shauna had taken up flying for the ATA, three had the audacity to try and board. None of them would trouble the allied pilots again.

"Oh, ho...what's that?" Shauna's voice reached me ear. I popped back into the cockpit to find her rubbing her eyes. "Tom? Are you near? Is there something out there, or am I seeing things?"

Pike in hand, I clambered onto the dashboard and peered into the night. Sure enough, through the smog, there was a flicker, like candlelight.

Weird, way up here in the airy night.

"Could it be another plane signaling?" I asked.

"Maybe," she said, frowning, "Though not a type of signal light I've seen before." A note of terror entered her voice. "But there's one I've seen. Jiminy Christmas, Tom! That's a Focke-Wulf!"

Sure as the sight o' green on St. Patrick's, the colleen was right. The clouds had parted to our left and moonlight shone on three aircraft, two bombers and a fighter. Enemy aircraft. Here, over England.

Me heart did an Immelmann of joy.

I extended me arm and me pike flew into me hand. Grinning me most ferocious grin, I shook it at the enemy. "Let 'em have it, laddie! Blow the enemy away!"

Only then did I remember that it was not Paddy flying the plane. Me heart drooped to me belt. There was no way me girl could shoot down the enemy before they did her in. Unless we could slip away unnoticed, we were a goner.

"Get out of here, ye wee wench! Don't let them see ye!"

"Right! I'll—"

There came a loud *rat-ta-tat.*

"They're firing on something!" Her voice rose shrilly. "On that strange flickering light."

"Great! Get away before they notice ye are here."

"Will do. Any idea how?"

"There's a thick cloudbank to the right."

"Roger."

More clouds parted, and we saw the enemy's target. In me time, I have seen a great deal of strange things. But I had never seen anything like this, not in all me days.

Through the break between the clouds ran nine tiny reindeer. Behind them, they drew an old-fashioned sleigh. In it sat a huge jolly fellow dressed in red and a great big sack. The front deer had a glowing nose from which issued the flickering light at which the German planes were firing.

"Merciful Mother of God!" Shauna slapped a hand over her heart. "It's Saint Nick!"

Rat-a-tat-tat. The enemy strafed the flying sleigh, striking one of the wee creatures. The little beasty arched its back in obvious agony and then fell limp in its traces. Shauna gave a sharp cry and grabbed her radio.

"Mayday! Mayday! Saint Nick is under attack."

Static. Then a calm male voice. "Repeat?"

"Saint Nick! Santa Claus! Father Christmas! He's under attack, I tell you!"

"Shauna, is that you? Did you have too much to drink?"

"The Germans are shooting at him!"

"Germans?"

"Three of them! A Focke-Wulf and two bombers."

"Where are you?"

Shauna told them.

"We're on our way."

❖

Silent as a cat treading on a pillow, Shauna negotiated another Immelmann and shot off in the opposite direction.

"Faith and Begorra, wench!" I threw down my green hat. "What are ye doing?"

"Slipping away. Like you said."

"Ye can't run out on Saint Nick!"

"Watch me."

"Ye ungrateful wench! 'Tis Santy for crying out loud!"

"What else can I do, Tom?" Shauna cried. "I can't fight three German planes."

"Only the fighter's a big threat. The other two are slow as cold butter compared to ye in this plane."

"But I can't shoot straight!"

Me ferocious grin claimed me face again. "Well, I can, lassie! There isn't a weapon this side of the grave that I can't wield with elegant precision!"

"You?" The plane swerved wildly as Shauna swung around to gape at me. "You can fire a gun?"

"With the best of 'em!" I drew me shoulders up proudly. "Yer brother declared me one of the best shots he had the pleasure to know."

"Really?" she blinked. "Truly?"

"True as toast. I swear it."

"You shoot." Shauna said, flipping the plane around yet again. "I'll fly!"

❖

No pleasure in this whole, great, wide world is as glorious as that of hunting down German aircraft (save maybe firing upon British planes, but then I have not had the pleasure.) And this evening was no exception. Rather the particulars of our situation made it all the sweeter.

Shauna shot upward and dove down over the top of the fighter, while I manned the guns. 'Twas easier this way. Even the best pilots have trouble both flying and manning the guns in these planes. Having a separate pilot and gunner gave us an advantage over the enemy pilots.

I fired at the Focke-Wulf. It took some careful maneuvering on both our parts. We did not want to overshoot and strike Santy or his wee deer.

My first several shots struck the fuselage and bounced off, leaving merely dents. Then the glass of the enemy cockpit shattered, spraying every which way like newly-opened champagne. And another pierced the side near the fuel supply. I saw dark liquid dripping out, illuminated by the silvery moonlight.

The Focke-Wulf tried to swing around and fire back at us. But its pilot was not the ace me sweet Shauna was. He tried a fancy move and stalled out, while Shauna flipped her plane like a flapjack and zoomed back, quick as a slim red fox.

"Go down in flames, ye manky Krauts!" I shouted, firing. I slapped me leather-covered rear. "*Pog mo thoin!*"

"Tom, watch your language! There's a lady present!" Shauna said. Her face glistened with sweat as she swung her whole body into her maneuvers.

"Begging yer pardon. I forgot who was flying. I'd tip me hat, but I'm busy showering the enemy with hot lead death."

"Shower away, Tom. Shower away!"

We swung by again. This time the Focke-Wulf outsmarted us. Instead of coming at us, it had swung around so as to put Santy and his reindeer between us. There was no way to fire at it without risking hurting the ones we were protecting, and if we flew above the sleigh to pursue the Focke-Wulf, we would be flying directly into its line of fire.

Bless me soul, me girl did not hesitate. She flew straight at the enemy's guns she did, her face as hard as shoeing nails. Bullets whizzed by us. One struck the wing to our left. Another dinged off something to the right. The stream of them seemed to come right at us. Shauna screamed, but she stayed her course. Even when the glass shattered around us, she did not so much as swerve.

What a brave girl!

Nor did I let her down. Straight through the broken windshield I shot, striking the pilot straight between the eyes. His plane nose-dived like a kestrel after a sparrow, spiraling away into the darkness. Then it was merely a matter of picking off the slower bombers.

By the time the squad arrived, there was only one bomber left and that one was limping. The RAF boys took it out and then circled, goo-goo-eyed, staring at the flying sleigh and its passengers. Saint Nick waved to Shauna and the boys and gave me a wink. Then he sped away, injured deer and all. Through the broken windshield, I swore I could hear him calling, "Merry Christmas to all, and to all a good night!"

⚜

The events of that night are not recorded anywhere. Even years later, after Shauna had married the wing leader of the squad that came to her aid, and the two of them were grandparents, they would sit by the fire on Christmas Eve and remind each other of this night only in whispers. (By then, I was the leader of a platoon of redcaps, patrolling an aircraft carrier commanded by Shauna's eldest son.)

But that was not the best part. That night, when Shauna finally got home in the wee hours of the morning, her stocking hung down so far, it brushed the bricks of the hearth. Inside there was an entire pound of sugar.

And there was still time to make the dollhouse for Anna—with a little help from yers truly.

AUTHOR NOTE: This story is dedicated to the nameless shopping center Santa who approached a friend at a book signing in Williamsburg and described a story he wished to write that included, among other things, German planes shooting at Santa during WWII.

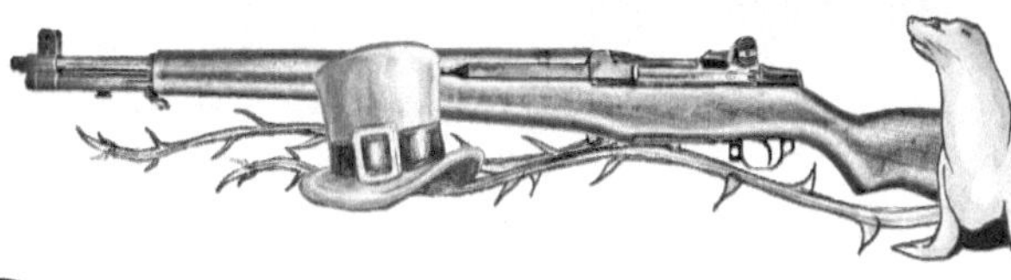

So Many Deaths

John L. French

THIS IS MY WORLD, THE LAND OF ETERNAL YOUTH. IT'S CALLED Tirnanogue in some languages, Faerie in others. I call it home. Once upon a time it was a gentle place, one of green hills and rolling valleys, where the Goddess ruled and all obeyed her quiet commands.

That changed of course, after the Folk fled here from the mortal world. No sooner did we settle than we began changing things, altering what had been an untouched world into something more to our liking. Felling trees and hewing stone, we built homes and castles that quickly grew into villages and kingdoms.

There is no perfect race of beings. For every angel, there is a daemon, for every noble there is a baseborne. We've had peace and war, just rulers and tyrants. And while for now we've entered into a period of peace and order, there are always those who would break our Goddess-given laws.

That's where I come in. My name is Fredag. I'm part of the Guard.

I was working Midwatch in the Artisan District, trying to find out who was selling a certain poison to the youths of the city. It was called White Angel, a powder that when dissolved in wine causes a momentary elation and feeling of divine bliss. Not a bad thing one would think. But over time more and more of the potion is needed to achieve the same effect. Soon the body craves it to the point that one will do anything to acquire it. When its use was limited to the lower quarters the City Wardens didn't care. But now Folk were being beaten and robbed so that the weak could afford to purchase what they needed.

The past night, guards of the Last Watch had brought in two purveyors of the foul mix and thrown them into a garrison cell. So far, they had refused to tell from whom they had obtained the drug. No matter; it was my case. I'd question them my way.

A mailed glove and a rod tipped with cold iron would loosen their tongues. And if that failed they'd be offered a choice between a clean death or one by torture. One way or the other they'd talk.

⚜

There was a new drug on the streets of Baltimore. That was the word at any rate. Faerie Dust, Super Juice, Red Angel, Tinkerbell—those were the names it went by. No one in the department had seen it or had anything solid as to where and by whom it was sold. It was still just a story and a rumor.

The usual dealers were no help.

"That rich-boy shit," said one.

"Ain't none of my peoples can pay two for a hit of that stuff," said another.

"Wish I had some," said a third. "Supposed be a bad-ass high."

The Feds didn't know or care about the drug and nobody was getting killed over it. At two hundred a hit it likely was some designer drug that wasn't illegal ye t. So that was as far as it went. With all the real dope out on the street, nobody worried about something that may not even exist.

⚜

My trip to the cells was interrupted when I was called into the Watch Commander's chamber.

"The scum talk yet?" Captain Rollo was not one for small talk.

"Not yet, sir, but they will."

"That goes without saying, Fredag. How were they found?"

"You know that Guard Conrad has trained a barghest to scent the powder." The captain nodded. "He let it loose in an area where he knew it had been sold."

"And it led him to those two?"

"It led him to three. Before he could pull it off the barghest had done for the third."

"Nasty beasts, those. Still they have their uses. Wonderful trackers. Maybe we should train a few more on White Angel and set them loose."

"That would be one solution, sir."

But it would not be mine, I thought. The dark hounds cared not who got in their way. Still, if the poison continued to spread, the City Wardens were certainly capable of letting them loose, no matter how many innocents might fall.

"That's not why I called you in, Fredag. I need you for something else. Let Stoinef work the White Angel."

Stoinef. Of course. Now that suspects were in hand and the case almost closed, of course they would give it to Stoinef. To him goes the glory and honor of closing the case after the rest of the Guard does all the work. He was the fair-haired princeling. It was common knowledge that he was the off-blanket son of a highborne and a kitchen wench. Despite this, or maybe because of it, he was favored by his father, and by those who sought his father's grace. The bastard would be my commander one day.

I said nothing. As a baseborne, it was not my place to comment on my so-called betters. I did my job and did it well and thus was allowed to keep doing it.

The look on the captain's face told me that the "something else" was one of those cases that required skills other than a well-placed parent. It would be one with no glory at its end but a posting to the Thieves' Quarter if I failed. I didn't like it but I'd taken the Duke's brass so I didn't have a say.

Rollo gave it to me straight. "Three highbornes are missing. At first it was thought that they'd flown out to their family estate. A messenger was sent but came back with the word that they had not been there."

I waited for more but that's all the captain said. Finally I asked, "Is that all we have, three missing young nobles?"

Rollo's answer made it clear where things stood. "It's all *you* have, Fredag. If they're in the city, find them. If they left, find out when and in what direction, then find them."

"And they are?"

"Nilus, Guibert, and Roisin."

The captain had saved the best for last. At his "You're familiar with the names?" I nodded. The whole damned city knew those names.

They were all members of the Clan Ademar, highborne flyers and one of the city's Five Families. Nilus and Guibert were cousins. Privileged youths with too much time and too much gold. They were not unknown to the Guard. Of course, their clan's influence meant that the Guard's sole role in their debauched escapades was to see them safely home and to advise the owner of whatever tavern they had destroyed to send Clan Ademar a bill for the damages, if they dared. Few did.

Roisin was another story. Sister to Nilus, her features were said to rival those of Cedric's famed sculpture of the Goddess. Whether that was true or not I couldn't say. She was kept out of the public eye. It was not for those like me to look on beauty such as hers.

"I need not remind you, Fredag, that the family is not to be bothered in this matter."

"Of course not, sir." Far be it from me to question the only ones who might know where the missing youths had gone. "Clan Odilo?"

"What of them, Fredag?"

As if he had to ask. Clans Odilo and Ademar had been rivals since the Goddess was a girl. And it was only Her Peace that kept them from hunting each other in the streets and slaying whoever got in their way.

"I presume that I am not to bother Clan Odilo either."

The captain's withering glare was all the answer I needed.

Detective Bethany Steele was working dayshift when the body was found. DOA in Patterson Park. Just another Sunday morning. "Stop at Hohn's, bring back donuts," McLarney yelled as she left to look at the dead body.

They'd seen it before; at the bottom of elevator shafts, beneath the JFX and on sidewalks below open windows fourteen floors above. Sudden impact trauma, gravity at work, that sudden stop at the end—whatever one called it, the body about five hundred feet from the Pulaski Monument bore all the marks of a fall from a great height. The only problem was that there was no great height anywhere around.

"Where did he fall from?" Steele asked the assembled uniforms and crime lab techs.

"Small plane?" offered one Southeast officer. "Maybe he jumped and forgot his chute?"

"Catapult?" suggested another. "I know these seniors over at Mount St. Joe who built one as a class project. Ever hear the expression 'When pigs fly?' They did that year. Course the landing was kinda hard on them."

"That was a trebuchet," Dolan from the crime lab added. "And it wasn't used to launch this guy. I got the animal cruelty call last year. Those pigs came in at an angle." She took another look at the body.

"This guy dropped straight down."

Photographs were taken, reports written, evidence collected. They put the death down as one of those things. Steele made a note to check with the Helicopter Unit for sightings of small aircraft over the city.

The ME's examination only deepened the mystery.

"Look at these." Dominic Jones pointed to long parallel gashes on the victim's back.

"Something from the landing?" Steele didn't remember seeing any jagged rocks on the scene. "They don't look like knife wounds."

"They are not," the pathologist replied, "As best as I can determine with the body in the condition it is in, both wounds are of equal length and seem to have been made from the outside in. But that may just be damage from the fall. I can tell you that they match...." Jones displayed a shirt. "...the tears on his upper clothing. And these were found in the jacket lining."

He held up a plastic bag containing several large white feathers.

"Any very big birds seen in the area, Detective?"

Barred from interviewing the victims' family or questioning the chief suspects in their disappearance, I left Rollo's chamber to begin my investigation, wondering what the billeting in the Thieves' Quarters barracks was like.

The first step was to determine if the three might still be in the city. That meant walking the wall. Twelve towers and five gates, all manned over four watches — that's a lot of walking. Using the captain's name, I put the duty on two of the younger guards. While they were about that business, I checked the alehouses, music halls and bordellos in case the cousins had caused any recent damage. They hadn't. Next step were the cells in each District and Quarter, just in case the two had been locked up by someone who didn't know or care who they were. If that was the case, that "someone" would no doubt take their place in lockup with no hope of release this side of the ground.

Without using her name, I also asked about Roisin. It was possible, although just barely, that she had joined her kinfolk in their carousing. It was rumored to be a fashion among the gentler young ladies to frequent those places from which they would be barred by good breeding and common sense. Some were even said to take a turn on the harlot's couch. True or not, there was no sign of the one I sought.

The guards who had walked the wall had no better luck. There were no reports of anyone answering the young Ademars' description leaving through the gates or over them.

With no evidence that the three had left the city, I proceeded on the theory that they were still within its walls, held somewhere against their will. Or that they were dead and their bodies carefully hidden.

There was a third possibility. The three could have opened a portal from this world to another. If that were so, there'd be no way of tracking them. I put this thought to the back of my mind, something to consider if all else failed.

I briefly considered putting out a citywide call for them, with every guard alerted to search for and detain all those who fit the descriptions. It would work, in time. It would also drag in too many innocent citizens causing them undue embarrassment and hasten my transfer to less enjoyable duties. I settled for sending their descriptions to the Necropolis and the Healers' District, just in case.

Without much of a home to go to I stayed late at the Garrison, trying to come up with a viable approach that would not offend any anyone of rank or influence. Failing that, I gathered my files on the White Angel case so as to be able to turn the report over to Stoinef in the morning.

White Angel. Confined still to the Lower Quarters, it was the one vice that the jaded gentry had yet to try. So far. But soon one of the younger winged nobles would wander into a tavern where it was available. He'd drink it down or sniff it up and soon it would be all the fashion, until one of them took too much. One or two dead highbornes and no doubt the City Wardens would set the barghests on the dealers.

Barghests. What was it the captain had said? "Wonderful trackers." Late as it was, I went to the barracks and woke up Conrad.

"Those hell hounds of yours, can they track anything?" I asked once he was awake.

"Given a scent, yes. Fredag, is that why you woke me up, because a prisoner has escaped?"

"Not a prisoner, Conrad, at least not one of ours. I'll need three of your best, with competent handlers, Midwatch tomorrow."

"Why, what do you have?"

"An idea, one that might solve my case and help me keep my job and position."

⚜

Two days later Jones called with the blood results.

"Tox screen is back. There was something strange in his blood."

"Drugs?" was Steele's obvious guess. It was a rare day when a homicide victim did not come back with something in his system.

"I do not know, detective. If it is, it is unlike any drug I have ever seen. It appears to be something like DNA."

"Something like? You mean animal DNA?"

"No, I mean it has the appearance of DNA, but it has a left-hand spiral and its base pairs are switched."

"Is that possible?"

"Not in this world."

I spent the next morning at the Ademar Estate. Not to visit or bother the family, but to convince the servants to break the law. It took a combination of pleas, bribes, threats of prison and promises of rewards but I managed to talk two valets and one lady's maid into obtaining items of clothing worn by my missing victims but not yet washed. Putting each in a separate sack, I took my booty to Conrad.

"I need each hound to track the owner of one of these items." I handed him the sacks.

"And what are you looking for?"

"Job security. I'm looking for three missing highbornes. So just make sure those beasts of yours don't eat whoever they find, or you and I will be their next meal."

Conrad took me to the stable where his barghests were waiting. For once I agreed with Rollo, nasty creatures they were — tall as a pony, black as the night; shadows given legs, teeth and appetite. I could well believe the legend that they had originally been bred in a realm with magic darker than our own.

The hounds were separated then given the scent. Dragging their handlers behind them, each took off in a different direction. I stayed in the stable, praying to the Goddess that I was right.

Conrad stayed as well, keeping track of his beasts. With an affinity which led me to suspect that maybe he too was from a different realm, he seemed to know exactly where each one was. Random streets at first, as each barghest worked to find the scent he'd been given. Then more purposeful as they hit on the smell and began to work.

"That's odd," Conrad muttered, more in a trance than awake. "They are...converging. Drogo from Thieves' Quarters, Dash from this

District. Now Bruno. All into the Merchants' Quarters. Back into the storehouses."

Conrad awakened suddenly. "They're together. Let's go!"

He ran out of the stable, moving as fast as one of his hounds after a hare. I followed as best I could, struggling to keep up with him.

The city is mostly a labyrinth, having grown around its citizens with no plan or reason. The Folk built homes and shops where they would, leaving only enough room for a cart to pass, sometimes not even that. The Merchants' Quarter is the exception. Built near the docks, its storehouses are laid out in straight rows separated by wide passages so as to make shipments and deliveries, both legal and otherwise, that much easier. Oddly enough, for one used to the maze of the city, its grid-like layout was somehow confusing.

So it was that it took me some time to catch up with Conrad and his hounds, all three of which were baying and scratching at the door of an extra-sized storehouse toward the rear of the Quarter.

"Thought we'd wait for you before going in," Conrad said. He looked at the crest above the doors.

I followed his gaze and cursed. The storehouse belonged to the Clan Odilo.

Somewhere gods were laughing. Whatever game they were playing had me as both pawn and jester. There was no way this was going to end well, not for me nor for the missing Ademar youths. Right then I was more concerned about myself. Even the right decision would land me in the Thieves' Quarters. I did not want to think what a wrong choice would bring.

As four men and three hounds waited on my decision I knew there was only one path to take. Politics and influence be as damned as I was likely to be. If the barghests were right, inside there were three young people in need of aid or vengeance, and as a member of the Guard it was my duty to see that it was provided them.

Still, it would not do to rush in. In the past, haste in these situations has led to Guardsmen passing into the Grey Mist.

I had Conrad take one of the hounds, freeing up a guard. "Go to the barracks," I told him. "Tell Rollo I need the Duke's Own—flyers for the roof, rammers for entry, swords and slings for those inside."

I had another thought. "Also send a runner to the Clan Odilo. Tell them that the Guard has found evidence of thieves and intruders in their storehouse and is moving to protect their property." The guard ran off.

"Intruders, Fredag?"

"Of course, Conrad. Surely you don't believe that the noble Clan Odilo is behind the disappearance of members of their close friends and allies the Clan Ademar?"

Whatever Conrad believed, he wisely kept to himself.

⚜

Jones's results were verified when a chemist from the Lab handed her the report on the feathers. It showed the same combination of human DNA and "other similar nucleotides." The only good news was that the Latent Print Unit had finally identified the body — Curtis Evans, a grad student at Hopkins, working on a Masters in Biochemistry.

At last, Steele thought, something that might lead to a logical explanation. College students mixing their own chemical pleasures was nothing new. Maybe, just maybe, when she checked out his apartment there'd be a reason for the tears in his back and clothing.

What Steele found in Evans's apartment were his three roommates floating a foot off the floor in a near unconscious state of bliss.

Three cell phones and a digital camera went off almost simultaneously as officers on the scene photographed the phenomenon. The flash of the camera was enough to wake one of the levitating students who promptly crashed on the foam mattress above which she was floating.

Later, grounded and sober, the three were taken to the Homicide Unit.

"Yeah, we were flying Red Angel," the girl admitted. "It costs like anything but the high...hell, it's better than anything, better than the best sex you could ever have. When you're flying it's like your whole body's tingling, especially your...."

Steele didn't care what parts of the girl were tingling. "Tell me about Curtis," she prompted.

"We bought two vials, cut four to one that would have been two hits each. But Curt couldn't wait. Wanted to know what a full dose was like. So he opened a vial in the park and downed it."

"What happened then?" A thought was forming in Steele's mind, an idea that wasn't possible, one she knew she was going to hear from the girl.

"He was shaking, then moaning, then he sorta started, I don't know, glowing, like a bright light was inside him. Then he screamed. There was this ripping and tearing sound and then we saw his wings."

"Wings?" That would explain Evans's wounds and the rips in his clothing. Still despite seeing three people floating in air, Steele was not yet ready to believe that a man could fly.

The girl nodded her head. "Yeah, wings. Once he realized he had them he flapped them twice then shot straight up in the air. We got bored waiting for him to come down so we went home and flew a little ourselves. We haven't seen him since. I guess he came down somewhere."

"He did," Steele said and told the girl about her friend's landing.

Knowing it would cut off their supply, the three students were reluctant to give up the name of their dealer.

"Besides," said one of the two male students, "it's not as if Faerie Dust is illegal. So you don't even have a reason to hold us." He then proudly told Steele that he was a law student, adding, "Charge us or let us go."

Always willing to cooperate with the public, Steele accommodated the young man. She offered to charge them with murder.

"Evans was found dead with two severe wounds in his back. You were the last to see him alive after purchasing drugs. And your defense is that he grew wings and flew away. Good luck with that."

Faced with the reality of jail, the three readily gave up the name of their dealer. He in turn, threatened with contributory homicide, gave up his supplier, who then provided the police with the address from which he obtained his Faerie Juice.

⚔

While most folk in the Guard come from every walk of life, the Duke's Own are an elite breed. They are all ex-military, having served their time on the outer edge of Faerie, in the Twilight Realm where the light merges with the darkness. These are the ones who stand against the stuff of nightmares and make our petty games of politics possible. They are both a joy and a terror to watch.

They responded quickly to my summons: four on the ground plus two flyers. Six men seem to be a small force, but there are tales of how just two once subdued a town that rebelled against the Duke. That town no longer stands, and of its few survivors, none are believed to be whole.

The sergeant in charge came up to me. "Your orders, sir?" As the Guard who summoned them I was nominally their commander. That meant I told them what needed to be done and let them do it. It also meant that the responsibility for failure rested on me.

I explained the situation and what, or rather who I hoped to find inside.

"And those other than the hostages?"

"Meet force with force, sergeant." They would anyway, but it had to be said.

"Very good, sir."

"One other thing. I'm going in with you."

It was my case, my responsibility. The sergeant nodded in understanding.

"With me then, sir. Once the way is open."

They began. The flyers, their crossbows armed with iron-tipped quarrels, would take down any who tried to escape by air. They would also watch the rear and sides. In the unlikely event that someone got past the raiding party, the flyers would hunt them down.

The sergeant drew his sword, as did one of his men. I had my long knife. The rammers did their job and forced the main door in three blows. We went in. The rammers followed, backing us with slings and iron pellets to take out snipers and other distant threats.

It was messy, brutal work. The baying of the hounds had given those inside ample warning and the pounding of the ram told them just what they faced. They fought to save their lives and to take ours.

As we expected, a few tried to escape through the roof hatch. Iron pellets took down one of them, leaving the others as sport for our flyers.

There were nine inside. I engaged one and by the time I wiped his blood from my knife it was over. Seven dead, two wounded and that was not counting what happened to the flyers.

We checked to make sure no one was hiding amidst the stores. It was a quick search as there was precious little product for a building of its size. What we did find were tables of what at first appeared to be alchemical equipment: scales, balances and weights, glass vials to be used for packaging and a strange transparent material full of a whitish powder.

The latter I recognized immediately. I had lived with it for several fortnights. I knew its effects and the tragedies it caused. It was White Angel.

Any joy I felt about the fact that this was one case that Stoinef was not going to be solving was tempered by the reality of where I was. Thanks to me, the source of a plague devastating the city had been found. And thanks to me, one of the major clans was implicated.

I was wondering if I'd be allowed to take my medal to the Thieves' Quarters with me when the sergeant came over.

"The storehouse is secure, sir. The prisoners have been bound. One's injured but in no immediate danger of dying. The other won't last the hour. Any further orders?"

I was just about to dismiss him and his troops with thanks when there came the sound of a thousand buzzing hornets. Outside the barghests let out howls that could not only wake every sleeping monster in the city but drive them from our midst never to return. Knowing what to expect, the sergeant and I turned toward an empty blank spot along the rear wall and watched as a portal opened.

"To me!" shouted the sergeant and the Duke's Own gathered, weapons drawn, ready to meet and repel whatever threat might emerge.

Portals are magic, a way of traveling from one realm to another. There is no way to tell what land is on the other side or who — or what — might be coming through.

The buzzing stopped and a shape appeared in the doorway. Seconds later, a man bleeding from several small holes fell dead on the storehouse floor.

"I recognize those wounds," the sergeant said as we stood over the body. "Only one realm can slaughter a man like that — Earth."

Earth. Earth was the home world, the place from which we fled when the God of the Tree supplanted our Goddess. The humans who dwell there are a short-lived, violent people with a tremendous talent for developing new and imaginative ways of destroying each other.

We turned the corpse and a face familiar to me stared up with dead eyes. The Lady's luck was not with me in this case. It was not one of the Angel dealers I'd been tracking. Rather it was one of three for whom I'd been looking — Nilus Ademar. And if the body on the floor was Nilus, his sister and cousin were, no doubt, on the other side of the door.

I looked into the shimmer of the portal as if trying to see through into the world beyond, wondering if they were alive or dead. Dead, probably, considering Nilus's fate. Either way it was not my problem anymore. The investigation was over—my part in it anyway.

"Sir?" The sergeant interrupted my thinking. His men were gathered around him and they all had the attitude of soldiers who had finished their duty and just wanted to go home. I dismissed him with thanks and a promise of a glowing report to his command.

"Thank you, guardsman." The job done, I was no longer his commander. "What of the captives?"

"Leave them with me, sergeant. We're almost done here. If we can, we'll take them to a Healer. Otherwise the ghouls at the Necropolis can have them."

The Duke's Own departed, leaving me alone with just the dead, the dying and my thoughts.

✛

"It's an old house in the northeast," explained Sergeant Thorndale, the man in charge of the Quick Response Team. "No attic, three or four rooms upstairs, the same on the first. Who knows what's in the basement. We go in at four. That time of the morning everybody's thinking about sleep. Nobody expects a knock on the door and a flashbang in the face. Jennings, secure the back, I'll follow the entry team and you follow me. That clear, detective?"

"Got it, Sergeant."

They went over the plan twice more before grabbing some rest. At four, they hit the house as planned; no one expecting trouble, each officer prepared for it.

No sooner had the first swing of the ram opened the front door than Thorndale and his men were inside. Steele followed just after, feeling awkward in the ballistic armor that was twice the weight of her regular vest. There were stairs as she went in, a QRT man standing at the bottom, his weapon pointed up. The living room was clear. Everyone was quiet, listening for any sounds of movement in the house.

Steele saw it first, a thin barrel edging around the doorway leading from the kitchen.

"Gun!" she shouted a second too late to keep a QRT man from taking a slug to the neck. He went down as automatic weapons riddled the wall and the man behind it.

The firing stopped. The back door burst open and Jennings ran inside. Eyes locked, heads nodded. Northway, the officer at the foot of the stairs, checked the fallen man and shook his head.

Steele reached for her radio.

"What are you doing?" Thorndale asked.

"Calling it in."

Cold anger was in Thorndale's voice. "When it's over. Right now, we finish it."

Now was not the time to argue procedure. Not with the sorrow over a fallen comrade driving the need for payback. Steele nodded.

Northway started up the stairs. "You're here," he told Steele. As the least trained, she was lookout and back-up. Thorndale led Jennings down the basement steps.

Gunfire below. Single shots followed quickly by more automatic fire. Silence, then...

"Clear," came the sergeant's voice. "Two down. We're both good."

"Clear above," Northway yelled from the second floor.

"Detective," Thorndale shouted, "get down here. We've got...damn, I don't know what the hell we've got."

The basement was one big room. From the middle of the stairs, Steele started looking around. In the front was what even a rookie cop would recognize as a drug lab. Vials of red liquid, packaged and street-ready. A tray of a red flaky substance, something Steele had seen on countless murder scenes—dried blood. Glassine envelopes with a reddish powder were stacked next to the tray.

A bad feeling began to grow inside her as she realized that still no one had called in. Too much, too soon. It was past time, she thought. Then she looked toward the back, past the bodies of the drug dealers the QRT team had put down. The feeling got worse and her radio was forgotten.

Three beds, three people strapped to them. Two of them, the men, had tubes running from their arms into plastic bags, their life's blood slowing dripping into them. They were pale but otherwise healthy looking.

The woman was worse. She too had a line in her. She was naked and it was clear that she had been sexually abused.

They should be cut loose, Steele told herself but couldn't form the words or the will to move. Maybe it was the shock of seeing them.

Maybe it was because those on the bed were three of the most beautiful creatures she had ever seen. Maybe it was the wings.

Angels, was Steele's first thought when she realized that the large feathery objects were not part of the bedding. But could one so bind an angel and would divine creatures bleed?

There is a point in a case when it all comes together. Sometimes that point comes gradually, a steady buildup of evidence and witness testimony that tells the story. And sometimes there's a sudden realization that leaps past the facts and goes right to the answer.

"Faeries," Steele whispered as it all came together for her. The floating college students, the dead boy who flew away and fell to earth. The names for the drugs. These were faeries. Faeries who came into this world and met the worst kind of humans, humans who somehow discovered the properties of their blood then captured, enslaved and abused them.

Again came the thought that it was past time to call this in, to let someone know what had happened, what they had found, to report that the world was not what it was this morning.

Having put down the bad guys, Thorndale and Jennings moved to help the victims. They took off their helmets, laid aside their weapons and moved toward the beds. Together they removed the IVs and loosened the straps binding the male faeries, then they turned to free the female.

Feeling someone behind her, Steele turned briefly and saw Northway.

"What are they doing?" he asked, removing his own helmet.

"They're freeing the...." Steele started to explain, but as she turned back toward the room she saw what he meant.

The faeries were free. Thorndale had picked up a blanket and was offering it to the naked female. She, however, made no move to take it or cover herself. Instead she turned to her companions and said something in a harsh yet somehow musical language. They nodded in agreement with whatever she had said.

Three sets of wings suddenly unfurled, filling the basement and knocking the QRT men aside. One of the males made a dash to a far corner of the room, came back with things sharp and shiny.

"Move," shouted Northway and pushed Steele aside. "Look out," he called to his fellow officers just as the faeries attacked.

Taking a long knife offered by her comrade, the female fell on Thorndale. Unarmed and taken unawares, the sergeant had no hope of defending himself. The faerie stabbed once, twice, and then a third time, the blade piercing Thorndale's ballistic armor and going deep into his chest.

At the same time a male faerie went after Jennings. Wielding a sword, he first slashed and partly severed the officer's leg, dropping him. As the officer fell, the faerie pinned him to the floor with a thrust though his stomach.

As Northway began firing, Steele did what should have been done with the first shot.

"Signal 13!" she shouted into her radio, "Officers down, shots fired." She then drew her Glock to join the battle.

The female went down, then one of the males. The other retreated further back into the basement.

Nowhere to go, Steele thought, down here there's no door to the outside.

Then the darkness in the rear of the basement lit up as a bright rectangle suddenly formed. It grew to more than the size of a man and the remaining faerie stepped toward it.

"No you don't, you bastard!" Northway yelled and rushed the glowing door.

With what seemed to be a look of hatred for all things human on his face, the faerie threw a knife that caught the officer in the right eye. Then he stepped through the door and was gone.

Steele emptied half a clip into the glowing portal, expecting it to close any minute. When it didn't, she stopped firing and asked herself why. Why was it still open?

There was only one answer. He was coming back and bringing friends.

Why? Steele asked in despair, looking at her slaughtered companions. Why did they do it? We rescued them, we were going to help.

They're not that much different from us, she realized. They thought we would be like the ones who had enslaved them. And Steele had to admit that they were not that far from being wrong.

A drug that could make men fly. Who would not want that? What government would not want flying soldiers? And all that was needed was the blood from creatures that were not of this world, that were not even human. No, they were not wrong at all.

Steele knew she didn't dare leave the basement. The door could not be left unguarded. The faeries would be back, looking for vengeance. If they got loose in her world, the slaughter would be horrific.

Two highborne clans, one engaged in selling poison to the folk of the city, the other involved in unauthorized travel to a dangerous world. Both capital offenses and each carrying the potential for scandal great enough to cost the Ademars and the Odilos much of their influence. If it came out.

That was not likely. The highbornes knew how to protect themselves. What *was* likely was a cover-up that included silencing those in the know. The Duke's Own? They were soldiers doing their job. They were unaware of the parties involved. Conrad and his handlers? They had stayed outside and knew nothing of what had happened in the storehouse. That left—me.

They would need my silence. A transfer to better duty might earn it, so might a promotion or higher pay. However nice that sounded, I knew there was only one way they could be certain that the story would never come out.

I looked toward the still-shimmering portal and for a moment considered taking my chances with whatever waited on the other side. A glance at Nilus told me what that would bring me, but maybe it would be a quicker fate than the one that awaited me in this world.

The thought of taking the quick path to the Grey Mist repelled me. So did making my report and calmly awaiting the inevitable decision. There had to be a third option.

I started thinking like a guardsman and quickly found it. Why, I asked, would an Ademar open a portal in an Odilo storehouse? There were two people who might have the answer and one of them near death.

I checked on my prisoners. At least one of them might make it to a healer. Then I called in Conrad.

"About time, Fredag. Can we go back now, the hounds are getting hun...." The sight of the battle inside stopped him cold. "By the Lady!" Then Conrad noticed the open portal. "What's that over there?"

"Best you don't know. We're almost through here. Just one more thing." I hesitated, needing but not wanting to take the next step. I consoled myself with the thought that it was my life against one who would soon be making his final journey no matter what I did. What was a small piece of my soul against my overall survival?

"Conrad, bring in one of the hounds, preferably the hungriest one."

"Fredag, what are you...."

"Like I said, Conrad, best you don't know."

It was my case so Conrad did what he was told and quickly brought in the largest of his hounds, a creature called Drogo. While he was doing that, I dragged my two captives closer to the center of the storehouse. I had just finished when Conrad came in with his barghest.

Neither man could take his eyes off the snarling blackness that was the hound. It was all shadow, excepting the red of its eyes and the white of its teeth. Seeing the men, sensing their weakness, it strained at its leash. Conrad was barely able to hold it back.

A foul stench filled the air; my captives had soiled themselves. This only served to excite the beast more.

I again asked myself how far I was willing to take this, what my life was worth. I decided its value was far in excess of the two men at my feet.

"The thing before you, gentlemen, is hungry. It has worked hard all day and has missed several meals. Right now, it sees you as food. Should I order it released? Or will you tell me for whom you work and how the Ademars are involved?"

The one nearest the hound was close to death but he would have spoken, had not the severity of his wounds, coupled by the shock I had just given him, left him unable to speak. His partner, somehow sensing that Drogo would go for his weaker friend, shook his head.

"Don't know. The one who hired us is over there, dead in the corner."

"Too bad."

I walked over to Conrad. "That one," I said and pointed to the one near death. Conrad let out the lead slowly. "You're next," I told the other.

The hound was inches away from his friend's feet when the healthier one shouted, "It was Ekbert, Ekbert Odilo. He was behind it."

I nodded and Conrad backed the hound off, using all his strength to pull it away from its would-be meal.

"And what, my friend, was Ekbert behind?"

Never taking his eyes off the barghest he answered. "Where that portal leads, that's where he sent the three he had us snatch off the street one night. Sent them right through he did. Said he'd made a deal on the other side. Said that the blood of the folk does things to mortals, makes them like us. Traded the three for a mortal drug, something he called 'hero wine.'

"Hero wine." Funny name for a white powder that was anything but heroic. "White Angel" did sound better.

The man was babbling now, his eyes still on Drogo, repeating what he'd told me over and over in an effort to earn my mercy.

It was late and I was tired. With what I now knew I could safely make my report. It wouldn't earn me any honors but neither would it get me knifed in the dark. Just a feud between clans, happens all the time. The Odilos would pay the clangeld, Ekbert would be banished and all would be as it was.

Except for the young highborne lying dead in the place of his enemy. Except for his sister and cousin, no doubt dead in a foreign land, their lost spirits far from the Grey Mist. Except for those whose lives were destroyed by a mortal poison. All might return to what it was, but that did not make things right.

The small piece of my soul I had traded for information found its way back to me as I remembered that it was the duty of the Guard to make things right. At least it was the duty of one of the Guard, at least for one night.

Drogo's growl told me how I could accomplish this.

"Can we go now?" Conrad all but whined. "He really is hungry."

"Go with my thanks, Conrad, and buy your pets a steak each. I'll pay."

"After tonight, you owe them each a cow."

"And after tomorrow I'll owe them a herd. I've more work for them."

Conrad gave me an odd look. "You're not thinking of going after Ekbert Odilo, are you?"

"Of course not. I'm thinking of going after the thieving murderous baseborne who invaded the storehouse of the Clan Odilo and dared to impersonate one of its noble scions."

I said this as if I meant it. I'd need the practice when I made my report to Captain Rollo.

"Go home, Conrad. Go back to your stables, feed and rest your hounds. Come Daywatch, send me fresh ones, and someone to carry a message."

"It is Daywatch, Fredag."

"Go home anyway. I'll be here. I've business to finish up."

If Conrad suspected what my business was he didn't say, just nodded and left, leaving me alone in the storehouse.

Not quite alone. There were the dead, and there were my captives. There was also whoever was on the other side of the still open portal. Had they left or were they still there waiting for us?

If what little I knew of Earth and its humans was true, I knew the answer to that question. At least I hoped I did.

I checked my prisoners. One had joined his fellows in death. The other was still alive, still hoping for mercy. That hope faded when I put my knife to his eye.

"This boss of yours, the one who calls himself Ekbert. What of his is here?"

Without the threat of the barghest he was less willing to talk.

"I can send you to the healers blind or with two good eyes. Or to the Mist right now. Your choice."

I moved the knife closer; let him feel its point.

"Ekbert, he kept a cloak on a hook in back. It gets cold in here sometimes."

"A black cloak?"

"No, deep red, lined and with a hood."

I checked, there was such a garment and of a quality that an Odilo might own.

There was nothing more to do but wait was fated for the Inquisitors' chambers and no one deserved that. I used my knife and showed him the only mercy I could.

✤

Alone in a blood-splattered basement, Detective Bethany Steele watched a door without a room and waited for it to open. When it did it would be her against who knows how many but backup was on its way — maybe. The basement walls were thick and Steele wasn't sure her call for help went out.

Again, she looked around at the bodies on the floor. Cops, dealers, faeries. Soon there would be more.

She'd hold them off as best she could, dropping them one by one until her ammo ran out. After that...Steele looked at the sword on the floor beside her. After that she'd pick it up and start swinging and hope to take a few of the winged bastards with her.

Again she sent out a "13," not knowing if the radio signal would pass through the basement walls. She gathered her weapons and waited.

The messenger arrived before the hounds. To my surprise it was Stoinef.

"Fredag, all is well?"

"With me, Stoinef, but the others here have had better days." As he looked past me at last night's slaughter I added, "The Clan Odilo has been apprised of the situation?"

He nodded. "They were deeply troubled by the news and trust in the Guard to protect their name and reputation and to bring those responsible to justice."

"Of course they do. If you would, please go back to them. Tell them that, as you can plainly see, the responsible parties are now facing the Lady's Justice, all but one. And that one will be brought to bay this very morning. I'm setting the barghests on him, and their justice will be less merciful than the Lady's."

Stoinef left and shortly after, Conrad's beasts arrived with two handlers. I gave Stoinef time to arrive at the Odilo Estate with my message, sure that Ekbert was paying close attention to what was transpiring.

When enough time had passed, I gave the handlers pieces I had cut from Ekbert's cloak. "Take these to the First and Third Gates then give the hounds the scent. If they find the one we seek, hold them back as best you can."

"Why those two gates?" asked the taller of Conrad's men.

I could have told them the truth and said, "Because they are the farthest from here." Instead I shrugged. "We have to start somewhere."

They accepted this and were off. And again I was left in the company of the dead and a still-glowing portal. I spent my time picking up useful things from the floor and the table with the alchemical equipment on it.

My wait was short. In the time it would have taken the barghests to reach the gates and be set to work, a highborne wearing the colors of Clan Odilo joined me in the storehouse. He was tall, with a proud set of wings and carried himself with a noble bearing. In the right circumstances, most would consider him handsome, but today his pale skin and worried countenance stole whatever looks he might claim.

"You are Fredag of the Guard?"

I admitted that I was.

"You set the hounds on me." It was more of statement than a question but I answered anyway.

"Perhaps I did. Who are you?"

"You know damn well that I am Ekbert of the Clan Odilo."

"Then you are mistaken, Noble Sir. I set the hounds on the vile baseborne who has claimed to be you; on the villain who abducted, debased, and caused the death of three of your honored allies of the Clan Ademar; on the purveyor of poison who spread a plague through this city. Surely such a one deserves his fate?"

Ekbert, to his credit, did not gainsay my words. "Call them off," he begged in a now quaking voice. "Call off the hounds and name your price. I swear by the honor of my Clan I will pay it."

"My price?" I walked over to where lay the body of Nilus Ademar. "Bring him back. Bring back his sister and cousin." I went over to the equipment table. "Undo the damage your hero wine has caused. That is my price."

Ekbert had no answer. He just stood there, no longer a noble flyer lording it over the common folk of the city. Now he was just a man without power, without influence, without hope.

In the distance came the sound of baying hounds. By the Lady those beasts were fast.

"Hear that, Ekbert, that is the sound of your fate, the sound of justice rushing toward you. And when those monsters from Hell burst through the door, I will step aside and let them have you. They will feed, consuming not only your body but your soul. No judgment after death, no voyage to the Grey Mist, only eternal suffering as a wraith in whatever daemon realm they were spawned."

Whether that was true or not, Ekbert believed me. As the baying came closer, he began searching for a way out. He glanced first at the roof hatches, thought about taking flight.

"Barred from the outside," I lied. It was then he saw the portal.

A drowning man will clutch at the thinnest thread to try to stay afloat. Ekbert saw the glowing doorway as his only escape and ran toward it. I made no move to stop him. Instead, I used the glove I'd taken from the alchemical bench to pick up three of the pellets used the night before. These I tossed into the doorway just as Ekbert entered. The cold iron disrupted the portal's magic and it closed behind him.

How long has it been, Steele asked herself. Backup should have been here by now. Even if the 13 didn't go out we're long overdue to check in.

Just then Steele heard the faint sound of sirens in the distance. But as she relaxed, the shimmering in the back of the basement darkened, then a shadow appeared in the doorway. Remembering the slaughter of her comrades, she readied herself. The shadow grew solid. She fired just as the door closed behind it.

It may have been my imagining but as the portal faded I thought I heard the sound of thunder come from within it. Three times I heard the thunder and it was followed by the sound of a man crying out in pain and death. Maybe it was my imagination, or maybe the humans were welcoming Ekbert in their own unique way.

I had cut three pieces from Ekbert's cloak, one for each of the hounds and a third I placed in the pocket of one of last night's dead. When the hounds finally did burst through the door they ravaged the corpse beyond recognition. So it was, to my surprise, revealed that the leader of the criminal gang had been dead all along. My informant must not have seen him die. Or so I surmised in my report to the Captain.

My version of the events was accepted by all. A gang of basebornes somehow opened a portal, conducted illegal trade with another realm and caused the death of three nobles. It wasn't the whole truth but it was as close as I could come.

Ekbert's been reported missing. Stoinef has the case.

I often wonder if it's over. If there were other so-called nobles allied with Ekbert who know of this hero wine and the gold that can be made from it. So many deaths, so many lies and possibly more of each to come.

The wise men tell us that we live in a land of eternal youth. Why then, at times, do I feel so damned old?

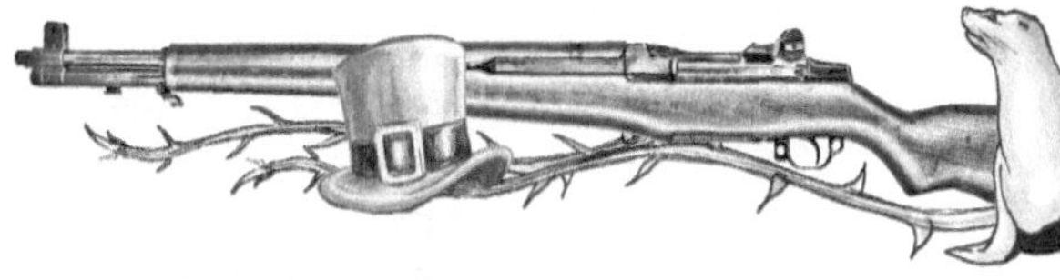

The Natural-Born Spy

James Daniel Ross

Some things are too close for a normal man to focus on at the time. Only decades after November, 1944, can I look back and realize the small stones in the road that diverted our lives so immensely. I could never know that when I walked into the professor's office at Boston College I was to begin a journey that would lead me to places I never imagined existed.

I was sitting at the desk, pads of paper thrown across the surface like machinegun fire, books opened to select pages and marked with new pads, pens, and other books. There was a quick rap on the door, and then it opened with a swing that spoke of impatient authority.

The man who entered was tall and straight, or maybe pressed. Yes, that was it: The man gave out an impression that if he were rolled over Niagara Falls inside a wooden barrel he would come out with every bone broken—but every crease of his suit intact. The man practically had starch in his walk and his shoes were shined to blinding brightness. The instant he entered the room, his free hand snatched the hat from his head, exposing only a furtive bristle of hair. His lantern jaw screwed his teeth more tightly together and his eyes narrowed as they took me in. In the non-hat hand there was a book, which he now pointed at me in accusation. "You're not Professor Levi Stein."

I blinked at him twice, swallowing hard as his disapproval smacked me across the face. "Um, no. I'm sorry. I noticed the appointment in the book for you, Mr. Smith. There was no telephone number so I decided to wait here to explain why the professor—"

Smith ducked his head out into the hallway, scanning both

ways quickly before retreating back into the office and shutting the door. Then he spun on me, his eyes as hard and cold as nails. "Where is the professor?"

I cleared my throat, fighting the tears trying to well up, "The professor is indisposed."

"How indisposed?"

Then I had to grab a kerchief from my pack and dab at my eyes. "Permanently, sir."

Smith glanced at the door darkly, but it was a moment or two before I heard a pair of shoes walk innocently by. He then turned back to me. "Who are you?"

"My name is Bruce Andrew."

He tossed his Stetson on the desk and leaned on the free hand, looming over me and—now I am convinced—reading everything exposed in an instant. "You're the professor's star pupil."

Maybe it was how quickly he dismissed the news of the professor's death, or maybe how successful he was at intimidating me in a place I had come to regard as a home. Whatever it was, it gave me a little steel of my own, which I threw into my voice, waving my paring knife in front of his broadsword. "That's right."

He tossed the book, thick, heavy, and at least two centuries old, down in front of me. "Can you translate Occitan?"

"Of course."

The grin on his face was not friendly or encouraging. "The pages are marked."

"And why should I?"

He glared at me as if I were a toy poodle barking at him from the safety of a rich woman's arms. Then he took out his billfold and pulled out five large bills as crisp as his pants. They fluttered to the desk carelessly, but when they landed they sounded like gold bars to me.

I only let them breathe there for a minute before snatching them up and stowing them in my front pocket. I opened the heavy tome, and saw page after page of pen-work easily dating back to the sixteenth century. Still his demeanor and the heavy bills in my pocket brooked no questions. I could only manage, "This will take a while."

He leaned in the corner and crossed his arms. "I'll wait."

And wait he did, though the longer I moved words across time and languages, the more I smiled inside at his foolishness. It was well past midnight by the time I put down my pen and handed him the sheet. I allowed myself a little smile as he took it. "No hidden treasure map there, sorry."

I started gathering my own papers into organized piles as he devoured every syllable I had recorded. Only once he was done did he refocus on me, eyes sharp. "Did you understand anything about this?"

I rolled my eyes and shoved my own books into my knapsack, leaving the one he had brought conspicuously alone. "I did an undergraduate paper on medieval belief in faeries and their ilk. They're really little gods and every culture has had them, like the house gods of Roman times—"

Smith made a motion like swatting away a lethargic fly. "You're an expert in myths and legends, then?"

I shrugged. "Myths, legends, and I read a half a dozen dead languages."

His eyebrows shot up. "Star pupil, indeed."

I nodded once, chin set.

He snatched up his book, translated pages folded within, retrieved his hat and nodded a thanks as he opened the door to leave. He paused. "Have you ever thought about joining the army?"

I hated that question, and it had been asked often the last three years. I did feel some need to go serve my country, and lord knows there were no more evil forces on the planet than Hitler and Tojo. Still, I was tall but thin, with an Adam's apple of prodigious size. My eyes were more attuned to reading letters than searching out Nazis. In fact, if there was someone less suited to armed conflict than I was, I had never met him. I just was not a soldier. I didn't know Smith, didn't much like him, and I never planned to ever see him again. So I settled on a terse, "No." without regard to what he might think of me.

Then he left, and I locked up the professor's office for the night. I went to his funeral the next Sunday. He was buried next to his wife in a beautiful ceremony. I stood by his grave for a very long time after.

The next day I received my draft notice. I tried to argue the point to anyone who would listen, but all I got were disapproving looks and olive drab walls funneling me into boot camp, where time ceased to have any meaning. I felt extra eyes on me the entire time, and extra attention paid to my training.

If you are thinking loving, paternal attention, think again. I was horribly out of shape, grotesquely inadequate with a weapon, and almost died on the first three-mile run. I could never keep my uniform clean enough. I was never able to properly express my ferocity. I never knew the right answers. I once stabbed a dummy with a bayonet and immediately fell over backward. I once passed out doing push-ups. The ten-mile marches were almost a death sentence. Let me be clear: I was a fantastic researcher, and an excellent linguist, but at six feet and one hundred and ten pounds, a hard-charging, bullet-chewing, Nazi-throttling grunt I was not.

It was something my drill sergeant never let me forget. He called me Ichabod...as in Crane. I was just glad they never found a pumpkin to throw at me as I suffered through the five-mile runs. Then, one night, I was pulled out of bed without warning. My scream turned into a cough as someone lovingly toed me in the solar plexus, emptying my lungs in one, fell *whoosh*. I tried to call upon my inadequately learned training and lashed out with hands and feet, earning a slap. My head was spinning as they efficiently shoved a cotton gag in my mouth, trussed me up with rough rope, yanked a bag over my head, and hustled me into the frigid night.

I stopped even trying to call for help once they threw me in the back of a jeep, and drove for miles. By the time the vehicle stopped, I had managed to convince myself that my bunkmates, the sergeant, or all of them together, had finally decided to pull a reenactment of Sleepy Hollow. Then someone pulled me out, dumped me on a floor like a sack of potatoes, and left. I cowered there for a while, wondering what kind of hell awaited me next. Beatings? Maulings? Was this how someone was flushed out of basic training?

But as the minutes ticked by, and the frigid December cold leeched into my bones from the ground. I came to realize that nobody was coming. Fear began to give way to anger, at being dumped here without reason, without instruction, and without even a pair of pants!

It was then I realized that the thick ropes were perhaps a bit too burly for the work of tying my thin wrists. It hurt, but it took only a few minutes of sliding my arms back and forth to move all the slack to the points I needed and pull an arm free. I tossed off the ropes, pulled off the hood, and yanked out the gag to breathe cold, clean air. But though I could see, I gained precious little information. I was looking at the inside of an abandoned barn, swept clean and devoid of animals or feed. The shadows were as dark as pools of crude oil, but between them knives of light slashed through cracks in the boards with unyielding brightness. Of course, looking outside between the boards only succeeded in blinding me. Spiders had been busy in every open area, but the ground had been raked clean at some time to obliterate any signs of passage.

It seemed an odd sort of prank. I had expected Jack-O'-lanterns honestly, but there was nothing but me in my underwear in the cold. Whatever was going on, I had no intention of playing along. The guard was conspicuously absent, so I simply tried the barn door.

Locked. Barred from the outside, actually.

Only after a once-over of the walls did I see a ladder leading up into the loft hiding in the corner like a young woman at a dance. Light was flooding in up there so I struggled up, rung after rung, and once there things got even stranger.

Light, indeed, slammed into the open end of the hayloft, obliterating the wooden tunnel that lead to it and turning it into an unearthly portal. I crept forward on tiptoes, afraid of any noise that might betray me, feeling increasingly that more was going on here than I understood. I took extra care to duck down as I came to the opening. Of course, that's when one, oversized toe caught a knothole in the floor and I stumbled forward onto the abbreviated platform jutting out into open space. I fought for my balance, a struggle I took personally, when that self-same traitorous foot found the edge of the platform. I lurched back onto my rump and just tried to come to grips with the strangeness.

Banks of floodlights punished my eyes mercilessly, causing them to stream without pause. The heat from their gaze fought with a cool breeze as I knelt down and felt at the edges that lead into open space. I stood there for what seemed an eternity before someone raised a bullhorn and in a perfect military voice said, "Jump."

All I could think was: *You have got to be kidding.*

I was at least thirty feet up, and I had no idea of the condition of the ground below. It was not just possible, but likely, that I was going to hurt myself badly if I followed the order, that was even now testily repeating itself. "I said, jump, recruit!"

Up until this point I had been marched, yelled at, smacked around, beaten up...and that was just the official stuff in boot. It was the middle of the night; I was tired, freezing, hungry, sore, and disoriented. There just wasn't room for fear in me, anymore. *Jump yourself,* I thought viciously.

I made to go back into the barn, but I knew nothing but a locked door waited me down the ladder. Jump into nothing or go wait, locked in a dark barn? None of this made any sense, none whatsoever. I began to search around the platform, eyes squeezed shut against the stabbing knives of light when, just beneath the left side of the rough balcony, I found a rope ladder bolted to the wall. I smiled to myself; *I will take option three, sir.*

I clambered down, out of the focus of the row upon row of lights, back into the uncomfortably cool darkness. To my right, underneath the platform, there was a massive, cushioned pad that would have caught me if I had obeyed the bodiless voice. It was at that moment that I knew my butt was going to be so completely chewed that I could have used it to feed baby birds. Still, that sinking feeling was made a little more bearable when my feet left the rope ladder and touched sweet Mother Earth.

I turned around, and there he was: the smartest officer, in the cleanest uniform, with the thinnest pencil moustache, I had ever seen. I recognized his Captain's markings and I snapped a salute. His hazel eyes twinkled and he smiled like a movie star as he thrust out a hand to me. "Welcome to the OSS, son."

I shook it, my head swimming. Reflexively I read his nametag: it said BLANCO. "I'm sorry, sir, there must be a mistake. I'm still in boot camp."

He cocked an eyebrow at me, "Do you want to be in boot, son?"

"No, sir."

"Then don't worry about it. Come with me and we can get you into uniform."

I was too busy floating on clouds at the prospect of never having to march in formation ever again to notice the frying pan was far, far above and it was getting rather hot and bright all around.

I can forgive myself, really. I was supposed to be finishing up my education, getting ready to start a career as a teacher in some college, somewhere. Instead I was inducted into the OSS.

It seemed forbidden and sexy, since I was technically inside of a department tasked with running operatives, agents, and assets, which is how people who do it say: spies. I was thrilled when they said I'd be given a task that utilized my language skills. Yet less than thirty days later all I could think was, *Office of Strategic Services, my left buttock.*

I spent most of my time translating radio-code gibberish from agents in the field into semi-English gibberish for those at command. I had nothing really to complain about, since nobody was shooting at me.

As the war began to wind down I began to suspect sitting around listening to radio traffic was a colossal waste of time. The Russians were sacking Berlin, and all but the staunchest Nazi hideouts were being rooted out across Europe.

Some small part of me believed that I should be off doing something, contributing in some real way to finishing off the war. I really didn't want to, understand, but since I was wearing a uniform I figured I might as well try to do my part. Instead, radio transmissions came in, became slips of paper, and disappeared into Captain Blanco's office. About the only excitement I got was letters from my parents in Ohio and my weekly jaunts across the Virginia compound to the base library.

But when I translated that last bit of radio traffic, my entire world changed forever.

I dropped it off at the captain's office as normal, but within an hour he had summoned me back. He gave me a set of typewritten orders and equipment kit to request from supply.

"I'm sorry, sir, where is this going?"

He smiled easily, one eyebrow dancing up and down. "It's there."

"No, sir, I mean who is this going to?"

"You have it." I glanced down at the orders, saw my name, and for a moment I was sure I was going to soil myself.

"But, sir, this says I'm going to France."

"Very astute, Lieutenant. Well, let's get used to calling you Captain Andrew until you get back."

"Captain? Sir, am I getting promoted?"

Captain Blanco smiled at me and leaned back in his chair. "Not as such, no."

"Sir, don't they shoot you for this kind of thing, err...pretending to be a rank you are not?"

"Well, we both work in the Office of Strategic Services, we keep secrets for a living, so I won't tell anyone if you don't."

"But, sir I can't—"

"Andrew, Command holds the position that you have unique qualifications vital to the success of this mission. Command also holds the position that they can send people to jail who use the word 'can't' in a war zone."

"Don't they shoot them?"

"Sometimes jail comes first."

Those cold words hung in the air for a minute, gathering potency and gravity. Then Captain Blanco dismissed the darkness of the moment with that lopsided, movie-star smile he *shoo*ed me out of his office. "Take heart, son, the fighting's been over in France for weeks. You'll be fine."

I left, but my stomach fell away as my eyes scanned over the paper in my hands:

HEADQUARTERS COMPANY, 3RD DIVISION, TO LT. ANDREW, BRUCE W.

PROCEED IMMEDIATELY TO LE CHATEAU EST MONTE LE CIEL. CONTACT PLATOON LEADER LT. RITTER OR SGT. KELLER CONCERNING REPORTS OF GROSS INSUBORDINATION WITHIN THE UNIT, INSTIGATED BY POSSIBLE ENEMY AGENTS—PERSON OR PERSONS UNKNOWN—WHICH HAS RESULTED IN CASUALTIES; AS OF LAST REPORT...

My eyes flicked to the calendar, even though I knew the date, but my eyes had to confirm it had been a week since the platoon had last made contact. A week in a war zone was a very, very long time.

...THERE HAS BEEN NO ADDITIONAL COMMUNICATION SINCE THEN. HOLDING MONTÉ LE CIEL IS OF THE HIGHEST PRIORITY TO THE WAR EFFORT. RENDER ALL AID POSSIBLE; PROCEED WITH CAUTION.

I am supposed to reinforce a platoon? Alone? How?

And the answer was, of course: *Command holds the position that they can send people to jail who use the word 'can't' in a war zone.*

ONCE IN EUROPE, SPEED IS OF THE ESSENCE; REQUISITION THREE INFANTRYMEN FOR YOUR USE AND SAFETY.

*I'm going to be in charge of...*Up until now I had only ever been in charge of the captain's laundry. The idea of having men under my command was at the same instant uplifting and terrifying.

YOU ARE TO DESTROY THESE ORDERS BEFORE YOU LEAVE CONTINENTAL US. FIND ATTACHED COPIES OF YOUR PUBLIC ORDERS AUTHENTICATING YOU AS A CAPTAIN AND ENSURING ALL NECESSARY AID FROM ALLIES ON THE WAY.

YOU WILL DEPART IMMEDIATELY.

As shocked as I was to be pulling a Thompson submachine gun, ammunition, a 1911, and captain's markings from supply, what came next was what really filled me with dread. I was flown over the sea by an empty army air corps C-54 air transport.

One: This was the last, very last, sign that this was not a prank. Two: These things never flew empty, it was simply too expensive, but there I was.

I reached England with a fluky stomach and a bad case of the jitters, but it was the boat ride from England to France that left me with an empty stomach and raging headache. I spent most of the time bent over a railing, heaving and heaving long after my last meal was nothing but a memory. That's how I wound up in France.

Once there, my 'official' — which apparently is OSS for 'fake' — orders were scanned by dozens of eyes at every stop. Allied troops jumped to offer me assistance. Everywhere I stopped, the man I passed the papers to would pause on the three-letter office designation and then size me up again. As I left, they would sometimes say OSS, more often they'd just whisper 'spy'.

Is that what I was? I didn't feel like a spy; my medieval literature professor, Dr. Goldstein, would have said I looked like a *schmuck*. I was beginning to believe that I had gotten much deeper into things than I had ever imagined and I had no idea how it had happened.

Don't get me wrong, I'd studied ancient cultures and languages. I was an expert at medieval texts. I'm not a dumb guy; I just didn't feel like much of a secret agent. At the moment, I couldn't even pull off soldier all that convincingly. Still, gates opened, supplies were handed out, and I even got my driver and infantrymen without complaint.

I was being chauffeured by a tow-headed mountain of a kid, Private Jimmy J. James. I didn't ask what the J stood for. I was afraid he'd tell me. The huge, corn-fed blond looked every inch like a soldier, and I took a bit of comfort from that. He was decently cheerful, but apparently he'd learned how to drive somewhere on the high seas.

The ragged jeep hit another patch of unstable, slushy dirt on the country road, churned into a rainy quagmire by the treads of untold Tiger and Sherman tanks. Private James howled like a wolf as we spun half-circle like a dog on ice. His big, meaty hands slung the heavily nicked wheel around but I wasn't sure if he was trying to stop the skid or make it worse. I slapped him on the shoulder in a signal he had learned through frequent use. He slid the beat-up car to a stop at the side of the muddy road and I barely managed to jump out to vomit...again.

Though they called it seasickness, apparently any significantly hilly, slippery type of travel will would do. *Lucky me.* From the jeep Martinez huffed, Hamilton snickered.

Private First-Class Alphonzo Martinez had been 'in theater' for nine months already, and it was almost as if he could smell the stink of fear on me. He said little, but he squinted at me more often than I was comfortable with.

Private Hamilton was a rat-faced man with teeth that looked like a fist full of broken dominoes. Every order was questioned, every job caused a miniature revolt. The only way to keep him in line was to constantly pair him up with Martinez or James. Marintez would stare at him until he did his share, and James would cheerfully do the whole thing himself.

I finished heaving, but as I got back into the jeep, the greedy mud sucked my boot right off my left foot. I lurched forward, socked foot coming down on a sharp edge projecting from the doorframe. A huge gash opened on the ball of my foot and I cried out as I tumbled back into the mud. I grabbed my limb and could do nothing but bite back on the tears. *Captains don't cry, do they?*

My men jumped out and came around to help me. James pulled me from the mud, Martinez retrieved my boot, and Hamilton just grinned. I was about to snap at the former when the latter broke into a gap-toothed grin. "Hoo dang! Cap'n, that looks like it smarts a fair bit."

I think the look I gave him would have cracked stone, but my glasses had fogged over and spattered with mud. In fact, I was covered with sloppy dirt from head to toe by the time I got back into the vehicle. It took several minutes for James to clean out the wound with the contents of his canteen, then break out a field dressing and the sulfanilamide. He dusted my foot to prevent infection and then wrapped it tightly. Only once he was done did I realize that Martinez was keeping watch in all directions with his rifle at ready, Hamilton was not, and I should have been the one to tell them both to do so. *Hoo dang, indeed.*

We hopped back into the jeep and roared off again. The burning pain in my foot distracted my stomach from the winding road, and at this point I was willing to take whatever victories I could. Then the smell hit me and I realized I must have fallen backward into my own pile of sick. *Wow, look at me, the secret agent.*

We pulled over an hour later in a little village, where I was able to muddle through with a polyglot of ancient languages I could actually speak to make myself understood to the French villagers. They took me to a veterinarian of all things, who drank heavily as he cleaned and sewed up my foot. The other two waited outside while James sat next to me the whole time, seriously confused, "Cap'n, didn't you say you could speak French?"

Maybe the doc had given me a dog's dosage of pain medication, because I could still feel the needle and thread as they pulled the ragged, angry, red tear closed. Not screaming was harder when I had to talk, *but captains don't admit such things, do they*? I gritted my teeth and replied anyway, "Middle French, James, (*gah!*); it's not exactly the same."

Private James looked around as if he expected a signpost to materialize in the animal doctor's office, "Well, I guess we're more south than the middle o' France, I reckon."

"No, Private, Middle French, like (*ow*) Middle English."

He stared at me blankly.

"...Old English (*yeow*)?"

His mouth gaped a bit.

"Shakespeare (*choke*)?"

Then his head bobbed like a blond boulder. "Aw, yeah, Cap'n. Shakespeare."

And, at last, we had found some common ground. An hour later, sutured, bandaged, booted, and miserable, we were back on the road. Two more hours after that, about the time my foot had settled into a dull throb, we saw Monté le Ciel in the distance.

"Glory be, Cap'n, that's an odd place for a hill to pop up like that."

I couldn't stop myself, "It's a motte."

"Well, I don't know how you say it in France, but in Kentucky, that there's a hill."

Hamilton snickered from the back seat.

The thing of it was, he was right. Centuries ago, a dauphin, baron, or king had gathered his conscripted serfs and pulled dirt from all over into a massive hill, or motte. After that, he had probably used a fair bit of his treasure and a generation of stoneworkers to build the magnificent, rambling structure as a testament to his military might. It was absolutely beautiful, white surfaces painted red by the fading sun, proud walls and graceful towers guarding stately buildings within. But as my eyes trailed over the castle, it became clear the Nazis had done some modification, mainly carving swastikas into every prominent position they could reach. Overall it reminded me of the movies Uncle Sam had showed us in boot camp...the ones where the poor soldier catches a dreaded social disease from a pretty girl. Someone had defaced a few of the swastikas, but it had been something of a perfunctory job.

The jeep ascended the ancient cobblestones with aplomb, but I felt my guts twisting tighter the closer we came to Monté le Ciel. We pulled up to the gate, which stood ajar, and my orders echoed in my head...*GROSS INSUBORDINATION WITHIN THE UNIT..., POSSIBLE ENEMY AGENTS...RESULTED IN CASUALTIES; AS OF LAST RE-PORT...PROCEED WITH CAUTION.*

As if reading my thoughts, Martinez readied his rifle, and it prompted me to do the same. I checked my Thompson to make sure a round was in the chamber. There hadn't been.

James brought the vehicle to a stop and honked the horn. He looked at me and shrugged before blowing the horn again. The shrill beep did-n't bring anyone to our aid, but it did seem to stop the wind from blow-ing, adding an eerie stillness to the tableau. I was telling myself it was all a coincidence as James' hand strayed into the back seat and took hold of his M1 Garand.

See, you're not the only one that's jumpy, I thought with relish.

James turned to me with wide eyes, his Adam's apple stuttering up and down a bit. "Well, Cap'n?"

Hamilton looked askance at the huge banners the way a toddler looks at liver and lima beans. "Yeah, Captain. Maybe we got the wrong place?"

Ignoring him was starting to take real effort. I took a deep breath and squared my shoulders. "I guess we better go take a look."

Hamilton made a whining noise, but Martinez moved without com-ment, and James' wide shoulders slumped a bit, but he clambered out of the jeep as I got out on the other side. Then the privates spun, guns raised, as I yelped and fell, my wounded foot giving out underneath me.

James raced around the vehicle to where I writhed on the ground. He helped me back into the jeep, his eyes flicking back and forth be-tween me, the open doors, and the wall of the castle above.

It was Hamilton that shrugged and tried the gambit, "Wow, Cap-tain, can you even walk on that thing?"

My foot felt like it was on fire. It throbbed up and down my leg and gripped painfully on my tendons, pulling them too tight. I wanted to say no. I needed to say no. But there, in the back of my head I heard every insult my drill instructor had heaped upon me in basic training.

I heard him call me Ichabod. "I can make it, but I have to go slow."

James looked up at the walls again, at the half severed eagle and broken swastika on the wall. "Slow is good, sir. I can handle slow."

Hamilton tried again. "Maybe we should go get you some real medical attention, sir?"

I did my best impression of Patton. "Move out, Private."

And while Hamilton grumbled, there was something in Martinez's eyes that may have been the tiniest little bit of respect. It was that more than anything that allowed me to lever myself to my feet. The pain washed over me again, but I was ready for it this time. I picked up my Thompson and motioned the soldiers toward the door.

When James spoke, I caught a note of sincere admiration. "Hoo dang, Cap'n, I guess you are a spy."

I took a step. I didn't pass out, but I wanted to.

The glorious façade outside was shattered once we cleared the massive front gates. Some enterprising B52 had come through here and dropped what appeared to be three bombs right on target. One had left the courtyard with an impromptu wading pond, one had blown a sizable chunk out of the north wall, and the last had found the south side of the keep. The entire side facing us had been scattered across the bailey, exposing the interior rooms to the elements. Recently, too.

I turned my attention to the exposed guts of the building, which was even more bizarre than I could have imagined. Every exposed floor looked like an amalgam of military barracks and a Knights of Columbus, or maybe a Masonic, Hall. Swastikas were everywhere, but instead of flags, they were on crests, shields, and carved into wood. I limped forward to get a closer look and my boot hit something with a 'clang'. It turned out to be a knight's helmet blown into the courtyard by the explosion. It was a weird mix of modern method and ancient design: rivets and highly polished steel and yet a very clear Waffen eagle stamped into the forehead.

What the hell had this place been?

Amongst the chest-sized stones flung from the bomb were numerous vehicles. The yard outside had several German trucks and Kübelwagens, a German motorcycle or two, an American jeep and an American halftrack. Even before the Allied platoon had arrived, this place had seen a lot of traffic.

I was wondering why when James snorted, "Speak of the devil, look, Shakespeare!"

Well, it probably wasn't Shakespeare, but it was a portrait of some Elizabethan scholar, noble, or rogue, amazingly intact and unmoved from the blast, clearly visible through a window-sized gap in a wall on the third floor. I made a mental note to visit that room, but before that I had to find the missing platoon.

"Hello?" I called.

Only Hamilton and James jumped, but all three of the men turned to give me dirty looks.

I shrugged and scowled at them, because I had no intention of exploring this place on a bad foot if I could avoid it. James and Martinez crept around the courtyard as I yelled once more at the open face of the castle, "Hello? I am Lieu—Captain Andrew of the United States Army...Hello? Is anybody there?"

Nothing.

With no direction from me, Hamilton patrolled from vehicle to vehicle, checking them each in turn. I'm not sure what he expected, but he tried to start a few of them up and got nothing more than dry wheezes in return.

"Out of gas...all of them." He hopped down and shrugged. Since nobody had come to find us, I had to check out (I was supposed to call it recon), the gate towers. Designed as a storeroom or gatehouse, it had only a door and no windows. I had to fumble with my Thompson until I could get out my flashlight and scan the corners. Inside there were stacks of American gear but no soldiers. I came back out and found everybody else...gone. I had a moment of sheer panic as I spun in a circle, right foot screaming as the stitches strained to hold the cut closed. My heart thundered like a mad metronome until the three of them popped up beyond a parked jeep at the corner of the yard and waved me over. "Here, Cap'n. Come see what Martinez found."

Fear rendered down into burning anger inside, a pool that smoldered as I limped the two dozen yards around to where he stood. But as I approached his crouched form, the sharp words at the tip of my tongue evaporated. Martinez held out a spent magazine in one hand, an even dozen snowy shells in the other. If I remembered correctly from boot, the combination said it was from a Browning automatic rifle.

"Someone had a firefight here, Cap'n."

He was right; the snow in this corner of the courtyard was trampled, carpeted with literally hundreds of empty shell casings, and spotted with more than two dozen magazines. James knelt while Martinez stood and examined the footprints with a trained eye born of long hours hunting in the woods. The walls, snow, and ground were splattered with dried blood. "Looks like he was surrounded—"

James stopped abruptly and dropped everything he was holding. He reached down, picked up a little red fragment of ceramic. I wondered what it had belonged to. *A cup? A bowl?* Then he turned it over, and I saw the patch of skin covered in regulation-length blond hair. James looked at me and I nodded, trembling.

"We have to get to the radio," I said, more bravely than I felt. He frowned, but he stood up and we all checked to make sure there were rounds in the chambers of our weapons. No matter where the artillery was raining down, there was no doubt we were now behind the lines, in enemy territory.

We crept across the yard to the collapsed section of castle wall. It was only the beginning of twilight, but it felt like ropes of thick, oily darkness were pressing in on all sides. The sensation was compounded by the castle proper, which cut off the sun with the suddenness of a guillotine. We both took out and turned on our electric torches, but they only illuminated the strangeness further.

In wreckage-strewn hallways, suits of Nazi-marked armor stood guard. The double thunderbolt of the SS and death's-heads appeared everywhere. On walls, ancient paintings were remade into a modern dystopia of red and black: Hitler in armor taking the sword from the Lady of the Lake; Nazi knights tilting (and winning) against dirty French and English freelances; glorious castles flying swastika pennants; Roman citizens giving straight-armed salutes to Caesar under Nazi flags.

I had spent my life studying the literature of these periods, and everything pictured here was patently false. A chill reached across me. Hitler was not just trying to subjugate Europe, but all of history as well.

We came across door after door leading to lecture halls, training rooms, and repair facilities. My modern German was sketchy, but they seemed to be teaching tailing and trailing, gathering intelligence, building up assets, and creating alternate identities, English, French, Spanish, and Russian. It seemed this place was a school for spies, which would make sense, but right next to these practical military rooms were machine shops for making and repairing medieval armor, classrooms set up to instruct in the proper methods for swinging a sword or using a lance. There was even a chapel that meshed Christian, Norse Pagan, and the deification of Hitler.

It washed over me all at once: This really wasn't a military base, it was a monastery, a cloister made to turn out monks whose prayer was deceit, and whose god bore a crooked cross.

"Cap'n?"

"Jimmy?"

I shut the door on the chapel and hurried as best I could down the hall toward James. Martinez's normally stern face looked cut from stone, now. Hamilton went to a corner to be quietly sick. A sour smell wafted to me, equal parts old milk and bad meat, it drew sharp claws across the back of my brain and whispered commands to turn and run. I had never smelt it before, but as I came closer I had no doubt of what I would find.

James was on his guard, rifle swinging back from one doorway to another in the large mess hall. Martinez settled his front sight on the opposing door and did not let it waver. Hamilton hung back in the hall-way, less conscious than I that there was nobody behind us anymore. James pointed toward a hasty barricade of flipped, bullet-riddled tables and then to a rather modern line of similarly damaged warming cabi-nets for serving food. I leaned heavily on the wall to take some load off my injured foot when my hand slapped into a light switch. I turned the thing, and the dusty, German-installed lights along the ceiling coughed into life.

"Well the generator's got fuel, at least." James tried to sound cheer-ful, but failed.

I limped to the counter and peered over, immediately choking down on what little food was left in my stomach as my eyes took in a battle-chewed body. He was bloated and torn, Thompson dropped like a bro-ken toy. His nametag and bars stood like a tombstone marking him Lieutenant Ritter. Then James pointed at the overturned tables. I painstakingly shuffled over there and found another body. This one was Sergeant Keller. I gimped my way back to James, who was also looking quite green. Even with the enhanced light, I felt the need to whisper, "I don't get it. Who were they shooting at?"

James gave me a long look, swallowing hard as he squared his lantern jaw. We both startled as Martinez growled at us both, "Captain, they were shooting at each other."

I looked toward Ritter's last stand, then to Keller. Indeed, they had been, but why? I motioned the privates on, and they were no less grateful to leave than I. Unfortunately, we only found more of the same. A Private Moore was impaled to a door by way of a bayonet through his chest. Scrawled in blood beside him were the words: 'Dirty Traiter'. Another room was burned to a crisp, the bodies of two soldiers, blackened beyond recognition, locked in a battle even in death. I saw their American-made helmets, and simply shut the door. Room after room, floor after floor, body after body, it became clear that nobody out of this platoon had survived. I was almost heartened when I found the radio set up on the top floor, but Hamilton reached behind and came out holding its innards in his hand. We'd have to leave if we were to make a report, and leaving was foremost on my mind. A nagging voice at the back of my skull reminded me I had not found Shakespeare, but with so many bodies about, it was easy to ignore. We were almost to the stairs when a warbling cry reached us.

"Help! Help me!"

We all froze, and Hamilton looked at me again, eyes wide. It didn't seem fair that this was my decision. I didn't want to go looking any more than they did. James was built like a mountain, Martinez was probably a crack shot, and Hamilton at least had two good feet. I could not ignore that one of our countrymen was out there, and he needed us. It came again, the words distinct, the gender and age muzzy, the direction hazy: "Help! Help me!"

I gritted my teeth and silently pointed James down one hallway, sent Martinez down the nearby stairs, and Hamilton up another, then took the other hall for myself. James went, Martinez made a face speaking volumes of his thoughts on my plan, and I didn't even give Hamilton a chance to complain before I limped off. The more I thought about it, the less I liked splitting up our group, but whoever was out there needed help as fast as we could get there. None of us considered calling out any longer, however. Abandoned rooms stood like empty tombs on either side, stone sarcophagi within which mad dreams languished.

The unknown dogface may have sounded like a lost and frightened child, Thompson gunfire, however, sounds like nothing else.

I spun and tried to run, foot screaming in protest as silk thread cut through flesh, opening the wound on my right foot, which bled freely. Debilitating waves of pain washed up my leg and squeezed my bladder. It seized up my whole side, but the sound of hot, fat forty-five caliber rounds spurred me on.

I limped into an eating hall where James spun in a circle trying to get a fix on the gunfire, when it stopped. He caught sight of me and almost got his rifle to his shoulder before he saw it was me. Instead he looked down each of the dozens of corridors in turn, nonplussed.

For my part I stayed as still as possible, letting the agony from my foot just wash over me. Then I noticed James was pointing his gun at me again. I hardly dared to breathe as the seconds expanded into eternity. Only once his expression dissolved into incredulous frustration and he moved his rifle to indicate '*You should be anywhere else.*' The sound of boots pounding on the stone floor pierced the fog in my head.

I stumbled away from the doorway as Hamilton exploded into the room. Arms flailing, weaponless, he had no idea we were there until he had taken five giant strides into the room. He somehow managed to come to an instant stop when he caught sight of the Kentucky private and his Garand, but he was so scared he was obviously still running on the inside.

"Private?" I tried, to no response. "Private? PRIVATE!"

Hamilton started, and seemed to see me for the first time as James lowered his rifle. His mouth flapped uselessly for a moment until a touch of color returned to his cheeks, but his voice brought no comfort, "Martinez is dead."

"Dead?"

He nodded. "Shot by a Thompson."

Losing our most experienced member was like being punched in the gut. Worse, the man had died doing what I had told him to do. I was the one who had split up our effort. I was responsible for his death. "Who? How?"

"I don't know, but somebody's out there, and they are going to kill us, Captain. We have got to get out of here." And he glared at me, daring me to deny it.

"OK. I have a plan."

From behind me, came the question, "What is it?"

Even with my foot creating a bloody swamp in my boot, even with Hamilton having a good three yards head start, I took cover behind Private James first. But when it turned out to be Martinez coming out of the passage, my terror turned to waves of anger. I got a hold of myself enough to keep from screaming, but there was no doubt of my murderous rage as I growled like a drill instructor at Hamilton, "The Pee Eff Cee looks pretty alive to me, Hamilton."

But Hamilton looked like he was seeing a ghost. He was even trembling slightly, paying no attention to me whatsoever. "He was dead," he whispered with a conviction near religious.

I turned to Martinez. "What happened?"

The swarthy man shrugged. "I was tracking down the voice and I fell over a body holding a Thompson, and the damn thing went off. I was sure one of those forty-fives had my name on it, but I'm still here."

Which is the most I had ever heard Martinez say. I glowered at Hamilton, giving him an expression that said *'Well, there you are'*.

"No. No. No. What happened to his coat?"

And it was true, the coat he was wearing was different, but Martinez let loose with a sour expression and spit into the corner, "I fell onto a dead body. It's ruined, covered in rotting blood."

I hobbled over to Hamilton but when he looked at me, I could have seen his irises through the eyes of needles. "This place is dark. There are bodies everywhere. I understand being scared, private, but we have a job to do and we are going to do it."

Hamilton was adamant. "He was dead, sir."

"Well, soldier, it looks like he's made a miraculous recovery." I backed away. "You and Martinez go north. See if you can find the voice, and if you happen to pick up a rifle, that would be good. James you're coming with me."

Hamilton started, realizing I had paired him with the dead guy. "Wait, why do you get Jimmy?"

I hooked a thumb at the massive Kentucky boy. "Because if I have to run after another wild goose chase I'm going to need someone to carry me."

"What if I need a weapon?"

I took a deep breath and tried hard not to let my injury bow me too far. "Private, there's nothing to shoot here."

And yet, as James and I left Hamilton and Martinez, the words of my long destroyed orders played through my head.... *REPORTS OF GROSS INSUBORDINATION WITHIN THE UNIT, INSTIGATED BY POSSIBLE ENEMY AGENTS – PERSON OR PERSONS UNKNOWN – WHICH HAS RESULTED IN CASUALTIES...*but the further I hobbled on a bad foot, the less and less I believed that this was some poltergeist or Deutschland superman, as the OSS implied, and just a case of plain old combat fatigue. We had been here less than an hour and Hamilton was already skittish. In another week, it was very likely that he'd start shooting at us with very little provocation. I was ready to make one more circuit of the damnable place and call it a day.

We came to a heavy door and James opened it. I frowned but he just shrugged. "We're still searching for that voice, right, sir?"

The disembodied voice, the one thing I had allowed myself to forget with Martinez's resurrection. I nodded an apology and waved for him to proceed, but it became obvious we were in a section of the castle that had not seen human presence for a while. The thin layer of dust exposed no human movement, or American GI exploration, but James went in anyway.

Room after room passed that way until far into the night. I began to secretly hate James a bit, both for his good feet and his limitless stamina. I cursed the heavy Thompson, and finally wound up slinging it over my shoulder. Finally, I could take it no more. "Where are we, Private?"

"We're almost back to the hall where we split from the others, I reckon."

"Once we get back there, we can meet up and get out of this place." James looked relieved that we were not even considering staying here the night. I momentarily felt bad I did not have plans to bury our American dead, but we'd be back with people better with shovels than ourselves. It was just then I discovered the advantage—perhaps the only advantage—of being in command was being able to make a command decision. "On second thought, let's just go, Private."

James' gap-toothed smile shone like the sun. "Roger-roger, Cap'n."

Like a dog on a leash, James used his long legs to get ahead, then even farther ahead. The corridors were punctuated with lights in Prussian precision, so I could easily see him ahead, but he was not slowing down.

Maybe it was that distance that caused me to take greater note of my surroundings. Whatever sharpened my eyes, the darkened corridor stood out like a picture of Shakespeare in a Nazi castle. I paused at the mouth of a dark spur James getting farther away as I fumbled with my electric torch. It clicked on like the snickering of a devil, and illuminated the passage beyond.

Ice water sluiced across every inch of my skin, and I could not feel my foot, the flashlight in my hand, or the scream I choked back from the edge of my throat. Once I swallowed the shriek, the words that followed were supernaturally calm. "James, get to Hamilton."

The farm boy turned around and saw how far behind I had dropped.

"James, get to Hamilton," I said again, voice rung out of all impression and expression.

Then he was there, beside me. James looked from my face, to the light, then followed the beam a dozen feet down the corridor to where Martinez lay, his body riddled with forty-five caliber wounds. Hours-old blood had clotted and turned black on the coat he had been wearing when we got to the castle. Completely on automatic, I repeated, "James, get to Hamilton."

And he was off, weapon in hand, a mountain of muscle moving like a Greek demigod. I struggled to keep up as he called out Hamilton's name, but within seconds he was out of sight, losing me again in the damnable echo-chamber of this house of the dead. I tamped down on the waves of pain coming up my leg and forced myself to run a few steps before I almost blacked out. That's when someone fired a Thompson again.

The massive, concussive blast of 30-06 bullets answered the Thompson, letting me know James or Hamilton was still alive and he was fighting. The Thompson stuttered to silence as I came around the corner to a staircase.

There was a slight pause, then the musical *ting!* of a spent Garand magazine hitting the floor for only an instant before James had his rifle blazing once more. I took up a half run again, misery blurring my vision as I brought up my Thompson. I definitely felt something important rip in my foot this time. I began to shout to my man, "James! Private! I'm coming! JAMES?!"

I got to the intersection and then something big and soft collided with me. We went down in a tangle of guns and limbs, two submachine guns went skittering over the edge and down to the second floor. I spent untold seconds in blinding agony from my foot, but when I looked up, I went numb with shock.

I was looking at me.

I remember my exact thought at that moment: *So this is what it's like to go insane.*

Then James stopped shooting and ran toward us, the sound of his boots echoing off of the walls.

Instantly, my simulacrum was on me. He slapped and punched, sending stars swirling in front of my eyes as his insanely strong hands ripped away my insignia. He kicked me in the stomach and grabbed my nametag, suddenly sharp nails ripping it from my chest and tossing it away. I pushed him off just as James came around the corner, faced with two of me lying on the floor, bleeding and panting. His eyes flicked back and forth between my doppelganger and myself before raising the barrel of his rifle to point between us.

My opposite painfully stood up, favoring his left leg.

I did the same.

I cleared my throat. "Private James, it's me."

The other me shook his head, then spoke with my voice: "Jimmy? It's me, Jimmy. Captain Andrew? The spy?"

Jimmy James shook his head like a horse bit by a bug. His barrel shifted toward me as my mind raced. Had I ever called James by his first name inside the castle? Had I ever mentioned being a spy? Had we been watched all this time? My mouth was filled with cotton, my head empty. I tried to think of something, anything that would get Private James to trust me. My mouth moved, but nothing came out.

The copy took a shuffling, apparently painful step forward, hands in plain sight, trying to speak soothingly. "Remember Shakespeare, Jimmy?"

James nodded, and his rifle centered firmly on my chest. "Yeah, Shakespeare."

I saw him aim; I could almost feel his finger tightening on the trigger. Whole new levels of fear raced through me, electric arcs that slowed time to a crawl as everything became very clinical, detached. Jimmy had rivulets of sweat moving down his face. A near miss with the Thompson had left a perfectly round hole in his Army-issue coat under his arm, missing him by less than an inch. Behind him, spread in several parts of the corridor, was Hamilton's body. It had been pulled apart like a cooked chicken, tendons and muscle messily trailing from wounds caused by nothing more than strength I could hardly comprehend. Then the reality of my death, and worse, the death of my men came to me all in a second and the magnitude of my failure collapsed inside my head. Clouds of fear flowed through me and I lost bladder control.

James heard the trickle, glanced down, and immediately shifted his sights to the fake me. He yanked the trigger, blowing the counterfeit captain, well the *other* counterfeit captain, back. He did it again, and again. Watching the private pump round after round into someone who looked just like me was surreal, and I found I didn't have the where-withal to move as the bullets rocketed right past me. Blood flew from the thing's wounds like macabre flowers. I swear, deep inside the crimson blossoms, golden flecks glittered. The eighth bullet slammed into the neck of the bogus me, pushing him the last foot and over the railing. He disappeared over the edge and down the stairs where he landed with the sound of a discarded bag of meat. James' empty clip hit the ground with a musical tone.

James reloaded like a flash, bounded forward and leveled his smoking Garand over the railing. He looked for three long seconds before nodding grimly. "He came down the hallway, lookin' like you, wavin' and smilin' 'fore he opened fire. I thought you had just gone loony like the whole platoon."

Slowly facts began to swirl in my head, and though I didn't have the pattern yet, I felt the tide pull me along and wash away some of the confusion.

Jimmy handed me my glasses from the floor, slapped me on the shoulder and brought me back to his words. "That was some quick thinkin', Cap'n! Peein' yourself like that so I'd see the pool of blood around your boot. You're one hell of a spy, sir!"

But all I could do was shake and shudder, words echoing inside my skull:...*person or persons unknown*...Sixty seconds spanned into infinity before I could ask, "Is it dead?"

James gave a bitter, lopsided smile as he went back to the railing. "Sure 'nuff. Martinez and Hamilton'd be proud. Got him in the gut, chest, and neck with eight rounds of Uncle Sam's finest. He's deader than dog...." His words lost conviction as he finished, "Shit."

I limped next to him and followed his gaze downward. The stairs were soaked in blood, but otherwise empty.

James began to shake as well. "Jeezus, Mary, and Joseph. Cap'n! What is that thing?"

I shook my head. "I don't know, but I don't think it wants us to get out of here alive."

"But if at least one of us gets out then we can bring back a huge group and wipe it out."

"No, they tried that the first time. It infiltrated their ranks and had them shooting one another in days."

"So what d'we do?"

We had searched the entire castle, and found no clue as to the identity of the creature. We had been everywhere, everywhere except— "We need to find Shakespeare."

"Shakespeare?"

"The picture! The picture of Shakespeare, we never found it. The answer has to be there. We have to find that room!"

"How?"

I gazed up into the country boy's eyes, understanding the fear there even as I told him in quiet tones what had to happen. He quickly got my gun from downstairs and I checked to make sure the safety was off and the chamber loaded.

"But Cap'n, bullets don't kill it."

"But they do hurt it. Use enough and you'll buy time to get away. As soon as I can find how to kill it, I'll come join you and we'll try to get away."

He didn't like it, but he hefted his rifle and ran off. All I could think was: *That is one, fine soldier.*

For my part, I limped toward the bomb-ravaged side of the castle. The wall was gone, and I dared not get too close to the edge. I was no engineer but I was willing to bet that the floor might collapse at any second.

I tried to watch every direction at once, but it wasn't until James appeared in the courtyard that I began to really breathe again. He clambered onto the roof of a truck cab so I could see him, and flashed his hand torch three times in the prearranged signal. I flashed back. Then he scanned the third floor until he found the window-sized break in the interior wall. He flashed twice, and I followed the beam of his light. I found the wall of the suspect room easily enough, but I wasn't happy with the idea of going out toward the broken edge to get to the hole. Instead I opted for limping deeper into the structure, following the wall to find the door. Every step erupted in a chorus of pain, but once I got back to the open-air broken wall, I had found no door whatsoever. James shrugged at me and I mimicked him back. I tried again, but no door materialized when I had come around to where I had started.

I sighed, and nearly cried, as I began shuffling toward James and out into no man's land. I stayed close to the wall, figuring that would be the place where strength would be at its highest. Truthfully, I should have leapt down, should have run away, should have jumped into the jeep and smiled like a madman as I puked all the way back to the American lines. Somewhere, somehow, I felt the shades of Hamilton and Martinez watching over me. To abandon this mission now would feel like the worst kind of failure. I may have been a fake captain, but I didn't have to be a fake human being.

I crept slowly, carefully, around under the naked sky only yards from the edge that plunged three long stories to the rubble below. I was so focused on down, I forgot completely about up until James yelled to me. I glanced, saw the hole, and began to climb painfully through.

It was not wide, nor was it even, so I shouldn't be surprised that my Thompson caught on the edge. I tried to lever myself though, tried again, and finally I had to slip the Thompson off of my shoulder. I maneuvered, fumbled, and finally watched in horror as the heavy weapon slid through my tired fingers.

It hit the block below with a sharp crack, and then a dozen stones groaned and fell into the waiting abyss. I leaned forward like a madman as the blocks tumbled away, crashing into the finely appointed office as a large part of the wall I had just come through disappeared into the night. I would have watched it go, I really would have, if I hadn't landed on my right foot and nearly passed out.

When I came to, James waved like he was seeing the President for the first time. I waved back tiredly and got slowly, ever so slowly, to my feet. I tried the light switch. Nothing. Cursing, I pulled out my hand torch and turned it on. I managed not to scream like a girl scout when the light illuminated the face in the painting, but I think it had more to do with fatigue than fortitude. This close I could see it was, indeed, a portrait of The Bard himself. While I puzzled that I studied the plaque at the bottom of the frame. It read:

'Ich werde mit Ihnen kaufen, mit Ihnen, Gespräch mit Ihnen, Spaziergang mit Ihnen, und so im Anschluss an verkaufen, aber ich werde mit Ihnen, Getränk mit Ihnen nicht essen, noch mit Ihnen beten.' – Shylock der Jude, Großhändler Venedigs, Gesetz I

Modern Language. Not my area. But just beneath it, on a small table sat another book titled *Ein Sonnenwende-Nachttraum* by William Shakespeare I opened it and saw THESEUS and HIPPOLYTA amidst the German. This was *A Midsummer Night's Dream.* I flipped through it. The pages where PUCK appeared were dog-eared. *What the...?*

Putting it down, I continued my investigation of the room. I found a German bolt-action rifle lying dejected in the corner. I checked the chamber, and found it empty. *Well, at least it's a club.* I slung it over my shoulder.

Next was a lever set into a blank space of wall. *You have to be kidding me.* I pulled it, and the blank wall swung open nearly silently. *A secret door? A REAL secret door?*

My eyes trailed around the covert office, landing less than a heartbeat later on an entire bookshelf, stuffed full of works that spanned from simply worn to truly ancient. I flipped through a few in awe. Many of them were handwritten, illuminated, and written in languages with which I had spent three years becoming intimately familiar.

'...COMMAND HOLDS THE POSITION THAT YOU HAVE UNIQUE QUALIFICATIONS VITAL TO THE SUCCESS OF THIS MISSION...'

The sons of bitches knew.

The Voyage of Bran by Meyer Kuno, *Faerie and Folk Tales of the Irish Peasantry* by W. B. Yeats, *The Druid Path* by Marah Ellis Ryan, *Pagan Papers* by Kenneth Grahame...More and more, in languages from English, to German, Occitan, to Latin, Old English, or Middle English. All of them about legends, or more precisely: Faeries.

The sons of bitches knew, and they didn't tell us.

Followed closely by a thought in Captain Blanco's voice: *Would you have believed them?*

I turned around and scanned the desk, which was full of reports of all kinds. I opened the center drawer and found two stripper clips of rifle bullets and two magazines for a German pistol I did not have. I pocketed the rifle ammo absently as I attacked the side compartments. I had to break one open with the butt of my new rifle but inside I found four more books, with any luck the four I was looking for. Each one of them was heavily dog-eared. Each page so marked dealt with changelings.

I opened one ancient, handwritten journal, the hand-printed vellum pages greasy in my hand. I scanned the first entry, effortlessly translating the words out of Occitan in my head.

'*The Changelyng is a nefarious creature, the offspring of an elfe that is brought by stealth and malice into a home where it is left in place of a newborn human child. The childe is then spirited away to be the servant of the Queen of the Faeries.*'

I had read these words before. Months ago, in Boston, in the office of my dead professor. Mr. Smith had brought an exact copy of this tome to me and I had translated this exact passage for him.

'*It is said that Changelyngs can be identified by a wizened visage, but this is a falsehood. When not killed in an oven, Changelyngs are oft left with elderly relatives by distraught parents, and the child grows to resemble these aged people...*'

I stopped reading and began scanning the first few lines of each paragraph. The copy Smith had brought was incomplete. This one had additional entries that went far beyond what he had paid to have rendered into English.

'...as it ages, its powers of mimicry shall grow, and will upon adulthood be able to copy any sound, face, or mannerism it observes...'

As my eyes sluiced over the words, visions of some otherworldly creature unspooled in my head. A fae creature stealing into a German home, taking a newborn babe, leaving something else behind...

'... malicious temper...wiser than human children...'

Was it given up willingly by the parents? Was it claimed by the Socialist government? With all the breeding programs and Aryan purity checks in Hitler's Germany it was sure to be discovered. Did anyone ever regret never putting it in an oven?

'...strength of thirteen men...an appetite that cannot be sated...'

Still here after so long? And then I realized the total sum of the horror. This child, brought from an alien crib to one of our own, was given to a government that would only see use of its full talents in pursuit of world domination. They would have suckled the child on propaganda, making its whole world revolve around the Nazi party and the hellish charisma of Adolph Hitler.

It was a super weapon, a natural-born spy that could go anywhere, steal anything, *become* anyone. The damage it could do would be incalculable, but then, before its training was done, the war blew past it on wings and treads. Now it was like this castle: broken and useless except as a monument to a conflict future generations would never truly understand. What else could it do, with its only tie to the outside world a political party on the verge of death?

And then I heard the gunshot.

I sprang to the window, but my right foot finally gave up completely. It skidded out from underneath me and I cracked my jaw on the new lip of the ragged hole. I tasted blood as I shook my head to clear it of stars. Below, Private Jimmy J. James was fighting for his life.

The creature was fast, so fast. Still dressed in the ragged uniform of an American soldier, it seemed to fly from shadow to shadow, from behind a door to behind a wall, behind a jeep to behind a truck. Jimmy was desperately trying to keep up, emptying his weapon, slamming rounds into the breach, and then emptying it again. He was calling to me, screaming for me to help.

I picked up the book beside me and continued to read.

'...of all weapons steel, copper, and bronze are of no use. One must find an aged blade of pure iron, to cause permanent harm to such a devilish creature. Even then, only by the Grace of the LORD our GOD shall thou prevail.'

I read that last bit again. *Iron? Where in the hell do I get IRON?*

The gunshots stopped. I heard Jimmy yelp, "Captain?!"

I glanced out the hole, and saw the changeling on the hood of the truck, hands on Jimmy's rifle where they struggled over it like a quarterstaff. Over six feet tall, a mountain of sausage-gravy fed muscle, his face was already flushed as he bent every ounce of power to the battle. The faerie wasn't even breathing hard. Its face melted into Jimmy's own, and he grinned nastily at the private.

Iron-Iron-Iron-Iron?

And then a weight shifted in my pocket, poking me with sharp teeth. Mindlessly, I reached in and pulled out the thin metal clip holding five rifle cartridges in a single line.

The bullets looked odd, dull, black.

Iron. Because in the office of the guy who trained the damned thing Hitler would be sure that there was a way to put it down.

I took the rifle off of my back and opened it up. The changeling pulled viciously and kicked Jimmy in the stomach. The air *whuffed* out of him but still he did not let go. The stripper in my hand settled neatly into a clearly made notch at the breach. In the back of my head, my drill instructor was screaming at me to work the bolt faster, to assemble the damn thing blindfolded, to breathe-release-aim-squeeze. Already my hands were shaking because I never was any good at any of those things.

I pushed the rounds into the weapon with one thumb as the creature pushed the Garand into Jimmy's face. I thought the crunching-celery sound meant his nose was broken. The bolt refused to close as I tried to push it again and again. I cursed bitterly, removed the stripper and tossed it aside. I slammed the bolt home.

Below, the changeling slung the butt of Jimmy's rifle around and smacked the private in the face. James went off the far side of the truck like a doll and into the shadows.

The creature spun the ten-pound rifle like a baton and shouldered it as I aligned my sights on his body. All the while, all I could think was: *I'm a crappy rifleman. I'm a crappy rifleman. I'm a crappy rifleman.*

And immediately, every joke, every cuff, every abuse of boot camp came back in an unending wave. They called me Ichabod. Ichabod Crane. I lined up the sights, front post on the target, between the back leafs and even across the top. I felt the trigger beneath my finger tighten, tighten.

The changeling pointed the rifle at the man under my command, the last man for whom I was responsible, the only survivor of my series of blunders, the only man who had unfailingly supported my command. I might have been a fake spy. I might have been a fake captain. I refused to be a fake soldier any more.

The trigger snapped cleanly. The rifle spoke loudly.

The 8 millimeter bullet entered the changeling's back and blew out his front. The fountain that followed was a stream of pure gold that sparkled and shredded into stars in the air. I racked the bolt and sighted again. The next blew out his left knee, and he fell on the roof, but still would not die. I racked the bolt again.

With palpable malevolence, the thing turned to stare at me, eyes glowing with a silver light that gave no warmth. A hum distorted the air around his head like a halo, building in intensity and shattering the windows in an expanding circle coming closer and closer. The vibrations from the hellish thing rattled my teeth and caused cracks to spread across my abused glasses. It raised the M-1 Garand in one hand and pointed it at me. I adjusted the sights on the warbling image of his distorted skull and pulled the trigger.

The creature exploded with the force of an artillery shell. The truck collapsed, windows shattering in a sparkling rain. Jimmy tumbled end over end away from the blast.

Golden stars burst out in every direction and the whole castle shuddered, shedding blocks into the courtyard. The room I was in bucked and rocked. Instinctively, I rolled back from the edge as more stones tumbled down and out of sight. A cascade of ceiling pieces gnashed at my retreating feet. I scuttled back further, further, as chest, table, and shelves spilled off the encroaching edge of oblivion. I crawled faster, clawing along seams in the floor while everything spilled outward, finally taking the desk and dumping into a pile of falling stone anvils. I clocked my head against the wall and sprang onto my feet. Bloody footprints disappeared in front of me as the edge came closer and closer, leaving me nothing to do but press into the edge of the wall and watch. The floor's decay became slower, and slower. Then it stopped, leaving me a tiny shelf to stand on as the frigid winter air washed over me.

Stars swam in front of my eyes when I remembered to breathe. Finally all I could do was stand there in the corner, set my head against the cold wall to my rear, and just hurt for a while. I had never mastered the military skill of sleeping standing up until that very moment.

I came awake with a start. Part of the wall swung inward, exposing Private Jimmy James beyond with his hand on the concealed catch. I nodded my thanks and smiled at him. He looked ruffled, torn, and the side of his face was swelled up like he had an orange in his cheek, but he was alive.

He helped me off the ledge and we sat down tiredly. It took several seconds of awkward silence until he could figure how to make himself understood around the lump on his face, "Hell of a shot."

"Yeah, they teach you that in spy school." My smile got a touch wider. "Happy to oblige, Private James."

"Shee...knew...git you.... talkin' proper 'fore.... too long."

I chuckled and just sat there, waiting for my foot to stop hurting, or at least until it stopped making me want to pass out.

But a shadow passed over his face as he asked, "Uh, Cap'n? What if sheresh two of shem?"

This time, I was sure my look could crack stone. "Shut your mouth, Private."

We made it back to an army camp sometime the next morning. The day after that, four platoons and intelligence specialists were back at Monté le Ciel. The heroes were buried.

Apparently, Hitler was dead, the war all but over, but all I was authorized to do was lay in a French hospital and try to fight off the raging infection that had set in the wound on my left foot. Private James was made Sergeant and given a cushy job in Briton. People in the know who spoke of him mentioned OSS...the rest of them just said 'spy'.

I had spent weeks studying the books I had caged from Monté le Ciel, becoming one of the world's foremost experts on faerie kind, I'm sure. I only set them aside once I received a letter from Captain Blanco.

'You succeeded where a large group surely would have failed. Your skills indeed proved invaluable to your country and the war effort....'

I read through the congratulations, and the promise of a top-secret commendation or three, but it was the last line that meant most to me:

'...So, Lieutenant, how did you take to the role of spy?'

I snatched up a pen to send back my reply, hastily scrawled on the bottom of his message.

'I don't know about being a spy, but I think I finally have the hang of soldier, sir.'

I sent the letter back and laid down for some well-deserved rest.

I dreamt the dreams of the just.

AᴛＴＨＥ Gʀᴀssʜᴏᴘᴘᴇʀ's Hɪʟʟ

Robert E. Waters

September, 1847. Near Mexico City.

Church bells brought Lubbick to Molino del Rey, but it was the scent of human blood that drew him to the barn. The pixie wiggled his long, sharp nose, guided his raven, Spindle, through a maze of wooden rafters, and touched down lightly on an oak beam scorched black with the heat and soot of fire. He sniffed again, and this time he could sense something more, something sinister and magical, something that he had not felt since the days of Montezuma II.

Word had reached General Winfield Scott that the Mexicans were violating their ceasefire by melting down church bells for new cannons, and Old Fuss and Feathers wanted it checked out. The general was tired of giving Santa Anna yet another reprieve to regroup and solidify his defenses in Mexico City. The final assault would come, and it would come soon, right here, at the foot of the Grasshopper's Hill: the massive rock fortress of Chapultepec.

Climbing out of Spindle's saddle and crouching on the charred beam, Lubbick felt that anxious feeling he often got right before battle. He was not afraid of war—or death. He had ridden to battle on the shoulders of great men: Alexander of Macedonia, Charlemagne, Genghis Kahn, Napoleon. He had killed scores of humans and *fae* alike in pitched combat. But what was happening below in the shadows made him angry. He wiped sandy grime from his face, took a deep breath, and leaned forward to view the awful scene.

The barn had been raked clean and a pit dug into its hard, dry ground. Around the pit, humans and *fae*, dressed in rich

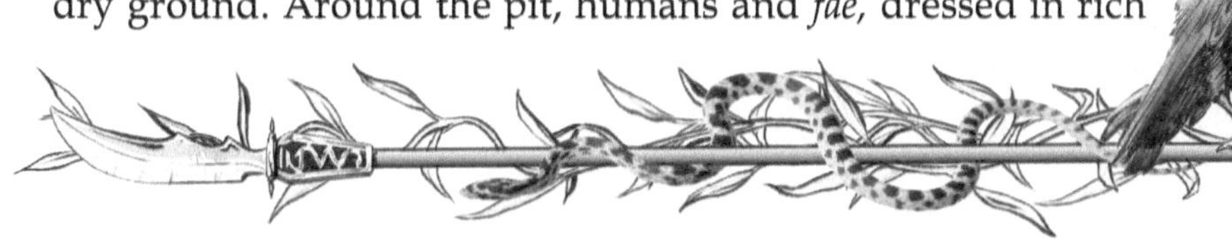

robes of blood red and gold, with eagle feathers tucked into headdresses and jaguar pelts over shoulders, stood with arms raised as if they were gathered in a revival tent in Alabama. But the raspy whispers escaping their mouths were not praise to a Christian Almighty. Lubbick strained to hear the faint words as they were spoken. *Nahuatl*. Without question. The ancient language of the Aztecs. What the words meant, however, Lubbick did not know. In his brief time with Hernán Cortez, he had picked up some simple phrases, but that was hundreds of years ago.

In the pit sat a simple stone altar, carved from crude granite. Over it lay an American soldier, dazed and brutalized, his blue coat and white shirt ripped away to expose his chest and stomach. His flesh had been scrubbed and shaved clean, but across his arms and shoulders dozens of tiny cuts leaked blood. He had obviously been bled near death and sustained only for this final moment.

Three other American soldiers knelt beside the altar, huddled in chains on the hard ground, their mouths wrapped tightly in blood-soaked bandanas. Though bruised, starved, and exhausted, they held their heads high in defiance, though Lubbick could see the fear in their eyes. He allowed a smile to cross his mouth. They were fine, *fine* men.

Beside the large stone altar lay another, smaller one, carved from granite and seemingly made for a mouse. On it laid a female pixie, bereft of clothing, her arms and legs tied to the altar base. Over her hovered a small imp, its red skin and horned face glowing with magical zeal and lust. Lubbick moved to the right to get a better look at the figure standing over the American soldier.

A human, certainly, covered head to toe in a pitch black robe, its hood pulled so far over the wearer's head as to obscure the light from a nearby kerosene lamp. The human wavered on sandaled feet, voicing the same Nahuatl being chanted around the pit. In its hand was a knife, black-bladed and sparkling like glass. Lubbick's eyes closed to tiny slits as he watched the figure turn and twist to a rhythm that only it could hear. It waved the blade in circles over the American's chest. Then, sharply, the figure stopped, howled the word, "Titlacauan!", and thrust its arms into the air. The thick sleeves of the robe fell down, exposing long, slender arms. A spike of light revealed the figure's face: Pale with thin black lips, dark Egyptian eye shadow, and teeth filed to sharp points. Lubbick knew her well.

Zarqa.

He leaped, like a lynx, onto Spindle's back. The raven responded in a shake of black feathers. Lubbick locked his boots into the stirrups, pulled on the reins, and drew an enchanted sword made from the rib-bone of a Mississippi catfish. He leaned into Spindle, patted the bird's long neck, and whispered, "Go for the knife, old friend."

Spindle squawked and launched, his large wings beating the smoky air. Lubbick held on tight, his sword raised high. He barreled toward the arm, his eyes fixed on the ancient sorceress. She had turned the knife down, and with both hands drove the sharp tip toward the breast bone. But just as it punctured the soldier's skin, Spindle slammed into her arm and sent the knife clattering across the stone altar and into the dirt. Lubbick slashed at Zarqa's wrist, found exposed flesh, and opened it to the bone.

Spindle tumbled but managed to keep his wings. He flew up and out of the pit. The sorceress screamed and struck out at the bird, nicking Spindle's tail-feathers and spinning him round. The inertia of the blow forced Lubbick's boots from the stirrups and he lost his hold on the reins. He twisted out of the saddle and flew through the air, tumbling over and over.

He generally kept his powers in check around humans; some grew nervous when he blinked in and out of sight, or flew through the air, or threw tiny fire balls from his hands, or set a candle aflame with a whistle. Blinking and flying through vast spaces was exhausting and drained his powers faster than he preferred; it was always best to ride a bird or some other kind of creature for distance travel. But in the current situation, that concern was moot. Lubbick blinked and immediately stopped tumbling through the air. He blinked again and reappeared in the pit, face to face with the crazed imp.

The creature pulsated light as flames flickered along the hot veins roping its dry ashen body. Lubbick could smell sulfur and molten rock oozing from its brittle skin. It was a construct of lava, no doubt forged out of the Pedregal lava field near Coyoacan. Only a sorceress as skilled as Zarqa could have made such a fiend. It roared and belched fire at Lubbick. The pixie thrust his free hand forward and shouted, "*Agua frio!*" A line of clear water sprang from his palm and doused the flame, sending sparks and black smoke swirling between them. The imp tried desperately to move away from the cold spout, but the water connected squarely in its chest. It shook as its veins popped and steamed. Lubbick propelled himself into the rafters. Below, the imp exploded.

The blast showered the room with shards, smoke, and fire. *Did it kill the Americans?* Lubbick wondered as he drifted above the chaos. But they weren't fighting conscripted Mexican soldiers having a bit of fun. This was Zarqa and her retinue of imps, boggarts, bogles, and knockers. This was a death room, and let death take it! If a couple of Scott's men fell in this service, they were heroes. Lubbick spit ash from his mouth, whipped his sword through the air to freshen its edge, and blinked.

He stood on the altar. Two American soldiers lay still and quiet on the ground. They had taken shards in the throat and face and were unrecognizable in a pool of blood. The other two were trying to free their hands and feet but were having trouble with the solid chain links. Lubbick swooped between them and drove his sword through the chains, cutting them like butter. White light flew off the enchanted bone sword as it sliced the metal clean. The chains fell to the ground.

"Get the hell out of here!" Lubbick said to the Americans as he turned to look for Spindle in the smoke.

"What about Johnson and Riley?" One of the soldiers said, pointing to the fellows on the ground.

"They're dead! And you will be too from my own blade if you don't move. Now go! That's an order."

The soldiers scrambled out of the pit.

He protected their retreat, and when they were safely out of the barn and away, Lubbick rose above the smoke. He smiled.

Spindle had survived the blast. The old bird was gouging out the eyes of a boggart just a few yards away. The pasty little goblin tried to shield itself from the sharp claws and thick, cutting beak. But Spindle had lived almost as long as Lubbick; he knew where to strike and how hard. The matter was over quickly; the boggart dropped like a lead ball and dissolved into dust.

Through the chaos of Mexican soldiers and faeries making for exits, Lubbick caught dark movement out of the corner of his eye. He turned, blinked, and came to rest in front of the sorceress. Zarqa stopped. Their paths had crossed enough over the centuries—she knew as well as he that it was futile to run. She lowered her hood and let her long, brilliant black hair flow down to her waist.

By the stars, she was beautiful. Lubbick had to admit it. The green sparkle in her eyes, the curve of her mouth as she smiled tenderly. Her perfect teeth, filed down to fine points like a jaguar. Her nostrils flared energy; her cheeks bloomed full rose-red. She was the perfect mix of human and *fae*. A rare thing indeed; one of only a few in the world. And one of the nastiest, most clever, and heartless creatures Lubbick had ever known.

"I thought I left you dead at Brandywine," Lubbick said, hovering before her.

"And I thought you froze to death in Russia," she replied in that dark, husky voice that Lubbick had once loved.

"The Emperor and I escaped...thankfully."

"Only to fight and lose another day, eh?" Zarqa chuckled. "Why are you here with the *gringos*, Lubbick? Are your pickings so slim?"

Lubbick squeezed the hilt of his sword to calm his mind. "I like winning."

"There's no guarantee that they will win."

Lubbick shrugged. "Their odds are better than half. But more importantly, what brings you so far south, chica? I thought you preferred colder climes."

Zarqa raised her arms to feign innocence. "I'm merely assisting my Mexican brothers and sisters against this unprovoked war of American imperialism."

She giggled, but Lubbick ignored her attempt to draw him into a political debate. War, indeed, was politics, and politics war. One could hardly separate the two, but Lubbick was not interested in political ideology. War, taken pure and unfettered by higher purpose and cause, was the greatest endeavor in the world.

"Come now, Zarqa. You don't give a damn about the Mexicans, or any of this. You're here to be a meddlesome bitch...just like always."

Zarqa's expression turned cold. Her green eyes faded to gray. She frowned and said, "It's good to see you again, Lubbick. When all this is over, when we are not slaves to our nature, perhaps we'll be together like we've always talked about. But now I must be off. The Lord of the Near and the Nigh awaits. And when he rises, my brave little pixie, I promise you, your precious American army will fall."

Lubbick's eyes hardened with rage. "Don't do this, Zarqa. You can't control it, you know that. It'll kill everything, everyone. It will make no distinctions. You *know* this."

Zarqa huffed. "Do I? Like you say, I'm just a meddlesome ol' bitch. What could I possibly know?"

Before Lubbick could answer, Spindle flew into his view, claws and beak flared out toward Zarqa's face. "Spindle, halt!" Lubbick roared, but the sorceress waved her hand and the raven tumbled across the barn, a twisted ball of black feathers. The bird hit the wall and fell into a lump, unmoving.

Lubbick growled and leaped forward. He held his sword above his head and aimed it toward her throat. Zarqa blinked and turned into a funnel of green smoke, swirling around and around. The rush of air pushed Lubbick aside. He strengthened his hold and leaped again, but the green smoke swirled upward and vanished through the hole in the roof.

Zarqa was gone.

Lubbick tucked his sword away and rushed to Spindle's side. The foolish bird lay limp in the dust. He knelt beside his old friend, wrapped his arms around its neck. He placed a hand against its soft, tiny chest. Though inconstant, he could feel a faint heartbeat. He was relieved, but angry. He raised a weak finger toward the hole in the roof. "I'll find you, Zarqa," he shouted. "I'll find you, and you will pay for this!"

He hugged Spindle tightly, and with all his remaining strength, blinked as hard as he could.

✚

"No church bells," Lubbick said as he dropped the obsidian knife onto the wooden desk in front of General Scott. "But I found this instead."

Scott's staff and Generals Quitman, Pillow, and Shields crowded around. They had all gathered in the small town of Tacubaya to discuss the Old Man's plans for the final assault. But now their eyes were fixed on the black, shiny blade that lay before them.

"What is it?" Scott asked.

"It's a Tecpatl," Lubbick said, "an Aztec knife used for human sacrifices. I returned to the barn after caring for Spindle to retrieve it."

Lubbick felt the increased tension in the air as the humans tried wrapping their minds around the concept. Such a thing was blasphemy to Christians, yet it was a very common practice in many ancient cultures, particularly the Mesoamericans and even as far south as Peru. "What was it doing there?" General Quitman asked.

Lubbick gave the full story. The room fell silent as he described the pit, the altars, the American soldiers, the lava beast, and Zarqa. When he finished, Scott stood and said, "My sympathy for Spindle, General. How is he?"

Lubbick cleared his throat and thought about his old companion. Memories of the Teutoburg Forest filled his mind. There, thousands of Roman soldiers had been slaughtered by Germanic tribesmen as they fled through the boggy ground. It was there that he had found Spindle, weak and near death, punctured through the breast by a Roman shaft. He had saved the great bird from certain death by giving it a bit of his own life-force. It was a dangerous thing to do, for each time he did that, he grew a little older. Eventually, it would catch up with him and he, too, would die. But Spindle was worth it; he had saved Lubbick's life many times since then.

"She knocked him for a loop, that's for sure. He's got a broken wing, a chipped beak, but he'll survive. Goddamn bird is even tougher than I am. But Zarqa wasn't trying to kill him. She was just trying to piss me off."

"It sounds like you and she go way back," General Pillow said. Lubbick turned to him and could see a wry smile escape the man's mouth. General Shields snickered and tried to bury his mirth behind a cough and a dirty hand. "Perhaps you have unfinished business with her in things other than war."

Others laughed. Lubbick waited until the giddiness subsided, then turned to General Pillow and smiled. "You're quite the funny man today, General. Some might say smoking hot."

The pixie blinked and fire burst from General Pillow's left boot. The man screamed and danced about, slapping at the flames. The room fell into laughter, as General Quitman and a black body servant tried pelting their unfortunate officer with a blue field coat. But the flames would not go out and the room quickly filled with smoke.

"Stop this pettiness!" General Scott boomed. "Lubbick, put out that fire. We don't have time for tricks."

Lubbick let it burn a few seconds more, then tossed a line of water from his hand onto the charred heel. General Pillow dropped into a chair, cursed, tore his boot off, and rubbed his smoldering sock.

The pixie turned to Scott and said, "Very well, sir. But I wanted to impress upon General Pillow the importance of the situation. Zarqa is not to be taken lightly. She's not here to engage in some ancient fun with misguided Mexicans. She's here to destroy."

Scott's expression turned grave. "How so?"

Lubbick dropped down beside the knife and gently ran a finger along its edge. Sparks flew from his skin. "She's working with the Unseelie Court again, and they are trying to raise a god."

That got the room's attention, but Lubbick could not decide if it was due to his mention of the Court or the god. Perhaps both.

The Unseelie Court was an organization of evil faeries. Lubbick had given General Pillow a hot foot; a pixie of the Unseelie Court would have lit him like a torch then laughed as his skin crisped. An entrenched Unseelie Court could cause great damage to their excursion into Mexico. Those gathered might not understand the full breadth of the danger, but they understood enough to remain silent. Lubbick could feel the temperature in the room drop.

"Santa Anna, that son of a bitch," Scott said, shaking his head and rubbing his rough face. "I didn't know he had it in him."

Lubbick answered grimly. "Sir, it's unlikely that General Anna knows about this. He's not the most competent general, I'll grant you, but he's no fool. Being a native, he would understand—more so than even we would—the grave danger inherent in raising a god from the Underworld. Don't forget, General: I walked the causeways of Lake Texcoco. I stood on the great pyramid of Tenochtitlan at the height of Aztec power."

"Yes, yes, I know. You never miss an opportunity to remind us."

That little insult drew a couple of chuckles from the room, but understanding what motivated it, Lubbick let it pass. General Scott was an aging veteran. He had served the American army longer than any other officer in its short history. He was a surly, arrogant man, prone to anger. But he was the best goddamned general they had, the best since Washington. The Old Man was simply trying to maintain control in front of his officers. Lubbick was the supreme commander in the room. Human authority did not recognize it, but the Seelie Court, the good court, did, and the laws of nature as well. There was no one in all the world senior to Lubbick in matters of war. In his heart, Scott knew this. So did the others present, though they were loath to admit it.

"What god are we talking about, Lubbick?" General Shields asked.

"I'm talking about the Lord of All, General," Lubbick said. He leaped into the air and hovered above the desk in a faint glow of light. "Titlacauan. Ipalnemoani. Necoc Yaotl. More commonly known to the Aztecs as Tezcatlipoca: God of obsidian, of smoking mirrors, of enmity. God of temptation and of sorcery, God of strife...and war.

"This is no simple creature easily tricked and confused into absolution, General. This is a beast that, if released, will sunder all in its wake. Americans and Mexicans, the near and the nigh, the sky and the earth. If released, it will take a generation to destroy, and even your Christian God will not be able to tame it."

Lubbick stopped and measured their expressions. Everyone was silent, yet he could see the doubt in their eyes, feel the uncertainty in their breath, the disrespect in their averted glances. They respected his military judgment. No one doubted the skills that he had shown over the centuries. But this new country, this America, this experimental Democracy, found it hard to accept the council of a pixie, especially in matters of the spirit plane. Despite the fact that humans had lived side by side with faeries since the days of the Pharaohs, many could not take their other-worldliness seriously.

Lubbick pressed the matter. "Sir, give me forty-eight hours and I will find Zarqa and eliminate this threat. Two days."

Scott sighed, turned and walked to a window. He stood there for a few minutes. Then he shook his head, and said, "No, sir. This matter is concluded. Washington wants a victory, and they want it now. I've argued against it myself, sent Polk's little spies crying back to the teat, but there's nothing more I can do. We go, today."

He turned quickly and pointed to his generals. "Sirs, get your men ready. In six hours, I want them in Molino del Rey. Church bells or no, the time is now. That is all."

Lubbick began to argue but Scott put up his hand. The pixie dropped back to the desk, legs planted and arms crossed. Rage consumed him until his skin turned deep red, but he held his tongue.

When all had left, he flew through the air to General Scott's shoulder. "You're a fool, old man. A fool, fool, fool—"

Scott tried to swat the pixie aside. "Quit your damned belly-aching, Lubbick, and pipe down." The general found his chair. Lubbick jumped off Scott's gold epaulette and hovered near the knife. "It will do no harm to get a foothold at the base of that damned hill. If this Zarqa is as smart as you say she is, she won't be there anymore. We have to take Molino now to learn the strength of General Anna's forces in Chapultepec."

Scott leaned in close. Lubbick could smell stale smoke and breakfast on the general's tongue. He wrinkled his nose but did not move. He had stood down a charge of Persian Clibinari; a little bad breath was nothing.

"I understand and believe what you are saying, my friend," Scott whispered. "But this matter must go forward. We'll take that village by nightfall, and then we'll hold. You have twenty-four hours, not forty-eight, to find your sorceress and stop her. Take a scout if you wish; I can spare you one."

"Then what will you do?"

"In twenty-four hours...we take that hill, or the Devil takes us."

Lubbick nodded, gave his salute, hopped off the desk, and walked outside.

Twenty-four hours. *Ridiculous!* Not enough time to scratch an ass, much less find a cagey sorceress. Human wars were human wars, and despite his involvement and guidance over the years, in the end, the decisions were theirs, no matter how bone-headed or short-sighted.

Twenty-four hours. Lubbick considered his options. Who could he get to help him track down the proverbial needle in the haystack? If she were close, Zarqa's "essence" could be detected, if he knew where to look and feel for it. But before that, he needed someone with a good eye, someone who could measure the lay of the land, sense the movement of enemy troops, avoid ambushes, locate and point out the best hiding places.

A tiny voice repeated a name over and over in his mind. He tried ignoring it, tried thinking of anyone else. There were many competent scouts he could call upon to help him track the sorceress, but their names kept getting lost in the constant hum of one man's name. A man that he had little desire to work with. Why him? But there was no denying the truth: He was the best.

A courier waited nearby. Lubbick motioned him over. The boy saluted, said, "Yes, sir?"

"Young man, find me Captain Lee."

⚜

Captain Robert E. Lee had recently been promoted to brevet Major for his excellent reconnaissance work at Cerro Gordo. But brevet status was a temporary rank, and so most still referred to him as a captain. He had come to General Scott's staff from the Army Corps of Engineers, having served that entity well in Georgia and Missouri. His most amazing feat (to Lubbick's mind anyway) was his traverse of the Pedregal lava field during the ordeal at Churubusco. Not only had he found a route for the cannon through that swath of deep ravines and sharp rock, but he had crossed it several times in a thunderstorm to relay word back to headquarters about Brigadier General Persifor Smith's intent on attacking the Mexican forces. These actions, along with many others, had won Lee a unique status in Scott's eyes, and the Old Man's unshakable trust. Lee was a thoughtful, soft-spoken man whose star was on the rise.

"You don't like me very much, do you, Captain?" Lubbick asked as they came to a split in the small path they were trotting. They had spent the better part of six hours circling around the Mexican army's position near Chapultepec, with Lee using his excellent sense of topography to keep them just out of sight and range of enemy spotters and cannon. Lubbick rode on the captain's shoulder and reached out with his senses, seeking the sorceress in every shadow, every crack and crevasse no matter how small. The ride was for the most part comfortable, but Lee kept twitching his shoulder and forcing the pixie to grab the lapel to keep steady. He's doing this just to annoy me, Lubbick thought as he repeated the question.

Lee stopped their horse and cleared his throat. "I respect your service, sir, and your rank. And I appreciate your duties to our army. But I must confess: My beliefs, my faith, does not consider you, or your kind, viable in the eyes of the Lord."

Lubbick sighed. *Christianity!* Ever since Emperor Constantine had seen the cross and had taken the oath, such had been the struggle between man and *fae*. In the days prior to that event, there had been true equality between them. During the Reformation, however, faeries had been hunted like wild animals and killed in scores. The Unseelie Court had given gullible and frightened humans aid in that endeavor, only to have the sword turned against them. Oh, how the blood flowed in the fields of Europe during those brutal early years of the 17th century! Now, there was a kind of cool acceptance, a grudging allowance of each other's space and presence. Some Christian generals simply ignored his offer to serve. George Washington had refused outright to even let him in the tent, not so much because he was overly religious, but because he felt that the physical existence of faeries was an abomination to the rational mind.

Thank God for Napoleon! Lubbick said to himself as Lee grabbed the saddle horn and dismounted.

Lubbick changed the subject. "You know, Captain Lee, you may become a general someday. If so, you'll have to learn how to be an ass. All good generals are assholes. Scott's a big one. Genghis Khan was an ass. Even Alexander, whom I considered my father, was an ass. Napoleon was as well. He cheated at cards. What do you cheat at?"

Lee dismounted and gave his horse a gentle nudge into the direction from which they had come. "Well, sir, I hope we both cheat death today."

Lubbick agreed wholeheartedly. "Tell me, Captain," he said, "what's our best route of approach?"

Their careful traverse around Chapultepec had brought them within sight of a dry grass field and wood. What lay beyond them Lubbick did not know, but he intended to find out.

Lee considered, then scratched his face and said, "Either way will get us to the other side of the field, sir. That direction is further," he pointed to the right, "but it guarantees the least amount of attention from Mexican scouts." He pointed directly into the field. "That's the most direct route, but I suspect it's guarded by General Anna's cannon. Though I must say, that dry grass would make an excellent screen if we keep low and move fast."

"Then that's the way we'll go," Lubbick said as he drifted off the captain's shoulder and dropped low to move behind the tall grass as they worked across the field.

Lee pulled a pistol and bent low. "Sir," he said, "could you give me an idea of what we're looking for?"

Lubbick nodded. "Certainly, Captain. We're looking for a way into the hill."

A low rock wall gave them cover. It ended at a patch of trees, where Lubbick swung up and onto a branch to see what lay beyond. Several yards beyond the trees lay a swampy glade, a bit dry now, but Lubbick could smell the moss and decay always present with warm, wet earth. Across from them, perhaps fifty yards, lay a gap in a pile of rocks which must have fallen from Chapultepec's heights years ago. Perhaps an earthquake or a mud slide had brought it down; the area was susceptible to both. Now it lay, shaped like a dome, near a dirt road which wound around and disappeared to the rear of the fortress. In front of the stones, two guards stood, dressed in Irregular brown and tan and white *sombreros*. Each had a knife sheathed to his belt, and the one puffing a cigar hefted a *pistola*.

"What do you suppose they are guarding, sir?" Lee asked.

Lubbick shook his head. "I don't know, but we're going to find out." Lubbick blinked and appeared on Lee's left shoulder. "Carefully now, Captain. Keep low and take us around yonder." He pointed to the right.

Lee cocked his pistol and stepped into the swamp, taking care to place his feet on the most solid ground. Lubbick held on firmly as they swayed up and down. Lee's boots sank into deep mud; he was careful to pull them free with minimal noise. They reached a patch of brambles as cannons sounded in the distance. Lee crouched behind the brush. The crack of muskets and men shouting echoed through the trees.

The battle for Molino del Rey had begun.

They reached a small hillock with sage brush dispersed through a line of rotting planks from an old fence. Lubbick tapped Lee's shoulder. "This is as far as you go, Captain."

Lee's face showed concern. "What are you going to do, sir?"

Lubbick dropped to the ground. "Pay our friends a visit."

Lubbick blinked and appeared between the guards, eye level. He smiled and said coolly, "Hello, my friends. May I have a smoke?"

The guards, confused by the pixie's sudden appearance, looked at each other. The one smoking pulled the cigar from his mouth and handed it over. "Thank you," Lubbick said, and took a long puff. He withdrew the cigar and let the smoke flow slowly out of his mouth, then turned his face upward as if he were sniffing the air. Then he coughed, spit, and let the cigar fall to the ground. "Sorry...not my brand."

The guards, finally realizing their danger, tried to seize him, but Lubbick moved too quickly. He thrust his blade into the eye of the nearest guard, pulled it out and watched as flashes of green sparks spewed from the jagged hole. Then he launched into the air, avoiding a swipe as the guard behind tried to knock him aside with a beefy fist. Lubbick somersaulted through the air, straightened, then dropped like a rock onto the head of the flailing guard. He ripped the man's *sombrero* in half and drove his sword through the skull. A shower of sparks flew from the puncture. The man gurgled a wet protest, sagged on his knees, then dropped hard.

Lubbick wiped his sword clean and put it away.

Seconds later, Lee appeared at his side. "Sir, couldn't we have just scared them away? Did you have to kill them?"

"They weren't human, Captain," he said sharply and pointed to the ground. "Look."

The bodies of the guards slowly dissolved into bright, brilliant pools of jade and turquoise dust. Lee shook his head. "How did you know?"

"I just smelled the air. No amount of cigar smoke could hide the truth. They didn't stink, and if there's one thing I've learned in centuries of war, Captain, it's that humans stink."

Lee nodded. "Very clever, sir."

Lubbick nodded his thanks. "I have my moments."

He turned away from the sizzling pools of dust and ran his hands across the thick wall of stone. He closed his eyes and pressed his mind through the rock. "Stand back, Captain."

Lee withdrew. Lubbick placed himself in front of the stones. He arched his back, drew a large mouth of air, and blew the stones away.

They cracked and tumbled, sending large clouds of dirt into the darkening sky. When the dust settled, Lubbick stared through a small entrance into the hill, a mere sliver barely large enough for a man to squeeze through.

"Okay, Captain," Lubbick said, running his hands across his chest and arms. From his touch, his skin glowed like torch light. "Let's go in."

"Is that wise, sir?"

No, it was not, but there was no choice. The hour was late. The cannon were sounding and men were dying. *What lay beyond this small entrance?* He wondered. He did not know, but there was no choice now but to see.

He perched on Lee's shoulder, his body light showing the way. "Lead on, Captain."

Lee breathed deeply, wiped his face, drew his pistol, and stepped into the gap.

Twenty feet down the steep passage, the entrance was suddenly sealed shut by an avalanche of stone blocks. The air grew stale and hard to breathe. Lee gasped, clutched his throat, and fell to his knees. Lubbick shoved at the stones. They would not budge. He used his breath spell, sending large gusts of wind crashing into them. Nothing.

A deep nausea gripped his stomach, and he dropped to the ground. The world spun.

The last thing he saw before blacking out was a slender foot slamming into his face.

❦

Lubbick opened his eyes. His body shook violently. The roar of cannons, though muffled, filled his queasy mind. He tried raising his arms, but they were caught somehow. He strained harder and still could not move. He tilted his head, looking left, then right. He was not being held down by anything; no bindings or clamps. Yet something held him firm. He put all his magical strength, all his energies, into breaking free. Nothing.

A figure appeared above him, tall and slender, cloaked and shadowed by torch light flickering along the stone walls. A coarse, female voice *tsk'd*. "My poor little Lubbick. You used to be the smartest pixie in the room. You fell too easily for the trap."

Lubbick blinked to clear his eyes and saw Zarqa's sharp grin. "Sometimes, witch," he said, "the fly desires the spider's web."

The sorceress knelt and ran a stone blade gently down Lubbick's forehead, around his nose, across his lips, and down his belly. She paused at his crotch. "The chase used to be more exciting, lover. Back when we were younger, less disciplined. But you've given away too much of your life-force. You're getting old. Are you trying to kill yourself, just to be rid of me?"

"If it were that simple, I'd have saved every soldier at Waterloo just to watch you burn."

Zarqa laughed. She lifted the blade and stepped away. Cannons boomed again, and dirt and rock dust fell from the high, domed ceiling.

They were in a cavern of some sort, deep beneath the ground. Under the Grasshopper's Hill? Probably so. The light was faint and torches went dark as the room shook again with cannon fire. Somewhere high above, through layers of earth, the battle raged. *How long have I been here?* Lubbick wondered. Had General Scott ordered the attack on Chapultepec already? Another cannon shake confirmed it.

Moldy-white skulls and discarded bones littered the floor. Broken war clubs, the tattered remains of jaguar fur and loincloth covered the broken hips of scores of ancient dead. This was a tomb, the resting place of hundreds of sacrifice victims. They had probably been tossed down a long shaft or brought in by the dozens, their chests ripped open and their hearts left to bleed dry on altars of Aztec kings. Now their bones served the deadly designs of a sorceress.

Feeble moans interrupted his thoughts. He turned his head to the left and saw, lying flat in the darkness, Captain Lee on a block of stone, his arms and legs tied tightly. He had been beaten, his face swollen, his lips crusted with dirty blood. "Let him go, Zarqa," Lubbick said, pressing against his invisible bonds. "This matter is just between us."

"On the contrary," she said. "You're both very important to my plans. Vital, I'd say."

Lubbick's expression grew cold, calm. "You planned this all along, didn't you? You knew I was here with the Americans." Then a more infuriating notion came to mind. "And you're the voice I heard telling me to choose Captain Lee. Admit it, you deceitful bi—"

Zarqa laughed. "Where there's war, there's Lubbick. You're easier to track—and *trick*—than a bleeding harpy. Especially when you're mad." She lifted a small, square object from the cavern floor. She turned it with her long fingers. Lubbick squinted and observed the smooth finish on each of its sides, the utter blackness of its substance. A perfect, richly-hued piece of obsidian. An Aztec mirror. "Now I have you both: The great war-pixie, the Soul of Alexander the Great, the right-hand of Scipio Africanus, the hero of Agincourt, King Frederick's Champion." She walked to Lee and placed the knife on his arm. "And Captain Robert Edward Lee, Scott's eyes in the dark." She leaned over and whispered in his ear. Lubbick strained to listen. "You've come a long way in a very short time, sir. You have so much potential that you glow with power. Why, I dare say that—"

"Let's get on with this, Zarqa," Lubbick said. "Your voice is making me ill."

She smiled and blew a kiss. Lee wiggled his head groggily against her warm breath. "Oh, very well. What a bore you can be, lover, when you're nervous. It doesn't matter anyway. I have you both, and there's nothing you can do about it. A drop of your blood and his will be more potent than all the life coursing through the veins of those men playing soldier above us." The sorceress clapped her hands twice.

Flashes of light burst around the room. One by one, figures appeared, dressed in red, green, gold, and black. Goblins, imps, harpies, boggarts, ogres, gremlins, and pixies, twisted and foul, hump-backed and holding staves and cudgels, walking canes and mahogany spears. A royal ensemble of *fae* from the Unseelie Court.

An ogre stepped forward, his bulbous, green body undulating strangely like a large sack of rocks beneath a coarse burlap throw. He slammed his staff against the floor. "Quickly now, Zarqa!" The sound of his strike matched the cannon blasts. "The battle rages."

She shot the beast an angry look, then turned, cut the cords holding Lee's right arm, and let it drop to his side. She placed the edge of the knife on his wrist and opened it with one quick motion. Blood dripped like rain. She placed the obsidian mirror beneath his hand and caught the drops, one by one, until they formed streaks of crimson running from corner to corner.

"O, great Tezcatlipoca," Zarqa said, raising the mirror toward the ceiling. Her voice was deep and threatening. "We, who are your slaves, bid you rise and reclaim your rightful throne on this mortal earth. Drink the blood of war, and rise!"

Looking at her smile, the upturned corners of her mouth, her sharp, dangerous teeth, Lubbick suddenly understood the truth. Zarqa was not trying to release a god for kicks, nor did she care a whit about the conflict that raged above. She was...

"You don't understand what's happening," he said to those of the Unseelie Court gathered round. "Do you not see what she's doing? Are you blind to her deceit? She's trying to kill you all. She's—"

Zarqa's hand crashed against Lubbick's face, dazing him momentarily. She hit him again, then grabbed his chin between thumb and index finger. She spoke softly so that only he could hear. "Quiet, my love. This is the way it has to be. Once they are all dead, we'll be free of our obligations, free of this ghastly, mortal world that binds us eternally to war. Then we can be together, forever, in peace."

Lubbick considered her words. The idea of destroying, or at least damaging considerably, the Unseelie Court did have its appeal. They had been a source of constant annoyance over the years. The world would certainly be better without them. The Unseelie Court was oftentimes the fountain from which human conflict flowed. They worked their schemes below ground, in the shadows. Why, the entire French Revolution occurred because Marie Antoinette refused a pixie of the Court a taste of her feminine wiles. Yet, putting them out of business would put Lubbick out of business. *That* was unacceptable.

"No we won't, Zarqa," Lubbick said. "We'll be dead as well, you damned fool."

"Our spirits will be free to do as we wish; to go where we want. Do you not desire that?"

"Ah, no!"

She chuckled. "You weren't so certain a thousand years ago in Egypt."

Before he could answer, she flicked a nail across his face. Bright, blue-green blood trickled down his cheek from the cut. Lubbick struggled, turned his head left and right, licked his face to swab away the blood, but it was too late. The sorceress ran her finger across the gash.

She pulled away, dabbed a bit of it on her lips, licked them clean. Then she ran her finger across the mirror, mixing Lubbick's blood with Captain Lee's.

Black, empty smoke began to swirl out of the mirror. "Rise, Night Smoke," she said, holding the mirror to the ceiling. "Come and claim your throne of blood!"

The smoke intensified, now billowing out into a cloud. "Rise!" Zarqa shouted, then tossed the mirror into the air.

It wobbled and twisted as it rose before falling. It struck the cavern floor...and exploded.

Blood-red and brilliant white light sprang from the shards. Zarqa herself was tossed away from the blast. Such searing heat Lubbick had never felt before. He clenched his muscles and fought against the pain. He thought of snow, of ice, the cold water of a fountain in Egypt he once bathed in with Cleopatra. It had no effect. The pain went beyond bearing. *Make it go away*, he pleaded to the dark ceiling.

It did not go away. Instead, it changed. The room grew cooler, darker, the pungent smell of rotting flesh and the age-old stink of bone dust choked the air. Lubbick forced his eyes open.

Before him stood a god twenty feet high at least, a-swirl with black smoke adorned in jade, diamonds, gold bracelets, neck, and nose rings. Over its massive, cinnamon-colored shoulders lay the largest jaguar pelt Lubbick had ever seen, and across its sharp face, lines of yellow and black war paint accentuated the deep, red eyes that flickered with fire and oozed green steam. In its left hand lay a war club lined with eagle claws. In its right a human heart, still beating and dripping blood as if it had just been ripped from the chest. Its left leg was thick and daunting, the sinews of its powerful muscles like cords of hemp reaching through its thick flesh, ending in a clawed foot. Its right leg was similar but ended instead in the long, scaled body of a python that swayed back and forth as its broad, forked tongue peeked out to catch a scent on the air.

The god looked around as if it did not know where it was, then saw the arcane carvings on the wall, the piles of dusty bones and battered skulls. It pulled back its head, drew in a long, tortured breath, then roared.

Whatever power that held Lubbick to the stone altar was now torn asunder. He flew through the air in the gust of foul wind that broke through the beast's sharp teeth. He hit the jagged wall, blinked himself away, and appeared behind the Aztec god. He reached for his sword. It was not there. Of course it would not be. Zarqa was foolish but she was not so stupid as to allow a *war pixie* to keep his magical weapon.

The truth of the sorceress's plan was beginning to sink into the thick minds of the other faeries in the room. But there was no way out. Some tried to snap their fingers, blink their way free, but the presence of such an ancient and powerful god set a barrier that could not be penetrated by simple spells. The only way out was to break this thing which Zarqa had called forth from the nether-world before it grew any stronger, but already it was beginning to feed.

A goblin waved its cudgel half-heartedly as the god sucked the tiny monster into its bloody maw. One deadly bite cut the goblin in two. Both halves slid down Tezcatlipoca's throat like fresh fish.

An imp, taking advantage of the god's momentary pause, drove its spiked tail into the beast's right thigh and brought it down to one knee. *Good shot*, Lubbick thought. The imp, however, delighted with its success, foolishly paused to gloat. The wide jaws of the python snapped out, caught the imp in its vise grip. Seconds later, the imp popped like a tick.

Others—pixies, boggarts, harpies, gremlins—fluttered around the room in chaos, some trying to thwart the beast, others banging themselves into the rock walls as if their efforts would prove fruitful. A terrified boggart cracked its skull against a wall and hobbled aimlessly into the path of the god. The beast bent down and took the boggart's head off with one snap.

Then Lubbick saw her out of the corner of his eye, Zarqa, her hands pulling on Lee's arms to drag him from underneath the altar on which he had lain. The altar was now nothing more than a pile of rock, the god's mighty roar having split it into a dozen rough stones. Lee lay limp on the ground, his face bruised, his body cut and bleeding. Even through the deadly morass that waged around Lubbick, he could smell the captain's fresh blood.

The strong scent caught Tezcatlipoca's attention. It crushed an elf beneath its solid foot, then turned and moved toward Zarqa.

Lubbick blinked and appeared in front of her face, curled his tiny fingers into a tight fist, and sent it across the sorceress's chin. He put everything into the blow, but Zarqa merely stumbled back a pace, stopped, adjusted her neck, and smiled. "I've grown much stronger since we last danced, Lubbick," she said. "More so than you can imagine."

She flung her hand out and an invisible wave of energy pushed him away. It felt like an intense rush of water shooting from a narrow pipe. He fought free from its path, fell to the floor, rolled, blinked, and came up behind her. He concentrated on his left hand, focusing on its shape, its malleable, white flesh. It changed before him, elongating and sharpening into a spike. It grew three times its normal size, and Lubbick howled and drove it into Zarqa's neck. The sudden attack caught the sorceress by surprise. The spike cut through her skin and a spray of blood showered her face. She screamed and clutched his wrist. He tossed her at the god's feet.

Lubbick turned to the beast and said, "Take *her!*" He pointed to Zarqa. "She's the one you want."

But Tezcatlipoca already had Lee trapped in the python's coils. The captain was awake and struggling to free himself from the serpent's grip, his eyes desperate and terrified. The snake weaved its way upward, and the god opened its mouth to accept its meal.

Lubbick blinked himself into Tezcatlipoca's mouth. Like a stick, he teetered among the sharp teeth, feet pressed against the lower jaw, hands against the upper palate. The god's bite was powerful, but Lubbick put all his strength into keeping its jaws apart.

"Bite the snake, Captain!" Lubbick yelled. At first, Lee was confused, uncertain from where the voice had come. "It's me, goddammit!" Lubbick barked. "Bite the serpent! That's an order!"

Lee turned, barred his mouth, and sunk his teeth into the scales of the python. Though his bite was small compared to the size of the snake, the sudden, sharp pain of it made the snake jerk and drop Lee to the ground. The python would recover soon from the bite, Lubbick knew, but he didn't need much time. He just needed a distraction.

He flew out of the god's mouth, letting the teeth slam shut behind him. The pixie swooped up and smacked Tezcatlipoca on the face just hard enough to get its attention. He smacked again. "You aren't so tough!" He struck again and again. The god twisted and turned its face, biting furiously, trying to snatch the pixie out of the air.

Lubbick flew up to the top of the cavern, up where dust and small chips were falling from the incessant cannon shots outside. Lubbick blew the god a raspberry, wiggled his nose, and screwed up his face.

"Catch me if you can, Smoking Mirror. I don't think you've got the guts or the balls!"

The god swung up with his club. Lubbick drifted aside as the club's eagle claws struck the rock and lodged deep. Tezcatlipoca pulled the club free and a huge gash appeared in the ceiling. The god swung the club as if it were trying to swat a fly. It struck the ceiling again and again, each time pulling more rock away. Another strike and an arch of light fell through the gap. Large cracks spread across the rock. The room shook. Lubbick flew down to Lee, who had crawled to safety.

Then the ceiling collapsed.

It felt like a tornado as the gap in the ceiling widened. Mexican cannoneers and their guns fell through, and Tezcatlipoca, seeing light and freedom, shot through the gap and into the wide world. Everyone, everything in the cavern, was swept up in his wake. Lubbick held Lee tightly as they flew through the air.

The entire right side of the Chapultepec fortress blew apart. American and Mexican soldiers, guns and huge chunks of mortar shot skyward as Tezcatlipoca swirled upward in a dervish of smoke and flame. Lubbick focused his attention on Lee, making sure that the captain did not strike the ground too harshly as he fell. He pulled with all his strength to slow their descent, and carefully, he laid the captain down. Then he turned back to the fight.

But those of the Unseelie Court who had survived were already surrounding the beast. Like a swarm of bees, they stung top to bottom, drawing strength from the air and rocks and fields around them, from the nearby trees and water. Unfettered now by the closed cavern, they were strong again. Lubbick moved away and let them be. He smiled. His plan had worked.

Slowly, the Unseelie Court drove Tezcatlipoca off the Grasshopper's Hill. Lubbick watched as they swirled away into the distance. Yet sounds of battle still raged around him.

The American assault, which had been momentarily halted by the explosion, now recommenced in the center. Lubbick turned and watched as a wave of Marines dashed up the hill to storm the ramparts, their muskets popping, their bayonets striking. Lubbick's heart raced. There was nothing so wonderful, or so pure, as a simple, uncomplicated charge of soldiers into battle. Despite all that had just occurred, this was what gave his heart joy and quickened him again against the loss of energy that he had expended in the cavern. This is what he had been hoping for. He jumped into the air and cheered the Americans forward.

The words caught in his throat. Suddenly, he felt crushed, constricted. Something held him in place, pressing in on him. He tried to turn, but his body was suspended, stuck and unmoving.

"You have stopped me for the last time, Lubbick."

Zarqa's fingers wrapped around him and pulled him close. Her hair and face were caked in blood. Her eyes were wild, confused. She had been crying, but Lubbick doubted it was from grief or pain. She only cried when her rage was such that no other release from the intense emotion presented itself. He had seen her cry before. It was terrible.

"Give it up, Zarqa. You've lost this one. Deal with it."

She held up a tiny sword in front of his face. His sword. It sparked blue magic. Its edge glistened sharply.

Lubbick flexed and tried to break free. Nothing. She had indeed gotten stronger. "Come on, Zarqa," he said, his voice firm and hard. "The game is *over*. Let it go."

"Do you remember the promise we made to each other on the Nile, Lubbick? That we would always be together and that we would always love each other? Do you remember that?"

He did. "That was a long time ago. And you've broken that promise many, many times. Enough, Zarqa. Let me go."

She held him by the scruff like a puppy. She ran the sword across his chest and drew a line of blood. "You don't understand what it means to be human, Lubbick. You never have. You don't know what it is to suffer, to feel like I do. My human side is a trap. I'm bound in this flesh and a slave to its weaknesses. You see the world through the eyes of a *fae*. I feel it through the heart of a human. You broke my heart, Lubbick, and now I will take yours."

She barred her sharp teeth, pulled back her hand, and drove the tiny blade toward his chest.

A shot rang out.

Zarqa's stomach exploded in a burst of blood and flesh. Her hand opened and Lubbick flew out.

The sorceress, her torso a black, smoking hole, turned to Captain Lee who stood nearby, a spent musket held in his shaking hands. She smiled; blood ran down her cheek. "Oh, you bad, bad boy," she said, stumbling forward. "You will die for that, I swear."

"No he won't!"

Before she moved, Lubbick swooped down and tore his sword from her hand. He flew across her face, turned the blade down, and drove it through her neck.

Zarqa screamed and clutched the wound. Blue flame from the blade sparked against her flesh and Lubbick could smell it burn as she screamed again and twisted in pain. He flew upward to keep from getting scorched by the fire that spread across her face and shoulders. Smoke billowed as she fell into a pile of smoldering ash.

A moment later, Lee lowered his musket and stepped forward. He stared at the charred pile. "Is she dead, sir?"

Lubbick drifted down and held himself above the mess. He waited.

Zarqa's remains shimmered like a thousand grains of sand on a hot beach. Then the ash coalesced into tiny molten chunks. From each chunk sprouted eight legs and the body of a spider. Each spider scampered away into the rubble.

"No, Captain, she isn't." Lubbick shook his head in disgust. "Damn it all!"

Yet quietly to himself, Lubbick whispered, *Goodbye, Zarqa. We'll meet again.*

Lee lifted his foot and tried stamping the spiders, but Lubbick waved him off. "Don't bother, Captain. Unless you can get them all, she'll live. Save your strength for the fight that's coming." Lee stopped and let the spiders scamper away.

The assault in the middle of the fortress had ended. Chapultepec had fallen, and now the remnants of its garrison had retreated back toward Mexico City.

Lubbick looked into the warm sky. "What day is this, Captain?"

Lee cleared his throat. "September twelfth or thirteenth, sir. I'm not sure."

"And the year?"

Lee seemed surprised by the question. "Eighteen forty-seven."

Lubbick shook his head. "I'm sorry, Captain. But when you've lived as long as I have, and have fought in so many wars, it all blends together." He blinked and appeared in front of Lee's face. He saluted. "Well done, Captain. Your service to me has concluded. You may return to General Scott."

"What about Tezcatlipoca, sir?"

Lubbick spit. "Let the Unseelie Court deal with it," he said. "Now that they know it's a mortal danger to their place in this world, they won't let it rest until it's been devoured."

Lee nodded. "Yes, sir."

Lubbick turned and looked into the horizon, toward the vastness of Mexico City. He sighed. "Captain, I suddenly find myself a little bored, so I'm going to hunt up General Pillow and see if he needs another hotfoot."

Lee tried to hide his grin. He said, "Yes, sir. May I join you?

Lubbick smiled. He blinked and appeared on Lee's left shoulder. "Yes, indeed. Let's get back in this war, Captain."

Lee stepped carefully through the rubble and headed for the advancing American line.

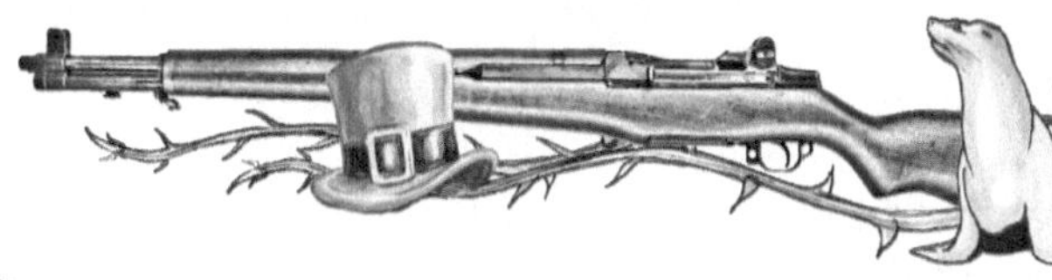

Selkskin Deep

Kelly A. Harmon

Cade Owen stood on the flight deck of the aircraft carrier *USS Livingstone*, watching the crew of an ammunition ship loading armaments on board. The night sea cooperated. Gentle waves in the Gulf of Tonkin lapped at the two navy vessels. Men from the other ship, the *USS Redoubt*, sent over bomb after bomb until a crewman from the *Livingstone* pointed to a large wooden crate and made a cutting motion with his hands, halting the transfer.

Cade itched to know what the man's agitation signaled. But from this distance, and under these lighting conditions, he couldn't make out the problem. The carrier needed those munitions. Without them, the fighter jets couldn't make their ordered strafing runs north of Hanoi in the morning, and he couldn't rendezvous with the other SEALs later in the week with the Biet Hai Commandos in Da Nang.

Thank Manannán mac Lir. And *President Kennedy*, he thought, who created the SEALs only recently. He hoped this special mission would grant him a reprieve from the boredom his nearly immortal life provided him, even if he had to live among humans to find surcease. Humans weren't a bad sort; he just couldn't fathom why they seemed to live their lives so intensely.

Didn't they realize that life is a series of up and down cycles? What made it so hard for them to accept that and move on? How can there be anything worth fighting over — dying over — when all things circle back in the ebb and flow of life?

He would love to discuss it with Friedman, but that would mean telling Friedman his bunkmate wasn't human. Perhaps they'd known each long enough to swim that current. Long

days confined together with the threat of war hanging over their heads had shaped their friendship far more quickly than a casual friendship might have. He'd give it some thought.

Until then, he would observe their intensity first hand. For now, he was just another man on the ship. And if he died serving? More the better, for it gave his life a purpose: something more than living and dying with the sea; yet, still living and dying *by the sea*.

The trident insignia of the Navy SEALs on his lapel gleamed in the moonlight. The brooding look on his face took on a more thoughtful aspect. He reached within his coveralls and pulled a small, rolled fur from around his neck. Shaking out the seal-shaped pelt, he moved into the darker shadow cast by an F4 Phantom and stripped out of his clothes. He draped the skin over his shoulders, letting the length of it drape down his back. Then, he grabbed the edges, pulling and tugging, smoothing the skin around himself until it grew large enough to cover him, turning him into a seal.

In an instant, the darkness disappeared, and Cade could see almost as well as if there were daylight. He opened his mouth, tasting the salty tang of the ocean on his tongue. He drew in a large breath, savoring the smell. He had waiting too long to return to true form. It always felt this way to him, after the change, like the sea wooed him back. If he were his human self, he would have smiled from the pleasure of it.

He dove into the water, falling forty feet through the air, cutting into the sea in a graceful arc. He plunged deep into the water, then surfaced and made his way around the side of the carrier and closer to the argument.

⚔

Cade slipped off his seal skin. In human form again, he climbed the metal hand-holds on the side of the *Livingstone* and popped his head over the edge of the flight deck. The ordinance officer was purple-faced with anger. He shook like a terrier, his hat sliding back to reveal short-cut grey hair. He turned to face the small crew on the *Redoubt*.

"These are goddamned comp B bombs!" he shouted across the water. "I can't take these on board."

The young officers from the ammunition ship looked like they wanted to be anywhere but facing down the old salt. One replied, "We don't know anything about that, sir."

"They're older than dirt. We can't use this shit."

"It's all we've got."

"We're the goddamned United States Navy. This can't be all we've got. Take 'em back. We can't use 'em."

"Can't, sir. Our orders are to deliver munitions."

Cade stole a look at the crates as they arrived aboard the carrier by way of the underway replenishment line. Black mold crusted the bottoms and sides of many of the crates. Several looked rotten. Cade saw the year *1935* stenciled on one. He swore softly under his breath.

Manannán mac Lir, help us, he thought. *These bombs were made half a decade before World War II, and WWII ended more than 20 years ago....*

He watched as an uncrated bomb advanced along the line and was lowered to the deck by a hoist. Cade recognized it by sight: round and wide, sailors referred to it as a *fat-boy.* The only time he remembered seeing one was in training class, having to watch the old black and white WWII footage, with the large bombs falling out of the back of planes.

Gods! he thought. Composition B bombs exploded full strength, not like modern munitions, which were built to blow at a lower rate if they went off accidentally.

Cade climbed back down to the ocean. As he swam away, he could hear the chief saying, "I really don't like the look of these things. I swear they'll go off in a heavy vibration. Hell! They're so decayed there's no telling what will set them off."

He didn't blame the ordinance chief for being worried.

"We took on four hundred tons of ammunition, Friedman," Cade said. "Some of them are so large, I don't know how they'll fit them to the jets." Cade tossed the nine of clubs onto the stack. "All of them are old and filthy — a few are rusting out of their casings. The ordinance officer was pitching a fit. He swore some were leaking." Cade moved all the clubs in his hand to the right side where he could reach them easier.

"Two cards," Friedman said. He dropped the three of clubs then laid his hand face down on the table beside his tattered copy of Heinlein's *Starship Troopers.* "Where'd the bombs come from?"

Cade played the king of clubs. "Guys on the *Redoubt* said they picked them up in the Philippines. They've been stored in Quonset huts: no walls, no nothing, out in the storms and heat all year round. They found snakes and tree frogs in some of the crates." Cade waited for Friedman to play a card. "I heard one of them say that these are the only thousand-pound bombs the navy has right now."

Friedman said, "And they could blow any minute?" He looked up at Cade.

"According to the ord-O, yes," Cade said. "And they're not sitting safe in some warehouse...they're right on deck, exposed to everything that could possibly set them off."

Friedman looked surprised. "The ordnance guys didn't stow them?"

"Too dangerous in the hold."

"The captain didn't have anything to say about that?" asked Friedman.

"I hear he wired over to the *Redoubt* and ordered them to give over newer bombs. They told him they didn't have any other ammo, and besides, they had their orders. *Livingstone* had to take them."

"Unbelievable," Friedman said, shaking his head.

"Do you blame them?" Cade asked. "Under ordinary conditions, the *Redoubt's* an explosion just waiting to happen. I can't imagine what they felt ferrying those garbage bombs to us."

Friedman tossed his last card on the stack, winning the game. "I'm out," he said, picking up his book and tucking it into his back pocket. "Pretty scary. But do they expect us to do our job with an extra four hundred tons of ammo on the deck getting in our way?"

"I don't know, Fried. I really don't know." Cade shuffled all the cards together and stowed them in his trunk. "I pulled steering duty in the morning...."

"Duty officer always treats you guys like parasites."

"You want to trade?"

Friedman's eyes lit up. "That's prime reading space."

Cade shook his head, smiling, as he said, "You're going to get caught, one of these days."

"Give me some quiet and a good book to read. I don't care if that room is no bigger than my pop's sedan," Friedman said. "I don't know how you can stand all the noise on the flight deck."

"Noise doesn't matter when I can be that close to the ocean."

⚜

On the open sea, seventy-five miles east of Ha Tinh Province, men swarmed across the flight deck of the *USS Livingstone*, preparing for an attack on a rail line in North Vietnam. They planned to disrupt enemy supply lines by both crippling the tracks, then burying them under an avalanche caused by bombing the nearby mountains. In order to accomplish that, the ordinance crew, the red-jacketed *BB Stackers*, loaded the thousand-pound *fat boys*—bombs larger than the planes normally carried—onto as many planes as they could for the first strike of the day. Crewmen loaded Zuni rockets—as many as twenty-four at a time—as well as Sidewinder missiles and Shrike or Sparrow III missiles onto planes when the fat-boys ran out.

Cade wore Friedman's purple jacket, just like the other *grapes*: men assigned to fuel the large planes. Hose in hand, he watched the crews load the composition B bombs under the wings.

Damn but they look like antiques, thought Cade, watching the ordies load, *but at least they're getting some of that ammo off the deck. I'll feel a little safer when* all *of it's gone.*

Just then, a rocket fired across the flight deck.

Lir! If anything blew, thought Cade, *I would have laid money on the fat-boys, not a rocket.*

As if in slow motion, he watched it launch from a starboard F4 at the extreme rear of the ship and fly at a forty-five degree angle across the flight deck.

It ripped by the safety officer checking armament on an F4, blistering his face and hands. Soaring hundreds of miles an hour, the missile headed across the deck toward Cade. It missed him, knocking him off his feet as it passed. He tumbled over twice, losing his grip on the fuel hose, and landed on his chest, scraping his hands on the deck.

The rocket ripped through the right shoulder of a red-jacketed ordnance man, severing his arm, and spinning him around like a top. Then it struck the fuel tank of an A-4 Skyhawk preparing for take-off.

Four hundred gallons of JP5 jet fuel spilled onto the flight deck. Flames engulfed several nearby crewmen as the blistering rocket exhaust whipped by them. The jet fuel on deck ignited. Wind, and exhaust from waiting jets, pushed the fire toward the rear of the ship. All of the A-4 Skyhawks parked on the port side of the ship caught fire. Fuel poured out of their gas tanks, adding to the flames.

Cade felt the heat of it on his back, burning as though flames already licked at his hair. He got to his feet, then grabbed the fuel hose, and ran from the fire.

Less than a minute later, one of the *fat boys* exploded on the deck. Ten thousand degrees of heat erupted, obliterating the entire firefighting team. A roiling cone of fire spouted high into the air, dragging burning fuel with it, creating near black-out conditions as smoke blanketed the immediate area. Shrapnel, burning oil, and debris rained down on the flight deck. The blast sent bits of planes, parts of the steel deck plating, tools, and machinery sailing horizontally across the deck, wiping out those men who survived the initial blast.

Cade reached the fueling station. *Shit! No shelter here*, he thought. He looked to *the island*, the twenty-foot wide command center located amidships. It loomed one-hundred and fifty feet in the air, widening out at each successive level. He ran toward it.

Once under the overhang, Cade dropped the fuel hose and beat at his shoulders and neck to brush off the burning debris. His seal skin, draped about his neck as always, sheltered him from the worst injuries.

"Oh, Manannán mac Lir," he prayed, "if you still possess your cauldron of life, now is the time to share it."

A second bomb exploded.

The fires spread beyond the port side of the carrier to the starboard side, where the old ordinance lay, and inched its way closer to the rear. Burning jet fuel pooled in the center of the deck, slowly expanding to the edges of the ship. Cade watched as men ran for shelter wherever they could find it: catwalks, down ladders and hatches, even jumping off the deck into the safety nets, racing forward away from the flames.

I could don my skin, thought Cade, *and escape this burning hell in the waters.* But he couldn't bring himself to do it. He had made a commitment to the Navy and he would see it through.

Even in the lee of the island, he couldn't avoid the danger. Planes burned, setting off the bombs they carried beneath their wings. Other munitions exploded, sending molten, shredded metal across the deck.

Dammit, he thought. *This boiling heat will ignite every last one of those bombs.*

The magnesium brakes on the wheels of a nearby plane ignited, sending a spray of sparks down onto the deck. *Lucky*, thought Cade, *that no oil pooled here. Lir!* he realized, *but it's everywhere else, and so are the planes.*

He shouted to the others taking shelter at the island, "We've got to move the planes." He pointed to the wheels of the burning Seahawk. "Magnesium brakes!"

Magnesium couldn't be extinguished. It burned at over four-thousand degrees, guaranteeing that if the brakes ignited, flames would soon overtake the entire plane, and any bombs or missiles loaded onto it. Foam could smother magnesium fires, but it was being used to put out the big fires. Tossing the ships overboard best solved the problem.

Men scrambled to the plane, pushed it to the edge of the flight deck and into the sea.

Good thing there's only a small amount of magnesium in the brakes, thought Cade, *or we wouldn't be able to get close enough to help.*

Another bomb exploded. Cade helped to push another plane into the ocean.

"Man your repair stations!" he heard over the ship's loud speakers. "Repair teams, re-man your stations. Put this fire out."

Cade looked around. The initial *fat boy* explosion had killed all the firefighters on deck. There was no one left to fight the fires. He pulled up the collar of his purple jacket and walked toward the fire, picking up a melting hose, and sprayed water at the flames. Burned hulks of F4s smoldered on the runway. Charred bodies lay strewn across the flight deck, but more worrisome to Cade were the lack of bodies. There should have been dozens more.

Then he saw the hole.

Sweet *Manannán,* he thought, an ache building in his chest. *The deck is open like a tin of sardines.* The burning fuel wasn't just cascading off the edges of the flight deck and into the ocean, it was pouring into the belly of the ship. He knew the berthing quarters lay beneath the flight deck. There were sleeping men down there!

"Deep peace to you," he murmured, knowing many shipmates must have died in their racks.

He pulled the hose over his shoulder to keep it from melting on the hot tarmac, and marched closer to the fire.

"General Quarters!" sounded the call over the speakers. "General Quarters."

GQ required Cade to report to the hangar deck with the other SEALs and wait for orders, but he was the only one on this hose. If he left it, the fire might spread.

"General Quarters! General Quarters!" The command repeated, followed by an alarm that bonged for fifteen seconds, then again, "General Quarters! General Quarters!"

Finally, men showed up to relieve him of the duty. He ran for his GQ, down a hatch and through a narrow, smoke-filled passageway.

❧

Thick smoke inundated the hangar deck. Dozens of men milled about, waiting for orders. Some, with injuries, sagged against the port walls. A large group of men crowded around the deck phone, awaiting orders and begging for information. Cade moved aft toward the fantail, where the deck yawned open over the sea. His lungs burned, he hoped to catch a breath of fresh air.

Another explosion rocked the ship, this one, close to aft. Cade felt the boat pitch downward with the blast. Vibrations surged up his legs, knees and hips throbbing with the force of it.

It feels like the entire ship is blowing up.

"Port steering's hit!" someone shouted.

Port? thought Cade. *Friedman's in port steering. And he traded for my watch. Lir, what have I done?*

He pushed his way through the men to the fantail, and felt his stomach drop to his knees when he saw the damage before him. The blast had occurred directly over the two-story tall steering shaft. The burning oil pouring over the rear of the ship had peeled away part of the plating.

"Port steering's taking on water," he heard another man say. The din quieted. Every man aboard knew the *Livingstone* was not in danger of sinking, but an open compartment meant a serious hit. Cade knew they felt for the men working there.

"Orders!" came a shout from a SEAL manning the phone. "Push any ordinance on deck overboard...and anything else: if it's on fire, toss it over."

Men surged inboard to the hatches leading topside. Cade moved with them, but went below. After a few yards, he came to a guarded, closed door. "I need to pass," he told the sailor.

"Captain's sealed the ship," the sailor replied. "No one gets through."

"Men are dying," Cade said.

The sailor looked grim. "Captain's orders. The door stays closed."

I could take him, Cade thought, looking the sailor up and down. These men didn't get the training he'd received as a SEAL. But he changed his mind. Fighting would only take time—time he wasn't certain Friedman had—and might attract the some unwanted attention. He let out a breath he hadn't realized he'd been holding. He turned back, then left down another passageway. He would make his way through on the port side.

Several moments later, he found an unguarded door. Cade could feel the heat emanating from the metal from ten feet away.

He sagged. He wouldn't make it to Friedman this way.

Still coughing, and wiping smoky grit from his face, Cade hurried back to the hangar deck, hoping to hear that Friedman survived. He would find another way to make it to him.

He arrived in time to hear a phone talker relay the damage to a small group of men. "They're hit pretty bad. The machinist's arm was severed, and the electrician's been hit in the head from debris falling down the shaft. They need medical help badly."

Injured and *taking on water*...Cade thought. *Can it get any worse?* Then it occurred to him. *If steering is taking on water, the bomb must have ripped a hole in the bottom of the ship.*

Cade ran to the fantail.

He pulled his seal skin from beneath his coverall and held tight to it as he jumped into the water. Then he began to change. He slid the skin around his body, felt himself return to seal form, then bellowed in pain. Several punctures and lacerations wept blood into the cool ocean. Tucked beneath his coveralls while he fought fires and moved planes, the seal skin had protected him. It had saved his human form from certain death, kept shrapnel from reaching his neck.

Now, he paid the cost in pain, as each of those injuries to the hide became injuries to his self when he took the seal form.

He dove beneath the water, trailing blood, and headed to the port aft steering compartment. It took him only a few moments to swim past the tremendous rudders of the ship and find the hole leading into the carrier. Cade found it, then swam through it and up into the steering chamber.

Friedman and two others were trapped in the eight-by-eight room. One of the explosions penetrated deep into the bowels of the ship, ripping large holes into the compartment, destroying the only ship-board access in or out, and cleaving open the hull. Sea water poured in from the bottom, flooding the narrow space. Munitions and flaming jet fuel poured into the room from the deck above. The smoke grew thicker, making it hard to see.

Neither repair parties, nor medics, could get here to save them.

"Where is the rescue crew?" Friedman phoned to control. "We can't breathe."

Cade looked at the machinist. Not one, but both arms were nearly severed. Someone—Friedman?—had put tourniquets on both. His arms still bled, pumping blood into the brackish water.

"Sir," he heard Friedman say, "we're dying."

Dead already, thought Cade, looking into the dull eyes of the electrician. Shrapnel protruded from his forehead.

But he could still save Friedman. Get him top-side for much-needed help.

He slipped his seal skin down to his waist, not daring to take it all the way off. The wounds transferred to his human self. His shoulders burned where the pelt had once been damaged. His legs were injured even more.

"Yes, sir. Right away, sir," Friedman said. He put the phone down. "We need to transfer steering control to starboard...," he said, looking around, "in case we're not here to transfer control later."

His eyes met Cade's, seeing him for the first time. "Cade. How did you get in here?" He smiled weakly, his teeth a white flash in contrast to his soot-covered face. "What happened to your uniform?"

"Long story, buddy. You look like you could use some help."

"Hydraulics have burned out. It'll take three of us to transfer control manually."

That wasn't the kind of help he meant to offer. "I can get you to safety," Cade said, swimming toward him. "But we've got to go now."

"First, we have to transfer steering," Friedman said.

"No time. This space is filling fast. Any more water and we won't be able to hold our breath long enough to—"

Another explosion rocked the ship. Water splashed up and over Cade's head. The wave knocked Friedman against the control panel. He cried out, and Cade reached out a hand to steady him.

The smoke started to clear, venting from a hole on the starboard side. But he could feel a current brush his legs. Was the water rising faster? He had to get Friedman out. Now.

"We need to get Grassi out, too," Friedman said.

"No time," repeated Cade. He reached for Friedman again.

"Steering first," Friedman said, brushing his hand aside. His eyes held steel. He would not be budged from his orders.

Humans! Cade nodded. "All right. Let's go."

Friedman said, "The drive shaft needs to be turned ninety degrees clockwise to line up with the starboard rudder. You have to swim down to where the shaft meets the port rudder and use the lever bar to turn it. Once you turn her ninety degrees, a bearing should drop into the opened slot and wedge it in place." He pointed to a spot on the chamber wall. "There's a lever mounted on the bulkhead near the ladder. I'll use the tiller arm to help turn from the top. When the bearing sets here...." He looked to the machinist, and then the instrument panels. "Grassi, can you make the switch on the boards?"

"With my nose if I have to," Grassi said. Cade hoped he could reach the panel when the time came.

"Okay," Friedman said. He coughed, and blood sprayed through his teeth and onto his chin. He wiped it with the back of his hand, smearing blood across his face and knuckles. "Let's do it."

Cade peeled the rest of the seal skin from his legs and wrapped it around his neck. Pain seared through his thighs where his pelt had taken the most damage. He could feel himself bleed into the water, enough blood to warm his thighs in the cold sea. He took a deep breath, and dove into the water, pushing hard with his legs and arms to propel himself down toward the rudder.

Darkness swallowed him. He found the lever by the bulkhead ladder and turned to the drive shaft. More by touch than by sight, he fitted the lever into the slot then pulled it toward him. The shaft didn't budge. He gave it a couple of quick yanks, felt it move, then realized he didn't have the leverage — even with the bar — to turn the shaft.

His lungs burned. He dropped the bar to the deck and paddled upward. He broke the surface and breathed deeply. "Not enough leverage," he said to Friedman. "In the water, I don't have enough weight to move the bar."

Friedman looked worse. Another stream of blood trickled from the corner of his mouth.

"Stand on the stuffing box," Friedman said.

Cade nodded. He took a deep breath, then dove for the bottom of the shaft. The shaft seal housing — the stuffing box — allowed the shaft to rotate the rudder while keeping water out. The shock of a bomb explosion must have misaligned the shaft and broken its seal. *Like taking a nail through a thin board and tilting it,* Cade thought. *That seal isn't doing any good now.*

Cade retrieved the lever and angled it into place. The placement of the stuffing box required him to push the lever, rather than pull it, clock-wise. He pushed, and the shaft slowly began to turn. The wounds in his thighs and shoulders ached. He could feel the strain in his back. His arms shook, his fingers burned as they gripped the lever. He opened his mouth and loosed a guttural scream, urging the bar to move forward more quickly. Oily water filled his mouth.

Finally, the bearing *thunked* into place.

Nearly spent, he spit out the water and pushed off the box with shaking legs. He surfaced, and breathed deeply.

Friedman lay hanging over his own lever, breath and blood rattling in his lungs. Grassi slumped over the switch panel, unmoving.

Friedman roused himself, then picked up the sound-powered phone. He relayed to Damage Control Central that the others were dead, but that the job was done. Cade could hear DCC continue to talk on the other end of the line, but Friedman dropped the phone and let it hang. His eyes were closed. It wouldn't be long.

"Don't be afraid," Cade said to Friedman, pulling his pelt from around his shoulders. Now pristine, the hide's injuries transferred to Cade's human form, he gifted it to Friedman.

Cade pulled the zipper down on Friedman's coveralls and pushed the uniform off his shoulders. Then he pulled the seal skin around Friedman's back, distributing the pelt evenly: tugging at the edges, smoothing and tugging, smoothing and tugging until he could pull it around Friedman, covering him. The pelt shimmered once in the darkness — a quick glow — and took shape. Once it did, Friedman disappeared. In his place, floated a seal.

Cade smiled.

Lir, he thought, as his own pain grew nearly unbearable. *Oh, Gods, it hurts. It hurts.*

But then his Navy SEAL training kicked in. *Pain is your friend. It lets you know you're still alive.*

He pushed the thought from his mind. He took a deep breath, and quashed his pain. It was there, he could feel it, but it didn't hurt nearly as bad as it had a second ago. He could endure it. He could endure anything, to get this job done. He could do no less than Friedman and the other men in steering had done to save the crew. *Life's not always a circle*, he realized. *Sometimes it's a line, with an end. And if you live it well, the end can have meaning....*

Despite the pain, he could feel himself smiling. He wouldn't need that discussion with Friedman after all.

It was a pity he wouldn't be able to show Friedman where the best oyster beds grew, and show him how to think like a seal. Friedman wouldn't be able to change back to human form — even if he knew the words to speak, he didn't possess the magic but at least he would be alive.

"Friedman? Friedman?" Cade heard from the phone dangling by its cord. Freidman's brown, whiskered face turned its big eyes toward it.

"Go," Cade said, pushing Friedman toward the water. "Down and out. Don't look back."

Friedman paused, and Cade knew that Friedman must have realized the finality of their good-bye. Friedman nodded.

Cade breathed a sigh of relief. For a moment, he thought Friedman was going to try to remain with him. Again Friedman must have realized he couldn't stay, because doing so rejected Cade's sacrifice.

Friedman barked once, then dove through the blackened water, down into the open sea.

Cade looked at the damage in the chamber, at the dead. He coughed once — waiting — giving Friedman a chance to find his own destiny. His lungs ached, his legs grew numb in the cooling water, but he could still feel eddies of blood run warm from his injuries.

The Navy would wonder what happened to the third man assigned at this duty station, but he'd be damned if he'd stay here and die when the ocean beckoned. He took a deep breath, glad the smoke had finally cleared, and dove, slicing into the cold water of the steering chamber with awkward human limbs. He wished he were a seal for one last moment.

He needed air. Lungs stiff and aching, he felt the pressure against his chest grow the deeper he swam.

But he pushed on toward the hole, working harder and harder the closer he came to the current roaring into the compartment. Muscles weakening, burning with fatigue, he swam tiredly against the battering water.

Finally, grasping the jagged metal edges of the open hull, he pulled himself through, cutting his hands and body, adding lacerations on top of the punctures in his injured legs.

He cried out, water filling his mouth. He blew it out again, and squeezing his eyes shut against the torment, he swam away from the carrier. Once he got past the initial shock of pain, he opened his eyes to the blackness of deep water, wishing again for his seal form, where darkness wasn't a hindrance.

He was free.

He blew the last remnants of air from his lungs, felt the bubbles rise, then swam in that direction.

Searing pain ripped through Cade's chest, and he knew he wouldn't surface before his breath gave out. He kicked hard, swimming, propelling himself upward, toward sunlight.

When at last his breath failed him, he thought he felt the hands of Manannán mac Lir, bringing him home.

It's Elemental

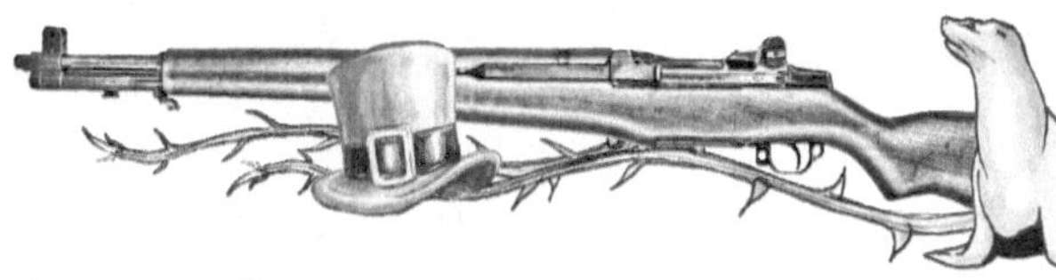

The Face of the Serpent

D.L. Thurston

He sat in the locker room, holding his face in his hands, a mask of green silk, eyes rimmed with yellow. The crowd called from the arena. Their voices bounced down the cinderblock halls of the building to his broken down locker room. The calls fed him. Losing was always a possibility, but tonight it was not an option. They had come to see him win. He dipped his head down into the only face the crowds ever knew, laced it grommet by grommet. The locker room around him was empty. He demanded it.

He looked into the mirror, straightening the eye holes. To those who called for him, the face was his own, that of his father, that of his grandfather. For decades he had dominated the ring as a fictional family. They didn't always win, but they won enough to be beloved, a family tradition that created generations of fans.

To them, he was *El Serpiente*.

For far longer he had been Xiuhcoatl.

"Serpiente! Serpiente!"

And tonight he would win.

"Señoras y señores!"

Today he would taste a glory he'd not tasted before. Not as himself. Not as his father. Not as his grandfather. He started up the cinderblock hallway that led to the arena, the cries of the crowd growing in volume with every step.

"Presentamos."

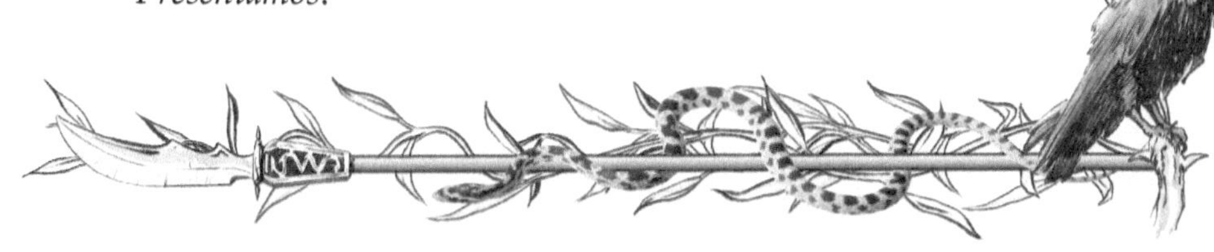

The energy and excitement of the crowd flowed through him. His muscles twitched in anticipation. Tonight he would become the winningest luchador to fight in the rings of Oaxaca.

"El Serpiente!"

And tonight, he would win.

He stepped through the end of the tunnel. Two cannons threw up sparks as he spread his arms. Blinding spotlights, the deafening crowd, the world around him was his and his alone. He strode down the aisle between two rows of seats and felt the hands that reached for him as he passed. These were his people, and he was their champion. As the lights swept away from his face and toward the ring, he saw them, the same faces as always. Jorge, who sold the churros in the stands, trying to earn enough money for a new car. The sweet cinnamon was the only scent that broke through the smell of human around him. Pepe, he dreamed of the day when he would have a mask of his own. He was always on the aisle, always hoping for a chest bump from his hero. Perhaps one day. Maria. Ah, Maria. Made up and pouting, she poured out of her favorite low-cut top. She could be his if he asked, but he had no interest in such things.

His faithful filled the small arena, nearly 500 strong, each touching his mind with their adulation. Children wore copies of his silken "face," eager to be more like the hero of the ring. More like *El Serpiente*.

His eyes burned as his true power coursed through his veins. The old memories of being Xiuhcoatl, the fire serpent, protector of the temples.

A thumping bass line struggled to be heard over the masses as he stepped through the ropes and onto the spring-loaded canvas of the ring. He shrugged off his cape and smiled at the ring boy who quickly gathered it up.

"Tonight!" The cry from the announcer hushed the crowd to awed whispers. "*El Serpiente* will fight for glory!"

El Serpiente flexed his muscles, and the crowd erupted again. He lacked the traditional inverse triangular build of the luchadores, but he still knew how to make men jealous and women excited.

"And for this battle, we have a special opponent. *Presentamos El Toro Del Oro!*"

The announcer sat on "*Oro,*" rolling it around his tongue as the lights swept across to the entryway and onto a pitiful man in a yellow mask. This was the Golden Bull?

As *El Serpiente* approached the record, the challengers had fallen away. Even among the other luchadores he was famous, beloved, and none wanted to see him lose. Many had refused to fight, either by not entering the ring, or by folding once inside.

The crowd rained down its displeasure on the challenger with boos and the occasional empty beer cup. *El Toro* hesitated before slowly approaching the ring, shoulders slumped and head darting around the crowd. He couldn't have been more than seventeen. This had to be his first fight in the center ring of Oaxaca. He fumbled with the ropes, which slipped out of his shaking hands. The crowd jeered at him, laughing at his troubles. *El Serpiente* couldn't help him, that wouldn't be right, that wouldn't be part of the dance of the Lucha.

"What do you say? Shall this battle be for masks?" The ring announcer begged for the approval of the crowd, and received it. *El Serpiente* always had the slight hesitation about masks, even when the victory was so clearly assured. None here had seen his face beneath the face. None here should.

"Very well! *El Serpiente. El Toro Del Oro.* Fight!"

There was a dance performed by matched opponents, circling the ring and each other, looking for the right opening and giving the crowd time to get excited. Against the boy they'd lined up for his victory bout, *El Serpiente* chose what mercy he could.

Make it quick.

He rushed forward, catching *El Toro* with a stiffened arm as the younger fighter turned to run. The springs sang out as *El Toro* hit the canvas, and the crowd leapt to their feet. *El Serpiente* bounced off the ropes, using them to reverse his momentum, and then dove down on the prone fighter, pulling his arms and legs back into a bent hold. The cheers of the crowd coursed through his veins, stronger than any drug. He rolled over, sending El Toro flying and sprawling onto the canvas face first.

The fighter in the yellow mask showed no resistance as *El Serpiente* stood and walked over. He put a foot on his opponent's back, not pushing down, but just for show and to signal an opportunity to cede the fight. *El Toro* made some show of resistance, but the fight was over. The kid was outclassed. *El Serpiente* knelt down and began unlacing the yellow mask, making a show of each rivet, calling to the crowd for their continued support. Had a typical fight been so short, they'd be screaming for refunds. This time, though, they all reveled in his victory. And he reveled in their love.

El Serpiente stood and displayed his trophy to the crowd as *El Toro* was led off in mock shame. He then called over the boy who had swept away his cape. It was the same move he made after every victory, asking for his tequila and lighter. He took a swig from the bottle then breathed forth fire to the delight of the crowd. He didn't need the alcohol or lighter for the flames, but his true nature would horrify those whose love he fed on.

And tonight he fed deep.

⚜

El Serpiente walked slowly back from his fight with *El Toro*. The locker room he left was sparse. The doors of the lockers were rusted, cobwebs hid the corners, and the ceiling hung heavy with water-stained acoustic tiles. The room he returned to was no better maintained, but now serpents of silk roses hung from the ceiling, great long green chains with yellow eyes and red tongues. Among the chains was a banner reading, "*Campeón.*"

The exhilaration of the moment flowed out of him. The adoration of the crowd just didn't last as long anymore. As his mood sobered, he was able to fully consider what he'd done. In the past he'd always been more careful. He had his winning streaks, but he made sure he lost before he got close to the record. Before he might draw any undue attention.

El Serpiente pulled the banner down and crumpled it up. He then unlaced his face and flung it across the room.

"*Tonto,*" he admonished himself. He'd been a fool. For months he'd planned his fall, intended to lose a match to a convincing opponent, but it became increasingly difficult. The power of the crowd was a drug, like the coca leaf was to the humans, and he needed more and more of it. Then a momentum had built up with the streak. The competition had grown weaker to the point where his own pride wouldn't let him lose to the men who faced him across the ring. The pathetic skeleton of a boy he'd faced tonight was the latest in a long line of jokes. Now, now perhaps he could line up a few real competitors. Someone he could lose to. Someone who would help make him look a little more human.

He picked up his face from the floor and looked into its empty, cloth-ringed eyes. Some still knew the name Xiuhcoatl, but they no longer believed. They might speak his name, but they no longer whispered it. They might study him, but they no longer worshiped him. However, every tongue in Oaxaca dripped with the name of *El Serpiente*. With this face, he was more than he'd ever been.

Without this face, he was merely a tool, an atlatl. But this face, this was the face of a god.

"Such dangerous thoughts," a voice behind him chided.

The locker room was his. That was the agreement dating back to when he had been his own "grandfather," and it was one that he had the clout to demand. He quickly held up his face and turned to the interloper.

The other man also wore the mask of a luchador, thick yellow and black bands stretching across his face. The mouth was bent in a mocking smile. The face was like that of a cat, but something larger, more menacing. A jaguar.

"Do not be angry, Serpiente. No one betrayed your orders for solitude."

El Serpiente finished lacing his face, but did not answer.

"You've been careless, Xiuhcoatl."

"I've left that name behind."

The man in the striped mask walked about the room. As he did, every other step fell with the clank of metal. *El Serpiente* knew this creature, knew this foot. It was the dark mirror, the jade jaguar, the god Tezcatlipoca. He'd lost his foot creating the world and had worn a false one ever since. The last *El Serpiente* remembered it was a bone foot; metal was an interesting upgrade. "We've had such difficulty finding you, *Xiuhcoatl*. I can see how that was possible, as you've chosen such..." he pulled down one of the silk rose snakes, and examined it, "base entertainment."

"They love me. Something I would not expect you to understand."

Tezcatlipoca roared like a wild cat. "I do not need love. I have fear."

"Had, Jaguar. You *had* fear. When was the last time your name made a man tremble, caused a mother to pull her child in close?"

"These people don't know who you are. They cheer for the mask."

"I am this mask now."

Tezcatlipoca shook the silk snake with disgust. "This is beneath you. You are the spirit of Xiuhtecuhtli. His dignity, all of our dignities, demand more than fake flowers and drunken cheers. You are more than this. You should be with us."

"In Xibalba?" He'd long left the ancient realm of the gods, realm of the dead, and land of perpetual torture.

"I will overlook the disgust in your voice. Thank me for that."

"To do what? Torture the same souls over and over again? We've lost. They brought their Christ from across the ocean, and they worship him now. Not us. Except for out there, in that ring. There I am worshiped." He held his arms wide, welcoming in imagined adulation. "And it's glorious."

El Serpiente twisted the knife further, "Out there I am a god."

Tezcatlipoca roared again, and stormed toward *El Serpiente.* "You are no god. Your *god* is Xiuhtecuhtli, and you will return to serve him."

"I don't believe I will."

Tezcatlipoca threw the snake to the ground. "You will change your mind."

The jaguar-masked god shook his head and walked out without another word. His false metal foot clanked and echoed down the hall, then the sound stopped all at once. *El Serpiente* picked up the discarded snake, smiled, and wrapped it around him as a boa.

Let Tezcatlipoca talk his talk. No amount of blustering from the obsidian god of discord could change what *Xiuhcoatl* was here. Here a mere spirit could be a god.

⚜

Another vanquished foe was laid out on the spring-loaded canvas of the ring. *El Serpiente* straddled him, one knee on each of his opponent's arms. The man was bigger than him. Stronger than him. But that's why the crowd loved their scrappy hero. Their screams drowned out even the pounding of blood past his ears.

"*Serpiente! Serpiente!*"

It was time for showmanship. In spite of the din, he held his hands up to his ears, calling for more noise. He got it. He pulled at the laces of his foe's blue mask. The string came free, and he held it up to the crowd before prying off the mask. His opponent was left without a face, disgraced to the crowd. *El Serpiente* let the man up to retreat in shame to the shadows of the arena. With a gesture he asked for his tequila and lighter. The crowd exploded with cheers mixed with screams of mock surprise.

El Serpiente returned to his corner of the ring as the crowd continued to chant his ring name. "*Serpiente! Serpiente!*"

"*Señores y señoras, sus campeón, El Serpiente!*" The master of ceremonies kept the crowd worked into a froth. It was a dance that would lead into the next bill of fighters. "Are there none who can defeat him? Are there none who are man enough to even face up to the challenge of *El Serpiente?*"

El Serpiente stood, waving to the crowd, beckoning anyone who would step into the ring for the challenge. Typically none did. Occasionally a man had enough liquid courage running through his blood to stumble to the mat and take a rapid beating.

He scanned the crowd and immediately saw trouble. There was the yellow and black jaguar mask grinning from the back of the crowd.

"*Mierda.*"

Tezcatlipoca rose from his seat, and a hush radiated out from him. None in the crowd had seen the likes of this sort of challenge, another luchador rising and taking on the challenge presented from the ring. Their cheers then redoubled. Of course this was fully staged, all part of the craft of the *lucha libre*, at least from the eyes of the assembled audience. Tezcatlipoca played it up as he worked through the crowd, shaking hands, accepting slaps on the shoulders, kisses from young ladies, and even entertaining a request for an autograph.

All the while, *El Serpiente* could only mutter "*mierda*" over and over, his new mantra in life. He was glad that attention was turned away from him, as it would do no good for the crowd to see anxiety in *El Serpiente*'s posture.

Tezcatlipoca reached the ring. *El Serpiente* strode forward to meet him, gripping the god's hand as hard as he could and pulling him close.

"What do you think you're doing?"

"You said this was fun. I thought I'd give it a try." *El Serpiente* tried to look through the mask, to see what was in the god's eyes. All he saw was the damnable feline grin turning everything into a sarcastic twist.

"*Señores y señoras*, we have a special for you tonight, a man who feels he has the mettle to take on *El Serpiente*. Presentamos..." the master of ceremonies trailed off.

"Titlacauan." The jaguar god had any number of names. This one meant "we are his slaves" in the old tongue.

"Titlacauan!" the MC repeated to the cheering crowd. "We fight until disqualification or submission. *Señores* to corners."

El Serpiente turned to his corner, out of his depth. Humans. Mortals. They could be defeated. But Tezcatlipoca wasn't one of them. He was a god.

"*Serpiente! Serpiente! Serpiente!*"

The chants flooded over him. There was only room for one god here. He lifted his arms triumphantly, sloughing off his silk cape. The crowd let loose with a pure roar. *El Serpiente* turned and didn't care if his eyes burned. Who would see other than Tezcatlipoca?

Let him see.

The bell clanged, merely a whisper against the crowd. Tezcatlipoca approached him, a rookie move. This was a dance, not a confrontation. *El Serpiente* circled the ring, moving from corner to corner, arms outstretched. At each corner he pumped his arms, pumped his crowd.

"You have no place here, Jaguar."

"This is beneath you, Snake."

"Go back to Xibalba."

"Not without you."

"I'll give you this one chance before I make you look like a fool." *El Serpiente* was certain he saw the yellow and black mask grin further.

"You appear to be an expert."

His circuit complete, *El Serpiente* charged Tezcatlipoca, propelled by cheers like they were rocket fuel. He ducked low as the god tensed against a direct blow. *El Serpiente* went between the Jaguar's knees with his head, straightened up, and sent Tezcatlipoca over his shoulder and bouncing to the mat. *El Serpiente* raised his arms for the crowd, keeping his back to the sprawled god. He didn't need to see his opponent, not right now. The crowd was his eyes. They quieted, they gasped, and he knew that the god was back on his feet. *El Serpiente* shot an elbow back and made firm contact with Tezcatlipoca's sternum, sending him back to the mat.

Again, the crowd was behind him.

El Serpiente dropped to his knees, assuring that he landed firmly on the jaguar god's back, pinning him. He leaned in nice and close. "You're out of your league, old man. You're not going to win. Not here."

A fat green bird darted by *El Serpiente*'s face, screeching in his ear as he did so. Sparrows or other small birds often got into the ring, but nothing like this. He turned, distracted, giving Tezcatlipoca opportunity to throw him off. He hit the mat hard to the displeasure of the crowd. He focused, first on the blinding light then at a looming silhouette.

The spring-loaded comfort of the mat slipped away as two muscled arms hauled him up. The world swam past, swirling and blurred, as he was carried to the edge of the ring. He saw the ropes below him. He struggled against it, but the god only gripped him that much harder, lifting him higher. The first row of the seats flew toward him, the audience scrambling to avoid *El Serpiente*'s airborne form.

He hit.

He intimately knew every aspect of the building where he reigned. The ceiling was pressed tin, the floor was cold concrete. What he hit was soft, yielding. Like dirt. The world coalesced around him. It was dirt. And leaves, and grass, and rot. He turned onto his back, knowing what he would see. Trees, a thick jungle canopy, dripping with blood and strung with human bodies.

And he knew he would see Tezcatlipoca there.

The god tossed his mask aside, revealing a skull of a face, neither human nor feline. Instead it was a horrible amalgam, elongated in with a jaw-full of horribly sharp teeth.

"Welcome home, Xiuhcoatl."

El Serpiente tried to straighten himself up, but a metallic kick to the ribs sent him sprawling again. "Why have you brought me here?"

"I'm taking you up on your challenge. You said I couldn't beat you in the ring. So I've brought you to Xibalba instead. Brought you home."

Another kick cracked his ribs, and pain shot through *El Serpiente*'s body. A third forced the air out of his lungs. He gasped, sucking in the fetid stench that wrapped over the ground like a blanket. His chances to act were slipping away from him. A liquid sound of shifting weight made *El Serpiente* whip around, ignoring the pain in his ribs, to grab Tezcatlipoca's false foot before it could strike him again. He twisted hard, loosening the foot in its mooring, but he lacked the torque to remove it entirely. Instead, he put his full force behind pushing, sending the god down into the muck and the mud.

El Serpiente stood gingerly, finding his footing as the god beneath him tried to gain some purchase with a loose foot and looser ground. The luchador could be taken from his ring, but the ring couldn't be taken from him. He crooked an elbow and fell toward the god, aiming at his chest. Tezcatlipoca tensed, and *El Serpiente* immediately saw his mistake. The god beneath him shifted into the jaguar beast of Aztec nightmares, claws and teeth flashing, white shards of pain awaiting a victim.

Even in this place of myth and legend, physics fought against *El Serpiente*. The world slowed as his fate played through his mind. Possibilities reeled. The first of the claws hit him, and fresh pain shot through his body. More claws dug into his flesh. His back arched.

And continued to arch.

His body became a lithe thing, rippled with long muscles and unencumbered by limbs. The world around him became hyper-real as his senses changed. The thing that launched toward Tezcatlipoca looked human, the thing that landed on him was the serpent spirit that still lived deep within his heart, set completely free for the first time in centuries. He writhed against the jaguar, letting its claws tear at his scaled skin if it meant being free.

He smelled blood. It excited him. His head shot forward, and fangs dug into yielding, warm-blooded flesh. Delicious. Part of him missed the taste. The jaguar god howled in pain and attempted to scramble away, claws digging into the bloody ground. As he did, *El Serpiente* twisted his body around the god's torso and squeezed. He came around again and bit at the jaguar's neck.

The jaguar screamed in a human voice, bucking up and back. The motion slammed *El Serpiente* into a tree. Bone and wood cracked, loosening the serpent's grip.

Tezcatlipoca prowled around to face *El Serpiente*. "Doesn't it feel good, serpent? Doesn't it feel right? We were never meant to be like them. We were meant to be us."

"What does it matter to you?" *El Serpiente* coiled and uncoiled, feeling the ground against his skin, warm and moist.

Tezcatlipoca sat on his haunches and cleaned his bite wounds. "We are incomplete."

El Serpiente lifted his head up, his body tensing, his spine cracking and popping. Deep within, he felt a heat in his body, working its way up from his gut. "I happen to like the niche I've found in the world."

"It's unseemly."

"I don't care." Flames rose out from his body, and he vomited them forth at the jaguar god. Tezcatlipoca jumped and howled, his fur crackling and adding a new stench to the horrid bouquet of Xibalba. The jaguar turned tail and ran through the woods, trailing smoke. *El Serpiente* gave chase, spitting flames at the trees as he went. "I'll burn this whole place down, jaguar. I don't care!"

"It's your home too, serpent!"

El Serpiente changed directions to follow the taunt, letting loose with another belch of flame. Bark peeled away from trees ahead of him, and wood cracked and popped in his wake. The destruction was beautiful to him. It felt right. It felt good.

But he knew the jaguar was toying with him like a cat with a mouse. It felt good now. But if he stayed in this place he'd again be just a minion. A tool, sent out to do the bidding of a god who had grown old and fat in his complacency. Cursed to do the will of a god who no longer had anything to do.

There was a cracking, so nearly blending in to the pop and crack of burning wood he almost missed hearing it. The jaguar again leapt at him with a roar and a flash of teeth and claw. Being a snake gave him certain mobility, but against the sidelong attack all he could do was attempt to double back. The jaguar god raked claws against him and was gone again into the jungle. *El Serpiente* spat fire in the direction Tezcatlipoca retreated, then he came around and created a circle of flame in all directions. The fire burned away a clean circle, leaving only dirt and ash behind.

"Come into my ring, Tezcatlipoca."

El Serpiente stood, regaining his legs, his body. He slapped his biceps, felt them twitch and shudder in anticipation of action. This felt more familiar to him. A defined boundary of conflict, the ground yielding beneath his feet. It wasn't spring loaded, but it would do. Around him he was aware of forms. The fat green bird alit on a tree, resolving into the god Quetzalcoatl. Around him a pantheon of creatures took their positions, settling in, ready to watch. The jaguar leapt out of the jungle again, passing quickly through the flames. It rose onto rear legs, once again taking form as Tezcatlipoca.

"So this is really all—"

"You talk too much." *El Serpiente* ran full speed toward the god. He slammed shoulder first into Tezcatlipoca's sternum, then spun around and kicked the god's feet out with a sweep of the leg. Tezcatlipoca fell, face first. *El Serpiente* stood over him, and heard the familiar voices of his fellow spirits cheering him on. In the ring, he would now go for the mask, unlacing it then holding it up for the crowd. But the mask was long gone, and he knew the jaguar god cared about something else much more.

He pinned the god and again gripped onto the false foot. The metal was cold and hard. As he twisted, Tezcatlipoca kicked at him with his free foot, tried to reach back, but *El Serpiente* had long ago learned how to keep a bucking opponent pinned. The foot grated and clicked as he twisted. Finally, it came free with a satisfying pop. *El Serpiente* held it aloft for the gods and spirits to see, before casting it to the jungle. He was certain he even saw Quetzalcoatl cheer.

He flipped the god back over.

"Submit."

Tezcatlipoca spat in his face. *El Serpiente* spat back, a quick shot of flame past the god's right ear. "Submit, jaguar."

"I am a god, I submit to no one. Certainly not to a spirit."

Another shot of flames, this time just to the left. A little closer, intended to catch some hair. "You've lost."

"I never lose."

"I've won!" His voice echoed as it would around the ring.

"Have you?"

El Serpiente punched the canvas. It rebounded with the familiar twang of the springs. He looked up, and the world around him was no longer Xibalba. Had it ever been?

Their battle had destroyed much of the arena. Smoke rose from seats, the ropes were singed, and the last remnants of the audience were those who hadn't been able to escape the rampage.

And there, on the mat behind him, was his face. It lay there like a rag where it had sloughed off as he shifted to his spirit form. He rose from his fallen adversary.

"They would learn your true nature eventually."

"Not like this." He climbed over the ropes, attempting to help some of the pinned and injured crowd members. There was fear in each of their eyes, even as he tried to help them. They scrambled away as best they could. He heard a scream that chilled him. Maria. He lifted a beam off her, tried to help her up, but she clawed at him as she scampered away.

He slumped, body and soul. He had been their god. Now he was their devil.

"There's only one place you belong, Xiuhcoatl."

He walked up the stairs, and found the place where the god's foot had fallen.

"Take it, serpent. You still can't run farther than I can chase."

El Serpiente broke into a sprint, taking the stairs two and three at a time until he was out of the seating area. Out of the arena. Out of the life he'd made for himself over generations.

"*Dragón! Dragón! Dragón!*"

He held his face in his hands. It was cheap red cloth, not silk, but this was his face now.

When you needed to find a place that didn't care who you were, there was always Mexico. And when you were already in Mexico and needed a place to run, there was always Tijuana.

One day, he might be tracked down again. He still had the foot, but he was certain Tezcatlipoca would find another. He just had to keep a lower profile. Perhaps in a few weeks he'd even lose.

But tonight he would win.

Tonight he would again taste victory.

He put on his face and rose.

El Dragón would be entertaining the crowd tonight.

LOOKING A GIFT HORSE

An early tale of Terrorbelle

Patrick Thomas

BRANCHES SLAPPING YOUR FACE HURT. IT DOESN'T MATTER IF you're on the ground or fifty feet off it. Flying through a forest is a particularly stupid thing to do, even if you have the option of blaming it on the fact that you're an eleven-year-old girl on the run from one of the gang of soldiers who killed you mother.

The soldier was chasing me, but no one besides me would blame him for it. It seemed only reasonable since I started things by stalking him and his partner. I had a good motive. A great one really. Those bastards and their friends... They did horrible things to my mother and made me watch. They made my mother watch as they did them to me and then killed her. I was lucky enough to get away. If you call being alone in Faerie and unable to sleep without waking up screaming from nightmares lucky.

I coped. One thing helped me continue to survive—the thought of all of those soldiers dead.

Seems he wanted the same thing for me, but so far that hadn't worked out for him. Mama's little Terrorbelle doesn't die easy.

Didn't mean that the damn graycoat stopped trying to kill me. And having pink hair made it easier for him to follow me. It sort of stood out among all the greens and browns.

It was down to which of us got the other first. The smart wager would be on the trained soldier, not the scrap kid. Even now I heard Mama tell me not to call myself scrap, that my parents were two different races didn't matter, but with a mama who was an ogre and a daddy who's a pixie, it was an apt term.

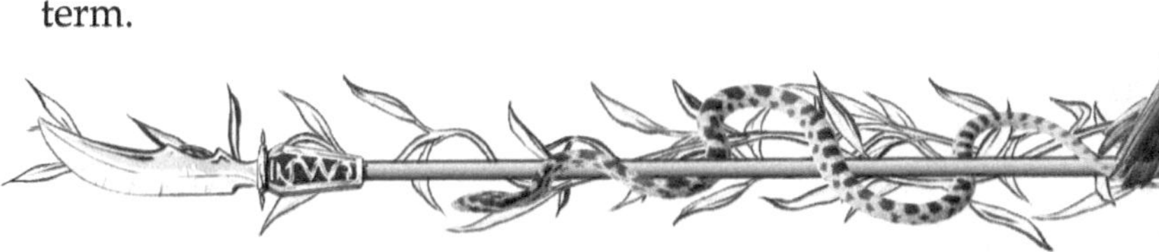

I'd bet on me, even if I haven't proved myself very good at killing yet, which was entirely my fault. This whole mess started when I found the graycoat soldiers' camp.

✤

It wasn't easy, but a combination of determination and luck led me to them. The black-hearted killers had been sent out on an extended patrol, just the two of them. No other graycoats to worry about getting in the way. It seemed like such a good idea.

I didn't know the graycoats' real names, but I'll never forget their faces. I gave them names, rather than figure out what their mothers had called them. It seemed unlikely that they even had mothers. If they did, how could they kill someone else's?

I called them Oaf and Tiny. Tiny was tall. My term of scorn referred to something other than his height.

Oaf and Tiny slept, not worried or smart enough to have one of them keep watch.

Getting into their camp was child's play. I stood over the mother killers, watching as the light from their fire flickered across their faces.

Neither looked to be the embodiment of evil that I knew they were. The knife I'd stolen during my escape from the slavers felt heavy, but it was barely the length of my forearm. It sat in my palm, just waiting to slit their throats. True, my wings were scrap like me. The beauty of pixie and the hardness of ogre. One flap and I could likely cut the mother killers' heads off without a knife, but the idea of using the only beautiful parts of me to kill made me sick to my stomach. More sick than the thought of killing alone.

And if the truth be told, as I stood over their sleeping forms I discovered something: killing two sleeping men in cold blood—even two of Thandau's soldiers—wasn't something I could bring myself to do, even with everything they'd done. Everything inside of me burned with the desire to see them dead for what they did to us. Yet killing for killing's sake was something that Mama had always taught me was wrong. I doubt my mother's killers would appreciate the irony.

I couldn't bring myself to end them while they lay helpless.

So I got stupid. I kicked dirt in their faces to wake them up so I could kill them while they were conscious instead.

It was an idiotic mistake of epic proportions. The soldiers snapped awake.

"What?" Tiny yelled as he grabbed his sword. The weapon was quite a bit longer than Oaf's. Babbey, my granny, would say he was trying to make up for something else. I missed the days when I only pretended to know what she meant.

Already alert, Oaf called out, "It's the winged scrap bitch. She got away!"

They had left me in a graycoat camp, a toy to be passed around among Thandau's soldiers.

"Damn right I got away from your slave camp. You won't be so lucky," I said. "I'm going to kill you for what you did to my mother."

Tiny leapt up and threw his bedroll aside as he held his sword in front of him. Oaf rose slowly and tossed his bedroll at me like it was a net. It covered my razor-sharp wings. He rushed at me, knocking me to the ground where he used his arms to pin my entangled shoulders and wings. I dropped my knife and couldn't reach it.

"Should have killed us while were sleeping," Oaf said.

At that moment, I couldn't agree more. "If I'd known I'd had your permission, I'd have done it."

"Smart mouth. Not the scared little thing you were last time." Oaf reached back and smacked me across the face. "I don't like smart mouths, little scrap girl."

Tiny was giggling, as he hopped back from one foot to the other. "Go easy on her." I was shocked. None of the graycoats had shown the slightest inclination for mercy before. "She came to us. You know what that means, right? The scrap didn't get enough the first time, and she wants more." Tiny dropped his pants and stepped toward me.

My nightmare had re-entered the waking world. Everything I could see turned red. Anger, not thought, controlled me as I smashed my forehead into Oaf's nose, making his world join mine in the red zone.

I got to my feet and struck Oaf with my elbow, then kicked him in a place I'd much rather be unfamiliar with. I may be scrap, but I was strong. The bastard fell to his side with only a brief pause on his knees.

I ripped the bedroll from me and tossed it away. Tiny came waddling at me with his sword, but having wings had its advantages. I flew up and over his head, flipping in the process to land behind him and pick up the knife I'd dropped.

Tiny spun with his blade aimed for my neck. I ducked as fast as I could, but his sword took a piece of my scalp and some of my pink hair as it whizzed by.

I stabbed forward with my knife. I'd like to say that the part of his male anatomy that I cut into was a target of convenience, but I can't for sure. All I know is it felt good, angry good, especially as Tiny let out a high pitched scream as he became a eunuch. He swung his sword wildly back at me—his missing bits must have made him forget his soldier training—but I was too close. His forearm hit me in the side of the head, letting me grab hold of the hilt.

I bit his arm, pulled, and the sword was mine. I took a step back and pointed the blade at him the same way he'd done to me. Tiny pulled a dagger from under his arm and lunged at me, but overstepped. He tripped, helped by the fact that he hadn't bothered to pull up his pants which still were wrapped around his ankles. I rammed the sword forward as he fell. His chest and the blade met, but I think it is safe to say that the sword probably got the better of the meeting, at least judging by the look on Tiny's face as the blade went in one side of him and out the other.

Tiny fell over, sliding off my blade like well-cooked meat off a spit.

I stood over him, holding the bloody sword, expecting to feel an angry pride, a fierce satisfaction that one of my mother's murderers had died at my hands. And I did, but what I felt much stronger was a vicious nausea from the pit of my stomach that didn't so much fight its way up as explode out my mouth and all over Tiny's corpse. The sight of so much vomit and blood led to a second wave of my intestines revolting, but this time I managed to turn so my gut emptied onto the ground.

I thought my first kill would make me tough, but all it did was make me realize that I really didn't know the meaning of the word.

I stood and dry heaved, barely hearing the footsteps behind me. I spun, leading with my sword and was lucky enough to block Oaf's blade on its way to slice open my skull. It would have been even more impressive had I known the proper way to hold a sword, but I didn't, and the impact knocked the blade from my grip.

Now I stood weaponless against a soldier with a sword. The fact that I was just a kid hit me hard. An idiot kid who thought she could take on soldiers by herself. My righteous anger was replaced by fear. I couldn't beat Oaf this way. My only hope for survival lay in getting far away from him. I flapped my wings and took to the skies. Or I would have if I could have. Their camp was in a clearing, but the treetops surround it formed a canopy that nothing larger than a bird was flying through. I had to fly on a path parallel to the ground, maneuvering through the branches and the trunks.

Oaf, who turned out not to live up to his name, pulled out a bow and a quiver. I flew faster, ignoring the branches as they tore into my face and skin.

The graycoat raced after me, managing to shoot and run at the same time. I think the running threw off his aim, but not enough for my comfort. I felt the air ripple as an arrow passed close to my face.

I ignored everything I could push and fly though. My face and arms were soon bloody, but I couldn't risk stopping to do more than look back.

There was no sign of Oaf, so I went faster, thinking I might get away, all the while blaming myself for being foolish enough to have gone after the graycoats with only a knife. And more so for not having slit their throats while they slept.

I needed something to even things up. With a bow, I could pick Oaf off from the sky. Unfortunately, other than knowing a bow had a string, I had no idea how to make one. Or shoot it. I told myself that if I survived this, I'd learn.

Suddenly, I wondered if I had hit my head because around me the trees seemed to move by themselves. I stopped and stood on a high branch. Far behind and below me, Oaf trampled through the woods. He was far enough away that he looked like an insect. Hidden by the tree trunk, I looked in front of me where the leaves seemed to dance as if invisible hands shook them. A high-pitched whistling sound teased my ears. I walked along branches until I got close enough to see beyond the woods.

A river with impressively choppy rapids raced by, so wide that the trees on the other side appeared to be the size of toothpicks.

Ckuf. I swam like a rock. My ogre and pixie heritage combined to make my muscles denser than water. Simply put, I sink.

From stalking Oaf and Tiny, I knew that more pairs of graycoats patrolled both upstream and down. I had no way of figuring whether Oaf had a way of summoning them or worse, if he already had. In the woods, I'd never get far enough ahead of him. Yet moving along the river might be an invitation for more graycoats to shoot me out of the sky.

My only chance was to get across that river. Even a good swimmer would have a rough time of it in those choppy waters.

I climbed to the top of the nearest tree that wasn't shaking. Fear made sure I was shaking enough as it was. Wind makes flying dangerous for someone my size. A good updraft could carry me for miles, while a bad downdraft could send me crashing.

The winds seemed to blow along the same direction as the river. That was good. If I caught it just right I could angle my air path diagonally and make it across the water.

I leapt into the air as high as I could. My feet more than cleared the trees in front of me and I was airborne.

Pixie wings don't work like birds' wings. We don't glide well. It's more akin to a bee or hummingbird, requiring constant work to stay up, with smaller movements to change direction.

There were no problems getting to the river. The problem was staying over it. The wind made a tunnel of the air, which kept pushing me aside. I didn't have the strength to punch through it.

But maybe I could go over it.

I pushed and climbed, but the wind didn't let up. If anything, it got stronger. One big gust flipped me over and spun me around. I couldn't tell up from down, left from right.

I stopped moving my wings. It took a moment, but I started to plunge. Now I knew which way down was. With any luck, I'd manage to right myself before I hit the water.

Luck wasn't in a helpful mood. I hit the water and kept going down. I pushed and kicked to speed it up. It might seem odd, purposefully heading in the opposite direction of air, but it made sense. I can't swim, but I can walk. I wasn't too far from land.

I picked my best guess of which way the shore lay and let the current push me as I ran along the bottom, pulling against the water with my arms. I went with the same diagonal strategy I tried in the air, hoping to have better luck. My wings were hard and worked just as well in the water as the air.

My lungs burned, begging for air, but I couldn't stop. I wouldn't. I refused to die until all those who killed my mother were dead too.

White stars danced in front of me in the water, then everything turned dark. I felt something brush against me, then bump me, not once but three times. I guess the third time was the fix because my head broke the water's surface. No nectar has even tasted as sweet as that first gasp of air.

I made it to the same side of the river I'd left, more crawling than walking, and moved as far away from the river as I could before my limbs gave out and dropped me on my stomach.

I lay gasping for air, but my breath was proving a more elusive quarry than I was. I heard hoof beats approaching. Quickly, I rolled over. What looked like an odd horse stared down at me. Odd because of the angular shape of its head, its overly large mouth, and its blue color.

"Not a good swimmer," it said, which was not particularly odd. Many animals in Faerie can talk if they make the effort to learn. "Seems a foolish thing to try, getting across my river."

"Your river?" I said.

"Oh, yes. Nothing can fly across it, although some call it Wind River. Few can swim across it except for little old Aughisky."

"You can swim that?"

"Oh yes. Didn't you see Aughisky out there helping you make it in?"

I didn't, but I felt his push. "I owe you my thanks, Aughisky."

"Yes, many owe Aughisky, but so few pay their debts. It's why Aughisky left the family lake and went out on his own. Other Aughisky thought him mad, but Aughisky proved them wrong. Crossing lake easy. Crossing river hard. People willing to pay to cross. Now would the little, winged girl like to discuss what she owes Aughisky for saving her?"

"What do you want?" I asked, nervously. I had never seen a horse with sharp teeth smile before.

"So if Aughisky tells little wing thing what Aughisky wants, wing thing will give it to Aughisky?"

"I'll certainly consider it," I replied. "If I agree, then what I owe you for saving me is paid?"

"Aughisky supposes." The horse's mouth opened wide and revealing even more teeth than I'd first thought. All of them appeared long and sharp. Aughisky stepped toward me. I scurried back. It continued to move so I reached out to look for a weapon – a rock, a branch, something to defend myself with. My hand found something, and I pulled it up, only to feel it squish between my fingers.

I looked and realized I was holding something brown and mushy that likely was the insides of a person or animal at one time. I realized

Aughisky had stopped his advance. I stood and the wind almost knocked me over again. I wasn't going to be flying any time soon.

"Liver is so repulsive. So unsavory. No good for no one, no good at all."

"How do you know it's a liver?" I asked.

"Aughisky knows."

"Do you know how it got here?" I asked, dropping it.

Aughisky had a hint of a smile on his long face that vanished so quickly I wasn't sure it was ever there. "How would Aughisky know that?"

I shook my hand, sending leftover pieces of innards flying. Aughisky jumped back like I had thrown a knife.

"Watch what you do. Aughisky did save your little life."

"And you want this liver gone?" I asked.

"Aughisky does."

I bent down and picked it up again. "Then we have a deal."

The horse's jaw dropped. "No. Wait. Aughisky didn't mean—"

But it was too late. I rushed down to the river and threw the liver in, but not before coating my hands in it, getting bits under my fingernails. The horse seems afraid of the liver, so it seemed wise. After all, our deal was for the liver, not any juices it might contain.

"Done," I said and started walking downstream, praying I wouldn't run into any graycoats before the wind let up or there was a way to cross.

I heard hoof beats and turned to watch Aughisky cantor up beside me.

"Little wing girl no want to cross river anymore?"

"Can't figure out how to do it safely here. I'll find another place that will work better," I said, walking faster. Aughisky kept up easily, an advantage of four legs over two.

"But Aughisky could take little wing girl."

"I'm not sure I could afford your price," I said.

Aughisky smiled again, this time wider. The sight of a horse with teeth as sharp as those of a dragon sent chills up my spine. "Aughisky always willing to negotiate. What do you have?"

"What do you want?" I countered.

"Perhaps little wing girl's name?"

"I'm a kid, not a toddler. I know better than to give you my name," I said.

"Aughisky told you his name. Be fair."

"I don't think Aughisky is your name. I think it is what you are," I said.

"Why little wing girl think that?"

"Because you referred to your family as the other Aughisky," I said.

The water horse laughed. "You smart. Aughisky foolish for letting that slip. Doesn't mean we cannot come to agreement for passage over Wind River. Gold is always good."

"I've no gold," I said.

"Silver then."

"None."

"Any coin?"

I shook my head. "Sadly, no."

The horse looked at my finger. "What about ring?"

It was pewter. Not worth much, but it had sentimental value. It was a gift from my pixie father on my last birthday. I thought about it, and I could hear old Thunderrod in my mind's ear telling me he could always buy me another so long as I survived.

"Deal. I'll give it to you once I'm safely on the other side," I said.

"No, too easy for you to run off, and then where will poor Aughisky be? Ring first before passage."

I took it off and held it. "Ring for safe passage."

The water horse reached out with his mouth and plucked the ring from my fingers with his lips. I had to force myself not to pull my hand back. "Ring for passage is what I said."

An arrow whizzed by my head, clipping my ear and Aughisky's mane. I turned to see Oaf lean out from behind a tree, notching another arrow. The wind probably just saved my life.

"Who be shooting at Aughisky?"

"One of Thandau's graycoats, and he's lining up his next shot. Time for running and swimming," I said.

"Aughisky thinks little wing girl is right. Get on!"

I did, and no sooner had I sat upon his back then we were off running down the shore. I barely got a hold of his mane before I looked back to see an arrow sticking out of the ground where we had stood.

Aughisky ran so fast and far that in moments, I could no longer see Oaf.

"Think Aughisky lost graycoat."

"Looks that way," I said.

"Foolish soldier, try to kill Aughisky. Not realize he on wrong side of food chain." Before I could say anything, he ran into the water. A rapid hit me hard enough to knock me over, but I didn't budge. I tried to move, but my lower limbs were caught fast.

"Aughisky, my legs—"

"Yes, Aughisky knows. Aughisky has special power, won't let rider get off."

I didn't like the way he said get instead of fall, but before I could question this, he dove beneath the water. I barely had time to get a breath before we sank to the bottom of the river where Aughisky ran as easily as he had along the shore.

The horse could breathe underwater but I couldn't. I tried to get off, but Aughisky had told the truth about his sticking power.

Drowning is not a good way to die. I didn't survive the damn graycoats to get killed by a swimming horse.

I wrapped my right arm around Aughisky's neck and pulled. Even underwater I heard some pops from his spine adjusting. I tried to move my arm, but couldn't. The sticking magic extended to his neck.

Good. I dug my liver-coated hand into the skin there and felt it start to burn as I jammed my fingernails in. I took my free hand and rammed it into Aughisky's left eye. The horse screamed and tried to throw me off, turning the magic stickiness off. If I fell, I'd be stuck at the bottom of the river, so I held on with my legs and arms.

"Up," I glubbed with some of my little remaining air as I squeezed harder and wrapped my fingers around his eye.

The water must have carried my words well enough because Aughisky swam to the surface.

"Your hands burn!" the water horse screamed. "Let go of Aughisky, you monster."

"Not until you take me to shore." I felt the water horse tense beneath me. "If we go under the water, your eye comes out. I may rip it out anyway just on principal."

"No, Aughisky needs his eyes. Aughisky make you a deal. You take hand from Aughisky's eye and Aughisky take you back to shore."

"No, I want to go to the far shore. And you will not get off that easily. You tried to kill me and broke our previous deal."

"Only because Aughisky hungry."

"You were going to eat me?" I said.

"Not all of you. Aughisky leave the liver. It is foul, poisonous thing."

"Well you better come up with something better to offer me than passage only," I said, squeezing his eye.

"Aughisky doesn't know what you want. You tell Aughisky, and it shall be yours. Promise. Is better than deal. Never break promise. Break deals all the time."

"Whatever I ask? Your word?" I said.

"Yes, Aughisky's word is his promise."

A plan began to form in my mind and I smiled. I told Aughisky what I wanted.

The water horse nodded. "Aughisky can do that."

"You better, or I will come back for you with a hundred livers," I said.

"No need to threaten. Aughisky's word is good."

The water horse swam to the far shore. I got both legs on dry land before I let go of his neck and eye.

Aughisky swam back into the river. Even if he broke his word, at least I made it past the river.

But the water horse kept his promise and went back to where we'd started. I kept pace with him on my side of the river. I made a little effort to pretend to be hiding, but knew the graycoat would still see me. I didn't want him to give up the chase at this point because he thought I'd gotten away. Oaf was still there trying to figure a way across. Aughisky offered his services. They made a deal, and the graycoat climbed on. The water horse reared up, causing the graycoat to try to grab onto his flank where Aughisky's magic locked the soldier's hands in place, along with his legs. I guess he learned his lesson from me.

I squinted and strained to watch as Oaf was taken into the river. I couldn't hear Oaf over the winds, but I saw his face contort in a scream as he was dragged under. The screams were much shorter than those of my mother. I couldn't tell if tears accompanied them like my own when he and his ilk attacked me, but these silent screams were infinitely more satisfying.

Moments later, Aughisky surfaced back on my side of the river, a limp Oaf still stuck to his back.

I stepped forward to examine the soldier. He looked dead, but just to be sure I pulled his sword out of his scabbard and ran it through his black heart.

"See, Aughisky kept word."

"So you did," I said, taking Oaf's bow and quiver, as well as his sword belt and dagger. Oaf's weapons were the last part of the water horse's promise to me. Now I had a bow, and I would be able to kill the rest of my mother's murderers from a distance.

"May Aughisky eat now?"

"First return my ring," I said.

"That was part of our deal for passage."

"For safe passage. You broke the deal. Return the ring," I said.

"Pewter ring worthless."

I held my hand out. "True, except for the fact that it is mine."

"Little wing girl fight Aughisky over worthless ring?"

"Not if you give it to me," I said.

The water horse laughed. "Aughisky likes little wing girl." He retched and out came the ring from his gullet onto the sand. "Have ring with compliments. May Aughisky eat now?"

"Yes, Aughisky may eat now," I said.

The water horse reached back with his mouth and opened it wide. His sharp teeth tore Oaf's hand off. The water horse chewed and swallowed it in three gulps.

"Meat doesn't taste right dry." Aughisky carried Oaf's body into the rapids.

I sat and picked up my ring, then watched as the waters turned crimson, then back to white. Aughisky did not surface again, but a lone liver did.

I headed in the same direction as the river. There were more of Mama's killers to find and make pay.

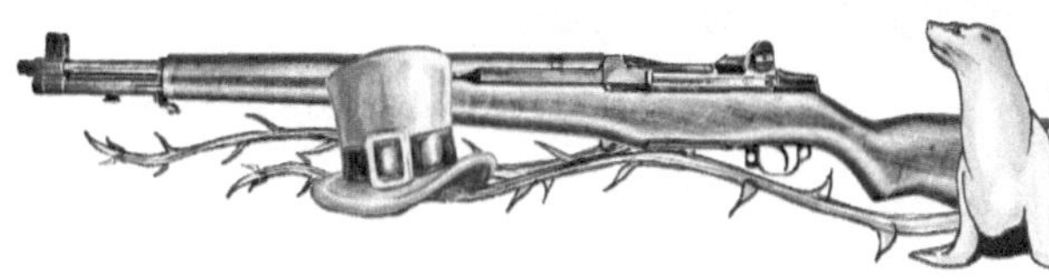

FIFTEEN PERCENT

Jody Lynn Nye

MARCEL DORNER FELT HIS COLLAR JERK BACKWARD AGAINST HIS Adam's apple. He choked. His hands flew to his throat to try and free the pressure, but it was as inescapable as the fierce, high voice that accompanied it.

"Lying in the gutter! Plastered to the gills, while some of us starve! How dare you!"

In panic, Marcel kicked out, feeling for the brick-paved street under his feet, but there was nothing in reach. He managed to pry open his gummed-up eyelids. His body dangled over the gutter in question. It wasn't that nice a gutter, but it was the one where he had landed among the horse droppings and discarded plastic go-cups, oh, how many hours ago? It had seemed like a good place to lie down. His body had felt way too heavy to walk all the way home, with its load of whisky and Hurricanes on board. The comforting glow had vanished with the shock.

Marcel gasped in a breath. He wiped dust and wet debris — probably vomit — from his mouth and drooping black mustache. His eyes traveled along the now friendly-seeming bend of concrete, up a narrow column of draped white linen that would have looked right at home on a fashion show runway, to the arm that held up his six-foot frame with no apparent effort. Behind the arm was a very disapproving and all-too-familiar face. To anyone else, the petite, pale-skinned female with long, flowing tresses of golden hair looked like the most beautiful woman in the world. To him, she embodied all the furies of Hell, the Internal Revenue Service, and every telemarketer ever born. Ninette was a *filandiere*. And she was his literary agent.

"Hi, Ninette," he choked out, trying to evoke a friendly smile, even though his head felt as if it swelled with blood. His eyesight narrowed to a pinpoint of light surrounded by blackness. "Uh, could you let me down?"

"*Aaaagh!*" she screamed. She turned and threw him against the wall of the bar, twelve feet away. Marcel winced at the impact, and slithered to the pavement. He hoped he could just lie there, but he knew better. She stalked over to glower down at him, and wound a hand in his wavy hair. He winced. "You let *me* down! Where is your manuscript? I need to turn it in!"

Marcel raised his hands to protect his face.

"I've been working on it," he assured her.

She let go of his hair and crossed her arms against her dress, the folds of linen as disapproving as her expression.

"Fine. Then, let's see how far you've gotten."

"Uh...."

She reached down and grabbed a handful of his shirtfront. Marcel felt his feet leave the ground again.

"That's what I thought! Come on!"

Carrying him like a rag doll, Ninette stalked toward the corner, where Toulouse met Bourbon Street. Even at this hour of the morning, Marcel knew half his friends would see them.

"Put me down," he pleaded. "Ninette, I'll do anything..."

"You do nothing," she snapped. "Leaving me to go hungry while you drink yourself unconscious!"

But she let go of his shirt. Marcel stumbled as he hit the ground. He thought about stepping into the nearest bar—New Orleans was full of them—and just shooting the breeze with one of his fellows until she got frustrated and went away. He didn't have the words that she needed. They both knew it. He wanted another drink so badly that he could feel it in every taste bud and every dry inch of his throat, but God alone knew what Ninette would do to him if he tried. Marcel sighed and trudged toward his apartment on the southeast edge of the French Quarter.

After three times being on the New York Times Bestseller List, young writers always wanted to ask Marcel for advice on making it as a writer. The truth was they only wanted to know how to make it big, talk-show big, fancy-car big, mansion and servants big. He always told them the same thing.

"It's nothing complicated, just work hard." Though he didn't follow his own words most of the time.

"What about Ninette?" the fans always asked, at conventions, libraries, and book signings. "We hear she's not only your agent, but your muse. You said in *Esquire* that she gives you inspiration for your books?"

"That is true," Marcel always admitted. But it wasn't the whole truth. "One more piece of advice. Never let a filandiere become your agent, even if she asks nicely. It's not worth it. You'd be better off going broke in peace."

"What's so bad about it?"

"She takes fifteen percent of everything," he told them.

"That sounds kind of high," some of them agreed, "but don't they all take that much?"

Trying to explain always made him feel desperate. "You don't understand. She takes fifteen percent of *everything*."

They *didn't* understand. How could they? It had never happened to them.

Marcel's apartment had one of the best views in New Orleans, on the third floor of one of the long buildings overlooking Jackson Square. Until Ninette had come along, he would never have dared to rent a place like that. He had always grown up with the tales of how no one ever spent the night on the top floor of the old buildings of the city because of the lonely spirits of those who had died there over the past three centuries. He heard strange noises in the night, sure, but nothing ever bothered him. If there were haunts, they were as afraid of Ninette as he was.

His computer stood on a low table right in front of the window. Slow, warm blues music wound its way over the sill as he sat down and flipped on the CPU. He felt the music infiltrate his soul, lifting it to heaven and beyond. His headache began to ease. There was no place on Earth like New Orleans for making a body feel at home.

Ninette hung at his elbow while he brought up the file. She frowned down at it. He shuddered. Here came the moment of truth. Ninette hit 'Word Count.'

"Eighty-three thousand?" she shrieked. "You should be at a hundred thousand by now! I have to give them your first chapters to append to the present volume. They want the rest of the book by this week. Get to work!"

He cringed, and started typing. Within the first few sentences, the familiar pearly haze arose over his keyboard.

"Ah!" Ninette exclaimed, leaning closer. The faerie inhaled. Tendrils of the white mist flowed into her nose and mouth.

Dissatisfaction formed a black and sour knot in Marcel's belly.

Since he had started to associate with Ninette, he had learned to see what she saw, and he didn't like it.

"You're a real poet, a true bard," she had said, in that soft, French-flavored lilt that he had found so entrancing. "A rare and precious thing. You should prosper far beyond those incompetent scribblers who call themselves writers. If you feed my soul, I can help you."

It had seemed like the perfect bargain. He wrote, she sold. But there was more to their relationship than that. She trained him to understand that what he typed had a reality, and a soul, of its own. As its spirit rose from the word processor like white smoke, Ninette absorbed some of it. The rest of it still stayed near his computer, hovering around it like a halo, but Marcel knew deep down that some of it was missing. Fifteen percent. And she took fifteen percent of the money, too. That didn't rankle as much, though.

At first he had not minded, but as time went by, he sensed the lack in his finished work. He felt pained that his readers couldn't see and would never know all the joy, pathos, anger, excitement, and everything that he poured out into his work. Some of it, perhaps the best part, was gone forever. The lack of that portion was killing him, devastating his creative soul. Her percentage was breaking him. That was why he kept going off to get drunk. And why she kept having to drag him back. She brought in the money, all right, more than he ever thought he would see in his life, but her sustenance was the magic of his words. When he didn't work, she didn't eat, and that made her cranky.

A high note from a trumpet distracted him from his keyboard. He looked out over the park, and his hands fell still.

Ninette looked at the screen.

"What about the ending?" she demanded. Marcel shrugged.

"I forget," he said. "I just can't remember what I was thinking of."

"You need to go back," she said at once.

The thought excited and terrified Marcel both at the same time. He nodded, clenching his hands in anticipation.

Faerie tales never really explained how really powerful faeries were in real life. Marcel had to hold onto his sanity as she spread her palms out, describing an oval on the air. Within that oval the air shimmered. The ancient, biscuit-colored wallpaper with its tiny pink Victorian flowers ceased to exist. Instead, he looked out over a broad waterway bounded by reeds that looked just like the bayou where he grew up on his Cajun family's houseboat, him and Mommy and Daddy and his two sisters. The scene looked like home, but it wasn't. Magic happened here.

Marcel had told his folks all about Ninette and the mystic doorway. He had believed it to be a gift from God to help restart a stalled career, him stuck down in the mid-list of writers, with no chance at the big time. Marcel thought he might end up working in a bar again to make a living, or hauling nets like his daddy used to on the shrimp boats. Now his family had a white-pillared mansion outside of Lafayette overlooking the Mississippi and Daddy fished for fun. They were proud of him. But they didn't understand how he suffered. They called Ninette a blessing and told him to thank God. He tried to tell them she was stealing from him, eating off him, but they paid him no attention.

His daddy had clapped him on the back and told him not to be a fool. "Eighty-five percent of something is still something. You could have one hundred percent of nothing."

The rest of the apartment vanished. Under a broad blue sky streaked by high white clouds, Marcel floated on the surface of the water like a spirit himself. He scanned the lacelike tracks of the weeds under the water for that doorway he had imagined long ago was there. What he came up with in his mind took on a reality in the filandiere's domain, took shape and dimension and a life of its own. Marcel loved the land he made as if it was his own child. The salmon maidens, the man-hawk who stood guard over the Marsh Lord's palace, all these things were from legends he had heard as a child or had come up with out of his own head. Telling their stories had made his career.

Ninette was a distant presence behind him as he reached the portal to his characters' kingdom. It waited amidst a stand of six cypress trees all leaning toward one another like six old aunties having a private confab. The door was made of wrought iron twisted like leafy vines. It was so beautiful that it hurt him to see it. The door opened onto a sunlit scene, diamonds of light glinting off the water. His characters were on the other side the way they always were. The final scene played out from the last moment he remembered. Orestes, his hero, had to face the betrayal by the witch whose life he had saved, but it was a ruse so she could save her daughter from a more terrible fate. Marcel had always meant for Orestes and the daughter to get together, and they did. He drank in the drama as if sipping prime whisky. It was delicious and warm. His readers would adore it.

"*Oooh*, a bard!"

The shrill voice broke in on his reverie. The leafy door slammed shut, making the Spanish moss in the cypresses dance. Marcel turned in fury at being interrupted.

A swarm of faeries sailed toward him over the surface of the water. Their gowns flowed and swirled. Their long, slender hands were outstretched, reaching for him. Their voices were a combination of Acadian French and broad Cajun patois, mixing like jazz clarinets and violins in the air. Marcel recoiled. One filandiere was more than enough. Twenty was a plague. He threw up his hands to guard against their touch.

A gorgeous, shapely female with charcoal-dark hair slipped through her companions and cuddled up to him.

"Well, honey, sing me some words." Her eyes bored into his, drawing him down into an infinite well of midnight blue. "You know just what I need to hear, don't you? Tell me what you saw inside that door. And don't rush it, darlin'. I like it slow."

A white blur interceded. Ninette slapped the other fae back like a horsefly.

"Back off, Mistinguette! He's mine!"

The newcomer's flesh warped disturbingly but snapped back into shape. She smiled over Ninette's shoulder at Marcel.

"He'd like me a lot better than you, you old sack of wind."

"You be no use to him," Ninette snapped. Her accent always turned to harsh Cajun when among her fellow faeries. "What you know about New York publishers? And sell-through, what you know 'bout dat?"

"Well..."

"I give him what none of you can! Now, go mind your business!"

To Marcel's relief, they faded away like so many bad dreams, leaving them alone on the water, with no sound but the wind and the distant calling of birds.

"Thanks," he said.

She smiled at him, prettier than anything he could even imagine. Her voice returned to its soft Gallic lilt. "I'll always protect you. You're my client."

That reminded him of his obligation to her and to his publisher.

"I need a minute," he said.

She never argued with that tone. Marcel took a deep breath. He concentrated hard on what he had seen, forcing himself to memorize it all, and secure it in his memory. Small details were already trying to escape, but he repeated them over and over again. Must not forget the ink-dark spells racing through the sky that the witch turned back just in time. Must not forget the jeweled brooch Orestes gave his ladylove.

Done. He nodded, and Ninette grabbed him by the collar. She dragged him backward, as if he were a bad boy leaning out a high window. The bright dream faded, and he was back in his apartment.

"That Mistinguette always tries to steal other faeries' bards," Ninette said, as Marcel looked around at the dull, faded furnishings. "I remember when she all but smothered Arthur Pierce when he started reciting poetry. Francoise shoved her so far down into the bayou it took her a month to clean the mud out of her hair...."

Just then, Marcel had no time to listen to her crap. The scene was fading. He had to capture it immediately. His fingers hit the keys like runners hearing the starting gun. They danced and pirouetted and stomped on the keyboard. Marcel stared at the screen, just barely conscious of the growing lines of black on the white background. Instead, in his mind he saw the landscape of Faerie, looking in on the kingdom that he had created, the reality of his life.

When he finally snapped out of the writing trance, he felt exhausted but absolutely wonderful. It was dark out. The clock on the screen said he had been typing for about nine hours straight. The book was finished! It was possibly the best thing he had ever written. He hit SAVE two or three times just to make sure.

Ninette lay draped over a chair at his side, a silly, blissful look on her face. Marcel's elation faded. He realized that once again she had been consuming his words as they came out of him. She had stolen fifteen percent of his glorious world. He felt the loss as if part of his body had been amputated. He was so disgusted he could have burned up like a torch.

"Get out," he snapped. "You're fired."

She looked up. The dreamy look on her face changed at once to fury. "*What?*"

"I'm tired of you stealing from me," Marcel thundered. "Who knows how great my work would be if you didn't keep eating it?

You've taken the best of all of it, and no one will ever know what it was like. I want my art intact."

She sputtered with rage, her tiny face red.

"Your *art?* You owe it to me! I've made your career! I pulled you out of the gutter in the first place. I made deals for you. I ran interference with your publisher twenty times when you went on a bender. I got you on the *Tonight Show!*"

"I know," Marcel said, waving his arms wildly. "I've paid you. God above knows I've paid you. But now the deal's off. Go batten on someone else." He went to the door and held it open. "Out!"

She stayed where she was. Her whole body shook with anger. She raised a tiny finger.

"I'll ruin you," she said.

"You can try," Marcel said, with a sour smile. "But I'm a true bard. All your little faerie friends think so, too. How about if I sign on with one of them, *hein?*"

"I'm the best!" Ninette squawked. With her yellow hair messed up, she looked like a little girl in a nightgown. "You can't do it without me! You still owe one book on this contract!"

"I'll do it without you!" He took the flash drive out of the USB port and thrust it at her. "You already got your...your pay for this one, but we're finished. Go! Take it! Get out!"

"Nobody leaves me," Ninette said. She drew back her fist, the one with the flash drive in it.

Marcel braced himself, but it was no use. She smacked him in the jaw so hard he fell down. Before he could scramble to his feet, Ninette leaped out of the window. He ran to look, but no body lay on the rippled pavement under the antique street lamps. A couple of musicians looked up at him and tossed him a jaunty salute. Bewildered, he waved back.

He sat down hard on his desk chair.

"I did it," he said aloud. "I fired Ninette!"

Finishing a book always left him exhilarated, but the extra success of ridding himself of her made him feel as if he could fly. He tripped down the ancient stairs of the building, and went out into the night, heading for his favorite pub. He had to drink to his successes.

⚜

"To Ninette," he said, raising his tenth, or maybe fifteenth glass. Light gleamed on the tumbler of amber liquid from the hurricane lamps behind the antique counter.

"To Ninette!" echoed his newfound friends at the bar. Marcel downed his drink. The whisky burned mellowly down to his belly. It felt great. He bought another round.

Thanks to her, he had plenty of money to get drunk on. He drank away the emptiness of having delivered his book, drowned his resentment, poured in one more shot and a Hand Grenade for luck, and staggered home again. He knew he'd have a killer hangover in the morning, but anything was better than having to deal with Ninette again.

In the morning—technically 11:45 A.M. was still morning—he sat down at the computer, all ready to go. Normally he liked a week or so in between books, but he felt so good he wanted to start on the next book right away. This one was going to be all his. She was entitled to the commission on it because she had negotiated it for him, but the ideas, the soul, were his. Once he turned it in, their relationship was over forever. He hit the keys, and saw Faerie open in his conscious imagination. Words poured out of him. He wrote until his fingers were hot and his eyes burned.

After he had gotten words down and broke for the day, he began to think about the future. Ninette was right. Marcel didn't have the first idea how to deal with what came next. He was a storyteller. All he knew how to do was write. He knew nothing about technology and distrusted social media. He hated doing business and publicity, and all the other things she had always handled for him. He needed new representation. It had to be easier with someone else, someone *human*, even if they couldn't get him more money.

Over a supper of gumbo and a beer, he started calling all his friends in the business. They all promised to call their agents. He had a good reputation and a hell of a record. Someone would take him.

The phone rang the next morning while he was reading over the previous night's work. As was his custom, he had left off in the middle of a paragraph.

"Hello?" he said, knowing he sounded a little distracted.

"Hey, Marcel," said Leon Dupres, an old friend from school who wrote media tie-ins. "Hey, man, sorry. My agent danced it a bunch, but he said he can't take you. I got it out of him, said your old agent told him you were a pain in the butt to deal with. He can't take a risk on someone who ain't gonna earn him money. Sorry, man."

"It's okay," Marcel said. Leon hung up, but other calls followed, all with the same news. Ninette had done what she threatened. She had spread the word among all her fellow agents that Marcel was trouble, that his books were always late, and she had to ride him to get work out of him. Nobody wanted to take him. Damn her!

He couldn't believe that no one else had ever tried to get rid of her before. He took out the agency directory and phoned some of the other clients on the list.

"Yeah, I tried to fire her," said Rod Skryzinski, one of his friendly rivals, a hero in the paranormal romance category. "She blackmailed me, the little bag of bones. I took her back in the end—I had to. I was going broke. Now she sits on my lap while I write just to make sure I produce."

"She broke my arm," said Anna Giles, who wrote Regencies. "But she's still the best damned agent in New York, maybe the world. She makes sure I get placement. I hit number three on the list even in the middle of the *Twilight* saga, and fifteen on the Amazon list. I'd rather be a vampire's bitch, but I can't argue with the results."

Marcel cringed. He vowed he would make do without Ninette. He had to.

But it wasn't going to be easy. His publisher refused to negotiate with him directly. "I'm sorry, but we only deal through a legitimate representative. We have always found our relationship with you a mutually beneficial one. Perhaps when you find a new agent...?"

The copyright lawyers had had the fear of God put into them by Ninette, too. No one in New York would take his calls.

Marcel kept trying to work after that, but the bad news depressed him so much that he couldn't write anything. For several days, he got up and sat at his computer with a cup of hot coffee, and ended up staring at the screen. The three and a half chapters didn't grow a single paragraph in two weeks. He knew all the signs of writer's block, and couldn't do a damned thing about it. He gave up shaving because he couldn't be bothered. He sent out for pizza and beer delivery. One day he decided he just didn't feel like taking a shower. Who cared if he was clean? He lay around in his robe and a pair of old jeans, watching whatever happened to be on television. One day the money would run out, but until then, why should he move? His career was over.

But a week or two into his deep depression, he caught a glimpse of himself reflected in the glasses of the boy who delivered carryout for him from the Gumbo Shop. Marcel was appalled at the scruffy, unkempt mess, and felt deeply ashamed anyone had seen him like that.

He couldn't just sit around feeling sorry for himself. That wasn't the way his daddy had raised him. Maybe he couldn't write, but he had to do something.

That afternoon Marcel showered, shaved, and put on a clean shirt. With his guitar under his arm, he went back to the place he used to play on Thursdays and Saturdays during college and before his books hit it big. The manager gave him a puzzled look.

"Got too big for yo' britches, now you come back to work for *tips?*"

"Tend bar, too, if you want," Marcel offered. "I just want to work. That okay?"

"Okay with me, brah," the manager said, bewildered but happy to help out an old friend.

Marcel played the late show two evenings a week and tended bar on four other nights, mixing Hurricanes for strangers and Bloody Marys for locals. On his day off, he spent it drinking with friends. It was a familiar existence, but not what he wanted to do. He was miserable.

"How could you let a girl like that go away?" a pal asked him, two or three beers into the evening.

All Marcel could do was shrug. Part of him was still glad to be rid of Ninette, but part of him wished he hadn't been so rash. And now that he didn't have her riding him, now that the words were one hundred percent his, he wasn't making any of them. He had no reason to coax them out from their cozy place in his imagination. She made him work!

He hated to admit it, but he missed her. She was his muse. She inspired him. She *made* him write.

"To Ninette!" he said, holding his drink up to the light.

"To Ninette!" his friends echoed.

Marcel clawed at his neck. Something was strangling him. He couldn't breathe! He pried his eyelids open, and daylight lanced in, piercing his brain. He flailed for the solid surface that he had been lying on. Air! He couldn't walk on air. He was dying.

"Sleeping in the gutter again! You waste your life!"

The hand at the nape of his neck shook him like a feather duster.

Marcel forced his head around to see over his shoulder. There was the radiant beauty, the shining golden hair, the spotless white dress that left so little of her slim faerie body to the imagination, the disapproving little face.

"Ninette!" he choked out. "I missed you."

She threw him down. He fell flat on his face, but made it onto his hands and knees. He looked up at her, drinking in the wonder of her presence. She grabbed him by the shoulder and hauled him to his feet.

"I'm happy to see you," he said. "Why did you come back?"

"You called me," she said. "And I was hungry. I wanted to be there while you wrote and drink your words, you're a true bard."

Without warning, she punched him in the nose. Marcel heard a crack and felt a warm gush flood over his upper lip. "*Never* do that again."

"Maybe I will," Marcel said defiantly, holding his sleeve to his face to stop the bleeding. She held a warning finger under the injured nose.

"You try it. You need me. I got you fifty thousand more for the next contract based on the manuscript you turned in."

"How much?" he asked, incredulous.

"Fifty thousand. But that's only if you work!"

"I love you," Marcel said, fondly.

Heedless of the blood, he picked her up and kissed her. She kneed him in the stomach. He moaned and dropped her. She brushed down her white dress. The red stains vanished like, well, magic. She gave him a look of disgust mingled with an unexpected softness.

"Stupid, sentimental man. Now, feed me! I want some words right now!"

She pushed him along Toulouse toward Chartres, one bony hand in the middle of his back.

Marcel plodded forward without complaint. Ideas were already percolating through his mind like the finest coffee brewing up fresh. She *was* the best. He'd learn to live without the fifteen percent, and like it. Eighty-five percent of something was a whole lot better than a hundred percent of nothing.

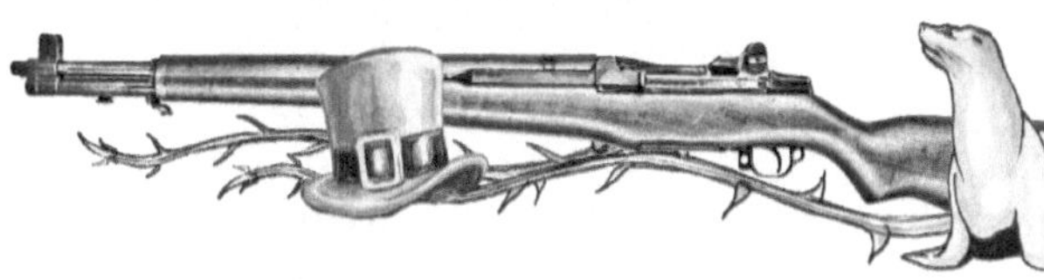

Bad Blood

Lee C. Hillman

Lee C. Hillman

ROXBURY, MASSACHUSETTS COLONY, 1659

Three more months to work off her debt. That's all she needed. Three months and she and Johnny would be clear to marry. If Mr. Davis honored her contract, that was. With Mistress Sarah expecting again, and so soon after losing the first babe, Toireasa O'Hara was none too sure her master would conjure a new reason to keep her on, indenture paid or no.

Sighing, she picked up the basket of clothes and brought it down to the well. Her freedom was only half of the problem. Johnny's own situation was far from settled. Oh, he wanted to provide for her, a little cabin somewhere near to his trapping grounds, out on the edge of the wilderness. That was not precisely her idea of a life, but if it meant they'd be together and free, then she'd make the best of it.

The well drew water from the fens, taking advantage of the runoffs fed by the Charles. Rarely was the water muddy or tainted, but sometimes, in late spring like now, some sediment came up and had to be strained through a cloth before it could be used to wash, or had to be boiled before it was safe to drink. Toireasa stretched a bit of linen over her bucket as she poured into her washbasin.

But the water didn't clarify as it passed through the linen. If anything, it grew darker, ruddy and thick with foam.

Toireasa dumped it out and drew another bucket. She strained it again with the same result.

"'Tis no use, child," someone said behind her. She jumped, yelping despite herself.

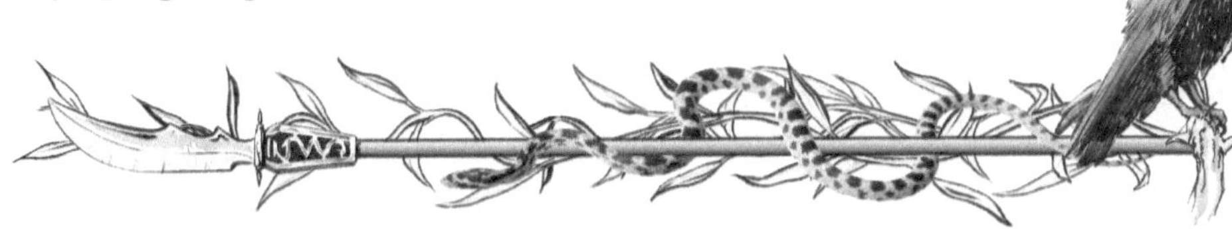

When she turned, she beheld a woman with white hair, pale skin, and grey eyes. She was dressed in a torn leine, the sleeves of which were dipped in red to the elbow, as were her hands. The woman looked to be only a few years older than Toireasa herself.

"Who are you? Is the well tainted?" If it were, then she'd have to inform Mistress Sarah, and the elders would need to know what had entered the supply upriver. It could be days before it cleared.

"I am you, sister," the woman replied, in a voice that sounded both like a whisper and a scream, and seemed to go directly into her head instead of through the air between them. "I am your future and your past and your present. The well is fine. 'Tis your lad who is not."

She pointed a red-stained finger at the shirt in Toireasa's hands. A moment ago, she would have sworn it was just a linen serviette, but now she looked more closely and recognized the cuffs, the pleated ruffs sewn in with blackwork, the bloused sleeve and back, the yoke and ruffed collar, and there where a man's breast would be, a dark red stain.

"This was Johnny's shirt," Toireasa said numbly. "I gave it to him when he left two weeks ago." She ran her hand over the bloodstain, saw the tear in the fabric, a rend just over the heart, as if an arrowhead had pierced it through. "Witchcraft," she whispered.

"Witch? No, not that. You know what I am," the woman said sadly. "You know the stories, Toireasa O'Hara."

"Aye, but they canna be," she answered. "He canna be —"

"Can be and is."

Toireasa held the garment to her lips, then tore away at the place where the arrow had opened the cloth. Screaming, the rawness of it tearing her throat from inside, burning her lungs and gullet with the pain, she stumbled away from the well, west, toward the pond. Blind to all who looked up, who offered to assist her, who questioned her health or sanity, or who tried to stop her, she ran to the banks and plunged the remnants of Johnny's shirt in the water before the weight of her own skirts pulled her under.

BOSTON, MASSACHUSETTS, 2011
NEW YEAR'S EVE

All things considered, Tara would rather have been home watching 'Doctor Who' instead of standing by the Charles on First Night. Duty being what it was, though, she kept her post on the Esplanade, hovering close to the iced-over river. A lot of creatures may have thought the holidays were a slow time of year for banshees. One night with Tara, and they'd change their tunes.

Tonight, for example: Sixteen degrees with the wind chill, but she had to be out by the river because several Winter Hill boys had promised to meet some Patriarca family members during the fireworks. Tara had lived in Boston for over three hundred years—two hundred of them as Chieftain—and she still didn't understand the rivalries or the need to set things off just when everyone was having a bit of fun.

She pulled the puffy coat out of the icy water and carried it, dripping, to the edge of the crowds. A young woman stood watching the skies, waiting for the countdown. She couldn't have been older than nineteen, but her skinny jeans and the ripped t-shirt she wore under her down parka didn't quite hide the early bump of pregnancy. Tara sighed.

"That wind is absolutely frigid," said a woman behind Tara, shivering.

"Sounds like a howling ghost, doesn't it?" answered the girl. "Sometimes I think we're nuts to come out here in the middle of the night like this, just to celebrate." She caught sight of Tara.

"Then again, it's always fun to ring in the New Year with a party, isn't it?"

Tara didn't answer. She smiled sadly at the young woman and handed her the wet garment. As she walked away, she heard the girl sputter in protest. Then came the gasp of recognition, and finally:

"EEEEEEEEEE! This is Johnny's coat! How did she get his coat?"

Ignoring the girl's attempts to find her, to ask her how she came to hold her lover's coat, how it came to be stained in blood, Tara strolled down the riverbank to her next appointment.

⚶

She handed out three more blood-soaked coats before the first hour of the New Year had passed. Wearily she made her way to the cozy apartment she and several of her sect shared. It was near enough the Harvard Bridge and the Charles, but it sure beat a hut with no central heat or cable. Ten years ago, one of her sisters had tried to live alone among the humans; it hadn't gone well. Nowadays it was easier. So much could be done online—bills, shopping, even food could be brought in with the click of a button. Tara had even encouraged them all to get paying jobs, though they mostly involved telemarketing. It was funny how phones didn't pick up anything supernatural about their voices.

Tara let herself in and stretched. The sounds of celebration filtered through the closed and insulated windows. She was exhausted. Before she could sleep, however, she flicked on the television.

"...In other news, Boston police report that their year began with a quadruple homicide. Four men were found shot and killed shortly after midnight. While police are not yet releasing the names of the victims, they suspect gang warfare...."

Tara knew their names: Johnny Malone, Patrick Flanagan, Sean Curtis, and his brother Robert. She changed the channel to something benign, feeling the same disgust that had settled in her gut with her first delivery of the year. Gangs. Mobs. Thieves. Soldiers. It was an endless, mindless cycle. The whole mess made her feel tired.

Perhaps the time had come for her to name her successor, as Adele had named her two hundred years ago. She had little doubt that her second, Finnoughla, would lead the clan well if Tara chose to pass on the responsibility. But quitting wouldn't solve the problem. It wouldn't free them all from their duties, just Tara. Besides, even abdicating *en masse* wouldn't stop the murders; it would just leave no one to herald them to the kinfolk left behind.

But something had to be done. When Tara had first taken up the washboard, there had been only three of her sisters in the whole colony of Massachusetts. She'd awoken the night after her accidental drowning in Jamaica Pond, after Adele showed her her own Johnny's shirt. She was doomed, as they all were, to walk the earth and bring others the same painful tidings they had received. For 15 years, she, Adele, and Muireann had been the only ones, from the Sudbury to the Charles, Walden Pond to Tiogue Lake.

When the War for Independence started, their numbers doubled, trebled, increased exponentially, and spread throughout the country, following humans as they always did. Following the men who killed each other, and for what? Fighting hadn't done her Johnny any good, no more than it had Johnny "Skates" Malone that New Year's Eve.

She knew better than to think men would ever stop on their own. *What would happen,* she wondered, *if someone* made *them stop? If they couldn't blame their rivals for the deaths of their comrades, would they give up?*

Not likely, she admitted. But it might be satisfying to try.

⚜

Two days later, she was riding the Red Line south to Braintree. The car was nearly deserted at 9:30 in the morning, just a few tourists and one job-seeker on his way to an interview. At Park Street, three hoodlums with shaved heads and too many prison tattoos boarded and lounged across the bench seats toward the rear. They paid the others no mind as they chatted.

"You gotta get the name right, man," one of them was saying to his buddies. "You just tell her you need your Oxy refilled, she'll know you're scamming. Me, I got a rapport with this nurse. You'll see."

The tourist family got off at South Station to wait for another train, the mother looking scandalized at the way the boys plotted openly. When the thugs exited the train at Quincy, Tara resisted the urge to follow. They were perfect candidates for her plan, except that they were Polish, Italian, one even had some Dutch heritage. Not of her clan; therefore outside her jurisdiction. Besides, she had her own business to attend, just then. It gave her an idea, though.

Her mission for the morning took some patience, some shoe leather, and some backbone to complete. There was an area where Adams Street crossed a tributary to Smelt Brook in a couple places, where the stream curved up and around and back south again. Tara arrived just before 10:00 a.m. and waited for the little daycare center to walk its students down to Adams Playground, right across her bridge.

"Miss Gina!" a girl named Bridget, age four and three-quarters, said to her teacher. "Miss Gina, tell the lady not to jump!"

"What lady?" Miss Gina asked the little girl.

Bridget pointed to Tara. "That lady there!"

Miss Gina bent down to meet her charge's wide eyes. "Bridget, there's no lady on the bridge," she began to insist.

"She can't see me, little one," Tara said over Miss Gina's breathless and concerned prattle. "Only you, girl."

She pointed to one of the boys in the line. He reached down to his leg, letting out a shout, as if he'd been kicked. At his startled cry, Miss Gina turned.

"Now, Thomas, what in the world...."

Tara reached into her knapsack. "This belongs to you, lass," she told the child.

"Not s'posed to. You're a stranger." Bridget said with a shake of her head. She backed away a step. The other children were watching Miss

Gina console Thomas while Miss Stephanie tried to figure out who had kicked him.

"Am I?" Tara replied, leaning down. "I know you, Bridget McKay. I knew your grandmother, and hers, and hers before her. I knew your father and all his kin. Take the shirt." She pressed the bundle of cloth into the four-year-old's hands. Without another word, she vaulted over the guardrail onto the ice below.

Bridget's shriek could have been due to Tara's leap, or the fact that she did not break through the surface when she landed, or to the fact that she disappeared under the bridge. Or perhaps it was because she recognized the tee-shirt her father had been wearing that morning, which she now held.

The young ones were the hardest. When the Sight skipped a generation, as it had for Bridget's mother, there was no one else to tell, but notifying a child like that turned Tara's stomach a little, and no mistake. It reminded her too sharply of Mary's bairn, two centuries ago, and how she had lost him and his father when she'd come to join this cursed existence. Her Padraig, his swaddling stained dark, and her Eoighan's coat as red as the soldiers' who'd killed them both—the patterns spreading on the cloth would dance behind her eyes all her days. Mary had told her that the moment she saw Tara, the white woman by the riverbank, holding out the rags, she had known Padraig was taken from her, had known Eoighan had paid with his own life and failed to keep their son safe. Like Tara, Mary had taken the garment with her into the water and drowned...and from that time to this, it had been her job to bring the same unwelcome news to countless women and girls.

That had been enough to break Adele, as it turned out. She'd gone with Tara to collect their new sister, wake her from her short sleep, and explain what was to become of her. When she'd heard Mary's tale, she told Tara that night of her intention. Under the next new moon, the two followed the river together, down to the bay. Tara bid her sister farewell, then watched as Adele waded into the surf. She swam out through the waves, let the salt of the sea take her, and dissolved into the ocean's eternal memory. Two hundred years, that had been, and Tara still missed her now and then. There had been too much suffering down the years, and no one to make it stop.

It had to stop. Tara had to stop them.

⚜

That night, Tara found a good spot near the Convention Center, where the Silver Line buses changed from wire to diesel and the bay flowed close to the tunnels around South Station. She hugged her leather jacket tight around her shoulders, though she felt neither cold nor wind. The amber streetlamps glowed steadily on her skin, while the white and red of car lights flickered across her face as they passed on the roads all around her. The last bus trundled up from underground; most of the passengers stayed warm and dry inside, but three got out to the sound of laughter and teasing.

"Man, I didn't think we'd ever get outta that lame-ass party," a boy in a Red Sox ball cap proclaimed. He slapped one of his friends on the arm. "You sure this dude's got the stuff?"

His friend laughed. "Nick's cool, man," he said confidently. "Just let me do the talking."

No, let me *do the talking*, Tara thought, but said nothing. She ghosted after them when they walked by, falling into step silently. They didn't see. They never did see their deaths coming, any of them, all assuming they would be able to cheat the reaper when no man ever had before. None but the Wandering Jew — and Tara had her doubts about him.

They walked along the wharf toward an industrial building with smokestacks and a fenced-in parking lot. Tara quickened her pace to draw alongside them. Their blood smelled rank with pollution — fast food, drugs, cigarettes, sweets, and alcohol — but underneath, she could feel the green of home. She learned their clans, their given names, and their life histories, with the breath of the wind. Reassured that these specimens were as good a set of targets as any, she sped forward to intercept them.

When she opened her mouth, the young men clutched at their ears and fell to their knees. Tara had expected the reaction and took quick advantage of disabling them with her voice, even if it meant they could see her now. She drew a long penknife from the pocket of her jeans and brandished it with menace. She wanted more than anything to explain why they had to die, but she knew that any attempt to speak would simply send them into new paroxysms of pain.

She slit their throats quickly, while they were still writhing on the frozen ground.

⚔

The news report the next morning made Tara smile. "The three men were all between the ages of eighteen and twenty-three. Police are not releasing their names, but did confirm that all three victims had criminal records, including arrests for possession of drugs."

Neil Walker, Brendan Smith, and Luke "Lefty" Moore had been their names. But Tara's sisters had not had to lament them, nor make their mothers regret the day they had birthed the miserable wretches. *Men* had not killed them. *She* had.

Her next decision was more difficult. She would add more names to her list, that much she knew. But whether to tell her sisters—that was something she was not sure of, yet. Would they understand? Would they condemn? After all, the mourning continued, whether or not women had any warning. By her hand or those of men, murder was still murder.

There was one difference. She had found satisfaction in delivering the blow herself. As if the sorrows of her three hundred years could be soothed, even for a little while, by the act of killing. And in the moments just before and after, she had felt...alive. Alive in a way she had never experienced, even when she walked as a human. That was both exhilarating and frightening to think on.

Perhaps she would wait before telling any of the others.

⚜

"Two more victims were discovered last night," the television reported a week later, "in what Boston police are calling a probable serial murder case. Both victims were male, between the ages of eighteen and twenty-four, and, police revealed, had a history of violent criminal activity. They were both found along the Esplanade under bridges. No evidence of robbery or a struggle was reported in either case. The deaths are believed to be related to three other murders a week ago. Police Chief MacArthur at a press conference this morning cautioned against walking the Esplanade alone at night...."

Tara kept her face deadpan as her sisters talked about the murders. They had been so simple to commit, she was surprised none of her kind had thought of it before. She had wondered whether her inability to speak to mortal men would become a challenge but instead, they seemed to find her alluring. It made it easy enough to lead them to a secluded spot along the river and then move in for the kill.

"Mrs. Jonson was devastated," Mary said. "She cried and cried. 'My Andy deserved better,' she kept saying." She snorted.

"Andrew Jonson probably would have died within a year no matter what his mother thought," said Colleen.

"Maybe, but Mrs. Jonson might make one of us someday. She's two more about to join up now that their brother's gone," Finnoughla countered.

"What do you mean?" Tara asked, tuning back in now that the news had moved to sports.

"Well, Rick and Devon, of course," Finnoughla said. "Can't you feel it? They want revenge. It's always the way."

"Revenge against whom?" Tara said angrily. "How can they know who did it?"

"*Psh*, when do men ever need to know who did it?" Colleen shrugged. "No matter what, they'll find someone to blame."

"Oh, aye, and then it's us who'll be keening and handing out bloody shirts and hoodies and jackets all the long night," Muireann agreed, coming to sit close to Colleen. "There's always someone else to be killed. Blood for blood."

Tara said nothing. She closed her eyes and tried to feel for Richard and Devon Jonson. Richard was only seventeen; his brother barely fourteen. But Muireann was right. Already their souls felt tinged with bloodlust.

She hadn't wanted to kill ones so young. Indeed, technically, they had not yet killed or even harmed. But, she realized, if her actions were to have any meaning, she must stop the cycle *before* it started. That meant making sure they could never kill, no matter how justified they thought it.

She would do it tonight, before they had time to try.

⚜

Charlestown was a tangle of narrow streets set on hills that Tara imagined would not have been out of place in a film about San Francisco. At night, the monument at Bunker Hill served as a combination of flood-light and map. Row-houses were packed so tightly that one could barely squeeze through the alleys. It was one of Tara's favorite parts of the city. It reminded her of home.

In one such brownstone, the Jonsons lived. Their flat was on the top floor of a walk-up that, Tara knew, once belonged to Mr. Joseph Templeton. He had left behind a wife, two sons, and a daughter when he robbed a bank, back in 1867. Desperate to put his business back in order, he had ended up with a bullet in his throat and the house had been sold within six months. His family scraped by until three years later when the two sons had also died in an attempted robbery. *Men in their desperation,* Tara thought, *never, ever changed.*

She brushed her fingertips over the doorknob and drifted up three flights of stairs. Devon's room overlooked the backyard, but Tara could hear music blaring all the way from the front door. The bass line pounded like a heartbeat, more pulse than sound. Devon didn't even look up when Tara opened his door; his eyes were fixed on his laptop screen and his fingers flew over the keys.

A window popped up on his screen and a girl's face smiled out at him. Devon smiled back. Then the girl saw Tara behind him, her eyes widened, and she shrieked.

Tara moved quickly, slapping the laptop screen. Devon snatched his fingers free from the keyboard.

"Hey, what the fuck—Who are you?" he shouted, rising from his chair.

"Devon? What's going on? Should I call 911?" the girl's voice, tinny through the speakers, cut over the blare of the music.

Tara realized her mistake: The laptop hadn't shut down completely. His connection was still open and the girl could still hear. But that also meant she could understand Tara.

"Tell him I know what he's planning," she said. Before her, Devon clapped his hands to his ears, hearing only shrieks.

"What? Who the fuck are you?" the girl shouted.

Tara shook her head. She pushed Devon aside and lifted the screen back up to speak to the girl directly. "Listen to me. I'm the woman who's going to kill your boyfriend if you don't make him understand it has to stop. Put your cell phone down, girl, it won't help," she added, as the teen reached for the device. "I'd stab his heart before you could dial."

She saw the girl's eyes widen a split-second before Devon's reflection showed in the screen. He was lifting a hockey stick over his head. Tara turned and snatched it away from him before he could strike, then drove the butt end into his stomach. He crumpled to his knees. "Tell him what I said, girl," she insisted again.

"Devon, she's nuts, okay? She's fucking insane. She says she's gonna kill you."

"Only if he goes through with what he's planning."

"If he goes through with—what? What the fuck is he planning? How do *you* know he's planning anything?"

"Please. Boys like your Devon always seek blood when blood's been spilt."

Devon, hands still wrapped around his middle, interrupted with a loud snort. "Erin, tell me you can't actually understand this bitch?"

Tara rolled her eyes. "That's quite enough language out of both of you, by the bye. Now, listen to me, girl. If you'd not been here, your man would already be dead. He can't hear a word, it's true, but you can. You've got to convince him not to go after anyone for killing his brother. It wasn't the gangs, it wasn't the police. It's not worth the revenge. And if he tries, I'll be there to stop him. Understand? He might just listen to you if you counsel him to let it go. You have the power, girl, to change his future. See to it that he gets to have one."

She dropped the hockey stick and looked down once more at the boy. On his knees, he looked impossibly young, almost like a supplicant at church. Too bad she knew otherwise.

She spat at his feet. "You never will stop, will you? You never have and you never will."

Tara glanced once more at the image of Erin on Devon's screen. "Someday you'll be one of us, girl. I'm so sorry."

She walked out of the bedroom and down the stairs, out of the house, to take up her vigil across the street.

⚜

Mary and Finnoughla were waiting for her. Their white hair glowed in the scant moonlight and their coats hung open despite the cold. "What do you think you're doing?" Finnoughla asked.

Tara pulled up short. A dozen replies flashed through her mind, ranging from snappish to glib, from deflections to outright lies. But the sad look in her second's eyes told her that denial was pointless.

"Someone had to do something," she said feebly.

"That's not our office, sister," Mary said gravely. "We canna play the reaper *and* the harbinger."

"Come with us," Finnoughla continued. She took Tara's arm and, with Mary on her other side, they walked down to the pier. "Sister, you are changing. Look at yourself."

Tara leaned over and looked in the water. In its dark reflection, she saw a visage at once like and unlike her own. Where she had been fair, this face was clouded, the eyes sunken and red. She looked at her arms, her hands which were stained with blood, but the flesh was no longer ghostly pale, but withered, charred black as if burnt.

"What is this?" she cried. "What's happening?"

"You've strayed," Mary said simply. "We saw that something was different days ago, but we did not know why. Then that story came on the news, and we realized that none of us had known it would happen."

"We followed you when you left." Finnoughla picked up the tale. "When we saw you leave that house, we could see it on you. Sister, you've become tainted."

Tara shook her head. "No, don't you see, I'm stopping them!"

"No. You are only making things worse."

"Think on it. That lad has now left and is gone to do murder. And why? Because of something you did."

Tara opened her mouth to protest. She wanted to rail at them that she could have stopped him if they had not drawn her away. But instead a high wail escaped her lips. "I thought—I thought perhaps..."

Finnoughla brushed Tara's hair with her fingertips. "I know. But it's not the way of our kind."

Tara turned her face into her second's shoulder and sobbed. She keened out her loss and her remorse, one over three hundred years old, the other raw and fresh as the new cut of a knife through skin. Her cries rent the air around them and, dimly, she could feel the humans nearby stirring in their beds, made uneasy by the howling wind which was all they could hear of her sorrow.

"Are you all right?" a new voice asked.

As one, the three sisters turned. Tara recognized the young woman, though her head was now covered by a beanie and her nose was a bit red from the chill air.

She recognized Tara, too. "Oh my God, you're that crazy bitch who was in Devon's room earlier! I knew when he didn't answer something had happened. What are you doing here?" She reached into her pocket for her cell phone.

"Erin Malloy," Mary said. "Before you dial, there's something perhaps you ought to see." She knelt over the water's edge and pulled out a dark, wet piece of cloth.

"Uh-uh," Erin said, backing away. "You're all crazy; you're crackheads or something."

"If you look at this you shall understand, child."

"Who are you?"

Mary cast a reproachful glance at Tara, then looked at the young woman with regret. "I am your future and your past and your present, sister. I am you."

Two gunshots cracked in the night, blocks away but unmistakable. Erin looked up the hill toward the white-spired monument, in the direction of the sound. Mary took a step forward, pressed the soaked material into Erin's hand, and looked back at Tara, who nodded her comprehension.

Without a word, she embraced Finnoughla a final time. Then, she turned away and walked to the edge of the pier. She stepped off its edge and felt the freezing water close around her. The moment she submerged, she could no longer hear Erin's cries of grief. She had only time to look ahead and see that Erin would soon become as she had been, and know that her office would continue without her. As she sank into the depths, the salt of the sea dissolved her flesh, dissolved her pain. She became one with the ocean's eternal memory, and knew peace.

HISTORICAL NOTE:

*Richard Davis, of Roxbury, married about 1654, Sarah, daughter of John Burrill, had Richard, born Jan. 5, 1658, who died next year; Richard, again, May 26, 1661 ; and Sarah, and he died March 6, 1663, his will of February 20, being probated March 19, of that year. But there is a posthumous child and the widow married Samuel Chandler, in 1664, and he died August, 1665. (Genealogical Guide to the Settlers of Early America, Whittmore, Henry B., 1898.)

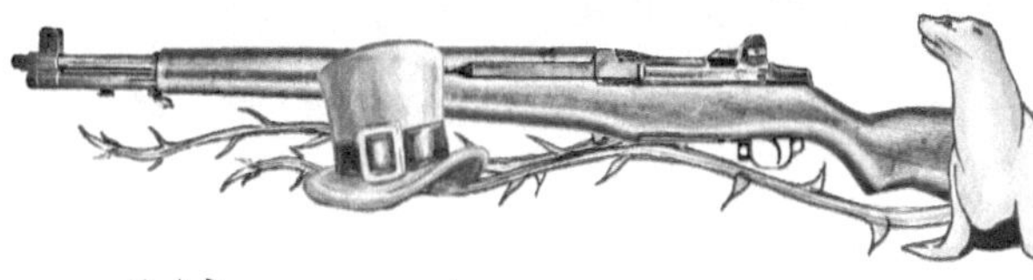

Melia's Best Wave

N.R. Brown

Melia caught her last Florida wave as the sun slipped beneath the horizon. It was late, but she was not alone on the water when the huge 15-footer, glassy and smooth, popped up. She and at least five others of varying experience took off to catch it. She hung back, watching as a young boy near her wobbled when he stood up on his board. She knew it was his first time, just like she knew everything that happened in her waters. She calmed the wave a bit to give him a smoother ride, and followed, bumping over the zigzag smile he left behind. He'd just gained enough confidence to shred the face, when a man cut him off. The boy overcorrected and tumbled off into the churning water. Melia used the water to push him forward and out of harm's way.

No one acted like that on her beach. Ever.

"Watch it, buddy!" She yelled. The other surfer just laughed, and it angered her. The water responded to her rage, surging forward in a ragged eddy. The man struggled when the unsettled water hit him, but kept his feet under him. While he fought to stay upright she cut down below him, racing along the bottom of the wave where the angry, white water should have slowed her, but it didn't. She was an Oceanid. The water loved her.

She eased her way past the snake, then cut up in front of him, using the water affinity that had been her father's greatest gift to propel her forward. She glanced back. The man's eyes narrowed. He hunched forward on his board. He was coming for her, and that angered her nearly as much as his original sin of being a jerk on her beach.

"My shore, my waves!" she shouted, and sent another eddy back to greet him. She felt rather than saw him lose control and tumble into her waters.

Back on the beach, she saw the regulars packing up after a long day facing the bone yard. She knew them all, but she tried to keep her distance when they had their land legs under them. On land, they didn't know who she was and the many times she dragged them to the surface after a crash or amped the waves on a dull day. On land, she was just a pretty good surfer, for a girl.

She pulled her board out of the water, up onto the beach, and upended it. The sand beneath her feet seemed to undulate, the hallmark of an awesome day. She dallied, loath to leave the beach, and wiped the water off her arms. The blue tattoos reaching up to her shoulders still marked her as a water sprite, maid of the ocean, a daughter of a Titan. No one could read them these days. Which meant no more favors, no more prayers, no strings, just honest to goodness worship when the land dwellers entered her waters. It suited her. She tugged her board free and headed to the parking lot where her rusty truck sat waiting for her.

"Dude, this place sucks. It isn't nearly as good as Mavericks." The surfer she'd dumped in the water walked across the sand toward the parking lot with some buddies. "I was there two weeks ago. Forty footers, and two guys died. It was awesome."

Melia stopped still. She knew Mavericks. Her sister, Eudora, had protected it since the dawn of man. A long time for an Oceanid to keep a shoreline. Usually they moved on, challenging one another for wilder and better spaces until they were knocked out of the Great Contest. Reduced in reputation without a shore to call their own, they'd return to their father and wait for his favor to turn their way. After all, what was the point of an Oceanid if she had nothing to protect, nothing to save?

If people were dying it didn't sound like Eudora was doing much protecting.

❧

Melia looked half a mile out to sea, beyond Pillar Point Harbor, California where the waves reared up to be ridden on the unsettled water. Mavericks, that's what that they called that water now. When she was young it was the Kraken's Teeth. The stretch of shore had been cold and rocky and unforgiving then. It was no better now.

The waves didn't break pretty or clean. They weren't friendly or easy. They hauled back, doubled up their fists, and pounded down on surfers' heads. Out on the breaks, tunnels closed with no warning, and eddies jumbled the faces of the waves like scars. Even the smallest could turn into a monster if you didn't watch it. She could see why the devout flocked here. They could spend their life in this church and never learn its secret. Or, just when they thought they'd tamed the beast, sacrifice themselves on its altar.

She hooked her thumbs in the band of her faded jeans and sauntered down to the dock at Half Moon Bay. Here humanity encroached, and the shore lay lifeless. The water ebbed and flowed, but her father was absent from the heavily polluted tide. A man-made reef created to keep mortal buildings and ships safe kept in the oil-stained, stagnant water, turning it to sludge. She felt a sense of sadness and a desire to be part of the ocean's currents again under all the pollution. She shook herself, pulled up every magical shield she had, but still felt the itch to fix this desecration travel up her tattoos and across her shoulders.

She ignored the slick, foul mess and concentrated on the distant waves. They felt challenging, wild and hungry, but she wasn't there to surf, just snoop. She wanted to know if Mavericks was worth the risk, because if she failed, the price would be steep. She closed her eyes and let her senses reach down to the floor of the ocean. She recognized her sister's touch, but only faintly. She ignored it and followed the flow of the water. Soon, she found what she sought. Beneath Mavericks waves sat an ancient battleground, a relic of the war between her father and the untamed ocean where wild magic still held sway. Melia listened to the song of the wild, intoxicated.

"Disgusting, ain't it?"

Melia startled and looked up. A young man stood in front of her in flip-flops and ragged jeans that dragged in the sand. His pale hair and bright eyes reminded her of her favorites back in Florida, full of life and laughter, made for surfing.

"Yeah, I guess it is," she said, narrowing her eyes at him. She wondered why he'd chosen to stop and speak with her. Perhaps he was one of Eudora's pets, set here as her buoy to ring a warning if someone came to poach her shore. Someone like Melia. She stood slowly, looking from the yachts to the condos and back again, searching for her sister. She did not want to be surprised.

"I've been trying to clean it up." He gestured to the waves.

"What?" She dragged her attention back to him.

"I'm organizing a cleanup for this place. We already do it on the beach, but the harbor needs serious work."

She noticed the clear trash bag at his side for the first time. It was filled with plastic bottles, diapers, and other bits and bobs the mortals left lying around.

"You're a good guardian," she said. "The ocean could use more like you."

He laughed. "I'm no guardian. If these shores don't stay clean, my view gets trashed. I'm Joaquin, by the way. You new here?" He bent to pick up a piece of plastic.

"Yeah, heard about the waves and had to come check it out. My name is Melia," she said, and then nodded to the water. "Looks like fun."

"Don't let them fool you. They'll kill you as soon as look at you." He moved away toward more trash. She followed.

"I think I can take 'em."

Joaquin ran a hand through his pale yellow hair. "Don't take this wrong, but I'm not sure you're up to it."

"What?"

"I've seen a lot better people challenge Mavericks. People with more experience and talent, and a lot of them are gone now."

Challenge. The word hit her in the gut, and she fought a wave of anger. Was this what her sister had turned the mortals into? These mortals that should worship at her shore, reduced to warring with the waters. She ground her teeth.

"What are you saying? You've never even seen me surf."

"It's not that, hon. It's this place. It's bloodthirsty." She started to protest again when he held up his hands. "Listen, nothing personal, I just don't want to see another person get hurt. If you decide to stay, come find me before you go out there, ok?"

"Ok," she said, hesitantly. He smiled and walked away. Perhaps she did need to think about facing her sister and Mavericks before throwing away her place in The Contest.

What if he was right? What if she wasn't ready for this? In Florida, 15 feet was amazing surf. Here it was a joke. Was she in over her head? Should she just go back home?

Some of her lesser sisters might be sniffing around her shore already, trying to make inroads with her chosen, surfing with them and bringing on good swells, but claiming it would take time. She could easily return and pick up where she left off. She could live another couple of centuries getting some pretty good waves and drinking in Florida's sun.

She drove up the hill to the cliffs overlooking Half Moon Bay. The trees thinned, the earth fell away, and the bare cliffs revealed a breathtaking view.

The bay stretched out below, edged by thin, sandy arms trying to embrace the deep blue of the ocean. The strips of sand thickened until they shouldered into a stony cliff face that occasionally crumbled into the shallow white-veined surf, leaving dark clumps of rock pointing jaggedly toward the sky. Tumbled boulders littered the surf — waves broke right into them, but the swells were amazing. Even better were the groups of families scattered along the beach reached up to her with their laughter. Despite all the pollution and harbor development it was beautiful — they made it beautiful, and they deserved protection. Her protection.

⚘

Melia found Mavericks daunting without her powers to help control the water, but she couldn't betray her presence to Eudora. Not yet. The first time she went out she nearly froze by the time she reached the rest of the surfers in the lineup. It was the middle of July, but the water was frigid. She had to adjust her core temperature even with a wetsuit.

Paddling out was a battle. Waves came at her from every side, and just as soon as she got the rhythm of the water it dumped her again. Rocks loomed out of nowhere, scraping her raw. She was thankful her sister was not here to witness this humiliation.

It wasn't until her second week there that the regulars finally acknowledged her. Some nodded, not the friendly greeting she expected, but a searing measurement of her as a surfer. The others didn't even do that. They watched the water, and for good reason: the minute you took your eyes off the swells, they hit back.

"Outside!" someone yelled.

She spun on her board. Too late. Everyone else was paddling. She was the last to dig in. She paddled toward the wave with everything she had. As she approached the sheer rise of the face, she had to pause and look up. The wave towered above her; a smoky blue ravaged by snaking white eddies. This was no peaceful bump to her father's tidal rhythms, but a scream cut short by gnashing teeth.

"Kook! You're gonna get killed!"

Melia realized she was the kook. She'd stopped paddling and was just sitting there like a rookie. She dug in again, panting in her effort to make it up the face before it broke. Halfway there, she heard the roar of the break. She knuckled down, gave it two more strong strokes, and dove off her board.

Trapped in the impact zone, a surfer had one choice. Melia cut through the wave. The leash strapped to her ankle went taut as she came up on the wave's backside. A mountain of water separated her from her board, but only for an instant. The wave curled and dumped her over the top of it. Sliding over the lip into the blinding white mist terrified her.

Is this what it's like for mortals? she wondered. *It's terrifying! Why do they surf if it's always like this?*

She struggled to gain control, or to at least make it to the surface. Without using her powers she bobbed like so much flotsam, and she wasn't about to betray her presence to her sister by calling on them. The wave landed behind her and pushed her up and out of the dead zone, but not without a price. She shot forward underwater, pin-balling off the submerged rocks and scraping herself raw. The foam confused her. Everything was white and blinding, and she could only guess which way was up. Another surge of water hit, and she and her board, still linked through the leash, tumbled as Oceanus's waters held her down. She crashed into a rock and scrambled to hold onto it until the crushing force of the wave passed. The moment the lull came, she launched herself to the surface.

Dragging in a ragged, choking breath, she heard catcalls and applause in the distance. Her sister's devoted didn't care for her, and neither did her sister's shore. Melia ground her teeth and inspected the damage. Her board floated in three large pieces around her. She screamed and slapped the water, swearing payback.

Joaquin waited for her as she dragged herself back onto the beach. He didn't smile or smirk; he smoked a joint as he watched the water behind her like she wasn't even there. She felt bad for ignoring him since that first day. The idea of getting help from a mortal stung a bit.

"You're stubborn for a girl," he said.

She ignored the comment. "You saw?"

"Yeah, dude." He took a puff and held it in. "Crash and burn."

"I'm not letting this stop me. You know that, right?"

"Yeah, so let's get rid of that trash and get you a *real* gun," he said, coughing out the smoke and pointing to the broken board in her hands.

She blinked. "What's wrong with my board?"

"It's broken," he said, laughing as he walked away.

When they got back to her truck, she reached for the brightly colored beach towel hanging from her driver's side mirror. She scrubbed her hair, setting the last few heavy drops of water free so the long black strands fell in straight lines down to her waist.

He nudged her. "You still aren't ready, you know that, right?"

"Then why help me?"

"I don't want you to die," he said, suddenly serious. He looked out toward the waves, pain written so obviously on his face she didn't need to ask what he was thinking.

Her anger toward Eudora's neglect rose, but she couldn't act on it now. "So, where is this new board?"

He shook himself. "In my car. Come on, I don't wanna miss the good surf."

Melia glanced back at the ragged waves that looked no better or worse than what she'd seen during the last two weeks. "Is this good surf?"

"Nah." A grin creased his face. "But it's comin'."

Melia scanned the horizon. It looked normal: azure sky filled with fluffy white clouds covering the face of the sun at irregular intervals. Then she narrowed her eyes and cast her gaze beyond the human pale. There she saw what she should have sensed when she was in the water earlier. Dark ribbons of power stained the horizon. Oceanus pushed a storm their direction. It would die out long before it reached them, but she could still feel the tidal energy out there heading right for them.

"How did I miss that?" she asked herself, more than a little incredulous.

"You're busy watching the waves and not feeling them. A new board should help that."

"How did you—wait, what you do mean I'm not feeling them? I feel them just fine." She wrapped her towel around her waist.

"That explains how that rogue caught you off guard," Joaquin said, inhaling around the words. "The board puts you on the wave, not in it, but we can fix that. Easy. Come with me."

Joaquin lead her toward an ancient woodie station wagon. Inside lay an exquisite and huge longboard. It was easily six feet, caramel colored, with wobbling veins of dark brown running its length. The nose was sharp as a pin, and the fins jutted from its belly, so thin as to be nearly invisible. She gaped as he planted it in front of her.

"It's huge."

"You'll need it to get on those monsters out there," he said and ducked into the back of his wagon.

"How do you even ride this thing?" she asked, tracing the board's edge.

"Like any other board," he said, and pulled out another one. This one was weather-worn, the wax on it thick and smooth. It would need to be cleaned soon. "It just takes a little more muscle."

The wax smelled of raspberries and sunshine. She smiled: These were good boards, she could feel it.

"You like it?" Joaquin asked, color riding high on his peeling cheeks.

"I love it." She grinned at him.

"Good, now let's get you out there and let you surf. For real this time."

She glanced back at the ocean toward the jagged line of mortal surfers crowded together in the lineup; each an individual mind but working in near harmony to catch one wave after the other. Perhaps it was time to take a page from their book.

⚜

She paddled out with Joaquin, the roar and the speed of the waves kept them from talking much, but a smile tugged hard at Melia's cheeks. The lineup was crowded. The waves rolling in were going to be awesome. The surfers made room for Joaquin even if they questioned Melia's presence.

She watched the horizon, and waited. Joaquin picked a medium-sized lump shaping up to be a pretty respectable catch. Not the biggest wave of the day, but she wasn't ready for that yet. They both dug in while the rest of the regulars lagged back and let them have this one. Melia paddled as fast as she could but still her partner outdistanced her. She felt the slow build of the water swelling up underneath her. The wave had caught them.

Joaquin yelled. She couldn't hear him, but she didn't really need to. It was time for her to drop in. They popped up over the shoulder of the wave, and Joaquin pulled himself into a crouch. His laughter drifted back to her in fits and starts, and she joined him. They sailed into the face of the giant.

She took a deep breath and tried to stand, and at the last minute she risked a look up the face of the wave bearing down on her. Her hands tightened, the sight terrifying and beautiful, but she wasn't going to let Mavericks win. She got to her feet.

For a moment, she floated like a bird, then she felt the pressure of the wave under her feet. It was thrilling, trying to outrun a force of nature like that. She wove back and forth, her attention focused completely on the point in front of her board and the feel of the wax under her feet. She slowed until the tube enveloped her, finding herself encased in a blue cave with only one exit. Then she shifted her weight and danced away as her cave collapsed. Ahead of her, the curling giant ebbed away, making room for the next set to come in. She almost lost it then; she almost pushed the wave, to keep her ride going. The tattoos along her arms itched and she drew in a breath.

"Melia!" Joaquin yelled.

She let the breath and the wave go at the same time. She shot out of the impact zone and back toward Joaquin in the lineup. She shook, adrenalin still flooding her veins.

"You ok?" Joaquin said.

"Yeah, I'm great."

"You did good out there, kook!" a blond man yelled from further down the line. She waved at him, and he smiled before he took off to catch his own liquid mountain.

"Yeah, we never thought you'd make it," a boy sitting near her said. "Good wave."

"Thanks." Melia looked down at her board, watching as the crazy wavy lines on it became even more muddled behind tears.

Joaquin drifted closer. "You wanna head in?"

"What? Not on your life, brah!" She wiped away the tears and jockeyed for position as another set rolled across the horizon toward them.

❧

Melia pulled her longboard from the back of her truck. The vehicle was still rusty, but it had two working wipers now and ran better than it had any right. She and Joaquin had started working on it when the waves weren't cooperating. Today, they were cooperating, and she couldn't wait to get out on them. It wasn't until she was carrying her board across the beach toward the surf that she noticed Joaquin.

He had his back to her, ramrod straight and clad in an expensive-looking suit. His long hair, usually wild and curly, was slicked back into a ponytail. The only familiar thing about him was the cloud of smoke wreathed around his head. She approached him cautiously.

"Joaquin?" she asked.

"Hey, Melia."

"What's all this? What's wrong?" Her stomach tightened and she spun, irrationally expecting to see her sister, but the only people on the beach were mortals.

"I had a friend; he got hurt just before you got here. He tumbled and was held under too long. It took us forever to find him. He loved this place, but she took her price." He drew a deep, shuddering breath. "A bunch of us are headed to the funeral."

His voice broke. Melia dropped her board and went to embrace her friend. "I'm so sorry."

"It's ok. I'm ok." He pulled away. "He wouldn't want me to cry. He died doing what he loved."

Melia watched, numb, as Joaquin walked to the water's edge and tossed a wreath of flowers into the rushing surf. "You gonna be ok?"

"Yeah, I'll be fine. I just can't look at her anymore today." He sighed. "It's hard loving something that doesn't love you back."

Melia stood and watched the waves for a long time after Joaquin left. She lost herself in the shifting blues, sinking into them until she felt their rhythm in her soul. Still, under it all was the pain of the worshipers mourning, which sang along her nerves like a knife blade.

It was time.

Melia drew a deep breath, planted her board behind her, and pulled threads from the air to clothe herself as an Oceanid should: white silk, arms and back uncovered, exposing the tattoos her father had embedded in her skin. Her long black hair was bound in traditional complicated braids on top of her head, and her feet were bare.

Melia reached out to Mavericks, and power flooded her. Her tattoos burned with it. She reached out for the waves, their lush, liquid glory reaching for the heavens and brushing the sand. She pushed them slowly up from below. She didn't want to catch the surfers out there off guard, she wanted to give them the ride of their life. She grinned when they recognized her work for what it was: a gift, an unexpected joy on an otherwise normal day.

The surfers jockeyed back and forth, catcalling and trash-talking until the waves came right up on them. Those left behind as the first one took off cursed and spun around to catch the next viable one. Those lucky enough to drop in on the gentle giants she'd created squealed with glee as they dared the crest to break over them. She held the waves together for them, pulling one back or pushing the other forward, smoothing the face from a snarl to a smile, and in one case pushing a kook out of harm's way.

It wasn't simple, holding onto this much water, but she was up to it. She'd been pulling the ocean's strings since time began. Granted, Mavericks was a little more vicious than she was used to, but it wasn't going to get the better of her.

She pulled more power to get a better hold on the water, but this time something pushed back. Eudora. Melia didn't have much time.

She collapsed one wave and then another, making sure her surfers were out of the way. She pushed away the set on the horizon and settled everything just in time for her sister to make her grand, rumbling entrance.

Rocks along the sheer face of Half Moon Bay trembled, and concerned families clustered together, fearing an earthquake. Melia rolled her eyes. The display was unnecessary and didn't impress her in the least.

"You!" Eudora erupted from the water, kelp and barnacles clinging to her pale skin. She wore tattered jeans and a threadbare bikini top. "Get off my beach!"

"Hello, Eudora," Melia said, invoking the family voice. It filled the air around them with the roar of storm surge. "You look well."

"Did you hear me?" Eudora ran right up to Melia. Melia did not flinch.

"Well, sister dear, if it is your beach, why haven't I seen you here before?"

"How long have you been squatting on my turf?" Eudora spat.

"Long enough to know you haven't been around."

"I've been around, but they don't care. None of them care."

"They would if you protected this place and its people!"

"I have been."

"You have?" Melia raised a brow. "Tell that to the trash littering the beach and the families here to mourn."

"How dare you!" Eudora's face twisted with an ugly, naked anger.

"How dare *you*? These people deserve better!"

Eudora growled, "Get. Off. My. Turf."

"Not before I say one last thing," Melia leaned in. "Eudora, I challenge you. Come fight me on the waves, and let's see who has the power to hold this place."

"You bitch."

"Tomorrow morning. If you aren't here, you forfeit, and Mavericks is mine."

"You'll never take it. Mavericks' heart belongs to me."

"We'll see." Melia looked at the mortals, still riding high from the surf she had provided.

Eudora said nothing, but stomped off, fading into the water before she'd even gone ten paces.

⚜

The air hung thick as Melia inspected her longboard. She'd waxed it the night before when she should have been sleeping. Now she was exhausted, but at least the board smelled comforting and familiar. She ran her fingers over the slightly tacky surface.

Mavericks didn't look happy. The grey sky glowered over the beach, and the constant roar of surf reached all the way to the parking lot. Even the mortals streaming around her to the beach were subdued. Their excitement at the swells was tempered by a patina of fear, as if everyone, sea included, knew a battle was brewing. She gathered her courage and tucked the board under her arm, then walked toward the beach.

She didn't look up as she made her way down toward the surf, but that didn't stop the regulars from greeting her and quizzing her on how she thought the day would be. They'd taken a while to warm up to her, but she'd really come to love them, and she was happy they thought enough of her to speak. She broke away from yet another group, and walked alone when she heard a voice.

"Well, there she is," Joaquin said.

"Joaquin! What are you doing here?" She ran to him and gave him a gentle one-armed hug.

He looked like he'd just awakened from a deep and restful sleep, with his hair sticking up at odd angles and his eyes half-lidded. His red-rimmed eyes told a different story. The hate she'd felt for Eudora flared again. She couldn't continue to let the people of this place suffer just because none of the other Oceanids had the guts to face their neglectful sister and reclaim this beach for the good of the ocean.

"I couldn't stay home. Mavericks is set to blow today! A hurricane off the coast is going to make the swells sweet. The best we've seen in years." His enthusiasm was forced, strained.

"Are you ok?"

"Fine." He looked down. "Sorry about yesterday. I didn't mean to unload on you."

"What? You're my friend, it's fine." She leaned in to hug him and realized with a shock that she spoke the truth. She pulled back to say something more when she felt more than heard Eudora's approach.

"Ready to lose, sister?" Eudora looked better this morning—no stray underwater animals were attached to her at least—but the hate in her eyes made her ugly.

"Joaquin, do we have plans to lose today?" Melia smiled, although her heart beat like it was going to break out of her chest. "You'll have to forgive me... I haven't looked at today's schedule."

"Uh, no?" Joaquin said, bewildered.

"Sorry, Eudora. Losing isn't on my agenda. Perhaps I can pencil you in for never?"

Eudora huffed off.

"Who was that?" Joaquin asked.

"No one."

❧

Out on the water, a shadow rolled across the horizon, a hint of something huge. Melia spun her board and dug in. Her long, tanned arms stretched down into the water, reaching for the sea floor. She risked a backward glance and wished she hadn't. A wave pulled up behind her, not the usual brilliant blue but a stony green that made her stomach flip. Next to her Eudora grinned, and Melia felt the surge of power come from her sister as the wave grew another ten feet without pause.

They were well matched, pacing one another as they raced to drop in. Their arms flashed. The water sprayed. The only thing Melia heard was the rasp of her own breath. She slid onto the face and stood up, triumphant. Eudora joined her. Melia growled and tipped her board forward, gaining speed. Again, her sister matched her.

They flirted up and down, both trying to claim the main rail. Both failed until Eudora cut over the tip of Melia's board. Forced to drop back, Melia cursed and hurried to catch up, but the wave carried Eudora away. Melia called to the water surrounding her and pulled back on the reins of this wild ride. The wave dropped in height and slowed enough to let her catch up.

This time Eudora cursed, fighting to bring the wave back to its previous intensity. All the while, Melia struggled to keep the water manageable. They tangled together on the elemental plane, both of them pulling at the water, each for her own purpose, while on the mortal plane they both jockeyed for the best position as the wave turned into a sheer, fearsome face.

Melia cut under and jacked up trying to catch Eudora unaware, but Eudora was quick. She fantailed her board, spraying Melia in the face to blind her. Melia wiped her eyes, but she'd drifted high and found herself being drawn into the curl of the now-breaking wave. It was a dangerous place, hanging just beneath a mass of foaming white fury as it tried to crush everything in its path.

Melia tried to calm her nerves, but the wave was a living thing breathing down her neck. She glanced down at her sister, envious of the relatively easy job she had maintaining the main rail. Melia crouched over her own board, determined to take back that prize position. She grabbed every stray mote of energy around them. Her skin felt swollen and her head buzzed. For a split second, she wasn't sure she could hold it together. Her board teetered.

She glanced out over Mavericks, beauty and danger locked together forever in a lovers' embrace. It taunted her with its pride and wild song, but she could feel the encroachment of man, the pollution, the development, and she remembered who was responsible for them. Eudora didn't deserve this place. Melia took a breath, pulled in a final burst of energy, and propelled herself forward. If she was going to be worthy, she'd have to risk it all.

Her vision flickered back and forth between the ethereal plane and the mortal. It was dizzying to see the ribbons of power streaming to the two bright spots in the world that she and her sister had become and returning to the ragged world of water and sky. She stopped trying to keep track of them and focused on getting in front of her sister. She drifted up until she was in danger of being flipped. She held herself there for a second, gaining speed, and then shredded down the face. She screamed like a banshee when she took the lead. Then again, so did her sister.

Melia settled into the rail, but she didn't have time to get comfortable. On the face, in front of her, a mortal struggled to stay upright. Melia gasped. No one should have been out there, no one should have been able to get a drop on this wave. Yet, there he was. He held on, but Melia knew that couldn't last. She blamed herself; she should have cleared the wave. She should have spared an ounce of energy to barrier off this monster, but she didn't. She'd been so concerned with winning that she'd forgotten.

She was trying to decide what to do when Eudora let loose with a blast. Melia braced for the impact, but it flew over her and spread out onto the water. In front of her, the wave buckled into moguls the size of boulders. She hit the first of them too quickly to correct, and it rattled her teeth. She pulled up, high onto the wave again, where it ran marginally smoother and she was able to still hold onto her lead. Unfortunately, ahead of her, the mortal had lost his battle and now drifted at the mercy of her father's ocean. If she could hold a little more, she could transport him out of the impact zone and back to safety. Melia reached out to pull in more power.

She hadn't drawn in much before she felt the strain, felt her control splintering. She could do nothing for the surfer caught in their behemoth, unless she was willing to lose. They bore down on him. He turned to look at her. It was Joaquin.

Melia gasped. Joaquin, the mortal who had taken pity on her. The one who had recognized her first among her sister's devotees. The young man who loved Mavericks enough to know it deserved better.

Time stretched. Melia dropped the threads of power, scattering them over the face of the already jagged wave. Eudora jetted forward while Melia slowed. The monster giving chase threatened to overtake her. She made herself as small as possible, tucking down on the board until she nearly bent in half. She didn't use any energy; she couldn't. Any faster and she'd risk missing Joaquin as she went past, any slower and the wave would eat them both.

She held out her hand. All she had to do was avoid hitting him with the board. If they touched she could get him out of the water. Just one touch. But one touch at 50 miles an hour was all she'd need to kill him if it was her longboard that connected.

She shredded over the eddies, forcing them to give way by virtue of her skill alone. Closer and closer, it seemed to take forever and only an instant at the same time. She was inches away from him when the water warped around her. Eudora manipulated the wave to suit her, and damned be those caught in her wake.

Melia's board danced under her like a fish caught on a line. She lost control and came up over Joaquin's head. She was going to kill him; her board was going to slice him in half. Panic bubbled up in her chest, and she screamed.

It came out as a word, ancient and mighty. A word she had not spoken since the dawning of man. Driven by instinct, raw, naked power responded. In force. It came from everywhere: the water, the ocean floor, the wind, the beings on the shore, the animals in the sea, and most of all, her sister. And it all came crashing into her at once.

Her human form tried to contain it, but it had not been made to withstand that sort of blast. Unable to hold herself together, Melia let her mortal self slide away. Her wings, hidden by skin for so long, broke free in a flare of blue white heat. Her skin grew cold and wet like the water she'd been born from. It darkened to the deepest, unforgiving blue, smooth like the heart of the ocean. Barbs from her spine split her back, pale white and deadly sharp. Her hair clumped together in slick green ribbons. The webs between her fingers and toes stitched together, and round suckers popped free from her palms and soles. Her true form revealed, Melia let the long undulating ribbons of her wings dance over the face of the wave, forcing it to behave for a moment.

She searched for Joaquin. The long-dormant tattoos on Melia's forearms writhed with the same light as her wings. Light arced from her fingers, piercing the water, and locating the pulsing human heartbeat beneath the surface. The twining bands of power pulled him to her. She lifted him easily onto her board and he cowered at her feet, prostrate like the early followers. It didn't feel right.

She lifted him. Joaquin found his feet easily, and she could feel his terror ebb away in favor of joy. She smiled. That felt right. Together they raced down the wave like an arrow. Ahead of them, her sister struggled to stay upright on a board that no longer responded like it should. Melia felt sorry for her. She'd already lost; she just didn't know it yet.

They passed Eudora easily, moving in perfect unison, leaning and ducking, ripping up the face like it was a 10-footer and not the size of most high-rise buildings. They neared the end of this ride when a wave of a very different ilk enveloped them. Its folds were full of emotion and power. Cheers of the onlookers from the shore accompanied its swell.

Joaquin crouched over the board, ready to battle the monster wave on his own, and Melia knew it was time. She stepped onto the water itself, letting him have the wave.

She held out her hand. Eudora slammed into it. Her sister caterwauled like a wet cat and fought just as wildly. Melia lifted her off the surfboard, letting it wander off down the face riderless. She looked in her sister's eyes, seeing fear for the first time. Eudora frantically tried to pull protection from the water surrounding them, but it was no use — there was none to be had. Mavericks' heart had been won, and it belonged to its protector now.

"There will be no mourning here today, and you will never revisit your sorrow upon us again." Melia spoke in the language of the elements, reveling in the feeling of the sounds tripping off her narrow tongue. "Do you understand?"

"Yes," Eudora said as her form fell away until all that was left behind was a wisp of blue-green light. That light dimmed until it nearly disappeared from sight. Melia released her sister, allowing her to return to their father's care.

In the distance she saw Joaquin, his joy as powerful as the wave he rode, and she knew she was home.

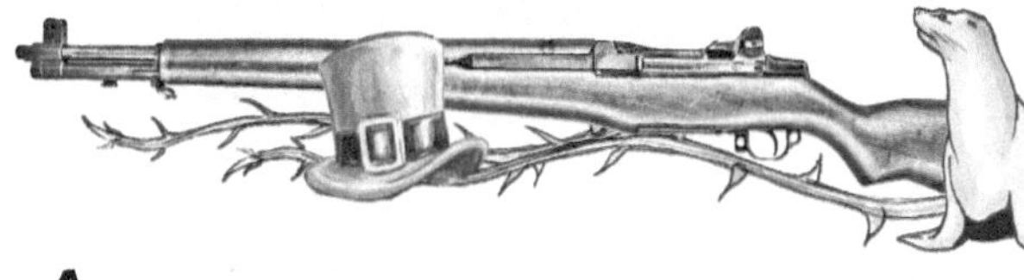

(in order of appearance)

Brian Koscienski & Chris Pisano reside in south, central Pennsylvania where Brian is often chased by angry villagers wielding pitchforks and torches due to his uncanny resemblance to Sasquatch while Chris can often be found in newspapers and magazines under the headline "Cro-Magnon Man Found." Their obsession with writing is pretty thorough; their compositions range from stories to articles to comic books to novels and even haiku. They even went so far as to start their own small press publishing company called Fortress Publishing, Inc.

Keith R.A. DeCandido has been writing fiction professionally for twenty-three years now, which makes him feel very old. Well, that, and his arthritic knees. He has written more than fifty novels, almost a hundred short stories, a mess of comic books, and a bunch of nonfiction, both in various licensed universes ranging from TV shows (*Star Trek*, *Supernatural*, *Sleepy Hollow*, *Doctor Who*, and tons more) to games (*World of Warcraft*, *Dungeons & Dragons*, *StarCraft*, *Command & Conquer*) to movies (*Cars*, *Resident Evil*, *Kung Fu Panda*, *Aliens*, *Night of the Living Dead*, *Serenity*) to comic books (prose featuring Spider-Man, Thor, the Hulk, the Silver Surfer, the X-Men, etc.), as well as in his own original universes. The latter includes fantastical police procedurals in the fictional city of Cliff's End, starting with the novel *Dragon Precinct*, and including several more novels and a mess of short stories, one of which, "House Arrest," will be reprinted in *The Best of Bad-Ass Faeries*, having appeared in the inaugural anthology in that series ten years ago. Keith also writes the *Super City Cops* series of cop stories set in a city filled with superheroes, urban fantasy tales set in Key West featuring Cassie Zukav, weirdness magnet, and 2017 will see the debut novel featuring Bram Gold, a nice Jewish boy from the Bronx who hunts monsters, *A Furnace Sealed*. Find out less at Keith's web site at DeCandido.net.

Adam P. Knave is the author of a few prose books (*Strange Angel, Crazy Little Things, Stays Crunchy In Milk*), some comics (*Agents Of The W.T.F., Black Decahedron*), webcomics (*Things Wrong With Me, Legend of the Burrito Blade*), and was one of the editors of the Eisner and Harvey award-winning Popgun comics anthology from Image comics. He lives in New York with his cat and spends his nights headbutting crime. In the face! You can find him at http://www.adampknave.com for even more madness.

Jesse Harris has always had a love for telling stories: either vocally, dramatically, or written; as well as a love for the mystique of Japan and its history and mythology. This opportunity proved to be a perfect launch point for bringing the two together. He lives in the Tri-State area with his wife and two children.

James Chambers is the Bram Stoker Award® nominated author of the original graphic novel *Kolchak the Night Stalker: The Forgotten Lore of Edgar Allan Poe*. He is also the author of *The Engines of Sacrifice*, a collection of Lovecraftian novellas described in a *Publisher's Weekly* starred-review as "…chillingly evocative…." and has written the story collection *Resurrection House*, and the dark, urban fantasy novella, *Three Chords of Chaos*. His tales of crime, fantasy, horror, pulp, science fiction, steampunk, and more have appeared in numerous anthologies and magazines, including *Allen K's Inhuman, The Avenger: Roaring Heart of the Crucible, Bare Bone, Chiral Mad 2, Dark Furies, The Dead Walk, Deep Cuts, Gaslight and Grimm, The Green Hornet Chronicles, Hardboiled Cthulhu, Kolchak the Night Stalker: Passages of the Macabre, Shadows Over Main Street, The Side of Good/The Side of Evil, Qualia Nous, Truth or Dare, Walrus Tales,* and the award-winning *Bad-Ass Faeries* and *Defending the Future* series. He has edited and written numerous comic books including *Leonard Nimoy's Primortals, Gene Roddenberry's Lost Universe, Isaac Asimov's I*Bots*, the graphic novel adaptation of *From Dusk Till*

Dawn, and the critically acclaimed "The Revenant" in *Shadow House*. His website is www.jameschambersonline.com.

CJ Henderson was the creator of both the *Piers Knight* supernatural investigator series and the *Teddy London* occult detective series among many others. He wrote over 70 books and/or novels, hundreds and hundreds of short stories and comics and thousands of non-fiction pieces. He was a master of hardboiled suspense as well as raucous comedy, and was not shy about saying so even when sober. He passed away on July 4, 2014 from lymphoma. For more on this truly fascinating teller of tales, stop in at www.cjhenderson.com.

Award-winning author and editor **Danielle Ackley-McPhail** has worked both sides of the publishing industry for longer than she cares to admit. In 2014 she joined forces with husband Mike McPhail and friend Greg Schauer to form her own publishing house, eSpec Books (www.especbooks.com).

Her published works include six novels, *Yesterday's Dreams, Tomorrow's Memories, Today's Promise, The Halfling's Court, The Redcaps' Queen,* and *Baba Ali and the Clockwork Djinn*, written with Day Al-Mohamed. She is also the author of the solo collections *A Legacy of Stars, Consigned to the Sea, Flash in the Can,* and *Transcendence*, the non-fiction writers' guide, *The Literary Handyman*, and is the senior editor of the *Bad-Ass Faeries* anthology series, *Gaslight & Grimm, Dragon's Lure,* and *In an Iron Cage*. Her short stories are included in numerous other anthologies and collections.

John Passarella co-authored Wither, which won the Horror Writer Association's prestigious Bram Stoker Award for best first novel of 1999. Columbia Pictures purchased the feature film rights to *Wither* in a pre-emptive bid. Passarella's solo novels include *Wither's Rain, Wither's Legacy, Kindred Spirit* and *Shimmer* and seven media tie-in novels: *Buffy the Vampire Slayer: Ghoul Trouble, Angel: Avatar, Angel: Monolith, Supernatural: Night Terror, Supernatural: Rite of Passage, Grimm: The Chopping Block* and *Supernatural: Cold Fire*. He lives in New Jersey with his wife and children. Please visit him online at www.passarella.com.

Jeffrey Lyman is an engineer in the New York City area. His work has appeared in *Sails and Sorcery, Trouble on the Water,* and in *The De-*

fending the Future anthology series, including the *Best of Defending The Future*. He was co-editor of *No Longer Dreams* and the *Bad-Ass Faeries* anthology series. He is a 2004 graduate of the Odyssey Writing School and was a finalist for the Writers of the Future Award.

Much to his embarrassment, **Bernie Mojzes** has outlived Lord Byron, Percy Shelley, Janice Joplin and the Red Baron, without even once having been shot down over Morlancourt Ridge. Having failed to achieve a glorious martyrdom, he has instead turned his hand to the penning of paltry prose (a rather wretched example of which you currently hold in your hands), in the pathetic hope that he shall here find the notoriety that has thus far proven elusive. His work has appeared in a number of anthologies and magazines, including *Bad-Ass Faeries II* and *III*, *Gaslight & Grimm*, *Betwixt Magazine*, *Daily Science Fiction*, and *What Lies Beneath*. In his copious free time, he published and co-edited *Unlikely Story* (www.unlikely-story.com) and the ever-timely *Clowns: The Unlikely Coulrophobia Remix*, as well as editing *The Flesh Made Word* for Circlet Press. Should Pity or perhaps a Perverse Curiosity move you to seek him out, he can be found at http://www.kappamaki.com.

L. Jagi Lamplighter is the author of the YA fantasy series: *The Unexpected Enlightenment of Rachel Griffin*. She is also the author of the Prospero's Daughter series: *Prospero Lost*, *Prospero In Hell*, and *Prospero Regained*. She has a brand-new short story collection, *In the Lamplight*, out through eSpec Books. She has published numerous articles on Japanese animation and appears in several short story anthologies, including *Best Of Dreams Of Decadence*, *No Longer Dreams*, *Coliseum Morpheuon*, *Bad-Ass Faeries* Anthologies (where she is also an assistant editor) and the Science Fiction Book Club's *Don't Open This Book*.

Her website is: http://www.ljagilamplighter.com/

Her blog is at: http://arhyalon.livejournal.com/ On Twitter: @lampwright4

John L. French has worked for over thirty years as a crime scene investigator and has seen more than his share of murders, shootings and serious assaults. As a break from the realities of his job, he writes science fiction, pulp, horror, fantasy, and, of course, crime fiction.

In 1992 John began writing stories based on his training and experiences on the streets of Baltimore. His first story "Past Sins" was published in Hardboiled Magazine and was cited as one of the best Hardboiled stories of 1993. More crime fiction followed, appearing in Alfred Hitchcock's Mystery Magazine, the Fading Shadows magazines and in collections by Barnes and Noble. Association with writers like James Chambers and the late, great C.J. Henderson led him to try horror fiction and to a still growing fascination with zombies and other undead things. His first horror story "The Right Solution" appeared in Marietta Publishing's Lin Carter's *Anton Zarnak*. Other horror stories followed in anthologies such as *The Dead Walk* and *Dark Furies*, both published by Die Monster Die books. It was in *Dark Furies* that his character Bianca Jones made her literary debut in "*21 Doors*," a story based on an old Baltimore legend and a creepy game his daughter used to play with her friends.

You can find John on Facebook or you can email him at him at jfrenchfam@aol.com.

A native of Cincinnati, Ohio, **James Daniel Ross** has been an actor, computer tech support operator, historic infotainment tour guide, armed self-defense retailer, automotive petrol attendant, youth entertainment stock replacement specialist, mass market Italian chef, low priority courier, monthly printed media retailer, automotive industry miscellaneous task facilitator, and ditch digger.

The Radiation Angels: The Chimerium Gambit is his first novel and is followed by *The Radiation Angels: The Key to Damocles*. He is also the author of *I Know Not, The Whispering of Dragons* (with Neal Levin,) and *The Last Dragoon. Snow and Steel* is his first sojourn into historical fiction. James Daniel Ross shares a Dream Realm Award with the other others in *Breach the Hull*, and an EPPIE award with the others appearing in *Bad Ass Faeries 2*.

Most people are begging him to go back to ditch digging.

Robert E Waters had been writing and publishing stories since 2003, with his first publication in Weird Tales. Since then, he has published over 30 stories in various print and on-line magazines and anthologies, including e-Spec's *Weird Wild West* and the *Defending the Future* Mil SF anthology series. Robert is also a frequent contributor to Eric Flint's alternate history series, *1632/Ring of Fire*, with several stories published in the on-line *Grantville Gazette*, and most recently in Baen Book's *Ring of Fire IV* anthology. Robert's first novel, *The Wayward Eight: A Contract to*

Die For, was released in 2014 under the Zmok imprint, and is a "weird wild west" adventure set in the Wild West Exodus gaming universe. Robert lives in Baltimore, Maryland with his wife Beth, their son Jason, and their cat Buzz.

Kelly A. Harmon used to write truthful, honest stories about authors and thespians, senators and statesmen, movie stars and murderers. Now she writes lies, which is infinitely more satisfying, but lacks the convenience of doorstep delivery. She is an award-winning journalist and author, and a member of the Science Fiction & Fantasy Writers of America. A Baltimore native, she writes the *Charm City Darkness* series, which includes the novels *Stoned in Charm City*, *A Favor for a Fiend*, and the soon to be published, *A Blue Collar Proposition*. Her science fiction and fantasy stories can be found in *Triangulation: Dark Glass*, *Hellebore and Rue*, and *Deep Cuts: Mayhem, Menace and Misery*.

Ms. Harmon is a former newspaper reporter and editor, and now edits for Pole to Pole Publishing, a small Baltimore publisher. She is co-editor of *Hides the Dark Tower* along with Vonnie Winslow Crist. For more information, visit her blog at http://kellyaharmn.com, or, find her on Facebook and Twitter: http://facebook.com/Kelly-A-Harmon1, https://twitter.com/kellyaharmon.

DL Thurston is a writer from Northern Virginia whose short fiction is available in the anthologies *Bad-Ass Faeries 4: It's Elemental*, *Steam Works*, *The Old Weird South*, and *The Memory Eater*. When he isn't writing, he can be found poking at a computer in his day job. He lives with his wife, daughter, cats, and a well-used copy of Nacho Libre. His website is at www.dlthurston.com.

Patrick Thomas has had stories published in over three dozen magazines and more than fifty anthologies. He's written 30+ books including the fantasy humor series *Murphy's Lore*, urban fantasy spin offs *Fairy With A Gun*, *Fairy Rides The Lightning*, *Dead To Rites*, *Rites of Passage*, *Lore & Dysorder* and two more in the *Startenders* series. He co-writes the *Mystic Investigators* paranormal mystery series and *The Assassins' Ball*, a traditional mystery, co-authored with John L. French. His darkly humorous advice column *Dear Cthulhu* includes the collections *Have A Dark Day*, *Good Advice For Bad People*, and *Cthulhu Knows Best*. His latest collection is the Steampunk themed *As The Gears Turn*. A number of his books were part of the props department of the CSI television show and one was even thrown at a suspect. *Fairy With A Gun* was optioned by Laurence Fishburne's Cinema Gypsy Productions. *Act of Contrition*, a story featuring his *Soul For Hire* hitman is in development as a short film by Top Men Productions. Drop by www.patthomas.net to learn more.

Jody Lynn Nye lists her main career activity as "spoiling cats." She lives northwest of Chicago with one of the above and her husband, author and packager Bill Fawcett. She has written over forty books, including *The Ship Who Won* with Anne McCaffrey, eight books with Robert Asprin, a humorous anthology about mothers, *Don't Forget Your Spacesuit, Dear!*, and over 115 short stories. Her latest books are *View From the Imperium* (Baen Books), and *Dragons Run* (Ace Books).

Lee C. Hillman died at the age of thirteen months. Since her death, and some would say suspicious return to life, she has been busy conquering worlds too numerous to mention. She has published stories in and edited all four *Bad-Ass Faeries* anthologies, *TV Gods,* and *TV Gods 2: Summer Programming,* and wrote the story "Under Pressure" for the *Defending the Future* series volume *No Man's Land.* She also writes fanfiction under the moniker "Gwendolyn Grace." Lee, or her alter-egos Gwen or Gwenly, is also an actor, singer, and songwriter. She is an avid fan and student of comparative media, a self-professed 'big damn geek,' a member of the Society for Creative Anachronism, and a past producer of conferences and events for the Harry Potter fandom.

For the past six years, her major online project has been writing and moderating the shared fanfiction-role-playing game "Alternity," found on Dreamwidth.org.

N.R. Brown has a passion for books. During the day she is a librarian, while at night she is a horror and dark fantasy writer and blogger. Her work has appeared in the anthology *Clockwork Chaos* and *Chiaroscuro* (www.chizine.com). An avid cook, geocacher, and improv performer, she lives in Maryland with her partner Day and two very spoiled Labradors.

Bad-Ass Backers

Adam T Alexander
Alan D.
Alexander "Guddha"
    Gudenau
Alexandra Walters
Allie ONeal
Anders M. Ytterdahl
Andreas Gustafsson
Annette Holland
April Freeman
Barbara deBary-Kesner
BC Brandt
Beth Lobdell
Brenda Cooper
Brendan Lonehawk
Brooke Starr
Carl Williams
Catherine Gross-Colten
Catherine L. Mock
Cathy Franchett
Chad Bowden
Cheri Kannarr
Cheryl Preyer
Chris Imershein
Christina R.
Christine Bell
Christine Czachur
Christopher J. Burke
Christopher Lee Washburn
Chuck Y. Newman

Curtis & Maryrita Steinhour
Daniel Lin
David "Handlebar" Kingsley
David Cooper
David Mortman
David Perlmutter
David Weinman
Debra Lieven
D-Rock
Edward S. Washburn
edward zagadinow
Elizabeth Inglee-Richards
Eva S
Eve Stein (not Einstein)
FoolSinc
Gavran
Graham
Heather Eberhardt
Helen Savore
Ivan Donati
J.R. Murdock
James Chambers
Janice Campbell
Janito Vaqueiro Ferreira Filho
Jeff Barnes
Jenn Whitworth
Jennifer Della'Zanna
Jennifer Park Washburn
Jeremy Reppy
Jessica Reid

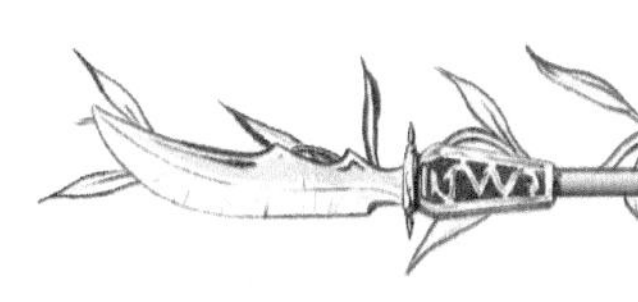

Joan Hoffman

Jody Lynn Nye

John Idlor

John L. French

John Passarella

Jorden Varjassy

Judy Waidlich

JW

karen diemer

Karen Zieman

Ken Mencher

Ken Winter

Kerry aka Trouble

Kevin "Wolf" Patti

Kierin Fox

Kiri Breese-Garelick

Kori Flint

Lark Cunningham

Laurie Hicks

Leshia-Aimée Doucet

Linda Pierce

Lisa Kruse

Literary Litter

Louise Lowenspets

Louise McCulloch

M.L.Falkenstein

M.Menzies

Margaret St. John

Mark Carter

Mark Lukens

Mat M-G

Matt P

Michael Blanchard

Michael Fedrowitz

Michael Skolnik

Mike Crate

mike smith

Missy Katano

Mullissa Willette

Neil Ottenstein

Nellie Batz

Patrick Thomas

Paul May

Paul Ryan

Paul van Oven

Peter Thew

Philipp J. Kessler

Rachael Jael Barcellano

Rhel

Rich Riddle

Rich Walker

Richard Novak

Robby Thrasher

Ronnie Baker

Roy Romasanta

Russell Ventimeglia

Sam murphy

Samuel Aronoff

Samuel Lubell

Scott Schaper

Shervyn

Sheryl R. Hayes

Stephen Ballentine

Steven Mentzel

Suragai

Susan Carlson

Svend Andersen

SwordFire

Tasha Turner

thatraja

The Wawrzynek Family

Thomas Bull

Thomas M. Karwacki Jr.

Tina Noe Good

Tomas Burgos-Caez

Tony Anjo

Tory Shade

Trace Hagemann

Trip Space-Parasite
Trystan Vel
V Hartman DiSanto

Vincent L. Cleaver
Y. H. Lee

www.ingramcontent.com/pod-product-compliance
Lightning Source LLC
Chambersburg PA
CBHW032101180726
48284CB00002B/397